THE MASUDA AFFAIR

A Sugawara Akitada Mystery of Ancient Japan

Eleventh-century Japan. Government official Sugawara Akitada finds a small mute boy on a deserted road. Akitada, still grieving for his own small son, determines to find the boy's parents. Meanwhile, Akitada's faithful servant Tora has troubles of his own: he has lost his new bride to a powerful man who pursues beautiful women and will stop at nothing to possess them. The trails of these two seemingly unrelated cases lead Akitada and Tora to the entertainers and prostitutes of the amusement quarter, and murder follows in their footsteps...

THE MASUDA AFFAIR

A Sugawara Akitada Mystery

J. Parker

Severn House Large Print
London & New York

This first large print edition published 2011
in Great Britain and the USA by
SEVERN HOUSE PUBLISHERS LTD of
9-15 High Street, Sutton, Surrey, SM1 1DF.
First world regular print edition published 2010 by
Severn House Publishers Ltd., London and New York.

British Library Cataloguing in Publication Data

Parker, I. J. (Ingrid J.)
  The Masuda affair.
  1. Sugawara Akitada (Fictitious character)--Fiction.
  2. Public officers--Fiction. 3. Japan--History--Heian
  period, 794-1185--Fiction. 4. Detective and mystery
  stories. 5. Large type books.
  I. Title
  813.6-dc22

ISBN-13: 978-0-7278-7953-0

Except where actual historical events and characters are being
described for the storyline of this novel, all situations in this
publication are fictitious and any resemblance to living persons is
purely coincidental.

Severn House Publishers support The Forest Stewardship Council
[FSC], the leading international forest certification organisation. All
our titles that are printed on Greenpeace-approved FSC-certified paper
carry the FSC logo.

Printed and bound in Great Britain by the
MPG Books Group, Bodmin, Cornwall.

A version of the story of the lost boy appeared previously in short story form in *Alfred Hitchcock's Mystery Magazine* under the title 'The O-bon Cat'.

ACKNOWLEDGMENTS

I am grateful to my readers, especially Jacqueline Falkenhan and John Rosenman, for their generous comments and suggestions. Amanda Stewart, publishing director at Severn House, deserves special thanks for her clear editorial eye. And, as always, the Akitada story would not have been told without my agents: Jean Naggar, Jennifer Weltz, and Jessica Regel of the Jean V. Naggar agency. Words cannot describe what their continued support has meant.

CHARACTERS
(Japanese family names precede first names)

MAIN CHARACTERS:

Sugawara Akitada senior secretary in the Ministry of Justice
Tamako his wife
Seimei an aged family retainer of the Sugawaras
Tora another retainer – young and of a romantic disposition
Genba a third retainer, middle-aged and with a love for food
Kobe superintendent of police

CHARACTERS INVOLVED IN THE CASES IN OTSU:

Lord Masuda an old and wealthy nobleman
Masuda Tadayori his dead son
Lady Masuda his daughter-in-law; first lady of his late son
Lady Kohime his other daughter-in-law; second lady of his late son
two little girls Kohime's daughters
Mrs Ishikawa their nurse
Ishikawa her son, steward to Lord Sadanori
Peony late courtesan kept by Masuda Tadayori
Little Abbess her maid

Mrs Yozaemon a poor widow in Otsu
Manjiro her teenage son
Nakano a judge
Takechi a warden
the Mimuras a fisherman and his wife
the deaf-mute boy the Mimuras' alleged son
Dr Inabe a physician
(also, a cat)

CHARACTERS INVOLVED IN THE CASE IN THE CAPITAL:

Fujiwara Sadanori a powerful nobleman and relative of the chancellor
Lady Saisho his mother
Seijiro her servant
Hanae a pretty dancer from the amusement quarter
Ohiya her dancing master
Mrs Hamada her nosy neighbor an elusive monk and assorted prostitutes
(also, a shaggy dog)

ONE

The Darkness of the Heart

He was on his homeward journey when he found the boy. At the time, caught in the depth of hopelessness and grief, he did not understand the significance of their meeting.

Sugawara Akitada, a member of the privileged class and moderately successful in the service of the emperor, was barely in the middle of his life and already sick of it. He used to counter hardship, humiliation, and even imminent death, with courage, and he had drawn fresh zest for new obstacles from his achievements, but when his young son had died during that spring's smallpox epidemic, he found no solace. He went through the motions of daily life as if he were no part of them, as if the man he once was had departed with the smoke from his son's funeral pyre, leaving behind an empty shell inhabited by a stranger.

The poets called it the 'darkness of the heart', this inconsolable grief a parent feels after the death of a child, a despair of life that clouds the mind and makes a torment of day-to-day existence.

Having completed an assignment in Hikone two days earlier, Akitada rode along the southern

9

shore of Lake Biwa in a steady drizzle. The air was saturated with moisture, his clothes clung uncomfortably, and both rider and horse were sore from the wooden saddle. This was the fifteenth day of the watery month, in the rainy season. The road had long since become a muddy track where puddles hid deep pits in which a horse could break its leg. It became clear that he could not reach his home in the capital, but would have to spend the night in Otsu.

In Otsu, wives or parents would bid farewell, perhaps forever, to their husbands or sons when they left the capital to begin their service in distant provinces. Akitada himself had felt the uncertainty of life on such occasions. But those days seemed in a distant past now. He cared little what lay ahead, and his wife cared little about him.

Near dusk he passed through a dense forest. Darkness closed in, falling with the misting rain from the branches above and creeping from the dank shadows of the woods. When he could no longer see the road clearly, he dismounted. Leading his tired horse, he trudged onward in squelching boots and sodden straw rain cape and thought of death.

He was still in the forest when a child's whimpering roused him from his grief. He stopped and called out, but there was no answer, and all was still again except for the dripping rain. He was almost certain the sound had been human, but the eeriness of a child's pitiful weeping in this lonely, dark place on his lonely, dark journey seemed too cruel a coincidence. This was the first night of the three day O-bon festival, the night when the spirits of the dead return to their homes for a visit before departing for another year.

If his own son's soul was seeking its way home, Yori would not find his father there. Would he cry for him from the darkness? Akitada shivered and shook off his sick fancies. Such superstitions were for simpler, more trusting minds. How far was Otsu?

Then he heard it again.

'Who is that? Come out where I can see you!' he bellowed angrily into the darkness. His horse twitched its ears and shook its head.

Something pale detached itself from one of the tree trunks and crept closer. A small boy. He caught his breath and called out, 'Yori?'

Foolishness! This was no ghost. It was a ragged child with huge frightened eyes in a pale face, a boy nothing at all like Yori. Yori had been handsome, well-nourished, and sturdy. This boy in his filthy, torn shirt had sticks for arms and legs. He looked permanently hungry, a living ghost.

'Are you lost, child?' asked Akitada, more gently, wishing he had food in his saddlebags. The boy remained silent and kept his distance.

'What is your name?'

No answer.

'Where do you live?'

Silence.

The child probably knew his way around these woods better than Akitada. With a farewell wave, Akitada resumed his journey. The rain stopped, and soon the trees thinned and the darkness receded slightly. Grey dusk filtered through the

11

branches, and ahead lay a paler sliver which was the lake and – thank heaven – the many small golden points of light, like a gathering of fire-flies, that were the dwellings of Otsu. He glanced back at the dark forest, and there, not ten feet behind, waited the child.

'Do you want to come with me then?' Akitada asked.

The boy said nothing, but he edged closer until he stood beside the horse. Akitada saw that his ragged shirt was soaked and clung to the ribs of his small chest.

A deaf-mute? Oh well, perhaps someone in Otsu would know the boy.

Bending down, Akitada lifted him into the saddle. He weighed so little, poor sprite, that he would hardly trouble the horse. He took the bridle again and trudged on. For the rest of their journey, Akitada looked back from time to time to make sure the boy had not fallen off. Now and then he asked him a question or made a comment, but the child did not respond in any way. He sat quietly, almost expectantly, in the saddle as they approached Otsu.

Ahead beckoned bonfires, quickly assembled after the rain to welcome the spirits of the dead. Most people believed that spirits got lost, like this child, and also that they felt hunger. In Otsu's cemetery tiny lights blinked, marking a trail to town, and in the doorway of every home offer-ings of food and water awaited the returning souls, those hungry ghosts depicted in temple paintings, skeletal creatures with distended bellies, condemned to eat excrement or suffer unending hunger and thirst as punishment for their wasteful lives.

In the market, people were shopping for the three-day festival. The doors of houses stood wide open, and inside Akitada could see spirit altars erected before the family shrines, heaped with more fine things to eat and drink. So much good food wasted on ghosts!

They passed a rice-cake vendor with trays of fragrant white cakes. Yori had loved rice cakes filled with sweet bean jam. Akitada dug two coppers from his sash and bought one for the boy. The child received it with solemn dignity and bowed his thanks before gobbling it down. As miserable and hungry as this urchin was, he had not forgotten his manners. Akitada was intrigued and decided to do his best for the child.

He stopped people to ask if they knew the boy or his family, but eventually grew weary of the disclaimers and headed for an inn. The boy had looked around curiously, but given no sign of recognition. In the inn yard, Akitada lifted him from the saddle and, with a sigh, took the small hand in his as they entered the 'Inn of Happy Returns'.

'A room,' Akitada told the innkeeper, slipping off the sodden straw cape and his wet boots and dropping them on the stone flags of the entrance hall. 'And a bath. Then some hot food and wine.'

The host was a stocky man with a dandified mustache above fleshy lips. He was staring at the ragged child. 'Is he with you, sir?'

'Unless you know where he lives, he's with me,' Akitada snapped irritably. 'Oh, I suppose you'd better send someone out for new clothes for him. He looks to be about five.' He fished silver from his sash, ignoring the stunned look on the man's face.

After inspecting the room, he took the child to the bath.

Helping a small boy with his bath again was unexpectedly painful, and tears filled Akitada's eyes. He blinked them away, blaming such emotion on fatigue and pity for the child. The shirt had done little to conceal his thinness, but naked he was a far more shocking sight. Not only was every bone clearly visible under the sun-darkened skin, but the protruding belly spoke of malnutrition, and there were bruises from beatings.

Judging by the state of his long, matted hair and his filthy feet and hands, the bath was a novel experience for him. Akitada borrowed scissors and a comb from the bath attendant and tended to his hair and nails, trying to be as gentle as he could. The boy submitted bravely to these ministrations and to a subsequent cleansing of his body with a bucket of warm water and a small bag filled with buckwheat hulls. Afterwards, while they were soaking in the large tub, as he had done so many times with Yori, Akitada fought tears again.

They returned to the room in short robes provided by the inn. The child's was much too large for him and dragged behind as he walked, clutching Akitada's hand. Their bedding had been spread out, and a hot meal of rice and vegetables awaited them. At the sight of the food, the boy smiled for the first time. They ate, and when

14

the boy's eyes began to close and the bowl slipped from his hands, Akitada tucked him into the bedding and went to sleep himself.

He awoke to the boy's earnest scrutiny. In daylight and after the bath and night's rest, the child looked almost handsome. His hair was soft, he had thick, straight brows, a well-shaped nose and good chin, and his eyes were almost as large and luminous as Yori's. Akitada smiled and said, 'Good morning.'

Stretching out a small hand, the boy tweaked Akitada's nose gently and gave a little gurgle of laughter.

But there were no miracles. The boy did not find his speech or hearing, and his poor body had not filled out overnight. He still looked more like a hungry ghost than a child.

And he was not Yori.

Yet in that moment of intimacy Akitada decided that, for however long they would have each other's company, he would surrender to emotions he had buried with the ashes of his first-born. He would be a father again.

Someone had brought in Akitada's saddlebags and the boy's new clothes. They dressed and went for a walk about town. Because of the holiday, the vendors were setting out their wares early in the market.

Near the Temple of the War God they breakfasted on noodles. Then Akitada had himself shaved by a barber, while the boy sat on the temple steps and watched an old storyteller, who was regaling a small group of children and their

15

mothers with the tale of how the rabbit got into the moon. His face was expressionless. Akitada's heart contracted with pity, and he looked away.

Beyond the busy market street, roofs of houses stretched towards the green hills: brown thatched roofs, grey wooden roofs weighted down with large stones, blue-tiled roofs of temples, and black-gabled pitched roofs of shrines. But, on the hillside behind the temple, a complex of elegantly curving tiled roofs rose above the trees and overlooked the town below and the lake and distant mountains beyond. Akitada idly asked the barber about its owner.

'Oh, that would be the Masudas. Very rich, but cursed.'

'Cursed?'

'All the men die mysteriously.' The barber finished and wiped Akitada's face with a hot towel. 'There's only the old lord left now, and he's mad. That family's ruled by women. Pshaw!' He spat in disgust.

Even without curses, there was no shortage of death in the world.

Akitada paid and they strolled on. The way the boy clung to his hand as they passed among the stands and vendors filled Akitada's heart with half-forgotten gentleness. He watched the boy's delight in the sights of the market and wondered where his parents were and if they were in despair by now. Perhaps they lived far away and had become separated from their son while traveling along the highway.

Or – a dreadful but reasonable thought – perhaps they had abandoned him in the forest because he was not perfect and a burden to them. The irony that this living child might have been discarded like so much garbage, while Yori, beloved and treasured by his parents, had been snatched away by death was not lost on Akitada, and he spoiled the silent boy with treats – a pair of red slippers for his bare feet, a carved horse to play with, and sweets.

No one recognized the child; neither did the boy show interest in anyone. Not even the odd figure of a mendicant monk, his entire head swallowed by a large basket hat made from straw, got more that a casual glance. The monk was playing a vertical flute with great skill, and Akitada, who played the horizontal flute, would have liked to linger a little, but the boy pulled him away to watch some acrobats tumbling in the street.

Only one odd thing happened later in the day. After having clung to Akitada's hand all morning and afternoon, the boy suddenly tore himself loose and dashed into the crowd just as Akitada was thinking of taking him to a nice dinner in one of the restaurants.

He felt a sharp panic that he had lost him forever.

But the boy had not gone far. Akitada glimpsed his bright-red shoes between the legs of passers-by, and there he was, sitting in a doorway, clutching a filthy brown-and-white cat in his arms. Akitada's relief was as instant as his irritation. The animal was thin, covered with dirt and scars, and looked half wild. When Akitada reached for it, it hissed and jumped from the boy's arms.

17

The child gave a choking cry, too garbled to be called speech. He struggled in Akitada's arms, sobbing and repeating the strangled sounds, his hands stretching after the cat. Akitada felt the wild heartbeat in the small chest against his own and soothed the sobs by murmuring softly to him. After a long time, the boy calmed down, but even after Akitada bought him a toy drum, he kept looking about for the stray cat.

They had a fine dinner of sea bream, melon pickle, rice, and sweet millet cakes with honey, and Akitada was happy that the boy ate well and with pleasure. When night fell, they followed the crowd back to the temple, where a stage had been set up for the O-bon dancers. The dancers, both men and women, wore brightly colored robes and gyrated in the light of colored lanterns to the music of a small orchestra of drums, lutes, and flutes. Akitada lifted the boy to his shoulders so he could see. His eyes were wide with wonder at the sight of the fearful masks and brilliant silk costumes. Once, when a great lion-headed creature came close, its glaring eyes and lolling tongue swinging their way, he gave a small cry and clasped Akitada's neck.

For a moment the colorful scene blurred as Akitada felt the small arms and hands against his skin. It was shameful for a grown man to weep in public, and he brushed the tears away, knowing that he could not part with this child.

He lost the boy almost immediately.

While thinking how to introduce this foundling to his wife, he became aware of shouting. The boy's arms tightened convulsively around Akitada's neck, and a sharp-faced, poorly-dressed woman pushed to his side.

'It *is* you, Jiro!' She glared at Akitada and demanded shrilly, 'What are you doing with our boy? Give him back.'

Akitada could not answer immediately because the child's thin arms had wrapped around his neck with a stranglehold.

A rough character in the shirt and loincloth of a peasant joined the woman. 'Hey,' he cried, 'let go of him. He's ours.' When Akitada did not react, he bellowed at the bystanders, 'Here. He's stolen our boy. Someone call the constables.'

Akitada loosened the boy's grip and saw the sheer terror on his face.

It was over quickly. Two constables pushed through the crowd. The couple burst into angry speech, confusing the two guardians of the peace and distracting the audience from the dance performance as a more exciting entertainment played out in their midst.

Akitada listened to the storm of accusations and demands, holding the trembling child against him, murmuring that it would be all right. But it was not all right.

The man's name was Mimura. The boy was his son. He was a fisherman on the lake and lived with his wife about a mile from Otsu, near the forest where Akitada had found the boy.

The constables turned their attention to Akitada.

'Do you know this boy, sir?' the first constable asked politely.

'No. I found him yesterday, abandoned in the

forest. In the rain. I brought him to Otsu to find his family.'

The constables looked at each other, nodded, and the first constable said contentedly, 'Well, you've found them, sir. Just give the boy to these people. I'm sure they're much obliged to you.'

Akitada looked at the Mimuras and frowned. 'He doesn't seem to want to go with them,' he said. The child's fear of the couple was palpable and obvious to anyone. Moreover, they did not act like loving parents. The man's low brow, mean eyes, and angry expression did not promise well, and nobody could find any maternal love in the coarse-featured female's manner. They did not look relieved to have their child back, safe and sound; they looked furious – and greedy. The crowd muttered.

Mimura caught their mood and put on an ingratiating smile. 'The kid's crying his eyes out 'cause his treat's over,' he explained. 'The rich gentleman has bought him pretty clothes and presents. And sweets, too, I suppose. I'm sure he likes it much better here than at home.' His voice took on a whining quality. 'We're just poor people, sir. Desperately poor. The child's gone hungry along with his parents. Why, I wager he thought he'd found paradise with you, sir. But he belongs to us. I lost a day's work, looking for him. I don't know how we're going to manage.'

Akitada looked at the constables and snapped, 'Before I turn this child over to these people, I should like to see some proof that they are indeed his parents.' But he had little hope of disproving their claim. The boy had recognized them. And

20

the fact that he had picked up the child in the forest near their home had already convinced the constables.

Since he was clearly a gentleman and the claimants were a ragged fisherman and his wife, the two constables decided to turn the matter over to the local warden. They all walked to the warden's office, Akitada still carrying the child.

The warden was a middle-aged man with an enormous mustache which he kept stroking as he listened to the constable's report. He looked them over, then took down everyone's name and dwelling place. When informed that Akitada was a senior secretary in the Ministry of Justice, he bowed respectfully.

The fisherman, Mimura, whispered to his wife. They looked like people whose fortune was about to be made, if only they played their game carefully.

When the warden had written down his last note with painstaking brush strokes, he turned to the child in Akitada's arms. 'Boy,' he said, not unkindly, 'are these your parents?'

Mimura's wife cried, 'No point asking him. He's an idiot. Deaf and dumb as a stone. He's ours all right. Who else would want him?'

'He is not an idiot,' snapped Akitada. 'And if you were his mother, you wouldn't call him that.'

The man came to his wife's aid. 'It's true, begging your pardon, sir,' he said. 'He's been a great burden to us, poor little cripple. But he's ours, and we take care of him as best we can.'

The warden sighed. 'Do you have any proof that he's yours?' he asked the Mimuras.

They looked at each other. The man said, 'We didn't know we'd need his papers. We just went searching for our lost boy. It's a fine thing when a father can't have his own child without carrying papers around with him.'

The warden sighed again. He turned to Akitada. 'You won't deny that you found the boy near the Mimuras' home, will you, sir?'

'No. But what parent would leave a child out in such weather in nothing but a thin ragged shirt? No real parent would treat a child in that fashion. And he's been beaten and starved.'

The warden heaved a third sigh. His expression spoke volumes about the naiveté of the wealthy when it came to how the poor lived their ramshackle lives. 'Can you find someone to testify that the boy is yours?' he asked the fisherman.

Mimura blustered, 'What? Now? This time of night? On a holiday? You don't mean I should go all the way home and walk back here with one of my neighbors, do you?'

But his wife was pulling his sleeve and pointing to the street outside. 'There's that monk again,' she said. 'He saw the boy at our place.'

The warden sent for the mendicant monk, perhaps the same one Akitada had seen earlier. He was still wearing his basket hat. The warden explained the situation and the monk turned to peer through a slit in the basket at the Mimuras and the boy in Akitada's arms. He spread his hands. 'I don't recognize the child, though I remember the woman very well.' He had a fine, deep voice and spoke like an educated man. His tone implied that their meeting had not been a

22

pleasant one.

The woman bit her lip. 'Jiro's wearing new clothes and is clean. You've got to remember him. I was telling you what a terrible thing it is to raise a child that's not right. Can't say a word, can't hear, and isn't right in the head, I said. We work and work to feed him, and there's never any money in the house.'

The monk inclined his head. 'I recall that conversation, and it is true there was a child there. It may be the same boy.'

It was good enough for the warden. Since Akitada made no move to turn over the child, one of the constables took him from his arms and handed him to the woman. The warden pronounced a warning to the Mimuras to keep a better eye on him in the future, the monk departed, and that was that.

But Mimura was not quite done. He now bobbed Akitada a bow. 'We're much obliged, sir,' he said. 'He's been treated like a prince. Just look at him weeping his eyes out, sir. He knows he's going home to a cold house and an empty bowl.' He paused expectantly.

Akitada looked at Mimura in disgust, but he reached into his sash and gave the man most of the silver he carried. It was enough to feed a large family for a month. The boy looked at Akitada despairingly.

'Be a good boy,' Akitada told him, tousling his hair. 'I shall come to visit you and make sure all is well.' He gave the Mimuras a sharp look and then turned away, unable to meet the child's eyes.

The woman snorted. 'He can't hear a word. No

need to bother yourself.' The Mimuras left.

Akitada followed them out, then stopped to watch them walk away. When they had gone a little way, the woman put the child down roughly. The father's broad back blocked Akitada's view, but he heard the boy cry out in pain and he clenched his fists. Both parents took the child's hands and disappeared into the crowd.

It had been foolish to give his affection so quickly and deeply to a strange child. Akitada's heart ached to see him dragged away, whimpering. The brutes had abused him and would do so again, but he had no right to interfere between parent and child. He hated this helplessness. He hated seeing the boy's hope crushed so suddenly and completely. And he ached because he had failed the child just as he had failed his own son.

For the next hour, he wandered despairingly about town, trying to think of a way to rescue the boy, knowing he should return to the inn, saddle his horse, and go home to be with his wife.

And then he saw the cat again.

TWO

The Courtesan's House

He recognized it immediately: the brown and white fur arranged in irregular patches; the scarred face with one eye half closed so that it seemed to be winking; the tear in the right ear. It sat on an upturned basket behind a vegetable stall, looking at him and twitching its tail.

Perhaps it was the festival's peculiar atmosphere, or his own confused emotions, but Akitada was suddenly convinced that the cat was his link to the boy. This time he knew better than to rush the animal. He approached slowly, making soft clicking noises with his tongue as he had heard his sisters do when they called their kitten. The cat winked, slipped down from the basket in one fluid motion, and strolled away.

Akitada followed, keeping his distance, waiting as the animal stopped to examine garbage in gutters and alleyways for bits of food. He had no idea what he would do if he caught the cat, and he did not worry about the peculiar figure he made, following a mangy cat up and down dark alleys in his heavy silk hunting robe and stiff hat. At one point the cat paused to consume a large fish head someone had tossed out of a restaurant.

Akitada hurriedly purchased a lantern from the shopkeeper next door, overpaying the man in his haste not to lose the cat. Eventually, the animal stopped scavenging and moved on more purposefully.

They left the business district behind. The streets grew darker, there were fewer people about, and the sounds of the market receded until they were alone on a residential street, the cat a pale shadow in the distance. A pearly moon cast its uncertain light as remnants of clouds moved slowly across it. Akitada picked up his pace. Occasionally, the light of lanterns or torches inside a walled compound threw weird shadows through the intervening trees. Puddles still glinted here and there in the potholes and cart tracks of the road, and Akitada hoped it would not start to rain again. He had the strangest sense that he and the cat moved towards some unearthly place, that the cat was leading him among the ghosts. He was being foolish, but in his misery, he relinquished his common sense willingly. It was a faculty that had never been particularly useful when it came to human emotions.

The cat appeared to have a definite destination. It kept up a steady and direct route towards the lake. The streets became darker, the lights from dwellings fewer. When they reached the road along the lake, Akitada saw that the wealthy people of Otsu and summer visitors from the capital had built their villas here to catch the cool breezes and have a view of the distant mountains. Their gardens were large, and the walls and gates in good repair. The sweet scent of flowers came

26

over the walls, made sweeter by the moisture which still lingered from the rain. Somewhere a reed warbler called and was answered. Charming rustic roofs peeked from the trees, or elegantly tiled ones, and occasionally, where a wall was low and the trees not dense, he caught a gleam of the moon-silvered lake.

Imperceptibly he relaxed and smiled to find himself on this adventure with a cat. Then, abruptly, the moon disappeared behind clouds, the street was plunged into sudden darkness, and he could no longer see the cat. When the moon came out again, he strained his eyes and started to run. The street lay before him, long, straight, and empty. The cat was gone. With a ghostlike suddenness it had disappeared into the darkness as if it had never been.

Akitada stopped and looked everywhere. Nothing. Panic rose for a moment, then abated into defeat. In the distance sounded a temple bell. He turned to go back to the inn.

When the ringing of the bell stopped, he heard the slow clacking of wooden sandals. An old man approached, paused, and produced a pair of wooden clappers which he beat together vigorously, calling out in a reedy voice, 'The Rat ... The hour of the rat ... The Rat.'

A night watchman. And it was the middle of the night already. Most decent people were in their beds.

Akitada called out, 'Do you happen to know who owns a brown-and-white cat hereabout?'

The watchman raised his lantern to look at him. 'You mean Patch, sir? Nobody owns him. He lives in the dead courtesan's house.' The watchman pointed to the gate of one of the lakeside villas. 'A visitor in town, sir?' he asked.

'Yes, a visitor.' Akitada looked at the wall and gate and saw that it did not match the neat appearance of the rest of the street. Plaster had fallen, exposing the wood and mud construction, and in one place a large section had collapsed, mocking the heavily barred wooden gate by allowing easy access to cats and humans alike.

Patch? The cat was spotted. Surely, the boy had recognized the cat and tried to call its name. 'The dead courtesan's house?' he asked the watchman, who seemed amused by the odd encounter on the moonlit street.

'Nobody lives there anymore,' the watchman said. 'It's a sad ruin. The cat belonged to her.'

'Really? Who owns the property? I might want to buy it.'

'Ah.' The watchman's curiosity was satisfied. The rich, not having regular work, kept peculiar hours, but that was not his concern. He shook his head. 'Dear me, not that place, sir. She killed herself because her lover left her to starve. They say her angry ghost roams the garden to catch unwary men to have her revenge on. I never go near it myself.' He produced a wheezing laugh. 'Not that she'll have much use for an old stick like me, but you'd better keep your distance, sir.'

Akitada looked at the watchman. It was the middle of the O-bon festival, and the old man was clearly superstitious, but somehow the tale of a haunted house fitted his own mood. 'How did she die?'

'Drowned herself in the lake. Pity. They say she was a rare beauty.'

'Were there any children?'

'If so, they're long gone. The house belongs to the Masudas now.'

Akitada thanked him, and the man resumed his rounds, making a wide detour around the broken wall and barred gate.

Akitada walked to the collapsed wall and peered into the overgrown garden. Trees and shrubs hid all but the corner of an elegantly curved roof. Up ahead the night watchman looked back and shook his head at such foolhardiness. Akitada waved and waited for him to disappear before scrambling over the rubble into the garden. He was trespassing and felt foolish, but was more determined to find the cat than ever.

A humid, stagnant atmosphere received him. Dripping vines, brambles, and creepers covered shrubs and trees. His feeble lantern gilded wet leaves and picked out a stone Buddha, half-hidden beneath a blanket of ivy. Strange rustlings, squeaks, and creaks sounded everywhere, and clouds of small gnats hovered in the beam of his light. The air was oppressive and vaguely threatening. The cat's coming and going had left a narrow track which soon disappeared under dense vegetation. Akitada followed it, but had to take detours and lost the way. His progress was noisy with snapping twigs, and he wondered vaguely about the neighbors. Surely no one else was out at this time. When he felt a tug at his sleeve, he swung around, his heart beating, but he had only brushed the branch of a gaunt cedar.

He would have turned back, if he had not heard the sound of a door or shutter slamming. Perhaps it had been the cat, or some beggar finding refuge in the deserted house, or even the wind from the lake beyond, but it was enough to make Akitada press on.

When he reached the house, he was covered with scratches, itching from insect bites, and his topknot was askew. But there, on the veranda, sat the cat, waiting.

The villa looked small, dark, and empty, its shutters broken, the paper covering its windows hanging in shreds, and many of its roof tiles had shattered on the ground. The balustrade of the veranda leaned at a crazy angle, and where there had been doors, black cavernous spaces gaped in the walls. It must have been charming once, poised just above the lake in its lush gardens, a nobleman's retreat from official affairs in the capital, or – as the watchman had implied – his secret love nest.

The lake stretched, dull silver, towards a distant shore that wore a necklace of tiny lights. People were still welcoming the return of their dead. Here, in this dark and deserted villa, no one had lit candles or set up an altar to welcome the spirit of the unhappy woman who used to live in it. Only the water lapped gently among the reeds along the bank, but Akitada suddenly felt a ghost-like presence and shivered. He looked about, then walked up to the ruined house. The cat watched him with unblinking eyes, motionless until he was close enough to touch it. But when he stretched out a tentative hand, it slipped away and disappeared inside. He called its name softly, but the animal did not reappear.

The veranda steps were missing, as was most of the floor. The house, which had been vandalized for useful building materials, had become inaccessible to all but cats. He was turning away, when he heard an eerie sound from inside, a soft wail definitely not made by a cat. He swung around and caught a movement inside.

He thought a tall pale shape – a woman trailing some diaphanous garment? – had moved past the opening to one of the corner rooms. Akitada felt the hair bristle on his neck and called out, 'Who's there?' He got no answer.

Walking quickly around the corner of the house, he climbed one of the supports of the veranda and held up his lantern. He directed its beam into the room where he had seen the woman. It was empty. Dead leaves lay in the corners, and rainwater had gathered in puddles on the remaining floor. In spite of the warm and humid night, Akitada felt a sudden chill.

When he jumped down from his perch, his foot landed on something that broke with a sharp crack. The lantern revealed a shimmer of black lacquer and mother-of-pearl: a wooden toy sword, proof that a small boy had once lived here. He picked up the hilt and choked with pain; the sword was identical to the one he had bought Yori during the last winter of his life. A costly toy, it had been lacquered and ornamented to resemble the weapon of an adult. Yori's delight in it, and the times they had spent practicing sword-play in the courtyard at home, had been more

31

than worth the expense. When the memory faded into the familiar bitterness, an irrational fear gripped Akitada. He stumbled away from the haunted villa, plunging back into the wilderness. He scrambled through as fast as he could, and when he reached the broken wall again, his heart was pounding and he was out of breath.

The street lay empty, the watchman long gone. Dejected, Akitada returned to the inn. He was no closer to helping the boy or making sense of what was troubling him. A courtesan's ghost, a feral cat, and an expensive toy? What did they mean? He was too weary to think.

In spite of his exhaustion, he slept poorly. The encounter with the child had brought back all the old grief and added new fears. He lay awake for a long time, thinking that he had abandoned the boy to his fate without lifting a finger to help him and remembering the guilt of having neglected his own son during the time of the pestilence. When he finally fell asleep, his dreams were filled with snarling cats and hungry ghosts. The ghosts had the face of the boy and followed him about, their thin arms stretched out in entreaty.

Towards dawn he woke, drenched in sweat, certain that he had heard Yori cry out for him from the next room. For a single moment of joy he thought his son's death part of the dream, but then he felt the tears on his face and knew he was gone. The dark and lonely room of the inn closed in around him, and he plunged back into despair.

Waking was always the hardest.

The final day of the O-Bon festival dawned

clear and dry. If the weather held, Akitada could reach the capital in a few hours' ride, but he decided to chance it and spend the morning trying to find out more about the boy, the cat, and the dead courtesan. He thought, half guiltily and half resentfully, of his waiting wife, but women seemed to draw on inner strengths when it came to losing a child. In the months since Yori's death, Tamako had quietly resumed her daily routines, while he had sunk into despair.

The sun sparkled off the waters of the lake, and behind him rose the green mountains, Hieizan towering above the rest. The surface of the lake was dotted with slender fishing boats and the large white sails of ships making their way both north and south, carrying goods and people. Otsu was a harbor for the capital and bustled with business. Today was the day of parting from the dead for another year.

Akitada set his mind on the needs of the living, on a small deaf-mute boy who might have a connection with an abandoned villa belonging to the Masudas. He left the business streets of the town behind and climbed the road to the green hillside overlooking it.

The curving roofs of the Masuda mansion rose behind a high wall. Its large gate was closed, in spite of the festival. Perhaps the Masudas feared their ghosts. Akitada rapped sharply. A window in the porter's lodge slid open, and a very old man peered out. Akitada gave his name, adding, 'I'm calling on Lord Masuda.'

'The master's not well. He sees no one,' wheezed the ancient one.

'Then perhaps one of the ladies will receive me?'

The window grate slid shut and there was the sound of steps shuffling off. After a moment, the gate creaked open, and Akitada was admitted to a large courtyard covered with gravel and shaded by trees. The splendor of the mansion amazed him. Blue tiles gleamed on the roofs, red and black lacquer covered doors and pillars, and everywhere he saw carvings, gilded ornaments, and glazed terracotta figures.

The old man led the way. They climbed the wide stairs of the main building and passed through it. Akitada caught glimpses of a painted ceiling supported by ornamented pillars, of thick grass mats and silk cushions, and of large, dim scroll paintings. Then they descended into a private garden. A covered gallery led to a second, slightly smaller hall. Here the old servant asked him to wait.

Akitada stood in the gallery and looked about him. This world was beautiful and remote from the bustle of the streets of Otsu and from the ragged boy. Great wealth had raised these many tiled roofs with their carved eaves and lacquered columns. Great wealth and exquisite taste had laid out the gardens that surrounded the halls and pavilions. But where were the maids, gardeners, stable boys, sweepers, cooks, carpenters, and pages who tended all this? The grounds were too quiet, almost deserted, though the buildings and the garden seemed in good repair.

An artificial stream babbled softly past the gallery where he stood, then disappeared behind a small hill and reappeared again, spanned by an elegantly arched red-lacquered bridge. Akitada stepped to the railing to look down into a small pond. Its clear water was quite deep. A frog, disturbed by Akitada's shadow, jumped in and sent several fat old koi into a mild frenzy.

The sound of children's laughter came from the garden, and two little girls skipped across the bridge, as colorful as butterflies in their silk gowns, their voices as high and clear as birdsong. A nurse in black followed more slowly.

Lucky children, Akitada thought bitterly, and turned away. *And lucky parents!*

The old porter returned eventually and took him to a beautiful room. Two ladies were seated on the pale grass mats near open doors. Both wore expensive silk gowns, one the dark grey of mourning, the other a cheerful deep rose. The lady in grey, slender and elegant, seemed to be making entries in a ledger; the other, younger lady had the half-opened scroll of an illustrated romance before her. The atmosphere was feminine, the air heavily perfumed with incense.

The lady in grey was no longer in her first youth, but still very handsome. She regarded Akitada for a moment, then made him a slight bow from the waist and said, 'You are welcome, My Lord. Please forgive the informality, but Father is not well and there was no one else to receive you. I am Lady Masuda, and this is my late husband's other wife, Kohime.'

Kohime smiled. She had a cheerful plain face and the robust body of a peasant girl. Akitada decided to address the older woman. 'I am deeply

35

distressed to disturb your peace,' he said, 'and regret extremely the ill health of Lord Masuda. Perhaps you would like me to return when he is better?'

'I am afraid Father will not improve,' said Lady Masuda. 'He is old and ... his mind wanders. You may speak freely.' She gestured towards a cushion. Akitada sat down. She nodded at the account book. 'Circumstances force me to take responsibility for running this household.'

Akitada glanced again at Lady Kohime, who nodded and said in a high, childish voice, 'Hatsuko is so clever. She can handle anything.'

So these two women were the old lord's daughters-in-law, and of the two, Lady Masuda had assumed the role of steward. She was apparently a remarkably capable and serious person. Lady Kohime, by contrast, smiled at him like a child who has been given an unexpected treat.

Accepting Lady Masuda's reticence, Akitada moved cautiously. He praised the town and its surroundings, and then expressed an interest in buying a summer place on the lake. He mentioned the beautiful setting and the fact that it was within easy reach of the capital. Lady Masuda listened politely, but he saw that her fingers moved nervously in her lap. Akitada got to the point. 'I was told that the Masudas own the abandoned villa on the water. The property would suit me perfectly. Is it perhaps for sale?'

She stiffened, and her fingers became still. 'The Masudas own half of Otsu,' she said coldly. 'I would not know the house you refer to. Perhaps—'

36

The cheerful Lady Kohime chimed in: 'Oh, Hatsuko, that must be the house where our husband's—' She gulped and covered her mouth. 'Oh.'

Lady Masuda paled and gave her a warning glance. She said brusquely, 'My sister is mistaken. In any case, none of the Masuda holdings is for sale. I am sorry, but I cannot be of assistance to you.'

Akitada was too old a hand at dealing with suspects not to know a lie. He was instantly alert to reasons why such an accomplished woman would resort to clumsy untruths. And that expression of distaste surely was because a courtesan had lived there.

Akitada's familiarity with courtesans was limited. As a young man he had not had the funds to visit the pampered beauties who sold their bodies only to the wealthiest and most generous clients. Nowadays, he tended to dislike them on principle for their greed, but in his youth he had been very tempted to find out what delights lay so far beyond his reach. He thought a wife would feel differently, especially if such a woman had stolen her husband's affections. In this case there were *two* wives. He glanced again at Lady Kohime, but met only the same bland and cheerful expression of interest.

The situation teased his curiosity. He wondered about the late heir, the husband of these women. And he wanted to know very much what had caused the courtesan to take her own life. The watchman had said it was because her lover had abandoned her. But if the lover had been the younger Masuda, neither he nor his family had made any attempt to reclaim the villa or to sell the valuable property. They had allowed it to fall to ruin in a tangled wilderness. Why, when Lady Masuda had kept the mansion in such excellent repair?

Kohime was the simpler of the two women and would surely pour out the story of the villa without much prompting, but he could think of no way to speak to her alone. Thanking the ladies, he left.

Outside, the old porter waited. 'Forgive me, sir,' he said, 'but there's someone hoping to speak to you.'

Akitada turned and saw an elderly woman in black peering over a large shrub.

'The children's nurse,' the old man explained. 'When I mentioned your name, she begged a few moments of your time.'

Akitada was puzzled. 'I don't believe I know her.'

'No, My Lord. But when her son was a student in the capital, he was accused of murder. You saved his life.'

'Good heavens! Don't tell me she's the mother of that—' Akitada gave the nurse another look. She must be near sixty, with anxious eyes in a careworn face. He had been about to call her son a rascal, but stopped himself in time. 'Er, young Ishikawa.'

'Yes. Ishikawa. That's her name.' The old man laughed, rubbing his hands, as if Akitada had been very clever to remember. 'When the gentleman is ready to leave, I shall be waiting at the

38

gate,' he said with a bow and trotted off.

Akitada had no wish to be reminded of the Ishikawa matter. It had happened a long time ago, in happier years, when Akitada had been courting his wife, but he sighed and stepped down into the garden.

On closer inspection, Mrs Ishikawa appeared to be a respected member of the Masuda household. Her black gown was of finely patterned brocade, and her grey hair was held by golden pins. He remembered young Ishikawa's haughty manner. They had been a good family fallen on hard times.

She bowed very deeply. 'This insignificant person is conscious of the great honor of finally meeting Your Lordship,' she said in a cultured voice. 'Our debt to Your Lordship has too long weighed on my conscience. I am the widow Ishikawa, mother of that unfortunate student whose life you once saved.'

'Please don't fret over the matter, Mrs Ishikawa. How is your son?'

Her face lit up. 'He is head steward for Middle Counselor Sadanori and lives in the capital,' she said. 'I'm sure he would wish to express his deep sense of obligation for your help in his difficulties.'

Akitada doubted it. Ishikawa, a thoroughly selfish young man, had been innocent of murder, but had been deeply implicated in blackmail and in a cheating scandal that had rocked the imperial university, and he had held Akitada responsible for his dismissal.

Perhaps she saw his irritation. Bursting into

long and passionate expressions of gratitude, she fell to her knees and touched her forehead to the gravel of the garden path.

Akitada looked down at the grey head and was glad he had spared someone the pain of losing a son, even if he was an unworthy one. He grimaced and bent to raise her. 'I'm very glad I could be of some small service to you,' he said. 'I assure you there is no need for such gratitude, but it is fortunate that I should have met you here.'

She brushed some dirt off her gown and looked at him uncertainly.

'You're the Masuda children's nurse, I take it?'

'Yes. I have served the family for many years. I raised both the son and the grandchildren of the old lord.' She flushed a little. 'After my husband died, I was in straitened circumstances and about to give birth. Lord Masuda is the head of our clan, and he took me in. His lady gave birth to her son soon after mine was born, and I nursed both boys.'

It explained a great deal. The student Ishikawa had been very poor, very bright, and very hardworking, but those qualities had failed to produce the rapid success he desired. No doubt being raised in a wealthy household, side by side with the heir, had contributed to his criminal activities at the university. Akitada felt sympathy for his mother, even if he could not excuse the son.

'Perhaps you can help me,' he said. 'There is an abandoned villa on the lake. I was told that it belongs to the Masudas.'

The old lady looked startled. 'You mean Peony's house? Lady Masuda would not wish to be reminded of that.'

Peony was a professional name used only by courtesans and entertainers. 'I take it that Lord Masuda's son used to keep this Peony in the villa on the lake?'

Mrs Ishikawa flushed and squirmed a little. 'We are not to speak of this.'

Akitada had put her in an impossible situation. Using her gratitude to extort information about her employers was disgraceful. He retreated instantly. 'I see. I will not trouble you then. But perhaps you can tell me about a cat I saw there, a white one with brown spots.'

'Patch? Could it be Patch after all this time? Such a dear little kitten. I used to wonder what became of it. Oh.' Shock at her indiscretion caused her to break off and clamp a hand over her mouth.

Half ashamed of himself, Akitada pounced. 'Was there not a little boy?'

'Oh, the poor child is dead. They're both dead and best forgotten.' When Akitada raised his eyebrows, she flushed. 'I did not mean it the way it sounds, but the story was so shocking that it is very unpleasant to think about it. You see, Peony killed her child and then herself.'

Akitada's face fell, along with his hopes.

Mrs Ishikawa misunderstood. 'Oh, forgive me for not saying any more. And please don't mention what I told you to the ladies. It was horrible, but there was nothing we could do. There is enough grief in this household as it is.'

From the garden came the voice of Lady Masuda calling for her. Mrs Ishikawa looked over her shoulder. 'I must go, My Lord. Please, forget what I said.' And with another deep bow she was gone.

THREE

The Dying Wisteria

Akitada stared after her. If she was right about Peony's child being dead, then the deaf-mute boy belonged to someone else, most likely to the repulsive couple who had dragged him away.

But here was a new mystery: why did Lady Masuda impose such secrecy on her household? Whatever jealousy she might have felt of her husband's concubine, such arrangements were common enough and accepted. Mrs Ishikawa had known Peony and her son and had been fond of them. Perhaps the elegant lady who had been bent over the account book knew what was in the interest of the Masudas, and the dubious offspring of a former courtesan was best assumed dead.

Whatever had happened, the Masuda problems were not his affair. Yet Akitada paused in his walk to the gate to look back thoughtfully at the Masuda mansion, testimony to the family's wealth, all of it belonging to an ailing old man without an heir. He wondered about the deaths of the courtesan Peony and her child. He also wondered about the curse killing the male Masuda heirs. Perhaps the years spent solving crimes committed by corrupt, greedy, and vengeful people had made him suspicious. Or perhaps his encounter with the wailing ghost had made him think of restless spirits in search of justice. He was neither religious nor superstitious, but there had been nothing reasonable about the events of the past two days.

For a few moments, the bleak and paralyzing hopelessness that had stifled his spirit lifted because he had stumbled on this mystery.

He asked the old servant waiting patiently beside the gate, 'When did the young lord die?'

'Which one, My Lord? Lord Tadayori died last year, and the first lady's son this year.' He sighed. 'Only the two little girls of the second lady are left now, but the old lord cares nothing for them.'

Akitada's eyebrows rose. 'How did the grandson die?'

'The great sickness, My Lord. Many children died from it.'

Akitada's stomach twisted. His son, that sturdy, handsome bundle of energy, had become a whimpering creature, covered with festering sores, as he watched helplessly. So Lady Masuda had also lost a son. And Peony and her son had died soon after. But their deaths were not clearly accounted for. A picture began to shape in Akitada's mind.

The story was not unusual. A wealthy nobleman falls in love with a beautiful courtesan, buys out her contract, and keeps her for his private enjoyment in a place where he can visit her often.

43

Such liaisons could last for months or for a lifetime. In this case, there had been a child. Had the younger Masuda really ended his affair or had his death ended it? What if Lady Masuda, after losing both husband and son, had become distraught with grief and jealousy and killed both her rival and her child?

But he was jumping to conclusions without facts. He could not even be certain that Peony's child had been Masuda's. He thanked the old man and left.

Crowds were already filling the main streets of Otsu to celebrate the departure of their ancestral ghosts. For most people, death lost its more painful attributes as soon as duty had been observed – when the souls of those who were once deeply mourned had been duly acknowledged and could, with a clear conscience, be sent back to the other world for another year. After dark, people everywhere would gather on the shores of rivers, lakes, and oceans and set afloat tiny straw boats, each containing a small candle or oil lamp, to carry the spirits of the dear departed away. One by one, the lights would grow smaller until they were extinguished.

Akitada's bitterness had hardened him to human emotions. To his skepticism for supernatural events he had added a cynical distrust for the professed grief of the living. His sympathies were with the dead. What of those ghosts whose lives and families had been taken from them by violence?

Feeling at odds with his world, he returned to the local warden's office and walked into a shouting match between a portly matron and two prisoners, a nattily-dressed man with a mustache and chin beard, and a ragged youngster of about fourteen. The warden was looking from one to the other and scratching his head.

Apparently, someone had knocked the matron to the ground from behind and snatched a package containing a length of silk from under her arm. When she had gathered her wits, she had seen the two 'villains' running away through the crowd. Her screams had brought a constable, who had set off after the fugitives and caught them a short distance away. The package was lying in the street and the two men were scuffling.

The problem was that each blamed the theft on the other and claimed to have been chasing down the culprit.

The ragged boy had tears in his eyes. He kept repeating, 'I was only trying to help.' He claimed his mother was waiting for some fish he was to purchase for their holiday meal.

The man with the whiskers was outraged. 'Lazy kids don't want to work and think they can steal an honest person's goods. Maybe a good whipping will teach him before it's too late.'

The matron, though vocal about her ordeal, was no help at all. 'I tell you, Warden Takechi, I didn't see him. He knocked me down and nearly broke my back.' She rubbed her substantial behind.

The warden shook his head. 'You should have brought witnesses,' he grumbled to the constable. 'Now it's too late, and what'll we do?'

45

The constable protested, 'Oh come on, Warden. The kid did it. Look at his clothes. Look at his face. Guilt's written all over him. Let's take him out back and question him.'

Akitada saw that the boy was terrified. Interrogation meant the whip, and even innocent people had been known to confess to crimes when beaten. He decided to step in. 'Look here, Constable,' he said in his sternest official tone. 'Whipping a suspect without good cause is against the law. And you don't have good cause without a witness.'

They turned to stare at him. The warden recognized the obstinate gentleman from the night before without much enthusiasm, but he dared not offend an official from the capital. He said, 'Do you have some information about this matter, sir?'

'No, but I have a solution for your problem.'

The warden suppressed a sigh. 'A solution, sir?'

'Yes. Make them run the same distance. The loser will be your thief.'

There was a moment's puzzled silence, and the warden's jaw sagged a little. Then the matron cried, 'A truly wise counsel.' She folded her hands and bowed to Akitada. 'A person of superior spiritual insight remembers that the Buddha helps the innocent.'

Akitada said dryly, 'Perhaps, madam, but in this case the thief got caught because his captor was the better runner.'

The warden expelled a sigh of relief. His face broke into a wide grin. 'Very clever, sir. Let's go

46

outside.'

They all adjourned to a large field behind the jailhouse, and the constables marked off the proper distance. Akitada watched the preparations with a frown. Taking the warden aside, he said, 'The culprit may make a break for it. You'd better have your two best runners keep an eye on the man.'

The warden glanced at Whiskers and shook his head. 'You think he's the one, eh? You may be right, sir, but with due respect, I'll have both of them watched. Frankly, I don't see it. He looks like a respectable citizen, while the kid's just the type to pull a snatch. This town's full of half-starved youngsters who make a living by stealing. Travelers passing through are in a hurry and rarely report the thefts. This one made the mistake of picking on a local woman.' He walked off to alert his constables.

Of course, Warden Takechi knew his town better than Akitada, and the ragged boy did look desperate. On the other hand, Whiskers had lost some of his earlier confidence. He moved his feet nervously and looked around. No, Akitada felt sure he was right about this.

The two suspects took their places and the race was on. The thin boy easily outdistanced the man. Halfway to the finish, Whiskers knew it too and suddenly veered off to make his escape. Several constables were on him in a matter of moments and dragged him back to the office to face charges. The crowd applauded and dispersed, well satisfied with their morning's entertainment.

The boy came to thank Akitada shyly. 'I don't know what I would've done without you, sir,' he mumbled, his eyes moist. 'Mother's not as strong as she was. She needs me to run errands and gather wood...' His eyes widened. 'The fish! Excuse me, sir.'

Akitada looked after him with a smile.

'Well, sir,' said the warden, joining him, 'I was wrong and you were right about that youngster. I'm much obliged. You saved me from making a bad mistake. Now, how can I be of service?'

Having established such friendly relations, Akitada introduced himself more fully and told him the story of the mute boy, the cat, and the abandoned villa. Warden Takechi's face grew serious. When Akitada reached the nurse's account of Peony's death, he shook his head. 'I remember. A simple case of drowning. Accident or suicide. They sent for me after she was found. Someone mentioned a boy, but we couldn't find him, dead or alive. Some think the *kappa* must've got him. Every time someone disappears in the lake, it's blamed on those water sprites. The dead woman had no friends, and no family either, as far as we could tell. The neighbors thought she was a loose woman from the capital. I can't see what the Mimuras have to do with that. They live in Awazu and wouldn't know anybody like that.'

It was a dead end, but Akitada could not leave Otsu without one last attempt to do something for the deaf-mute child. He said, 'The boy was terrified of them. You must have noticed?'

'Expected a thrashing for running away,' the

48

warden grunted.

'No doubt. He was covered with bruises from head to toe,' Akitada snapped.

The warden shook his head. 'Folk like the Mimuras live hard and raise their young ones hard. It's what they've got to look forward to in life. Prepares them for hardship. Forgive me for saying so, sir, but a gentleman like you would naturally mistake that for abuse. The boy will be all right. They're raising him to give them a hand with their fishing business. I expect they've already got him mending nets and weaving traps when he's not gutting the catch.'

Akitada shuddered. 'I gave the man money to feed him properly. Could you have someone check on the boy? If he needs anything, I'd like to know. I'll leave you information on how to contact me.'

The warden looked dubious, but nodded. 'As you wish, sir. But it's best not to spoil them. They get lazy.'

Akitada trusted neither the Mimuras nor the Otsu constabulary and planned to come back to check on the boy himself.

In the office, a constable was taking down information from the thief and the matron. People were waiting, and one of them, a tall and handsome young man in a neat blue robe and black cap, detached himself from a wall.

'I don't believe my eyes,' he said to Akitada. 'Here you are when I've been looking everywhere. I came to check with the warden in case he'd picked up your murdered corpse on the highway.' He laughed at his joke, flashing a set of handsome teeth and stretching his thin mustache almost from ear to ear.

Akitada said sourly, 'Nonsense, Tora. You know very well I can look after myself. Why are you here?'

'Well, you were due back two days ago. Your lady was upset.'

That was probably untrue. Tamako had made it abundantly clear over the past six months that she had lost all interest in him. Most of her anger dated from the death of their son. She blamed him because he had refused to listen to her warnings about the epidemic. But in truth their problems had started before. They had begun growing apart after Yori was born. She had undermined his efforts to teach the boy, and his wishes had no longer seemed to matter to her. After Yori's death, the bitterness between them had become physical separation. They maintained a coldly polite distance these days.

'I was delayed,' he said vaguely, canceling his plan to visit the Mimuras. He could not risk explanations because Tamako would take his interest in the mute child as another example of his indifference to her and their dead son. The fact was that he would have welcomed any excuse to delay the return to his empty home.

It was not literally empty, of course. Beside his wife, it housed his retainers – Tora, Genba, and old Seimei – as well as a cook, a maid, and at times a young servant boy. But with Yori dead, and the bitter recrimination he saw in his wife's face whenever she looked at him, he felt alone and unwelcome there.

Fortunately, Tora asked no questions. They ate a light meal in the market and then separated. Tora went to get his horse, and Akitada returned to the inn to pay his bill. They met again outside Otsu on the highway to the capital, leaving behind the glittering lake and Otsu harbor.

Tora chattered away as his master rode silently, hardly listening. The road led into the mountains. After a while, Tora gave up and fell silent. They crossed the eastern mountains at Osaka-toge and stopped at the barrier station. The sun was already getting low, and the trees cast long shadows. In these peaceful times the station was unmanned, but small businesses catered to travelers. They watered their horses and stretched their legs. Then, over a cup of wine, Tora tried to find out what troubled his master.

'Is all well, sir?' he asked.

'Why shouldn't it be?'

'You haven't said much. We ... I'm thinking it's time you got back to normal, sir.'

Back to normal? A moment's anger seized Akitada that Tora should think Yori's death was so easily brushed aside. He scowled ferociously, saw Tora's face fall and the pity and concern in his eyes, and sighed instead. 'It's not so easy, Tora. Let's go on. I'd like to get home before dark.'

It was his loss that caused him to yearn so desperately for the child. He wanted to buy the boy from the Mimuras, and his greedy parents would sell him gladly, but he was afraid to take him home to Tamako. But that he could not share with Tora.

51

They descended the mountains in glum silence. The hillsides opened up before them and revealed the great plain, cradled in green mountains and traversed by wide rivers. In its center, like a jewel, lay the capital, the roofs of its palaces and pagodas glittering in the setting sun. Akitada always paused at this point of the journey to drink in the sight and to let his heart fill with pride at the greatness of the nation he served. He did so now, and Tora came up. He looked cast down.

Akitada felt guilty and said, 'I came across a curious story in Otsu and almost meddled again. You rescued me just in time.' He forced a smile and saw Tora's face light up.

Back on the road, Tora asked, 'But why not meddle, sir? It might take your mind off ... things. And I could help.'

Tora's enthusiasm for prying into the secrets of total strangers made him a valuable assistant and sometimes a nuisance. It would not do to give him false hopes now. 'I'm afraid not,' Akitada said. 'It's none of our business, and there doesn't seem to be a case. It's a matter of a courtesan who drowned herself and may or may not have killed her child at the same time.'

'There's more to it than that, sir, if I know you. Why did she kill herself? And her child! Pitiful, that.' He shot a cautious glance at Akitada's face. 'Boy or girl?'

'A boy. Five years old.'

Tora sucked in his breath. 'Do you want to tell me about it, sir?'

Akitada told him what he had learned about

52

Peony and the Masuda family. As they passed the Kiyomizu temple, Tora said enthusiastically, 'That's some story. I'll bet there's more there than meets the eye. That much money, and all the heirs die.' He paused. 'What made you go to that empty villa in the first place?'

Akitada shot him a glance and looked away. 'Oh, nothing much,' he said vaguely. 'To have a look at the lake. The view, and a cool breeze. Did I mention that the nurse is Ishikawa's mother?'

'Ishikawa?'

'You remember the student involved in the cheating scandal at the university?'

'The one who blackmailed his professor and then tied him to a statue so the killer could cut his throat?'

'Well, he didn't intend that.'

'Brings back memories,' said Tora. 'That was when you were courting your lady.'

Akitada regretted having raised the subject.

Tora grinned. 'You even wrote her a poem and had me take it to her.'

Akitada grunted.

'A morning-after poem!'

'That's enough, Tora.'

They reached the Kamo River and crossed it at the Third Street Gate. It was not far from here to Akitada's house, and Tora had caught the bleak look on his master's face and subsided.

The Sugawara residence was substantial and rubbed shoulders with the homes of the wealthy, but it was old and had seen better days. Akitada's poverty during much of his career had made it impossible to do more than keep a roof over their

53

heads, and sometimes not even that. Recalling the Masuda mansion, Akitada looked at his home now and felt the old sense of inadequacy. He had let his family down. The stable was new, thanks to a case that had brought a generous fee, but the mud and wattle wall that surrounded the property had lost most of its whitewash and sections of plaster, and the roof of the main house needed new shingles. He knew the gardens were badly overgrown, and no doubt things were worse inside. Since Yori's death he had simply not cared.

Genba opened the gate and greeted them with a broad smile. 'So you found him, brother,' he said to Tora, and to Akitada, 'Welcome home, sir. We were worried.'

Akitada reluctantly accepted the fact that his people might be genuinely fond of him and care about his well-being. As he dismounted, he looked at Genba more closely. If he was not much mistaken, the huge man had lost weight. 'Are you quite well, Genba?' he asked.

'Yes, sir. Why?'

'You look ... thinner.'

Tora glanced at Genba and said, 'His appetite's gone, sir. He's been grieving for Yori. We all have.'

Bereft of speech, Akitada turned to go, then managed a choked, 'Thank you.'

Tamako was not waiting for him. He went to his study and shed his traveling robe, slipping instead into the comfortable old blue one he wore around the house. Then he went looking for his wife. The house seemed to be empty. In the kitchen, he finally found the frowzy cook. He disliked the woman intensely. Not only was she ill-tempered and lazy, but she had deserted them when Yori had become ill. She had returned later and wept with contrition, claiming that she would starve in the streets if he did not take her back. And he had done so. Now she looked up from chopping vegetables and scowled. 'So you're back. I'd better get a fish from the market then.'

The woman was impossible, but being in a softened mood after Genba and Tora, Akitada simply nodded and asked, 'Where is everybody?'

'Your lady and the old man are in the garden. Don't know where the silly girl is.'

The 'silly girl' was Tamako's maid. Akitada went outside. The service yard was neat, thanks to his two stalwart retainers. He could hear their voices from the stable, where they were tending to the horses. He entered the main garden through a narrow gate of woven bamboo.

The trees and shrubs must have put on a burst of new growth over the summer. He looked in dismay at a massive tangle of greenery that reminded him of the courtesan's garden. It was high time something was done or the garden would swallow the house. Hearing voices, he made his way along the narrow path, its flat stones barely visible any longer, and came on Tamako and Seimei. They had not heard him.

Seimei sat on the veranda steps, huddled in a quilted robe. Akitada frowned. Even after sunset, it was too warm to wear such heavy clothes. He saw how frail the old man had become and remembered with a twinge of guilt how, in his raving grief over the loss of his son, he had questioned the justice of a fate that snatched the youngest and let the old survive.

Tamako wore an old blue-and-white patterned cloth robe. She had turned up its sleeves and tucked the skirt into her sash so that he could see her trousers underneath. Her long hair was twisted up under a blue scarf. She was cutting dead wood from the wisteria vine. A large pile lay beside her.

It was a day for uncomfortable memories. Akitada had fallen in love with Tamako when she had worn a similar blue cloth gown. They had been sitting under a wisteria-covered trellis in her father's garden. Under the ancestor of this very same wisteria. And the poem Tora had carried to her the morning after their first night together had been tied to a wisteria bloom from that plant.

'Why don't you let Genba and Tora do that?' he asked sharply.

They both jumped. Seimei rose shakily to his feet and bowed, crying, 'Welcome home, sir. We were worried.'

Tamako said nothing. She gave him a searching, earnest look, then turned away.

He stared at her back. 'There is no need for you to do such heavy work,' he said. 'I can still afford to hire people.'

'It is dying,' she murmured vaguely, touching the shriveled twigs that remained on the plant. 'I have tried, but it keeps dying. A little more each day.'

'Nonsense. It just needs water. Or something.'

'There has been a lot of rain.'

Seimei sighed. 'Too much rain. It causes rot, and healthy things shrivel up and die.'

Tamako turned. They both looked at Seimei and then at each other and wondered if the old man was talking about the wisteria.

FOUR

Tora's Secret

In the stable, Tora and Genba unsaddled the horses.

'How's the master doing?' Genba asked, reaching for a rag to rub down Akitada's mount.

'The same, I think.' Tora leaned against his horse for a rest. He felt very tired all of a sudden. So many problems. He sighed. 'He did talk a little about some mystery in Otsu, so maybe he's taking an interest again.'

Genba brightened. 'That's good. So, did you tell him?'

'No.' Tora led his horse to his stall and tied him up. 'It's too soon. He's still brooding.'

Genba glanced at him as he scooped some grain into two leather buckets. 'Time's passing,' he said, taking the buckets to the horses. 'You've got to do something soon.'

Tora sagged down on some straw and did not reply.

'Besides, there's work to be done here. The place is falling apart. I can't do it all by myself. This can't go on, Tora. It's not fair to her or to our master.'

Tora was saved by the stable door creaking open. The cook came in. Tora groaned.

She put her hands on her wide hips and glared at him. 'So you finally show your face again. What's the matter? Are the girls fed up?'

Tora said, 'I hope you haven't been looking into the stew pot again, Turnip Nose. I hate curdled stew.'

'I hope it gives you a bellyache.'

Tora made a face at her. 'It will. You'll kill us all one of these days.'

'You think you're so smart. Here —' she held out a stained basket — 'run to the market and get a good-sized bream for your master's dinner. And be quick about it. He'll want his food as soon as he's had a bath.'

'For Buddha's sake, woman,' Tora cried. 'I just got back from riding all the way to Otsu and beyond.'

'Then it's time you made yourself useful around here.' She pushed the basket at him.

'Aiih!' Tora jumped back in mock horror.

'It's the fish basket, stupid!'

'I know. I meant *you*.' He gave a bellow of laughter, and she threw the basket at him with a curse and ran out, slamming the door behind her.

'You shouldn't tease her,' said Genba.

'That one brings nothing but joy,' Tora grumbled, bending for the basket, 'when she leaves.'

'She's a good cook. Give me the basket. I'll go.

58

You look dead on your feet.'

Tora relinquished the basket. 'She's short, fat, stupid, ugly, lazy, and mean. A woman like that is spitting into the wind of fate. And her bad karma is ruining our lives.'

'Get some rest, brother. You'll feel better.'

Tora collapsed on a pile of straw. 'You're right. Thanks.'

Genba swept up the basket with one hand and trotted out.

Akitada retreated from the scene in the garden to his study, and Tamako turned back to her work. Seimei watched her for a moment, then got up from his seat on the veranda and shuffled after his master into the house. He found Akitada seated behind his desk, drumming his fingers on the lacquered surface and scowling.

'Will you have some tea now, sir?' Seimei asked.

'Yes. Thank you.'

Akitada continued drumming, while the old man lit the coals in a brazier under the water pot and selected a twist of paper with powdered tea leaves and orange peel.

'Was your journey successful?' Seimei asked.

'Hmm. What? Oh, that. Quite successful.'

Seimei eyed his master. 'I was afraid there were problems when you were gone longer than expected.'

Akitada sighed. 'I found a small boy, Seimei. And I lost him again. Don't mention the matter to your mistress because it might upset her, but I'm worried about that child.'

'Ah.' Seimei cocked his head at the kettle, gauging the moment when the steam would whistle from the spout. Not yet. He poured a little of the powder into a cup and glanced at Akitada. 'You are worried, sir?'

'Apparently, he belongs to a fisherman and his wife. He has been beaten and starved, Seimei. I saw his poor body. It was covered with bruises, and he was just skin and bone. And he's such a nice little boy. Do you think I should buy him?'

'Buy him?' Seimei's jaw dropped. 'To do what?' The water came to a sudden rolling boil, sending a hissing thread of steam from the narrow spout. Seimei snatched the kettle up and poured. Stirring the tea with a bamboo brush, he brought the cup to Akitada. 'What did you have in mind for the child, sir?'

The question was uncomfortable. 'I don't know. I suppose I thought he would be company. That I could teach him. He's deaf-mute, you know. Or perhaps just mute. I'm not sure.'

Though he had not been invited to do so, Seimei sat down on a cushion. 'You miss Yori,' he said firmly. 'It is quite natural to feel such a loss.'

'You think I'm acting like a fool,' objected Akitada. 'I felt sorry for the child. He needed help. Is that so hard to grasp?' He saw the pity in the old man's face and threw up his hands. 'Oh, very well. Have it your way. All I know is that for the day and night I had the boy I felt whole again. And now that he is gone, I ... have nothing – except a dreadful fear of having abandoned him to the brutality of his parents.' He stared bleakly

60

into the cup of tea.

'You cannot replace a child the way you would a dog,' Seimei said.

That made Akitada angry. 'Forget it. You don't understand. How could you?'

Seimei bit his lip. 'Drink your tea.'

Akitada drank. They looked at each other. Akitada felt demoralized. He groaned. 'Everything I touch breaks in my hands. My life is cursed. What am I to do, Seimei?'

'Her Ladyship—' began Seimei.

Getting up abruptly, Akitada said, 'Never mind. Thank you for the tea. After a bath, I shall work on the household accounts for the rest of the day.'

Seimci sighed and left.

Tora was too worried to rest long. He decided to forego the evening rice. Since Akitada was bathing, he told Scimei he was going into the city. The old man was arranging the household accounts on Akitada's desk and seemed preoccupied. He barely looked up.

Tora's destination was a quarter near the Eastern Temple, a far distance for a tired man, but he walked quickly. This southernmost corner of the capital was almost rural. A few great estates mingled with a large number of very modest homes and small farms. The small houses clustered around and between the large, tree-shaded and walled compounds and belonged mostly to the owners' retainers and servants. Children played in the street, and laundry dried on bamboo fencing.

The rain had left puddles in the streets, and

some ducks scattered as Tora passed. Doves cooed on the wooden eaves, and behind one of the mansion walls someone played a lute. Tora's spirits lifted and he started to whistle.

Near the southern embankment of the city he turned into the yard of a tiny house and carefully closed the bamboo gate behind him. As always, he stopped to gaze at his home. The new roof was thatched and set the wooden house, little more than a one-room shack, apart from its flat-roofed neighbors. New steps led to a small porch at the front door, and a morning glory vine covered with deep-blue flowers and buzzing bees twined around its railing. Tora thought about adding a beehive next year, and then turned his attention to the little vegetable garden. His cabbages and radishes, planted in neat rows, looked well. The soil was good here, and the recent rain had caused a spurt of growth. He smiled as he walked along the path to the house. On the new step sat a fat white cat cleaning one front paw and barely pausing to purr when Tora bent to scratch its head.

He straightened and called, 'Hanae? I'm back.'

Immediately, a loud yelping sounded from behind the house. It changed to excited barks, and then a cloud of squawking and fluttering chickens erupted around the corner, followed by a large grey creature making the sharp turn on scrabbling paws. The creature transformed itself into a shaggy dog, who flung himself on Tora in a paroxysm of joy. Tora staggered back and stepped on the cat's tail. The cat yowled, spat, and jumped on to the railing, where it clung, hissing and twitching its tail.

Tora fended off the flying paws and lapping tongue. 'Down, Trouble. Down, you big useless monster. Down. You broke your rope again. Where's your mistress?'

The dog sat, the remnants of a straw rope still attached to his neck, his tail beating a drum roll on the wooden boards. He pricked up pointed ears and looked attentive.

'Hanae?' Tora called again.

The dog's ears twitched, and he looked around expectantly.

'Stupid dog,' said Tora. 'That's what I bought you for. To watch your mistress. Don't you remember where she went?'

The tail thumped apologetically.

Next door, a middle-aged woman came out on her porch. 'That you, Tora? Hanae's gone to the market. She should be back soon. Is that big brute loose again? I don't want him after my chickens.'

'Hello, Mrs Hamada. I'll tie him up. He doesn't mean any harm. Just has too much energy.'

She sniffed. 'That dog's a fiend. Better get rid of him. You here to stay?'

'Not yet.' This was a sore subject, and Tora hoped the nosy biddy would go back into her house.

But she slipped her bare feet into wooden clogs and waddled to the fence between their houses. The dog, recognizing an arch enemy, growled. Mrs Hamada fixed Tora with an accusing look and said, 'Hanae's talking about taking a job. In her condition! You know she's not very strong.

How about asking that grand master of yours to take her in? Hanae works hard, and she's good with children.'

Tora shook his head. 'Can't. The master has no children.'

'No children?' She gaped at him. 'In a noble house? How can that be? Your master isn't ... you know?' She waved a limp hand.

'No, he isn't,' Tora snapped. 'They had a boy, but he died from the smallpox in the spring.'

'Oh.' She relented, as Tora knew she would, having lost her husband and one of her own children in the epidemic. So many had died. It was the reason the small house next to her had become available. She gave him a shrewd look. 'You aren't afraid to tell them, are you?'

Tora stuck out his chin. 'Of course not. We'll manage. I'll find a way.'

'That's what you men always say. In the end it's us who have the babies and then have to scrimp and save to put food in their mouths. And nine times out of ten, we end up feeding their father while he squanders his money on wine and loose women.'

Tora was getting angry, all the more so because he could not antagonize Hanae's neighbor. 'I'm not like that,' he growled.

Encouraged by Tora's tone, the dog burst into furious barking.

Someone called from the street, 'Tora?'

They turned and saw a young woman with a large market basket over her arm. She was slight and very pretty, with a tiny waist and such fragile wrists that the basket seemed much too large and

64

heavy for her.

Tora gave a whoop of joy and rushed to meet her, the dog at his heels. Taking the basket and putting it on the ground, he swung her up into his arms, while Trouble danced around them, yapping with pleasure.

'Tora, let me down,' she protested, laughing. 'What will the neighbors think? Oh, and Trouble is loose again.'

'I don't care,' he said. 'I don't care what anybody thinks. You're my wife. Why shouldn't I do as I want with my own wife?' He swung her around, and she giggled.

At the fence, Mrs Hamada watched, a sentimental smile softening her face. Young love.

But even young love must come back to earth. Tora put his wife down and picked up the basket instead. Hanae caught up the dog's broken rope and waved to Mrs Hamada.

They walked together through the gate and retied the dog. Then they went inside the small house, closing the door on neighbor, dog, and cat.

Tora took the basket into the small kitchen. 'A fish?'

'Yes. For our supper. With some of your cabbage and a few mushrooms.'

'It's still early,' he said, reaching for Hanae again.

She blushed. 'Let me at least start the vegetables.'

'I'll help you.' He rummaged in a box and brought out a couple of knives, passing one to her. They worked side by side at the wooden counter, scraping and chopping quickly, and when she had tossed the last handful into the black kettle and hung it from the chain over the fire, Tora stirred the coals and added a little more wood.

'We're almost out,' she said, glancing at the wood pile.

He turned to look at her, aghast. 'You want me to split wood, too?'

She chuckled. 'No. Of course not. Later.'

He took her into his arms and carried her into the main room they used for eating and sleeping. There he knelt, laying her gently on the single thick mat in its center. He untied her sash and parted her gown.

Later they lay side by side, smiling. Tora felt almost dizzy with love. He turned on his side and put his hand on her still flat belly. 'A son or a daughter, do you think?' he asked, looking down at her with a besotted expression.

'A son, of course,' she said. 'How could it be otherwise with such a strong tiger for a father?'

'Hanae,' he said, suddenly serious, 'you're quite well, aren't you? That heavy basket. Let me bring home the food next time.'

'Nonsense.' She sat up, rearranging her robe, and tied her sash. 'I'm very strong. And it's early still. But I thought we'd better make some plans...' She stopped. 'I forgot. Did you find your master?'

'Yes. In Otsu. In the warden's office. Busy solving some minor crime.'

'Did you tell him about us?' she asked anxiously.

'I'm sorry, Hanae, I just couldn't. It was the O-

66

bon festival. He remembers.'

'Yes. Poor man.' She touched his cheek. 'Don't worry. You'll find a time.'

Tora was not at all hopeful. Akitada's mood had become very morose and bitter. He either ignored the other members of his household or flared up in sudden fury at the most minor infractions. But Tora did not want to worry her or make her think that Akitada was a cruel tyrant, so he changed the subject. 'He did tell me a strange story on the way back. It happened in Otsu. A courtesan drowned herself and her child in the lake. He thinks the death is suspicious. If he's taking an interest in murder again, he may be getting better. Anyway, it made me think of you.'

She flushed. 'Me? I was never a courtesan, Tora.'

'No, of course not. But I thought you might know something about her. She was bought out by a nobleman. Her name was Peony.'

'Peony?' Hanae frowned. 'There was a famous Peony who disappeared suddenly. I wonder if it could be her. But it was a long time ago. Maybe six or seven years.'

Tora had an idea. If Hanae could get information about this woman, Akitada might be interested enough to look into the matter, and that might give Tora a perfect excuse to introduce Hanae to him. 'It's possible. Very possible. Are they still talking about her? Tell me what you know.'

'Well, she was a *choja*, a courtesan of the first rank, which means she was very beautiful and talented, so, yes, they're still talking about her. A

67

woman like that can choose among many great admirers and is invited to private parties in noble houses. But one day she was gone, and she was never heard of again. They say she owed a hundred bars of gold at the time. I've always wondered what happened to her.'

'A woman of the quarter that famous doesn't just disappear. If she ran away, there would've been a search for her. Can you find out more? Like who held the debt?'

'I'll try. Maybe she bought her own way out and left the profession.' She paused. 'Some of us do, you know.'

He looked hurt. 'I gave you all the money I had. You wanted to buy this house instead of paying off Ohiya immediately.'

'We needed a place to live. And you know you like it here. I was starting to make good money, and I thought if we lived here I could save enough to pay Master Ohiya off in six months. But now there won't *be* six months. I'll have to stop dancing soon.' She let her voice trail off and touched her belly.

Hanae was an enchanting dancer. Tora had fallen in love with her the first time he had seen her. She had studied under Ohiya and had already been the most sought-after among the entertainers when she had agreed to be Tora's wife. Her success still made Tora uneasy. He suddenly remembered something Mrs Hamada had said. 'What's going on?' he asked suspiciously. 'Is there something you haven't told me?'

Hanae got up and started towards the kitchen. 'I can smell the vegetables. Time to cook the fish,' she called over her shoulder.

Tora followed. 'Hanae? Mrs Hamada said something about a job. What job?'

She turned around. 'Tora, you know I won't be able to perform much longer and I still owe Master Ohiya a lot of money. I've asked around for another job and...'

Tora's stared at her in profound shock. 'B–but I thought you were done with all that,' he stammered.

The 'quarter' was the pleasure quarter, where men could hire entertainers and prostitutes. Hanae was not only much in demand as a dancer at private parties, but she sang, too. Tora was afraid that she would become a great success and leave him. He still marveled that she had been willing to forego fame and fortune to share his humble life. No woman had ever made that sort of sacrifice for him, and he was both shamed and dizzy with pride. But now he might lose her after all. He clenched his fists in helpless misery.

She said gently, 'It's not that kind of job, Tora. I'm hoping to work as a nursemaid in a noble house. They have many servants so there won't be any heavy work. My debts are almost paid, and when the time comes that I get too big and clumsy to dance, I'll have somewhere to go to earn the rest of the money. And when Master Ohiya hears that I'm working for Lord Sadanori, he will be patient.'

Tora stared at her unhappily. It had taken all of his money and Genba's savings to pay for most of their little house. He had hoped to pay off the rest by the end of the year. If he could have taken

Hanae home with him, the money they saved could have paid off her debts. But that was impossible. Akitada had always disliked Tora's affairs with women from the quarter. He would not understand that this time it was different. And now that there was to be a child, Tora was doubly afraid because it might stir up fresh grief and more anger.

Hanae eyed him nervously. 'It will be all right, Tora. You'll see,' she said in a small voice. 'We're young. Many people started life with less.'

'We won't be together. How will I see you? Who is this Sadanori? What do you know about him?'

'He's Fujiwara Sadanori. Very important in the government. And it will only be for a few months, and you can visit any time. I shall be back in the capital before you know it,' she added softly.

'Back in the capital? What do you mean? You aren't going away?'

'Not very far. Just over the eastern mountains. Near Uji. The roads are good, and it's very pretty countryside. Very healthy, too. Much better than this great, dirty city.' She was babbling, but she broke off when she saw Tora's face.

'No,' he roared. 'I forbid it. I'll find the money. Somehow.' It was an empty promise, and they both knew it.

Hanae turned away and occupied herself with their supper. Tora stormed outside and split wood so furiously that even Trouble kept his distance.

They ate their meal in silence. Tora could not stay the night. Even with Akitada's indifference to household matters it was risky to be absent for too many nights. So when they were done, he said, 'Tell me more about this job.'

She knew that this amounted to a surrender, but it saddened her to see the pain in his eyes. 'Lord Sadanori,' she said, 'is an imperial counselor and used to be steward to the empress's household. He's very rich and powerful and has big houses here and in the country. One of his wives will give birth soon. Someone from the quarter recommended me to him.'

Tora stared at her. 'What? He found out about you in the quarter? And you want to go to live in his house?'

She flushed. 'I tell you, it's not like that. He knows I'm married and expecting your child. That's why he offered me the job. He sent a very respectable woman to talk to me. She came in a sedan chair with a servant and wanted to know if I had taken care of children before and how far along I was. Besides, who would take a pregnant girl for a concubine?'

Tora grumbled, 'He may be odd. Some men have strange fancies when it comes to lovemaking.'

She stifled a snort. After a moment, his mouth quirked and he leered at her. They burst into laughter.

'How soon will you know if you have the job?'

'I'm to go for a visit tomorrow.'

'I'll take you. To make sure you'll be safe.'

Hanae gave him one of her enchanting smiles, and a short but passionate interval later, Tora took his leave.

71

FIVE

The Fishing Village

Akitada slept better than he had expected, and this time dreamlessly, but the moment he opened his eyes the memory of the boy was back with him.

He got up and opened the shutters. Sunshine and birdsong cheered him, and suddenly he knew what he must do. His spirits lifted. He was going back for the child. He would have no peace otherwise and would imagine, in lurid detail, the boy's suffering for every moment of his waking hours. His Hikone report to the ministry could wait another day. The minister would assume that negotiations had taken longer.

As he dressed, he thought about his wife. In all justice, he must let her know of his decision to bring a new member into their household. Besides, she needed to make preparations for the child. The conversation would be painful to both of them, however.

Akitada was pacing when Seimei came in with tea and rice gruel. He returned an absent-minded, 'Good morning,' and then said, 'thank you.'

Perhaps he should suggest to his wife that they needed a youngster to help her in the garden? But the boy was too young to be much use, even if he had learned to mend nets and gut fish. Could he appeal to Tamako's pity for his condition? That would have worked in normal times, but a woman who had recently lost her only child could hardly be asked to devote herself to someone else's – and the boy would need a great deal of care and teaching. Perhaps the best thing to do was simply to inform her of his decision and let her choose her own way. Once the child was here, Tamako would either open her arms to him, or ignore him. If the latter, Akitada would make up for her neglect. Her opinion of him could hardly get any worse, but he had no wish to cause her unnecessary pain or make unreasonable demands.

Seimei came in again and cleared his throat.

'Eh?'

'Your rice gruel and tea are getting cold.'

'Oh. Yes.' Akitada looked at the food absent-mindedly.

'Cook has complained about Tora. She says he spends his nights in the city with some female. And he is very rude to her.'

Akitada grimaced. Tora's love affairs were legion, though to give him credit, he did not have to pay for his pleasure. 'Cook is an ill-tempered female,' he said. 'What do *you* think?'

Seimei sighed. 'He has been getting very unreliable, right when we need his help badly. The roof leaks in several places. Both house and garden have been neglected for too long.'

Part of that responsibility lay with Akitada, but he did not care to discuss it. He said irritably,

'Very well, I'll put a stop to whatever Tora is doing.'

Seimei bowed and withdrew.

Abandoning his morning meal, Akitada went to look for his wife. He found her in her room, sewing with her maid. The floor was strewn with piles of fabric, mostly ordinary cheap stuff, and Tamako was again wearing a plain cloth gown herself.

He stared at the scene in puzzlement. Surely they had not become so poor that they had to dress like common people. It occurred to him that grief had caused her to make some religious vow of simplicity. The Buddhist priests occasionally preached such doctrines, no doubt so their congregation would donate their wealth to the temples. He had always thought that their expensive stoles belied their vows of austerity. Heaven forbid that his wife should decide to become a nun.

He blurted out, 'What are you doing?'

Tamako flushed at his tone. 'We're sewing new robes, trousers, and shirts for Tora and Genba, and a few everyday clothes for Cook, Oyuki, and me. Did you wish me to do something else?'

He wanted to pursue the subject of his wife's working like a servant, dressed in servant's clothes, but decided against it. 'I have something to discuss with you.'

The maid, a dainty and very neat woman who had been with Tamako since both were young girls, pushed the needle into the fabric she was working on, bowed, and left the room. Akitada looked after her, wondering why Tora had never

74

seemed interested in her. She was still quite pretty, even after an ill-conceived marriage had ended in widowhood.

Bringing his attention back to his errand, he said, 'I am leaving for Otsu this morning.'

'Again?'

'Yes. There's something I left undone.'

'I see.'

'Er ... it concerns a child.'

'A child?'

'Yes. There's a child, a boy. He's about five years old.'

'I don't understand.'

Why was it so difficult to speak to one's wife? Akitada fidgeted, then burst out, 'I have decided to raise him.'

Tamako gave a small gasp and rose, the fabric on her lap falling to the floor, along with thread and needle. 'What boy?' Her voice was tight with shock. 'Five years old? In Otsu? You never mentioned...' She had turned quite pale.

So much for breaking the news gently. 'I'm sorry, Tamako. I should have told you right away, but I didn't want to upset you further. I have thought and thought how to tell you about him.' He pleaded, 'The child needs a loving home and someone to teach him and raise him properly. He's a very nice little boy.' Seeing her face contract with pain, his heart sank and he muttered again, 'I'm sorry.'

At least she did not burst into angry speech, as he had expected. She said tonelessly, 'Of course you must bring the child here. He will be welcome.'

'You won't be troubled,' he promised anxiously. 'I can look after him myself.'

She gave him a searching look and seemed to want to say or ask something else, but in the end she merely nodded.

'Thank you,' said Akitada. 'I hoped you would understand.'

Tora had to be woken to saddle his master's horse.

Akitada, for once conscious of his surroundings, eyed him with a frown. 'Another late night?'

Tora blinked. 'Not really, sir. Long day yesterday.'

Akitada, who thought he had had an equally long day, had no pity. 'You might as well saddle yours, too,' he said. 'We're going back.'

'Back?' Tora stared at him in dismay. 'To Hikone?'

'No. A place called Awazu, a fishing village on the lake just beyond Otsu.'

Tora had promised to take Hanae to Uji today. 'Will we be gone long?' he asked, a futile question, for they would certainly not be back in time, even if they turned right around. Tora's face grew longer.

In a deceptively calm voice, Akitada asked, 'Am I interfering with some personal plans of yours?'

'In a way.' Tora was too preoccupied to notice his master's growing anger. 'I had promised to take ... a young lady to Uji today. I was going to put her on a horse behind me.' In an afterthought,

76

he added, 'It'll give the horse some exercise.'

Akitada exploded. 'Don't make up lame tales about exercising the horses when you want to take one of your doxies on an outing. I regret to interfere in your plans –' Akitada's voice dripped icy sarcasm – 'but I must insist.'

Tora flushed. 'That's all right, sir,' he muttered and glumly finished saddling the horses.

'Take a sword. I'm carrying gold on this trip.'

Akitada led his horse into the courtyard and mounted. Tora remained in whispered conversation with Genba, who kept shaking his head.

'What is it now?' Akitada snapped.

'Just asking Genba if he can get a message to Hanae ... that's the young woman's—'

'Genba has better things to do than to carry messages to your women. Hurry up. I'm waiting.'

Tora obeyed, but he maintained a hurt silence all the way out of town. Akitada ignored him and kept up a good pace. They crossed the Kamo River against a stream of farmers who brought their produce in heavily laden ox carts or in huge baskets slung on their bent backs and headed for the mountains, still shrouded in morning mist.

Akitada had brought a large amount of gold because he suspected that he would not get out of the transaction cheaply. The gold was the reason Tora was with him and why they were both armed. The highways were not safe these days.

They reached the pass before Akitada awoke to his surroundings. He recalled stopping here the day before and turned back to make some comment to Tora. The words remained unsaid when he saw Tora's face.

'What's wrong with you?' he demanded. The scene at home came back to him, along with Seimei's report on Tora's absences.

'Nothing, sir.'

'You're angry with me when I should be angry with you.'

'And why is that, sir?' Tora asked bitterly. 'Yesterday I came to find you as ordered by Her Ladyship. Today I follow you back, as ordered by you. In what way have I offended?'

This was not the sort of answer Akitada had expected. Happy-go-lucky to a fault, Tora always shrugged off minor reproofs with a smile and an apology. It was this cheerfulness that Akitada had always liked about him. Their very different personalities complemented each other, and this morose Tora was unrecognizable. Akitada reined in his horse and said, 'Cook complains that you are rarely at home any more. Why is that?'

Tora did not like his master's tone, and his worries about Hanae got the best of him. He snapped, 'I hope that goblin-faced female goes to the hell where they cut out your tongue before they throw you into the flames.'

'Answer my question.' Akitada was getting angry again.

Tora glowered. 'I had private business. Since you never have any instructions for me or Genba, I thought I was free to take an evening off now and then.'

Being reminded of his own shortcomings did not improve Akitada's temper. 'Evenings, nights, and whole days. Apparently, you hardly ever sleep at home any more. And you're never there when you're needed.'

Tora's face froze. 'Oh, am I to be Cook's errand boy now? I don't believe you made that very clear, sir, when you took me on.'

They were stopped in the middle of the roadway, glaring at each other. Two pilgrims in white robes and straw hats gave them a wide berth.

Eight years ago they had met on another highway, where Tora had saved Akitada and Seimei from bandits. Akitada had taken him on as his servant, in spite of Tora's expressed hatred for titled officials. He had put aside his own sense of correctness to tolerate Tora's improper familiarity and ramshackle ways for the sake of his good nature and friendship. Perhaps he had gone too far in letting him have his way.

Akitada said coldly, 'I hired a servant, and I pay a servant to serve. When I saw my house yesterday it was clear that you had not done any work for months. I found my wife in the garden, hacking away at overgrown trees and shrubs like a common laborer, while you spend your days and nights in the amusement quarter. I should beat you.'

Tora's eyes widened. For a moment he said nothing. Then he nodded. 'Fair enough. You can beat me, but to be clear, it wasn't Genba's fault. He wanted to mend the roof and fix the wall, but it takes two to do it, and I wasn't there. You needn't pay me for the rest of the year, and I'll do my best to get the work done.'

'Another empty promise,' grumbled Akitada,

his happy anticipation of bringing the boy home spoiled by Tora's unaccountable behavior. Tora knew very well that Akitada would never beat him and took advantage of this. They continued their journey in disgruntled silence.

This time they bypassed Otsu and made straight for the fishing village. On this bright and sunny day, the forest where Akitada had met the boy was neither ghostly nor threatening. Sunlight filtered through the pine trees and spilled green patches of light on bracken and moss. Instead of an impenetrable dark crouching like a monster under the trees, the distant lake shimmered through the pines. Akitada had not noticed the dirt track to Awazu in the rain.

They took the twisting path to the lake and found a scattering of poor wooden houses covered with boards. Nine or ten of these weather-blackened dwellings clung to a narrow strip of land between lake and forest. The lake was a silver mirror reflecting the midday sun, and along the shore weathered boat docks extended into the fierce brightness. Broken dinghies, masts, torn sails, oars and rudders lay about, and fishing nets, floats, and baskets dried against brush fences. Gulls swooped and shrieked hoarsely while children played among the reeds, and two women were drying small silvery fish on grass mats.

The boy had not strayed very far at all. Akitada could see the warden's point. Children will roam from their homes without their parents' knowledge. And the poor are often malnourished. But he had not been mistaken about the bruises on the child's body.

Most of the men were probably out on the lake. The surface of the water was dotted with white sails and rowboats as far as the eye could see, almost to the blue mountains in the distance.

They passed an old woman sitting in the doorway of the first house. Like a piece of driftwood, her black clothing was bleached a dirty grey that blended into the weathered wood behind her. She was weaving bamboo strips into fish traps, but had stopped to stare at them.

Akitada said, 'Go ask her where the Mimuras live.'

Tora dismounted without a word and walked over to the old woman. A conversation ensued. The old one shook her head and talked, her toothless mouth like a knothole in an ancient tree. She scowled, gestured, and spat. Tora returned. The old woman got up and limped to the fence to look after him.

'She didn't seem very friendly,' Akitada commented.

'Hates Mimura,' Tora said. 'A devil, she calls him. I wouldn't trust a man that his own neighbors curse. Anyway, it's the third house from the end, and he's not home.'

Tora was evidently still angry. 'We'll have to manage without him then,' said Akitada, trying to re-establish working relations. 'It does seem strange that he should have made such bitter enemies in his own village.'

'I wouldn't know.'

Akitada realized that he had not yet told Tora about the boy, but they had reached their destination and there was no time, so he merely said,

'I'm trying to buy a boy from them. They starved and abused him.'

That got Tora's attention. 'A boy? You're buying a boy?' His expression suggested that Akitada must have lost his mind. 'But ... there are plenty of starving boys in the capital. Why come here?'

Akitada dismounted. 'Later. First let's make sure the child is here and safe.'

There was a strong smell of fish in the air. The walls of the decrepit wooden house, built on stilts like the others, were so weather-stained that they were nearly black. The small porch and steps leaned precariously, and the roof was covered with ancient, ragged boards, which had grass growing from them. Nearby stood a smaller, but much newer, storehouse.

Smoke came from an opening in the roof of the house, and the door stood open, so somebody was at home. Down on the shore, the children paused in their play to stare at the visitors, but the boy was not among them.

'Mrs Mimura?' Akitada called.

The frowzy female from their last meeting appeared in the doorway. She wore a new, boldly patterned robe tied around her thick middle with a bright-orange sash. Squinting into the sun, she recognized Akitada when he walked towards her. She was not at all pleased to see him.

'Mrs Mimura,' said Akitada, looking up at her, 'I came to speak to you and your husband about the boy.' Her eyes flicked towards the storehouse. Akitada was certain now that she was afraid of him.

'My husband's out fishing,' she said. 'He's taken the boy with him. What did you want to talk about?'

Akitada did not answer right away. The children, two boys and a smaller girl, joined them. They were sturdy, tough-looking children with flat round faces and looked nothing at all like the deaf-mute boy. 'Are these your other children?' Akitada asked.

'Yes.'

It seemed a very short answer for a mother to give. She was anxious to get rid of him, and he was beginning to be uneasy. 'You say your husband has taken the little boy. Surely he's younger than these children.'

'He was begging so, my husband took pity.'

Neither her tone nor her smile was convincing. Akitada frowned. 'I thought he was deaf-mute. Surely he's not much help on a boat.'

The oldest boy guffawed. 'Moron,' he said.

'Shut up.' His mother glared at him. 'It's true he isn't much help, poor cripple,' she said, turning back to Akitada. 'My husband lets him ride along for a treat.'

'Ah.'

She flushed. 'We're taking good care of him, sir. We give him only the best, thanks to your kindness, only the best. He eats like a prince. The other children are jealous. Aren't you, my pets?'

The children ignored her. Akitada was undecided. He looked out over the lake, wishing Mimura's boat would return. Overhead swooped white gulls with raucous cries; higher up, two black kites performed their slow circles silently.

83

Several gulls had taken up position on the roof of the storehouse, where they were walking back and forth with watchful eyes.

And then Akitada heard the sound of sweeping from somewhere beyond the storehouse.

Mrs Mimura heard it too and said quickly, 'We always tell them it's to make up for his being deaf and dumb. We all look after him like a little treasure, don't we?'

The children looked at their mother in surprise. The oldest said, 'Huh?'

Akitada looked at the storehouse. It was solidly constructed on sturdy timber supports. The sweeping sounds continued. 'Tora,' he called.

Tora dismounted, tied up the horses, and strolled over.

Mrs Mimura raised her voice a little and started down the steps. 'I'm sorry that my husband isn't home. Or the boy either. You've wasted a trip. How about coming back another day? Or maybe we could bring him to you in Otsu. Say tomorrow?'

Akitada bent to peer under the storehouse. It was raised several feet above ground on its supports, perhaps in case of flooding from the lake. In the shelter under the building, Mimura stored tools of his trade: spare oars, parts of a boat, three-pronged spears, and bamboo fishing rods and lines. Fishing traps, like the one the old woman had been making, and baskets hung from nails, and a large net was strung between the supports. But Akitada saw movement behind all of these objects, on the far side of the storehouse.

'Go see what's behind the storehouse,' he told

84

Tora.

Tora walked off, and the woman went flying after him to grab his sleeve. 'Wait,' she cried. 'We keep a vicious dog back there.'

Tora flung off her hand. 'Don't touch me, woman!' he snapped. 'I've dealt with dogs before. And with troublesome females.' He disappeared around the storehouse in two or three great strides, the woman on his heels. The children followed.

'Oh no, you don't,' she cried. 'You've got no right...'

For a moment there was silence. Then Tora's voice, strangely tight, shouted, 'Sir? Would you come back here a moment?'

Akitada ran around the storehouse and came to an abrupt halt.

It was a weedy area where Mimura cleaned his fish and dumped unsold wares and other garbage. The rotting fish was piled in a stinking mound beside an old basket. Flies buzzed everywhere.

And there was the boy. He held a broken broom in his small hands and was once again dressed in a filthy rag. New bruises, including a black eye and a swollen lip, had joined the old ones. His eyes were wide with fear.

But what made Akitada's blood boil was that he had a heavy leather collar around his thin neck. From the collar, a rusty chain about ten feet in length led to one of the supports of the storehouse, where it was fastened to an iron ring.

The child had stopped sweeping the malodorous mess of fish entrails; his eyes were on Mrs Mimura.

Tora cursed softly.

Barely controlling his rage, Akitada turned to the woman. 'Is this your vicious dog?'

She cringed away from his face. 'He will run away, sir,' she wailed. 'It's for his own good. You know he runs away.'

'So you tie him up like a dog? Worse, for I see neither food nor water bowls.'

'He eats in the house. He's only been here a little while. I've got work to do and can't watch him all the time. It was just for a little while until I got supper started.'

Akitada gave her another look that made her quail and went to the boy. The child whimpered and backed away. Akitada spoke to him, soothing meaningless phrases: 'Don't be afraid. It's only me again. You remember me, don't you? We met in the forest. It was raining then, but you rode to Otsu with me. I bought you a rice cake and we stayed at the inn. Do you remember?' The boy gave no sign that he understood. His eyes shifted to Tora, who had come up beside him, and he jerked away in fear.

'Hold still, little one,' Tora said gently. 'Let me take that collar off. You've done enough sweeping.' But the boy ran.

Mrs Mimura, perhaps trying to be helpful, snatched at his chain and jerked it sharply. The boy flipped backward with a strangled cry and hit the dirt hard. Almost at the same instant Tora backhanded Mrs Mimura so viciously that she screamed and tumbled to the ground, holding her face with both hands.

Neither Tora nor Akitada paid attention to the

blood spurting from her nose. They knelt on either side of child – who lay curled into a ball, clutching at his throat – and got in each other's way trying to undo the collar.

'That she-devil,' Tora grunted. When the collar finally parted, they saw bloody welts on the boy's slender neck.

Ignoring the stench and filth that clung to him, Akitada took the boy in his arms and held him, murmuring endearments, while Tora stood by. Behind them, Mrs Mimura got to her feet and ran back to the house. Her children ignored her and remained to watch.

When the boy stopped whimpering and relaxed against him, Akitada rose. Carrying the child, he said in a shaking voice, 'Come, Tora. We're taking him with us now. I'll be damned if I'm going to pay those monsters a single copper for him.'

When they got on their horses, the woman ran from the house, holding a rag to her face. 'Where are you taking him?' she cried. 'You can't have him. Not without pay.'

Akitada glared. 'Count yourself lucky if I don't have you and your husband arrested.'

She screamed, 'Help! Help! Thieves. They're stealing our child.'

The Mimura children shouted, 'Thieves,' and, 'Help,' and laughed at the excitement.

A small group of people from the village stood near the old crone's house. They watched with detached interest. No one made a move to come to Mrs Mimura's aid or stop them. The old one gave them a toothless smile and a wave as they passed.

Akitada held the trembling child and spurred his horse. He wanted to get away from this place of horror as fast and far as possible. They reached the road and turned into the forest.

There was no one else about, but after the rains the road surface was too treacherous for their current speed, especially as Akitada was distracted by the child and did not guide his horse as carefully as he should have. His mount stepped in a deep rut and stumbled. Akitada reined in. He was fond of his horse, a fine grey stallion he had brought back from the North Country, and realized with dismay that he was limping badly. Tora dismounted to inspect the damage.

'A sprain,' he said, feeling the animal's right front leg. 'Don't know how bad.'

'It was my fault,' muttered Akitada, stroking the animal's neck.

'Take my horse, and I'll walk yours to Otsu,' Tora offered, even though he knew this meant he would not get back to Hanae tonight.

Akitada looked at the boy and saw that he clung to him and was watching the woods as if he expected monsters to emerge at any moment. 'Very well,' he said. 'We'll go on to Otsu, spend the night at the inn there, and continue in the morning. If necessary, we can rent a horse.'

Tora reached up, intending to lift the boy down, but the child panicked and fell into the mud. He got up immediately and clutched at Akitada's boot.

Akitada's heart contracted with pity and love. He got down and lifted the boy, a muddy, malodorous bundle, into Tora's saddle before mounting behind him. They continued their journey at a slower pace.

SIX

Arrested

The innkeeper's jaw dropped when Akitada walked in, holding the same ragged child by the hand. He wrinkled his nose at the stench of rotten fish and eyed the filthy tatters with disgust. 'Don't tell me, sir,' he said with a sneer. 'You want a room, a bath, hot food, and new clothes for this boy.'

Akitada glared at him and passed across a handful of silver before signing the register. 'My servant is bringing an injured horse. We will need stabling for two horses and the services of a groom who knows about sprains.'

The innkeeper nodded and led the way to the same room they had occupied before.

And as before, they bathed, and then ate. The child had new bruises – bad ones – from the punishment he had suffered since Akitada had relinquished him to the Mimuras. And he clung more desperately to Akitada, eating little when the maid brought their meal.

Though filled with anger and guilt at the child's condition, Akitada was also deeply content. He

89

talked to the boy about Yori, about the home they were going to, about Tora, and Seimei, Genba and the cook and maid. And also – a little uncertainly – about Tamako. The child watched his lips with wide eyes and smiled a little now and then, and soon fell asleep. Akitada covered him with a blanket.

Tora arrived shortly after. They moved away from the sleeping child and talked softly, for Akitada was becoming more and more convinced that the boy could hear at least some sounds. Tora reported that the horse was having a poultice applied to the injured leg and that the groom was hopeful that the swelling would recede by morning.

He looked at the boy, shook his head, and muttered, 'That female! She isn't human. She's an animal. No. Wild animals wouldn't do that to their young. How is he, sir?'

'As you see. When we get him home, he will be fine.'

'You said you'd tell me about him.'

Akitada did. Tora became excited when he heard about the cat, the deserted villa, and the toy sword. 'It was your karma, sir, and his,' he said. 'All of it. You finding the boy. The boy finding the cat. The cat taking you to the house. Maybe his poor mother's ghost turned into that cat, looking for her child. And what about the little sword being like the one you bought for Yori? The gods have a hand in this.' He paused, looking a little embarrassed. 'I had something to tell you. About the courtesan Peony. At least – it's about a courtesan with the same name. But now I think it must be your Peony.' He gestured to the boy. 'That poor little fellow's mother.'

Akitada had made some of the same assumptions, but suddenly there were too many coincidences, too much supernatural manipulation of human affairs. A man like Tora would believe there was a spiritual link between the boy, the cat, and a dead woman, but then Tora was absurdly gullible when it came to ghostly phenomena.

No, the boy probably belonged to the Mimuras, or at least he was an abandoned child who had become a burden to some starving peasant woman or streetwalker. It was better that way. If he belonged to someone who wanted him back, he would lose him again. That cat had been one of thousands of feral cats, finding shelter wherever it could. And the broken toy sword meant nothing. There were plenty of those about, too. But Tora had got over his sullenness, so Akitada nodded and said, 'What about the courtesan Peony?'

'Hanae says about six or seven years ago a *choja* vanished from the capital. She left a debt of a hundred gold bars.' He paused for effect. 'Her professional name was Peony.'

Akitada shook his head. 'A dubious tale, Tora. A hundred bars of gold is a great fortune. What did she need the money for? Who would lend that much to a courtesan? If she was indeed so deeply indebted, her creditor would have demanded a thorough investigation. This has all the earmarks of legend. No, a hundred bars of gold is quite an outrageous value to put on a prostitute. Besides, if she was indeed famous, she could not have disappeared without a trace. Her new lover would have bragged, her former lovers would have discovered her whereabouts, and then her creditors would have taken the case to court.'

Tora's face fell a little, but he was not giving up so easily. 'I think it could be the same woman, all the same. A hundred bars of gold is not so much when you think of their expenses. They invest a fortune in their gowns alone. And then there's jewelry, cosmetics, scents, and servants. A high-ranking courtesan has a maid to carry her things and a man servant to hold her large umbrella. And if she sings and dances, she'll have to pay the musicians. And what of her house? Courtesans don't live in tenements or rent rooms over shops. Besides, she may have taken up the life because of her parents' debt.'

Akitada raised his brows. 'You're extremely well informed about loose women. Perhaps it would be better if you looked into the cost of lumber and found the name of a good carpenter.'

Tora flushed. 'We were trying to help. Hanae's promised to ask around for you. She knows people in the quarter. There must be someone who knew this Peony. She'll find out for us.'

'Who is this Hanae? As if I couldn't guess.'

Tora bristled. 'Hanae is a dancer, a very good one. She's no courtesan, but her work takes her places where the best courtesans go. That's why I know a little about that life. As soon as we get home, I'll talk to her again.'

'Spare me. You've spent most of your waking hours with such women. We just discussed your regrettable habits this very morning. No, I think you'll be better employed working at home for a while.'

'Sir, I can't,' Tora cried in alarm. 'I promised.'

Akitada glanced at the sleeping child. 'Shh! What do you mean?'

'I'm worried about her. I meant to speak to you...'

Akitada had had enough. 'Not another word. You will, for once, make yourself useful. As long as we're here, you can talk to the neighbors of the dead woman and report back to me tonight. But when we get back to the capital, I absolutely forbid another visit to your paramour until all the chores around the house are done. That should occupy your time for the next month or two.'

Tora stood up, stared at Akitada for a moment, then left.

Akitada thought, he no longer even bothers to bow when he is sulking. Then he lay down beside the boy. Like Yori, this child had a fragile, helpless beauty in his sleep, which made one want to protect and shelter him. Half afraid of the future, he listened to the child's soft breathing and stared at the ceiling, wondering how to patch up his marriage, his household, and his relationship with Tora.

Eventually, he must have dozed off, because a noise at the door startled him into wakefulness. Someone was whispering. Tora had closed the door, but now it was open by just a crack, and he thought he saw an eye peering in. He was about to get up and confront those outside, when the door flew back and several people poured over the threshold.

'There!' cried Mrs Mimura, pointing a triumphant finger at him. Beside her stood the solid figure of the local warden. The innkeeper and Mr Mimura peered over their shoulders, and several others, constables and assorted strangers, pressed in behind them, trying to catch a glimpse of the room. Their expressions ranged from avid interest to disapproval, shock, and anger.

Outrage seized Akitada. He felt the frightened boy creeping into his arms and responded by pulling him close. Someone snickered. 'What is the meaning of this?' he demanded.

Warden Takechi looked embarrassed. He glanced down at Mrs Mimura, who looked more repulsive than ever with her swollen nose and mouth. 'Er, this woman has laid charges against you and your servant, sir.'

Akitada bit his lip. Of course. The miserable creature was vengeful and greedy enough to make trouble. He should have known. If it had not been for his foolish haste, they would be well away from Otsu by now, perhaps even at home in the capital. The child in his arms trembled. Akitada patted his thin back and said, 'Don't be afraid. I shall take care of this,' before putting him back on his blanket and standing up. The child instantly clasped his leg and began to sob.

'Warden,' Akitada said, 'I can explain, but these people are frightening the boy. Make them wait outside and close the door.'

'Oh, no, you don't,' Mimura cried, pushing his wife aside and stepping forward. 'I'm his father and I want to hear what's being said. There won't be any deals this time. We can all see what's going on here. If the so-called "good people" think they can go to an honest working man's house, beat up his wife, and steal his son for their foul pleasures, it's time we stood up for ourselves. No, Warden, this time I'm laying charges against him. I demand that he's arrested, along with his servant, and put in jail until we can get a hearing before a proper judge.'

There was a murmur of agreement from the people in the back. Even the innkeeper nodded his head.

'Don't be ridiculous, Mimura,' Akitada snapped. 'We took this boy away from your place because he was being abused. Your wife attacked my servant and he defended himself.' It was not far from the truth. 'You're lucky I didn't lay charges against both of you right away. Since you have conveniently brought the warden with you, I think I will.'

The warden cleared his throat. 'Well, er, if you'll come along then, sir?'

'My servant isn't back from an errand. As soon as he gets here to look after the child, I'll walk over to your office.'

The warden shook his head. 'I'm sorry, sir. As I said, charges have been laid against both you and your servant. And the boy will be returned to his parents.'

'You must be joking! I will not permit it.'

'It's not for you to say, sir.'

Akitada saw that the man was quite serious. He felt an icy knot of fear in his stomach. 'You cannot turn this child over to the people who tormented him. Look at him.' Akitada leaned down to tip up the boy's chin and expose his black eye. Then he stripped back his little jacket and pointed out the new wounds on his neck and back.

Mrs Mimura cried, 'We never did that. He did it. He's been hurting our child.' She burst into tears and started forward. Akitada snatched up the boy and retreated.

'Sir,' pleaded the warden.

'Give me my child,' clamored the woman.

'Arrest him!' shouted Mimura.

By now a crowd had squeezed into the room and formed a threatening circle around Akitada and the child. If the boy had not clung to him so tightly, Akitada might have found the melodramatic scene comical. It certainly was beneath his dignity, but he could not think of a good way out of it. Where the devil was Tora?

'Sorry, sir. I have to do my duty.' The warden gestured to his constables and took the boy from Akitada.

Tora reached the capital before sunset. He went directly to his and Hanae's small house, and tied his tired horse to the fence post. The house was locked and empty.

Trouble was in the back, on a triple rope he had wrapped so many times around a tree that he now sat pinned to it, his tongue hanging out and his eyes nearly popping from his head. He whimpered when he saw Tora and wagged his tail weakly. A broken broomstick lay nearby.

Muttering under his breath, Tora struggled with the knots and finally got the dog loose, but Trouble acted strangely, cowering and hanging his head. When Tora called to him, he finally came, crawling and skirting the broomstick, and licked his boots. Tora saw that his neck was a mass of raw welts from the rope. It reminded Tora unpleasantly of the boy in Otsu. Convinced that Mrs Hamada had used her chance to tie and beat Trouble, Tora fetched the dog some water and then shouted for Hanae's neighbor.

Mrs Hamada trotted over to the fence.

'That miserable cur got loose and went after my chickens again,' she said immediately.

Tora swallowed down his anger and asked, 'Where's Hanae?'

'Hanae waited the best part of the morning for you. Finally, Lord Sadanori sent a sedan chair for her. She said she'd be back as quick as possible.'

'When?'

'How should I know?' Mrs Hamada added slyly, 'Some gentlemen show a pretty young woman a lot more respect than you do. She may decide to spend the night.'

Tora glared. 'That's a lie. She's to be a nurse-maid to one of the children.'

Mrs Hamada cackled. 'You're a fool, Tora. Hanae's much too pretty for any lady to hire as a nurse.'

'And you're an evil-mouthed hag,' Tora snapped. 'And something else: next time stay away from my property. It's cowardly to beat a poor dumb animal that can't defend itself.'

She flushed with anger. 'Good riddance to you and that monster,' she cried. 'He killed one of my chickens, and you'd better pay for it.'

'I don't believe you. Where is it?'

'It's in the soup. Poor people can't afford to give a chicken a proper funeral.'

'Then I hope you choke on it.' Tora turned away in disgust.

She cursed after him as he walked away.

Tora's anger at Akitada faded. Now he was sick with worry. The neighbor had an evil tongue, but Tora was beginning to doubt the nursemaid story himself. He did not like the idea of the sedan chair. Being too edgy to wait in the little house, and not wanting to leave the dog to Mrs Hamada's cruel care, he cut a length of rope, looped it loosely about the dog's sore neck, and got back on his horse.

It was dusk when they reached the Sugawara residence.

Genba let them in, looking anxious when he did not see Akitada.

'He's spending the night in Otsu,' Tora said. 'With a small boy.'

'With a small boy? What's going on? Why are you looking like that?'

Tora did not answer. He dismounted and took the horse to the well to water it. Then he tied the dog to a tree.

'Whose dog is that?' Genba asked, his voice a little louder. 'And the horse looks worn out.'

Tora sagged down on the well rim and put his head in his hands. Where was Hanae? How could he find her? And what was he going to do about Akitada? He had walked out of the inn room in Otsu too angry to think straight.

'Tora?'

He looked up at Genba. 'I've made a mess of it,

brother. But the devil only knows what a man is to do in my case. The master wouldn't let me get a message to Hanae, and now she's gone, the gods only know where. I was supposed to question people in Otsu, but instead I went home to Hanae. The dog's name's Trouble. He's mine. Our neighbor beats him, so I couldn't leave him there.'

'Trouble?' Genba's eyes grew round as he worked through this garbled response and grasped the salient part. 'You left the master in Otsu? Without telling him? That's not good. What's this about a boy?'

Tora rubbed a hand across his eyes and told Genba what had happened at the Mimuras.

Genba's face lengthened. 'But that means the master still has the gold with him. And you left him to ride back with all that gold, and with a small child, on an injured horse?' Genba's voice rose with anxiety. 'How could you? You've sworn to serve and protect him.'

Tora grasped his head again. 'I know, I know. I meant to go back as soon as I talked to Hanae. But what am I to do now? She's gone. Abducted. Hanae's my wife, and she's going to have my child. I just thought she needed me more than he did. He's got his sword. And he should've let me explain. Genba, what good is my life if I'm not allowed to look after my own?'

Genba shook his head and sat down beside him. 'I'd go myself,' he said, 'but somebody's got to look after Her Ladyship and the house.'

'I have to find Hanae.'

'What happened?'

99

Tora explained his suspicions about Lord Sadanori and how she had been taken away in a sedan chair.

Genba brightened. 'It's probably nothing. If she says she's to be a nursemaid, then that's what she was hired for. She'll be back later or tomorrow and tell you all about her visit. You need to go back to Otsu.'

Tora shook his head. 'I've a bad feeling about this. Something's wrong. I wish I knew where to look for her. If she's been abducted, she's not going to be in Uji.'

In the end, Akitada was arrested. He even had to bear the humiliation of having his hands tied with a constable's thin chain and his feet hobbled so he could not run away. The latter would not have happened if he had not made the mistake of snatching up his sword to keep the warden from taking the boy. Raising a weapon against a duly appointed officer of the law while he was carrying out his duty was so serious an offense that Akitada's rank did not protect him from the ensuing indignities. In any case, the sword was as useless as his arm after one of the constables had disarmed him by delivering a sharp blow with his iron rod.

During the night, which Akitada spent on the floor of one of the cells, his forearm became swollen and throbbed. He slept fitfully, in pain and sick about having been forced to abandon the child again to the vengeful fury of the Mimura family. He was also afraid that Tora would not come back.

Warden Takechi came to see him in the morning. Akitada did not bother to rise. He answered the other man's greeting with a harsh, 'I shall see you prosecuted by the law if anything else happens to that child. After I told you about the Mimuras, I expected you to make certain the boy was safe.'

Warden Takechi raised a hand. 'He spent the night with my family. It was too late to make other arrangements, but my wife will look after him until the matter is settled.'

Akitada got to his feet. 'Sorry, Warden, I did you an injustice. That was good of you and your wife. What happens next?'

'The boy's in the office. Would you like to see him? To make sure he's all right?'

'Of course.'

In the office, another surprise awaited him. The youngster who had been arrested for the theft of the matron's silk was waiting with a short elderly woman. The woman held the boy by the hand. When the child saw Akitada, he turned his head away.

Akitada's heart sank. He went to the boy and said, 'I'm so glad to see you well this morning.' The child hid his face in the woman's skirt. It was a moment before Akitada remembered to greet the youth. 'I'm afraid I don't know your name,' he said.

'Manjiro, sir. This is my mother, Mrs Yozaemon. We heard about your troubles and came to see if we could help.'

Akitada was touched. Here he was, a prisoner in Otsu, without a friend or servant, and these

101

two strangers had cared enough to come to him. 'You honor me,' he said, choking a little, and bowed to both of them. The mother bowed more deeply and began to thank him. Akitada interrupted her. 'Thank you for coming, but I hope to settle this ugly matter quickly and return home with the boy.' He looked at the child again, but met only a baleful stare.

The woman said, 'Poor little tyke,' and stroked the child's hair.

'At the moment he's in the warden's care. I'm worried that he may be returned to the people who tormented him.'

'We could take him for a while, your honor,' she said shyly. 'I'm alone except for Manjiro, and the child would be company when Manjiro's working. I don't get about much because of my bad back.' She paused. 'We're poor, but my little house is as clean as I can keep it. We eat simple food, but he would never go hungry.'

Akitada looked at the warden, who nodded. 'I don't see why not. Until we know what happened to the child. The parents have a claim on the boy, you know.'

'*If* they are his parents,' said Akitada. 'And even then, I believe they have lost the right to this child. I'll pay Mrs Yozaemon for his care, but I have only a few silver coins and coppers on me. My saddlebags are at the inn.'

Mrs Yozaemon said, 'Oh, you don't have to pay us. Not after what you did for Manjiro.'

'Thank you, but I insist.'

The warden pointed to a corner of his office. 'Your things have been brought. The innkeeper wanted the room for other guests.'

The man had been in a hurry to get rid of his notorious guest. 'What about my horse? He is valuable, and I have no intention of losing him. And what happened to my servant, Tora? He was supposed to return to the inn last night.'

Tora was accused of a brutal attack on Mrs Mimura, and so the constables had scoured the town for him, Akitada learned. They had given up when a groom from the inn reported that he had left Otsu on horseback shortly before Akitada's arrest. Only Akitada's horse remained in the inn's stable.

This blow was unexpectedly painful for Akitada. Tora had abandoned him without so much as an explanation or a farewell. Distracted, he looked at the boy again, perhaps in the hope that the child would somehow make up for it. But he turned his head away again. Why was he angry? What had Akitada done apart from trying to save him – and suffering dire consequences for a simple act of charity? He cradled his swollen arm and ground out, 'So what is next?'

'You'll remain our guest,' the warden said, 'until the case can be heard.'

'I want to speak to the judge now,' Akitada countered.

Warden Takechi scratched his head, but agreed that he would see what could be done.

At least the boy seemed to like Mrs Yozaemon and Manjiro. Akitada went to his saddlebag to pay her. The warden caught a glimpse of the gold, and he had to explain that he had meant to pay the Mimuras for the child.

Warden Takechi looked shocked. 'You'd give that much for the child?' Akitada flushed at the implication. The warden shook his head, 'If he finds out what he missed, Mimura will beat that stupid wife of his.'

Mrs Yozaemon and her son departed with five gold pieces and some loose silver, taking the boy with them, and Akitada bent his mind to solving his predicament. He hoped to convince the judge to release him. The warden had no such authority, but a judge could make exceptions for men of rank. One problem was the 'fugitive' Tora. Unless Akitada could produce his 'partner in crime', the judge might balk at letting him leave.

He returned to his cell to pace and brood over Tora's desertion. Tora was no humble and obedient servant, but he had always been loyal. Akitada was angry and hurt that he had been left in a cell, with an injured arm, under the eyes of three constables, who stared at him periodically through the opening in the cell door.

Tora's rebellion must have something to do with his newest girlfriend. Had Akitada missed some clue there? Doubts began to plague him. Perhaps he should have listened to Tora. But forgiving him was an altogether different matter. This time Tora had gone too far.

The warden returned with a soberly dressed corpulent gentleman he introduced as Judge Nakano.

Nakano looked at him and frowned. 'Surely,' he said to the warden, 'this confinement is not necessary. I doubt Lord Sugawara would run off like a common criminal. Take us to a private room.'

A more hopeful Akitada was soon seated across from Nakano in a small back room where the warden stored his documents. But if he had thought that this promising beginning would lead to a rapid dismissal of the charges against him, he was disappointed.

Nakano stared at him for quite a while before he said, 'I am afraid the charges are serious. Very serious. We have had such cases before. Apparently, there is a call for small children – boys, I should say – in some circles in the capital.' He made a face. 'So far the villains have been common criminals. Yours is a peculiar case.'

Akitada, who by now had a very good notion of what he was being accused of, snapped, 'I have no idea what you are talking about. I found this child a few days ago. He was wet, hungry, cold, and apparently lost. I bought him food and dry clothing, and when his alleged parents finally remembered him, I returned him to them with a gift of money to take care of him. Today, I found him tied by his neck like a dog behind their house. He was bruised and cut from a recent beating. My money had been spent on new clothes for Mrs Mimura and heaven knows what else. I was outraged and took the child away with me. That's all.'

'Hmm. The parents maintain you stole the boy from their village and spent the night with him in the Inn of Happy Returns.'

'I found the boy on the highway.'

'But you spent the night with him?'

'What else should I have done? Abandoned

him in the street in the rain?'

'But then you went back to get him again, and again you took him to the inn. Why did you come back for the boy? Warden Takechi says you intended to buy him. For what purpose?'

Realizing belatedly the unfortunate name of the inn, Akitada flushed. 'I lost my son this past spring,' he said stiffly. 'It pained me to see another boy mistreated.'

'Hmm.' The judge regarded Akitada fixedly. Silence fell. Nakano clearly did not believe that a man of Akitada's rank would bother to adopt the ragged, deaf-mute child of a fisherman.

'You are charging the Mimuras?' Nakano began again. 'With what?'

'Torturing the child. Stealing him. Taking my money under false pretenses.'

Nakano considered. 'The last one might work. Dubious, though. I think you'd better drop the charges and hope the Mimuras are willing to forget your behavior in return for some payment for their pain and suffering.'

Akitada fumed. 'Absolutely not! What about the child's pain and suffering? And what will become of him?'

Nakano sighed. 'This cannot be very good for your reputation, sir.'

'Let *me* worry about my reputation.'

They glared at each other. Nakano looked away first and said, 'You are senior secretary in the Ministry of Justice?'

'Yes.'

'It would be quite wrong to hold you here, under the circumstances. On the other hand, we

106

must make certain that you will attend your trial. Feelings in the community run high in this case. Shall we announce that you will deposit a certain sum in gold as surety for your return?'

Relief washed over Akitada. 'How much?'

Nakano pursed his lips and then mentioned an amount that was surprisingly close to what Akitada had in his saddlebag.

Akitada agreed.

Nakano rose and bowed. 'Delighted to make your acquaintance, My Lord,' he said. 'I trust we shall meet again when the time comes to clear up this matter to everyone's satisfaction.'

Akitada got up, too. 'What about the boy? I am anxious to have custody of him.' Seeing Nakano's lips tighten, he added quickly, 'To take him home to my wife.'

'Impossible.'

Akitada clenched his fists. For all he knew, he had made the boy's fate worse. 'Can he remain with the people who are caring for him now?'

'Why should he not be returned to his parents?'

'Because they beat him. If you return the child to the Mimuras, I'm convinced he will die before the cases can be heard.'

'Surely you exaggerate.'

'No. And I will not leave Otsu until the child is safe. In fact, if I hear that he is being returned to the Mimuras, I shall be back. With reinforcements. And I shall use my influence in the capital to investigate how children are treated in Otsu and its surroundings and what measures have been taken by the authorities to protect them. I gather from what you said that this district has a history of crimes against children.'

Nakano opened his mouth and closed it again. Drawing himself up, he said stiffly, 'I invite such an investigation, sir. In my view, children belong with their parents. But in this case, I will permit a temporary – mind you, temporary – arrangement until we know where we stand. I trust you will not try to see him in the meantime?'

Akitada bowed. 'Thank you. That is all I ask.'

Akitada returned to the capital, poorer by the gold he had carried to Otsu, and without the child.

SEVEN

The House on the Uji River

Tora did not return to Otsu. His fear for Hanae and his unborn child outweighed everything else. Akitada, who was armed, was well able to defend himself, while Hanae was helpless.

Too ashamed to tell either Seimei or Tamako, he left on foot. He had lost the right to use Akitada's property. He stopped at their little house, hoping against hope that Hanae had returned. She had not, and he set out for Uji.

Without money to rent a post horse, he fell into a steady pace walking south on the Nara highway. Night fell quickly, and most travelers on the road were headed for their homes in the capital. He scrutinized each sedan chair he met. Once or twice he got in trouble for lifting a curtain to look inside.

The road was lined with pines, snaked away towards black mountains.

Taking the extraordinary and painful step of leaving his master had been much like cutting off his arm or leg, and his stomach still twisted at it. That bond had been made for life. He had walked away from a debt he could never repay and made a lie of the solemn oath of loyalty. By all the rules he lived by, he was dishonored.

He no longer blamed Akitada. As his master, he had a right to expect unquestioning loyalty and obedience.

Tired and discouraged, he was tempted to lie down under a tree to sleep for a few hours, but his worries about Hanae had increased a hundred-fold. She should have been home a long time ago. He thought again of Sadanori's reputation and of Hanae's beauty and popularity. Sending a sedan chair was an unlikely courtesy towards a prospective servant, and Mrs Hamada's opinion that no wife would tolerate such a beautiful maid or nurse in her household gnawed at him.

At Uji, the mountains loomed ominously above him, and the river rushed through the narrows with a sound like thunder. Tora felt a kind of panic, a fear of real disaster. Oh, Hanae, he thought, why did you run away from me into such danger?

He had hoped to find an inn open to ask for directions, but all the houses were dark. He passed a shrine and walked across the bridge. The sound of the river was deafening, and the rushing waters made the massive timbers shiver beneath his feet.

Tora followed the highway along the river until the mountains fell back and a vast plain opened before him. Here he saw a great complex of buildings. When he reached the gate, a dog inside set up a loud barking. Someone shouted at the animal. Encouraged, Tora struck the bell by the gate with its wooden clapper.

There was more shouting, a yelp, and the dog fell quiet. Then a small window in the gatehouse opened a crack and a disembodied male voice asked impatiently, 'Yes? What is it?'

'Is this the villa of Lord Sadanori?'

'Are you mad? This palace belongs to the regent. I thought you were a messenger from the capital. Go away.'

The window was about to shut, but Tora cried, 'Wait! Sorry to trouble you so late, but I have to find Lord Sadanori's villa. I have an urgent message for His Lordship. From his lady. A matter of life and death. Can you at least point me in the right direction?'

The voice grumbled, 'They shouldn't send messengers who don't know the way.' Then added, 'Go back across the river. It's upriver from the shrine. There's a willow by the gate. You can't miss it.' And the window slammed shut.

Tora trotted back the way he had come, followed by more barking and another yelp from the dog. He thought of Trouble, left for Genba to look after. Would Akitada, in his anger, drive the beast out to join the other starving creatures that roamed the streets? In his tired and exhausted state, Tora was unable to achieve the smallest shred of his former optimism. Wifeless and masterless, he would join the mangy dogs scavenging for food in the market, kicked, cursed, and beaten by the more fortunate beings in the world. The image of Hanae intervened – a desperate Hanae fighting off the groping hands and wet lips of a repulsive male in an expensive silk robe.

He found the Sadanori villa quickly after a steep climb, because it perched on a hillside above the river gorge. The wind had picked up and whistled through the pines around him. The house was more modest than a palace, but still substantial for a summer residence. The wealthy loved such places, remote from the bustle of the capital and close to nature. In this mountainous area, the river rushed and gurgled through picturesque gorges. Tora wondered why a man would want to live in a place where the river and the wind made such a din that you could not hear yourself talk.

The faint moonlight played on the swaying branches of the willow by the gate, but the buildings lay darkly under their cedar-bark roofs. Tora suddenly felt, with absolute certainty, that Hanae was not here.

He pounded on the gate anyway, and this time someone came quickly. A faint light glimmered above the tall fence and a voice called out, 'Just a moment, Master Ishikawa. We'd given you up already.' Before Tora could reply, the gate opened. A stout, middle-aged man stood there, holding a lantern, a welcoming grin on his broad, bearded face.

The grin changed to a scowl. 'What do *you* want?' the man growled.

Tora was too tired for small talk. 'I'm looking for my wife, Hanae. Lord Sadanori sent for her, and she hasn't returned to the capital.'

The servant made a rumbling sound in his throat that Tora took for laughter because the man's belly shook. 'You mean you walked all the way from the capital in the middle of the night to fetch your woman home?' the fat man asked, grinning.

Tora put his hand on his sword. 'It's not funny. Send for her this instant.'

The servant stopped grinning. 'Don't threaten me. You've wasted your time. She's not here. Go home. Maybe she'll come back.'

Tora whipped out his sword and put its tip under the bearded man's chin. The other man backed away, his eyes bulging and his mouth half open in surprise, and Tora followed. When they were well inside the courtyard, he lowered the sword. 'Now will you do as I say?'

The man gasped, 'You're crazy. What do you think you're doing? If I call for help, they'll cut you to pieces.'

Tora raised his sword again and bared his teeth. 'Call then!'

The stout man's eyes rolled in panic. 'I tell you, she's not here. There's nobody here but Her Ladyship and two maids. Lord Sadanori lives in the capital.'

'Then my wife's with your mistress. She came

112

about a job as a nurse.'

'Nurse? She lied to you. Lord Sadanori's mother has no need for a nurse.'

Tora stared at him. 'Only his mother lives here? Is that the truth?'

'Yes, I swear it. His ladies are in the capital.'

Slowly, Tora lowered his sword. 'My wife said she was to go to Uji. Lord Sadanori sent a sedan chair for her. Where could she have gone?'

'Well, she's not here,' the servant said resentfully. 'Now will you go away and leave us alone?'

'No, I've come too far. I'll have some answers first. And since you don't seem to have any, I'll speak to your lady.'

'You can't. She doesn't see strangers, and it's the middle of the night. She's asleep.'

'Go wake her.' Tora raised his sword.

The servant muttered something, then said, 'All right. Wait here.'

Tora went to sit on the steps that led to the main hall. He was exhausted and glad that the servant had not put up a fight. Apparently, he was the only male in residence. It was clear that Hanae had been taken somewhere in the capital. The whole story had been a pack of lies. Hanae had been abducted, and he was already too late. Tora clenched his fists in helpless misery.

By the time the servant returned, Tora had worked himself into a fury against the Sadanori family. The fact that Sadanori's mother was willing to speak to him in the middle of the night did not settle his temper. Seething, he followed the servant along a covered gallery to a pavilion that perched like a bird on a ledge above the rushing and tumbling river. The servant knocked at the door, waited to hear a woman's voice call out, and entered, Tora on his heels.

The room faced the river gorge. Its doors were wide open to the night air and the sound of the rushing waters. A tall candle flickered in the air current. Lady Sadanori was in her sixties and still very handsome in a haughty way. She sat in the middle of the room, voluminous gowns draped around her. Her long hair was streaked with silver and perfectly tidy, and her large eyes were fixed on her visitor. A maid had apparently put away her bedding and now knelt in the background. Strange shadows moved over walls covered with paintings of the landscape outside.

Having taken Tora's measure, the lady said, 'Seijiro claims you have come here for your wife?' Because of the sound of the water, she had to raise her voice.

Barely remembering his manners, Tora bowed and said loudly, 'Yes. My name is Tora. My wife Hanae was to become a nurse to Lord Sadanori's expected child. She was taken from our home this morning in a sedan chair to travel here and be introduced to his household. Since she has not returned, I have come to take her back.'

There was a long silence. The old lady studied him and bit her lower lip. Finally, she said, 'There must be some mistake. She is not here.'

'If I have come to the wrong house,' Tora said, 'if there is another place in Uji where she might have gone, I'm sorry to have disturbed you, but ask that you direct me. Hanae is pregnant, and I worry about her.'

'Pregnant.' He almost did not catch the word. She closed her eyes for a moment, then nodded and said more loudly, 'That does you credit, young man. Who exactly are you? Where do you work?'

Tora no longer worked for anyone, but that was not likely to impress this great lady, so he said, 'I'm a retainer to Lord Sugawara.'

'Sugawara Akitada?' Her eyes sharpened and she compressed her lips. 'I think you must have been given the wrong information, Tora. There is no one here but myself, and I have had no visitors in weeks. My son does not have another house in Uji. And lastly, none of his wives is with child. Could you have mistaken the name of the family?'

Tora looked at her and around the room. She seemed honest. Could Hanae have been confused? He decided not. Hanae was a level-headed girl. He said, 'No, My Lady. Hanae was very certain about it. I questioned her because I worried for her safety.' He paused and added an explanation for his concern. 'Hanae is very beautiful and well-known as a dancer and singer in the capital.'

The lady's expression changed, closed, looked weary. 'I have no information for you,' she said curtly and turned away to look into the darkness outside. Tora followed her glance, but saw nothing apart from the trees tossing in the wind, the night sky, and the black abyss of thundering waters. He suddenly felt sick.

The servant plucked at Tora's sleeve. Sadanori's mother did not acknowledge Tora's bow, and he left without thanking her.

Outside, he stopped the servant, who was hustling him towards the gate to get rid of him as quickly as possible. 'Where is your master's house in the capital?'

'In the Sanjo quarter, between Muromachi and Karasuma Streets. Everybody knows that.' The servant was becoming defiant again.

Tora snapped, 'Not me.' Then he put his real worry in words. 'What about other houses? Manors? Farms? Hunting lodges? ... Places where he keeps his paramours?'

The servant chuckled richly. 'Ah, you finally caught on. It won't do you any good running after her. Take my word for it, she's made her choice. If she's as beautiful as you say, she's long since tasted His Lordship's favors – if you know what I mean.'

Tora hauled back and put his fist into the leering face with such force that the heavy man's feet left the ground and he flew across the courtyard. Then he let himself out.

Hoof beats approached as he stepped from the gateway, and two horsemen appeared out of the darkness. They stopped when they saw Tora coming from the gate, sucking his lacerated knuckles.

'Who are you?' asked the taller man.

'None of your business. Get out of my way,' snarled Tora.

The man moved his horse to bar his way. His companion approached also. 'Seijiro,' shouted the tall man.

The fat servant came staggering out through the

gate. He was holding his mouth. 'Master Ishikawa,' he mumbled, looking up at the taller man. 'Thank heaven. This man pushed his way in and forced Her Ladyship to see him. Then he beat me when he didn't get what he came for.' He took his hand from his face and spat out some blood.

The tall man looked at Tora as if he were a poisonous snake. 'You! Back inside,' he snapped.

His companion drew his sword, and this time Tora backed into the courtyard. When he was inside, Seijiro put out his leg and tripped him.

Tora lay on his back on the gravel and looked up at the horsemen. The man called Ishikawa looked familiar.

'Bring a lantern,' ordered Ishikawa. He and the other man dismounted and stood looking down at Tora, their swords ready.

Tora sat up. He also had a sword, but hoped to avoid an uneven battle. 'I was looking for my wife,' he said. 'The servant insulted her so I taught him a lesson.'

Neither man responded. Tora started to get to his feet, but the shorter man used his boot to push him down again.

'Look,' said Tora, 'all I wanted was for someone to tell me where Sadanori has taken my wife.'

Ishikawa said, 'That's Lord Sadanori to you, scum.'

Seijiro returned with a torch and held it uncomfortably close to Tora's face.

'I know you,' Ishikawa said. 'By heaven, aren't you...? Yes, you're Sugawara's servant. I remember that silly mustache. Apparently, you still lack proper respect for your betters. I believe I'll have you beaten.'

Tora also remembered. 'That's Lord Sugawara to you, Ishikawa.' He tried to get up, but Ishikawa's companion pushed him down again. This time Seijiro singed his hair with the torch. 'Hey!' Tora protested, 'get that damned thing out of my face.'

The servant sniggered and singed his other temple. Enough was enough. Tired as he was, Tora rolled away, under the legs of one of the horses, and jumped up on the other side. He drew his sword and, keeping the horse between himself and the three men, he said, 'That's better. I can see you now, Ishikawa. You're the student who cheated and was accused of murdering his professor. How did you manage to find work after they expelled you?'

Ishikawa's face darkened. 'Why you...' He took a step, raising his sword. Tora slapped the horse hard on the hind quarters with the flat side of his sword. The animal whinnied and reared. Ishikawa jumped back. 'I am His Lordship's steward,' he snapped. 'I'll have you arrested for breaking in and attacking one of our people.'

'You'd better not.' It was an empty threat, but as long as Ishikawa believed that Tora still worked for Akitada, he might hesitate to risk a confrontation.

'What's this about a wife? What are you really after? Has your master sent you?'

'What if he did? He talked to your mother in Otsu. She's the Masudas' nurse, isn't she?' It was what Hanae had meant to be – if it had not been

118

for a lecher who had other plans for her. The thought filled him with a black rage again. He was prepared to kill all three men to find out the truth. He gripped his sword more tightly.

A voice called sharply, 'Ishikawa.'

Sadanori's mother stood on the veranda of the main house and looked down at the scene in the courtyard. 'What is this unseemly noise?'

Ishikawa went to make her a deep bow. 'I'm very sorry, My Lady. This person forced his way in and attacked Seijiro. We arrived just in time. I'll have him arrested.'

'You will do nothing of the kind. He came looking for his wife. Let him go.' She looked at Tora. 'Go home and try to forget this night. It was all a mistake. I'm sure your wife will be waiting for you at home.'

Tora did not believe her. What was more, he was convinced that she did not believe it herself. But there was nothing else he could do here, and so he put his sword back in his sash and left.

Trudging down the hill to the bridge, he wondered what Ishikawa was doing here in the middle of the night, but he was too tired, and his mind was a blank except for the thought that he was too late to save Hanae.

In the east, the sky was getting lighter. The night was almost over, but here in the river gorge, the darkness pressed in on him from all sides. Ahead lay the long road back to the capital. The wind wailed as he left the valley. The waters hissed and roared, and the sound echoed from the mountainsides.

EIGHT

Rotten Wood

Akitada arrived home safely, a fact that – perversely – irritated him more because it made Tora's desertion less serious. He fully expected to be met by a contrite Tora, full of explanations and apologies, but Genba informed him that he had stopped only long enough to leave his horse and a dog and had then walked away.

'Walked away? Did he say where he was going?' Akitada asked, temper battling against bitterness as he slid awkwardly from the saddle.

Genba shook his head. His massive body communicated distress, from the mournful eyes and sloping shoulders to his nervously shuffling feet. 'No, only that he was looking for Hanae ... Is something the matter with your arm, sir?'

'An overeager constable used his truncheon on it. I was arrested in Otsu for child stealing.'

'What?' Genba's eyes popped open.

'Later, Genba. I'm very tired and just want to rest for a while.'

'Of course, sir. Shall I send for Seimei? To look after your arm?'

'No.'

Akitada left an unhappy-looking Genba and

went directly to his own room. There he took off his sword and outer robe and sat down behind his desk. He was not sure how he had got home or what he was to do with himself now that he was here. The journey had passed without his taking notice of it. His thoughts had chased each other so confusedly that he was only dimly aware of them even now. Some had concerned Tora's desertion, but most were about the boy and Yori.

He rubbed his sore arm. One by one, he was losing the things that mattered most. First it had been his wife's love and support, then his son's life, and now Tora.

He felt incredibly tired, both physically and mentally. For months now, he had tried to keep despair at bay by working harder. He had volunteered for difficult assignments, and he had put in long hours at the ministry in the hope that work would distract him during his waking hours and that exhaustion would bring him a few hours' sleep and brief oblivion at night. This strategy had not worked.

Until he met the mute child.

However odd their meeting, for a few brief moments he had felt joy again. The dreadful loneliness had lifted, and the ice that paralyzed his soul had thawed a little. Even now, his heart melted at the memory of those small arms wrapped around his neck and the soft cheek pressed against his.

But he would lose the boy and, when the scandal of his alleged perversion with a small child reached the ears of his enemies, he would lose his position in the ministry.

Seimei broke into his gloomy thoughts with the inevitable tea. 'Welcome home, sir,' he said cheerily and looked around the room. 'Are you alone?'

'Yes.'

Seimei's face fell. He looked at Akitada more closely. 'Is anything wrong?'

Not much point in postponing bad news.

'If you're wondering about the boy I had planned to bring home with me, the authorities would not permit it. And Tora seems to have walked out on us. I have no idea where he is and at the moment I don't care.'

Seimei sat down. 'Oh, dear. That is not like Tora at all,' he said, shaking his head and looking at Akitada anxiously. 'Something is very wrong, sir. I hope you will reconsider. Does Genba know anything?'

'Ask him yourself. Tora seems to get all the attention here.' As soon as he said it, Akitada was sorry. He felt resentful and was taking it out on Seimei. Dear heaven, what had happened to him?

'You look very tired, sir. Drink some of your tea.'

Wine was what Akitada wanted. A great deal of very strong wine to drown his misery. He said, 'I'm sorry, Seimei. I'm concerned about Tora, but this has not been a very good day for me.' He reached for his teacup with his left hand and drank.

'What is wrong with your right arm, sir?'

And that, of course, brought out the whole story of his disastrous visit to Otsu. Seimei got his case of medicines and listened.

Seimei's ministrations soothed Akitada's feelings more than they did the pain. Seimei clucked as he searched through his case of powders and ointments. It was not clear if he reacted to the tale of troubles or to the swollen arm, but it did not matter. Someone cared. Mollified, Akitada asked about Tamako.

'She is visiting your sister, sir.'

'Akiko?' Silly question. Only Akiko, the older of his two younger sisters, lived in the capital. She had married a wealthy, much older nobleman and was the proud mother of a small son. Akitada wondered how Tamako could bear to visit there and be reminded of her own loss, but then he remembered how he had held the lost boy and felt whole again. Perhaps it was the same for Tamako.

Seimei also thought of the boy. After applying a soothing salve to Akitada's swollen and bruised forearm and wrapping it, he gave Akitada a sharp look. 'This boy must be very special for you to take such trouble, sir.'

No doubt they all wondered about this. Hardly anyone but Akitada would find him an attractive child, let alone lovable. He was skinny, dirty, and silent – a boy who could not communicate because he was mute, and possibly deaf. But to Akitada he had become special because no one seemed to want him. 'I think I have grown very fond of the child,' he said. Only, the child had turned his back on him.

Seimei nodded. 'I'm sure that is quite natural. The child needed protection, and you needed someone to protect. But such a suggestion of

123

misconduct is really outrageous.'

Akitada correctly took this to refer to the charges brought against him. 'The charge is ridiculous, but it can do some real damage if it reaches the right ears. I'm convinced the whole thing is a form of blackmail. The Mimuras want money, a great deal of it, and I refuse to pay them for tormenting the child.'

Seimei refilled his teacup and pursed his lips. 'I wish Tora were here. He would find a way to snatch the child and bring him here.'

Akitada pointed out that this was what had got him in trouble in the first place.

'Your lady would be so pleased to have a child in the house again,' Seimei said wistfully.

That seemed doubtful. Akitada recalled Tamako's shock when he had proposed adopting the child. No doubt she had felt obliged to acquiesce. They all tried to appease his moods and only managed to irritate him even more. But in any case, Tora was gone, perhaps for good. He asked, 'Have you ever heard Tora mention a woman called Hanae?'

'Hanae? I don't think so, but I may not have listened. Tora is always talking about girls.'

'Exactly. And the wrong kind, the kind that gets a man into trouble. Why can't he find a well-brought-up young woman?'

'It's a mystery. I've tried my best with him. Our Oyuki would have been much more suitable than the loose women in the quarter. But that's where he spends all his time lately. As they say, the barley at the neighbor's tastes better to him than the rice at home.' Seimei expressed his disapproval of Tora's lifestyle more often, and more sententiously, than anyone else, but now he regarded Akitada very pointedly, as if the proverb had a more personal application.

The list of Tora's shortcomings would this time – Akitada strongly suspected – be followed by a lecture on his own neglect of Tamako, including a reminder that it was high time he produced more children of his own instead of running around stealing those of other, most unsuitable, people. When Seimei cleared his throat, Akitada said quickly, 'My arm feels a little better, but I'm very tired. I'll try to get some sleep. Wake me when Tamako returns. Or Tora, of course.'

Foiled, Seimei left, and Akitada stretched out and tried to rest. Seimei had stirred up unpleasant thoughts. They all considered him remiss in his responsibilities. He had not visited his wife's room since their quarrel early in the year. He had neglected the accounts, which had shown poor returns from their farms, and then had left nearly all of his funds in the hands of Judge Nakano. It was not likely that he would get anything back. No doubt, Nakano would bestow most of the gold on the Mimuras and keep the rest for 'expenses'.

As he lay on his back with his eyes on the ceiling, Akitada added another dereliction of duty to the list. Telltale black water stains had appeared on the wooden boards. The roof they lived under was probably close to falling down on top of them.

With a sigh, he got up again and unlocked the iron-bound chest that stood against one wall. As expected, only three gold bars and a little silver remained: hardly enough to begin large building projects. But he could at least see what needed to be done. He changed into his old robe and began an inspection tour.

Some time later, he had found enough urgent repairs to require double the money he had. Over the main hall, where guests were entertained and the family and friends gathered for celebrations, the cedar-bark shingles needed replacing. In summer the rains would finish the damage, and in winter the snow would melt and make its devious way into the house. Damaged railings, loose boards, and broken shutters were everywhere. In one gallery, the rain had come through and rotted out the flooring.

Akitada put off visiting Tamako's room until last, and then he knocked to make sure it was empty. It was. His wife had taken her maid on her visit to Akiko. He wondered what they were talking about – no doubt how difficult Akitada had become to live with.

He found more water damage. And when he raised the woven reed blinds to let more light in, the entire contraption fell with a loud crash and a cloud of dust. He muttered to himself. This sort of thing was dangerous. On closer inspection, the blind was not worth remounting; the reed strands were so dry and brittle, they had disintegrated when they fell. He wondered how Tamako had managed to use it.

Angry at himself and his family for not keeping an eye on things until it was too late, he kicked the blind aside and strode out on to the veranda to inspect the outside of the pavilion. The boards sagged alarmingly. Such repairs should have been done by Tora and Genba. He growled and looked up at the eaves. At that moment, the board he stood on decided to give way, and he plunged downward, ending up in a splintered hole.

He cursed at length.

A swallow had built a nest on one of the eave brackets. Swallows' nests were a good omen, but this nest was empty and long since abandoned by the bird family. He was still staring upward, bemused by this new symbol of the decline of his fortunes, when Tamako appeared in the doorway.

Her eyes widened when she saw her husband, oddly foreshortened by his fall. 'Are you hurt?' she cried.

Akitada's injured arm hurt because he had used it to break his fall, and one of his ankles had been jarred. But mostly he felt ridiculous. He snapped, 'No.'

Tamako raised a hand to her mouth and giggled.

He scowled and made an attempt to extricate himself.

'I'm sorry,' she said quickly. 'If I had known that you were coming to my room, I would have warned you.'

An implied criticism? He was hampered by having the use of only one arm, but managed to boost himself up enough so he could get a knee on the veranda. Tamako extended a hand to him. He looked at it doubtfully for a moment, then took it with his left hand and got both feet on the veranda. She smiled.

'I was inspecting the house,' he explained.

'You looked very funny.'

He glowered. 'No doubt. Why haven't you brought the condition of your quarters to my attention?'

Her smile faded. 'You've been working very hard lately. I mentioned the veranda to Genba, but he has his hands full with the horses and other daily chores.'

'And Tora is never around any more,' he added bitterly.

'Are you sure you aren't hurt? You're holding your elbow.'

Akitada had been cradling his throbbing arm and now dropped it quickly. 'It's nothing. I had a run-in with some constables in Otsu.'

Her eyebrows shot up. 'Constables? You?'

'Yes. They took the boy from me. It seems the people who claim to be his parents accused me of stealing him for improper purposes.'

Her eyes widened. 'Improper? But how...? They *claim* to be his parents? You mean you could not prove your own rights?'

'What rights? I don't suppose I have any, except common humanity. The child was in a pitiful state each time I saw him. Oh, Tamako, if you had been there, it would have broken your heart.'

'I don't understand. This was not ... you had no claim on him?'

'Of course not. Except—' He had almost said, 'Except that I love him.' He choked on the words and turned away. Stepping to the edge of the veranda, he looked into the garden. His eye fell

128

on the brown stump that had been the wisteria vine, and he shuddered. Tamako's silk gown rustled softly, and he felt her hand on his arm.

'Akitada?'

Unintended tears rose to his eyes. He did not want her to see him like this: broken, hopeless, and useless to her and to himself.

'I'm so sorry,' she said. 'I didn't know.'

'Don't be sorry,' he said harshly. 'It was my fault. All of it.' He glared at the dead vine. 'Everything I touch dies. My own son died because of my neglect, and when I tried to help another child, I just made matters worse.'

'You mustn't say that. You mustn't think it. None of it is your fault.'

He turned to her. 'What?' he asked bitterly. 'Not even Yori's death? Have you changed your mind about that?' He saw her eyes filling with tears also. She started to speak, but so many bitter words had passed between them, followed by dreadful silences filled with unspoken recriminations, that he had a sudden horror they were about to begin the entire searing process again. 'Tamako,' he said, 'I am so tired. I don't want to quarrel again. Please don't remind me of Yori. I don't think I can bear it.'

She raised her hand to touch his cheek. 'Oh, Akitada,' she murmured, 'please forgive me for what I said. And for what I thought.'

He put his hand over hers. The tears in her eyes brimmed over, and he took her in his arms. They stood, clinging together, under the empty swallow's nest.

After a long moment, he said, 'There's nothing

to forgive. This has been very hard for you, too.'

She clutched at him. 'I said those terrible things because I wanted to hurt you. I thought you did not love us anymore.'

At the time he had in fact turned away from her and given his heart to another woman, a woman of whom he still sometimes thought with a desire that heated his body. He did not know any longer what he felt for Tamako. Struggling with his cursed honesty, he let pity overcome the urge to stop a scene that was rapidly disintegrating into something he was not ready for. He said nothing, but held her a little closer and stroked her hair.

After a moment, she disengaged herself with an embarrassed laugh and brushed the tears from her face. 'Your arm? Has it been seen to?'

'Yes. Seimei put some salve on it.'

'Please come inside and tell me what happened in Otsu.'

They sat across from each other near the fallen blind, and he told her. He added, 'Genba asked what happened, but I was too tired to deal with his questions or to discuss Tora's absence, which seemed to trouble him more.'

'Genba is worried about Tora?'

Akitada was a little hurt that she should be distracted so easily from his problem to Tora's. Her lashes were still wet from tears and her nose was pink. For a moment, she reminded him of the boy. A ridiculous notion. He pulled himself together and said, 'Tora seems to have left my employ.'

'What?' This time the shock in her voice and face was palpable. 'Akitada, what happened?

Something must be dreadfully wrong for Tora to leave you.'

He snapped, 'Nothing out of the ordinary. Tora is once again besotted with some whore from the quarter. He has no control over his sexual urges the moment a loose woman makes eyes at him.'

She flinched at his language. 'Tora has a kind heart,' she said. 'He does not make distinctions.'

He snorted.

'Please don't be this way, Akitada. I think you must have misunderstood something. This isn't like Tora.' When he shook his head stubbornly, her eyes flashed and she cried, 'Oh, Akitada, think! Whatever Tora has done, don't forget what you owe him. He saved your life. He came for you in Sado. He fought beside you. You must find him and bring him back. Neither of you will ever be happy again unless you do.'

He was surprised at her urgency and digested this in silence. She was right, of course, and that rankled. He had thought himself the injured party and was still not altogether convinced that he wasn't. 'What do you suggest I do?' he grumbled. 'Do you want me to question every madam, porter, and whore in the quarter until I find him? And then apologize because I have found his work unsatisfactory lately?' He turned and pointed an accusing finger at the ragged hole in the veranda floor. 'This would never have happened, nor this –' he gestured towards the stained ceiling – 'nor all the other leaks in our roofs, nor the crumbling outer wall, nor the gods know what else, if Tora had done even a part of the chores he owed me.'

She closed her eyes briefly before his anger, then said, 'You're right, but you must find him all the same. There are more important things owed between you. Do you really want to lose Tora, too?'

He brushed a weary hand across his face. 'What does it matter? What does anything matter?'

'Oh, Akitada.' Tamako jumped up and stamped her foot. 'It matters to me. It matters to Tora. It matters to all of us who care about you.'

His resistance crumbled. He looked up at her uncertainly. 'You really think I should look for Tora?'

'Of course.'

'But what about the boy?'

'You said he was safe. Find Tora first. The rest will fall into place.'

'Well...'

'Please.'

Akitada saw the entreaty in her eyes and sighed. 'Very well. But if he doesn't have a very good explanation for this latest stunt, I'll be done with him.'

'Thank you.' She smiled.

His heart lifted a little. Whatever Tora was up to, the search would take his mind off his other troubles. He rose and glanced towards the veranda. 'Stay off those boards until they are mended. If you and Seimei will make a list of repairs and leave it on my desk, I will see what can be done. I'll try to be back for the evening rice.'

NINE

Lord Sadanori

The sun was up when Tora got back to the capital. He was limping badly and put one foot in front of the other by sheer willpower. There was a hole in one of his boots, and the sharp gravel of the highway had cut his foot. He was no longer hungry, though he had eaten nothing since the previous morning, but the lack of food and sleep made him light-headed.

Perhaps he had made this dreadful trip for nothing. Perhaps Hanae would receive him with a hug and a smile. She would make him sit down on the front steps beside the morning glory vine and take off his boots. Then she would bathe his sore feet and bandage them, feed him some warm rice gruel, and hold him in her arms.

But Hanae was not home. Only the white cat greeted him, mewing plaintively and rubbing against his legs. The cat was Hanae's, just as Trouble was his. Ordinarily, the cat did not care much for Tora, whom it seemed to consider an interloper. Trouble did not discriminate. He loved both his owners equally. But now the cat, an opportunistic creature, was distraught and, thinking it had been abandoned by its mistress, it

133

greeted Tora effusively.

Followed by the mewing cat, Tora limped to the backyard. He drank at the well and washed his face and hands. Then he filled the dog's dry water bowl. The cat drank daintily, twitching its tail. It preferred fish broth.

'Make yourself useful,' growled Tora, taking off his boots to wash his wounded foot. 'Catch some rats. Your mistress always said you were a good mouser.' The cat pressed its head into his hand and purred. Tora thought of Hanae and felt pity for the animal. 'I'm hungry myself,' he said apologetically.

The boots were in bad shape, but he had no others. Barefoot, he limped back to the veranda, found the key where they hid it under a rock behind the vine, and unlocked the door. The stale air and silence of emptiness greeted him and made his heart heavy again. He took off his sword and hung it on its nail. Since he was no longer in the service of a noble family, he could be arrested for wearing a sword in the capital. Plus, if Hanae returned, she would know he had been here. The mewing cat had followed him inside and was investigating both rooms for its mistress. Tora found a worn pair of straw sandals and cut inserts from these for his boots. Then he wrapped his lacerated foot in old rags and slipped the boots back on. In the kitchen, he rummaged about for food, but Hanae had cleaned up and the larder was bare.

'Come on,' he told the cat. They went back out and Tora re-locked the house and hid the key again. With a sigh he left, closing the gate carefully behind himself. The cat jumped up and over and mewed loudly. Tora kept walking. When he reached the corner, he glanced back. The cat had followed him halfway along the block and sat in the middle of the road looking after him.

Near the market, he used his last copper to buy a rice cake from a street vendor and ate it on the way. Following the directions from the fat servant in Uji, he reached Sadanori's residence quickly. He did not expect to find Hanae there, but hoped to learn something about its owner.

The nobleman's large compound occupied an entire city block and was walled all around. Its main gate on Muromachi Street stood open on a scene of great activity.

A small crowd had gathered on either side of the gate, and Tora joined them. They watched as a train of porters and carts tried to deliver building supplies, while inside grooms and servants clustered around an ornate, painted ox-drawn carriage. An irate little man in the white clothes of an upper servant jumped around in front of the train of porters, waving his arms and shouting for them to stop, to go away, to back up, to go around to the other gate. The men at the head of the train stopped, but the others were pressing forward from behind. In due course, trouble ensued. Two porters were crowded aside by a cart backing up and dropped a load of planks on someone's foot. Cries and curses followed. A mule shied and galloped into the cluster of servants, shedding roof tiles from the basket strapped on its back. The servants scattered, frightening the ox. The ox made for the stable building with its handler hanging on to the reins and digging in his heels to stop him. Outside the gate, the lumber bearers faced off against the tile carriers because one man had been trampled by a member of another group. Boards and beams lay everywhere, and large baskets spilled clay tiles into the street. The watching crowd cheered.

Tora used the fracas to slip into the courtyard undetected. When the ox had pulled away the carriage, it had revealed a nobleman in a rich red silk robe and black court hat. He wore a sword and held a gilded fan, with which he fanned a round, pale face with a small mustache and chin beard. Beside him stood Ishikawa, a head taller and much slimmer and still in the clothes he had worn in Uji. Both stared at the commotion with identical expressions of shock and disbelief.

Tora ducked behind a pile of stacked firewood, squatted down, and peered around the corner. The man in red must be Sadanori. Ishikawa had ridden back from Uji posthaste to report Tora's visit. The temptation to confront the great lord and wipe that smug, superior expression off his face was great, but Tora resisted. He wished he knew what they had talked about, but was even more curious about His Lordship's intentions. Had he just stepped from the elegant carriage, or was he about to leave in it?

Eventually, order was restored, and the ox driver backed the carriage to where it had stood before. The workmen and porters gathered up their mules and scattered goods and left, and Lord Sadanori and Ishikawa walked around the carriage. After some more words with Ishikawa,

Sadanori got into it.

There was a chance, a small chance, that the bastard had hidden Hanae elsewhere, but had spent the night in his own residence. And now he was reporting for duty at the palace. Tora knew very well what full court attire looked like.

The carriage turned and headed out the gate, the front runner shouting, 'Make way,' the red silk tassels on the black ox bobbing, the green-and-gold carriage swaying between its two huge black-lacquered wheels, and a retinue of servants in white jackets and short, full-legged pants trotting along on both sides.

And then the gate closed after them.

Tora sat behind the wood stack and thought about what he had just witnessed. Hanae was not likely to be in Lord Sadanori's women's quarters, playing nursemaid to his children and discussing her future duties with the pregnant wife. There was no pregnant wife, according to Sadanori's mother. And Ishikawa had dashed back here to report Tora's visit. All of this suggested that Sadanori had indeed abducted Hanae and that she was hidden elsewhere. Had Sadanori given Ishikawa instructions about her?

Tora peered around the wood pile. Ishikawa was walking towards the inner gateway. Tora could see the tops of trees beyond. From the distance came the sound of hammering. Ishikawa had probably gone to check on the arrival of the pack train at the other gate. Wherever Hanae was, Sadanori must think her well-hidden.

'Yoi!' a voice shouted practically into his ear. A bearded man was looking down at him over the

137

top of the wood pile. 'What do you think you're doing there, you lazy turd? Sleeping in the middle of the day? Move your sorry arse and go to work.'

Tora shot up. The man was the senior servant who had tried to stop the pack train. 'Er,' Tora stammered, trying to think of some explanation for what he was doing there.

'You thought you could just hide back here and then show up tonight with the rest of them to collect your wages,' the servant said, waving an accusing finger. He eyed Tora's blue robe, no longer neat or particularly clean after his excursions, but still better than the average laborer's shirt and loin cloth, and frowned. 'Who are you anyway? You with the supervisor's staff?'

'Yes,' Tora lied. The building project, whatever it was, needed professional supervision, and Sadanori's servants must be used to strangers roaming about. He yawned hugely. 'Sorry,' he said with a grin. 'Been up all night writing changes and checking orders. I was just grabbing a little shut-eye until they get unloaded.'

The servant looked at Tora's red-rimmed eyes and tired face. 'Oh. Sorry I woke you, friend. Go back to sleep.'

'Thanks, but now I'm awake, I'll stroll over and see what's happening.'

'Keep to the far side of the lake. The ladies don't like strange men walking about near the house.'

Tora gave the man a wave and set off towards the inner gate. He tried not to limp too noticeably. All this talk about sleep had made him realize how tired he was. But now that he was in the badger's den, he was not about to leave without seeing everything there was to see and perhaps learning a few things in the process.

The smaller gate led on to a wide inner courtyard that stretched between the main house and its two wings all the way to an artificial lake. Tora considered ignoring the servant's warning, but if he got caught near the women's quarters, all hell would break loose. So he followed the path around the lake to the sounds of sawing and hammering.

A separate hall was nearing completion. The framework was up, and so was the roof. Beyond the construction site was the east gate, where the pack train had arrived and was unloading supplies. Sadanori did not spare money on his projects. At least twenty carpenters with their assistants were at work on the building. They were raising more columns, sawing boards for floors and verandas, and carving banisters, railings, brackets, and ornaments for the eaves.

Ishikawa stood in front of the building. He was talking to a short, corpulent man in a plain gray silk robe. The man held a roll of papers in one hand and gesticulated with these from the goods to various groups of craftsmen. Tora guessed that he was the building supervisor. It all looked harmless and normal enough.

He crept a little closer. At the gate they were still unloading and stacking boards. The supervisor interrupted his conversation with Ishikawa and turned to one of the carpenters. Ishikawa scanned the area. Tora busied himself picking up remnants of wood and other building debris, hoping Ishikawa would not pay attention to a mere worker.

When he heard a shout, he jumped and risked a glance, but the supervisor's anger was directed at a carpenter, who rose from his labors and stood, shaking his head. Evidently, he was in trouble. Ishikawa joined them. The supervisor pointed to the gate. The carpenter pleaded. Ishikawa became impatient. He said something to the supervisor, turned, and stalked off in the direction of the main house.

Tora considered following Ishikawa, but the supervisor cut off the carpenter's pleading and went to talk to another group of workers. The carpenter, an elderly man, gathered his tools and walked out of the east gate, his hanging head and slumping shoulders showing his dejection. Tora followed.

The gate opened on Karasuma Street. The carpenter turned south. Tora caught up with him at Sanjo Avenue. 'Hey,' he called out. The carpenter did not turn; he appeared sunk in despair. When Tora touched his shoulder, he stopped and looked up. On closer inspection, the man did not look very promising. Tora took in his emaciated frame, the rheumy eyes, the toothless mouth, and wondered if he had darkened his thin hair to appear younger. He bit his lip, no longer sure what to do.

'Sorry to rush after you, uncle,' he said, 'but I heard what just happened. You got fired, didn't you?'

The old man nodded. He ran the back of his

hand across moist eyes. 'I'm a good carpenter,' he said sadly. 'The best. And I work fast. But my back's bad, and I can't lift heavy beams. So I'm no good anymore.' He looked sorrowfully at his wooden toolbox and sighed. 'I'll have to sell my tools for a few coppers.'

'Don't do that. I know where there's some work.'

The carpenter looked up, hope in his eyes. 'Where?' he asked. 'I'll do anything. May the Buddha reward you! We've almost no food left at home.'

'I'll tell you, if you'll tell me about Sadanori and Ishikawa.'

The old man blinked. 'The great live above the clouds. I'm only a simple man.'

Tora had never been troubled by his own lowly status and had little respect for men who behaved like Sadanori – or Ishikawa. 'If you keep your eyes and ears open, you learn things,' he pointed out. 'What did Ishikawa and your supervisor talk about before you got fired?'

'The hall. Mr Ishikawa complained about the money and how long it was taking. As if the great lord didn't have all the money in the world!'

'What's the hall for?'

'They say it was meant for a favorite, but was never finished. Now he wants to live in it himself. Calls it the Lake Hermitage.'

Nothing in that. Nobles were always pretending that the world wearied them and they only wanted a simple life. 'Did Ishikawa say where he was off to in such a hurry?'

'He's riding to Otsu.'

141

'Otsu? Why?'

The carpenter did not know. Tora decided that Ishikawa had gone to visit his mother. 'You hear any talk about Sadanori's affairs?' The carpenter looked blank. 'I mean with women. Courtesans, entertainers?'

The old man grinned. 'The great lord spends time in the pleasure quarter. Is that what you mean?'

It was hot, and the sun was already high. Tora felt light-headed with exhaustion and lack of food. He was frustrated that he was not getting anywhere, but some remnant of pity for the old man kept him from shouting at him. 'You were there yesterday. Did you see a sedan chair delivering a young woman? About the middle of the morning?'

'No. I think the ladies come and go by the north gate.'

So much for that. Tora did not really believe that Sadanori would bring Hanae to his home, anyway. 'What about Ishikawa?'

'Ishikawa's the *betto*. He runs everything. Him and the lord are like this.' The carpenter put two fingers together. 'He's the lord's eyes and ears.'

Tora sighed. 'All right. Go to Oimikado Avenue and ask for the Sugawara residence. When a big man opens the gate, tell him Tora sent you to do some work on the house.'

The carpenter bowed deeply. 'You are a saint,' he said. 'I bless you. My wife blesses you. My sons, who are soldiers, bless you also, wherever they are. And so do my grandchildren and their mothers.' He grasped Tora's hand and kissed it.

Tora snatched his hand back. 'Go on,' he growled. 'And make sure you do good work for them. They're my people.'

He crossed Sanjo Avenue before the old man could embarrass him further. While the relationship between Ishikawa and Sadanori was something to keep in the back of his mind – Tora believed the worst of both of them – he still did not know how to find Hanae.

Worse. He was at the end of his tether. He had no patience left. Only sheer dull willpower kept his legs moving. The linings in his torn boots had shifted, and his bare soles were again scuffing the dirt in the road. Tora sat down on the other side of Sanjo, took off both boots, and examined them and his feet. One foot was bleeding through a crust of dirt and gravel; the other had developed a large blister. He had lost the straw inserts. No matter. He must go on. Re-wrapping his feet, he put the torn boots back on and limped towards the pleasure quarter.

He should have gone directly to Hanae's dancing teacher, but Master Ohiya was one person Tora preferred to avoid. They were acquainted, but not on friendly terms, and for very similar reasons. Each despised the other, regarding him as Hanae's certain doom, as a seducer and destroyer of something precious. Tora thought Ohiya no better than a pimp who trained innocent young girls to become prostitutes. While he had nothing against prostitution in general, he was not so tolerant about his wife's activities. Ohiya, on the other hand, knew that he had discovered and perfected a fine talent with prospects of a

143

great public career until a low-class yokel had ruined her. Their contest over Hanae had ended with Tora's victory and Ohiya's bitter enmity.

Tora trudged through the quarter, from wine house to wine house, asking for Hanae or one of her friends. Nobody had seen his wife recently. He had expected that. But finding and speaking to the girls who might know something because she had worked with them brought him more trouble than he had bargained for.

It was afternoon, and the women were either still asleep or dressing for their nightly engagements. Tora was exhausted, dizzy from heat and hunger, and in pain. His appearance was no longer reassuring. His clothes looked dirty and wrinkled, his boots gaped, revealing dirty toes, he was unshaven, and his hair had come loose. Besides, he had developed a manner of glowering at people from bloodshot eyes. He was not welcome. Doors were slammed in his face. No longer able to draw on his stock of charm and flattery, he resorted to demands and threats. One woman cursed him and emptied a bucket of night soil on him when he turned away. Most of it missed, but enough soaked the back of his blue robe to add a fetid stench to his other unlovely attributes.

When he finally found a girl who knew Hanae, she looked at him askance and suggested that Hanae must have come to her senses and left him. To emphasize the point, she told him that Sadanori had shown a great interest in Hanae. And she said that he should ask Rikiju if he didn't believe her.

Rikiju took pity on him. Tora found her in a rented room in the back of a disreputable restaurant. She was in her thirties, an example of what happened to women in the pleasure quarter if they did not find a lifelong patron before their youth faded. Her old robe hung open, revealing too much of a bony figure. From a hook hung her only good gown: the silk stained and torn, and the embroidered flowers faded. She wore no make-up, and her face was both haggard and puffy from late nights and too much cheap wine. But she commiserated with him and offered to share the modest meal she was eating.

'You look terrible,' she said. 'Eat just a little.'

Tora thought the same of her and shook his head. He told her what had happened.

'Well,' she said dubiously, sucking the last bits of food from her bowl, and then wiping it with one of her fingers, 'if it's Sadanori who got her, she won't be getting back today.' She licked her finger and wiped it on the sleeve of her robe. 'He goes to that much trouble only when he's serious.'

'He's done it before?'

'So they say.'

'I know he took her, and I'm going to get her back if I have to fight him and a thousand armed guards.' Tora trembled with rage at the thought of Sadanori raping his Hanae.

She eyed him with concern and shook her head. 'You won't find her. He's probably taken her to a private house. He's done it before. The best thing is to wait for her to come back. He gets tired after a while. They say he's one of those men who

145

want what they can't have. It's not getting a woman that heats his blood. Until she's his, his fire burns hot; then he'll lose interest quickly and send her home. Smart thing to do for Hanae is to let him have his way.'

'Bite your tongue.' Tora glared at her. 'My Hanae will fight the bastard to the death.'

Rikiju looked away. 'Hanae's a sensible girl. She'll be all right. Now I've got to get ready for work.'

'What do you mean, she's sensible?'

She sighed and got up. 'Nothing. Don't worry. Go home, Tora.'

After that, Tora was no longer quite rational. Back on the street, he pushed people out of his way and snarled when he asked for information. Most of those he accosted fled or slammed their doors. He had only one name left before he had to crawl to Master Ohiya.

The dancer Kohata was Hanae's rival. The two women often appeared at the same parties and they competed for work. Tora tracked Kohata to the best restaurant in the quarter. To get this information, he threatened an old woman who had been hobbling out of Kohata's home with bodily harm. She told him that the entertainer had left the previous evening for a party with important clients and had not returned yet.

At the entrance of the Fragrant Plum Blossom, Tora cornered a maid and demanded to speak to Kohata. The maid ran from him, and the restaurant's owner arrived and threatened to call the constables. Tora pushed the man aside and went in. A young boy with the knowing face of an incipient pimp was sweeping the floor of the corridor. Otherwise the place seemed to be empty. The owner made the mistake of grabbing Tora's arm. Tora whipped around, grasped the man's jacket with both hands and slammed him against the nearest wall, which, being paper-thin, collapsed. Then he turned on the boy.

'Where's Kohata?'

The boy backed away. 'She ... she's in the "Willow Pavilion".'

Tora grabbed his shirt and twisted. 'Where, you brainless oaf?'

The boy gasped, 'In the back. Through the garden.'

Tora pushed him aside and stormed out of the restaurant's back door and into the garden. Behind him, the owner and the boy were shouting at each other.

Tora ran to the small building under the willow tree and burst through its door without knocking. The room was empty except for a pile of silk robes and two naked lovers in an interesting configuration of entangled limbs. Under normal circumstances, Tora would have taken notice of their inventiveness, but in his mind's eye he saw Sadanori embracing Hanae, and he went to seize the woman by the arm and pull her away from the man.

Kohata was furious. She shouted at Tora. Her frightened client, a fat old man, grabbed frantically for his clothing and stumbled into it.

Tora attempted to calm her down enough to ask her about Hanae, but his time had run out. Footsteps and shouts sounded outside. When he turned, he saw red-coated constables armed with chains and wooden clubs. Behind them came the restaurant's owner, the boy, the maid, and assorted strangers.

Tora abandoned Kohata and dashed out through the back, vaulting over a balustrade and then scrambling over a fence. Outside, he ran for blocks until the sole of one of his boots came loose, caught, and tripped him. He fell headlong and hard, scraping his left cheek and both elbows on the gravel.

The pain cleared his head a little. He sat up, took off the ruined boot, and tossed it away. Then he got to his feet and limped to Master Ohiya's house.

Ohiya's young male servant answered, then tried to slam the door when he saw a disheveled, bleeding man outside. Tora snarled, 'Out of my way,' and pushed him aside. He found Ohiya by following drumbeats to a large room at the back of his house. Ohiya himself was beating the drum, seated cross-legged on the wooden floor while a young girl went through a dance routine and three others awaited their turn.

The girls were very young, under fifteen, and they squealed when Tora burst through the doorway.

Ohiya looked up, cried, 'Oh!' and stopped drumming. In a shaking voice, he asked, 'What do you want?'

Tora cast a glance at the frightened girls huddling in a corner and said, 'Sorry. I need a word.'

Ohiya's eyes blinked, then narrowed in recognition. 'Tora? What is this? How dare you burst in here like this!'

'Hanae's gone. Stolen. I know who has her, but I don't know where she is. You've got to help me, Ohiya.'

Ohiya got to his feet. He was a slender man in his forties who whitened his face and touched his lips with red safflower juice. Today he wore his working clothes: a black silk robe under an embroidered jacket. The jacket was sufficiently feminine that, in spite of his tall figure and the male hairstyle, it and the make-up made his gender vaguely dubious. This was one of the reasons Tora despised him.

Now Ohiya curled his lip and said, 'You look disgusting. What dog has dragged you out of the gutter?'

Tora bared his teeth and advanced on him. The girls squealed again and put their arms around each other. 'Don't play with me, Ohiya. Either you help me find her or I'll know you had a hand in this.'

Ohiya skipped a few steps away. 'Don't you dare touch me, you brute.'

Tora backed the dance master against the wall. Leaning forward until they were practically nose to nose, he snarled, 'Tell me where Sadanori's hidden her or I'll make sure that you never dance again.'

'I know nothing,' Ohiya squealed. 'Don't touch me, you monster!'

Tora held a fist under his nose, and Ohiya screamed for help. Outside, other shouts answered. A moment later the room was full of burly men, some of them constables. Next, Tora was clubbed over the head and thrown on the floor, with two hefty men sitting on him and an excited babble of voices dinning into his ears. Waves of pain, fragments of Ohiya's complaints, prattle from the four little maidens, questions by constables, and excited chatter from neighbors and bystanders washed over him like a deluge – along with the knowledge that he had bungled the most important job of his life. He closed his eyes.

TEN

The Willow Quarter

Akitada eyed the sleazy painted banners and garish paper lanterns with distaste. In his view, prostitution undermined the family structure and contributed nothing to the welfare of the country. Tora was an excellent example of how it corrupted promising young men.

Not to mention women.

A very young girl rushed from the door of an adjacent house and almost collided with him. She was hardly more than ten or twelve, and already painted and garbed like a courtesan. For a moment they stared at each other, then she raised her painted fan and smiled at him over it, while her dainty little figure performed a perfect replica of a seductive wiggle. He scowled so fiercely that she lowered her fan, gathered her skirts, and ran away down the street.

Akitada had not set foot in this part of the capital in years, and even then he had only come in search of a killer. In broad daylight the quarter was hardly romantic, in spite of the many willows that gave it its name. After sunset the many-colored lanterns hanging from trees and doorways would be lit to suggest that the visitor had wandered into the abode of heavenly maidens. There would be music then, too, and laughter, and beautiful women dancing – or what passed for beautiful women in that light and in expensive silk gowns. But their business was anything but heavenly.

At the moment only old women and plain-faced maids were out, sweeping or shopping for food. Now and then a poorly-dressed youth ran down the street, carrying a message to one of the courtesans or purchases from silk merchants, comb makers, or incense shops. Inside the shuttered houses, the 'beauties', no doubt, still slept after the night's labors, or gathered in their wrappers to gossip about their customers.

The encounter with the young girl had not improved Akitada's temper. The day was hot already and humid. Akitada's formal robe clung uncomfortably to his back and waist, and his arm still ached. Sweat gathered beneath the silk ribbons of his hat and itched. He had no idea how to proceed in his search, but thought that Tora's latest flirt would be fairly easy to find. In all likelihood, Tora was with her, and if he was not, then she would know where he had gone.

Satisfied with his reasoning, he asked a messenger boy for the office of the warden. The warden maintained a record of all the prostitutes registered in the Willow Quarter.

A neatly dressed constable stood under the lantern that identified the ward office. He bowed and ushered Akitada into a large room, where they interrupted the warden, a fat man in a blue silk robe, in his midday meal. A large number of savory-smelling dishes surrounded him and reminded Akitada that he was getting hungry himself. The warden took in Akitada's appearance and suppressed his irritation. He put down his bowl and bowed.

Akitada cut through a long string of flowery phrases of welcome to demand information about Hanae.

The warden raised his brows. 'A courtesan?' he asked. 'We have so many. The name doesn't ring a bell. She's not of the first or second rank.' He gave Akitada an oily smile. 'One gets to know the great beauties quickly, and we have the best. I could easily put your honor in touch with a very reliable person to advise and arrange a meeting?'

Akitada glared. 'I am not here to buy an hour with a prostitute,' he snapped. 'A member of my household has disappeared. The woman Hanae may know his whereabouts.'

'I doubt that one of our ladies is responsible, but if it is indeed an urgent matter, I could search the records.' The warden glanced at his half-eaten food. 'It might take a while,' he added pointedly.

Akitada did not like the man and cared nothing

152

about spoiling his meal. He sat down and stared around the room, while the warden pulled down document boxes and ledgers from shelves. This warden's office looked more like a gentleman's study than a place where the law was enforced. Cushions awaited guests; a brazier and wine flask stood ready. Whatever tools of trade the warden used must be neatly tucked away in wooden trunks so as not to frighten away good clients. Akitada scowled. An immoral business corrupted even the authorities.

'How do you keep order in a place like this?' he asked irritably.

'Oh, I have my system, sir,' chuckled the warden, patting his fat ledger affectionately.

'I was referring to keeping order in the quarter. There must be a good deal of drunkenness and violence.'

'Heavens,' the warden cried with a hearty laugh, 'you make the Willow Quarter sound positively dangerous. It's nothing of the sort. Our clients, after all, come for a pleasant evening. I keep my eye on things personally. Should someone have a bit too much wine, we see him home safely.'

Akitada did not believe a word of this. 'You? In person?'

Another laugh escaped the warden. 'Oh, no. One of my constables. No, trouble is the last thing we want here. This is a place to enjoy music and good food and wine, to spend time with beautiful women, skilled in song, poetry, and dance. Here one relaxes and forgets his troubles.' He rubbed his hands and smiled like a

153

personification of the god of good fortune.

Akitada looked back coldly. 'I see. So what about this girl Hanae?'

'No courtesan by that name works in the quarter at the present time, sir. She may, of course, be an irregular. If so, she works here illegally. But that isn't very likely. My men are very vigilant, and so are the regulars. The ladies don't tolerate competition.'

It occurred to Akitada that Tora might have insisted his lover stop working. Most likely he had. 'What about a woman who has recently left the, er, trade?'

The warden bent over his ledger again. After a few moments, he said, 'No, not in the past year. But I do recall now that we have a professional dancer by that name. She's not a courtesan at all. Not yet, anyway. The dancers perform for large parties and are not supposed to spend the night with clients. Might the young woman be an entertainer?'

Akitada frowned. 'Possibly. Tell me how to find this dancer.'

The warden opened another ledger and ran his pudgy finger down the page. 'She lives in the southern ward. Between Shinano and Karasu-maro Street. I hear she's been doing well for herself.'

Akitada was disappointed. A first-class entertainer would hardly waste her time with Tora. But he had the warden write down directions to the house and the name of her dancing master. Then, on the point of departing, he asked, 'By any chance, do you recall a former courtesan by the name of Peony? She is said to have been quite famous and worked here about five or six years ago.'

'Of course. The beautiful Peony left very suddenly. Ah, there were many broken hearts.' The warden folded his hands and cast up his eyes. 'We'll never see her likes again. They say one of the great nobles wanted to make her his wife, but she turned him down.' He sighed sentimentally.

'How strange. I was told she left huge debts behind.'

The warden laughed. 'Peony? Hardly. She was a very rich woman by then.'

So much for that. Whoever the Otsu Peony had been, she had been dependent on Masuda support. Akitada thanked the warden and left.

Outside, he stood undecided. Should he follow up on the dancer or scour the quarter for Tora? He decided to take his chances in the quarter, distasteful though it was.

The willows swayed in a slight breeze from the river, doves cooed on the roofs, and the colored lanterns looked bright in the sun, but Akitada saw peeling paint and dingy whitewashed walls. Garbage still lay piled in odd corners. A mangy dog sniffed at some vomit in an alleyway and passed on to lift a leg against a tall stack of earthen wine jars at the back door of a restaurant. Akitada knew there were much worse looking wards in the capital, places where people lived and slept under a few leaning boards covered with brushwood. There men killed for food, women lay down in the fields to let strangers have their way for a copper or two, and children died faster than the rats or flies that were better nourished than they.

When Akitada saw a wine house open for business, he went in. Although it was still early in the day, two women sat in a corner, drinking wine and chattering loudly with the owner of the place. Akitada called for some chilled wine and looked at the women disapprovingly. One was middle-aged and dressed in black silk, the other a girl in pink. The older woman dominated the conversation with an irritatingly shrill voice. Akitada decided that she was the young prostitute's bawd. He rose and walked over to them.

'I'm looking for one of my retainers,' he said curtly. 'His name is Tora. Perhaps one of you may know him?'

Both women shook their heads, but his host said, 'I think I remember him, sir. Haven't seen him for weeks. A handsome and cheerful fellow with a small mustache? The girls liked him a lot.'

Akitada nodded sourly. The description fit.

'We'll keep our eyes and ears open, if you like,' offered the man.

Akitada left his name and directions and returned to his wine. He had barely sat down and raised his cup when the young woman in pink approached with the sinuous gliding motion of the trained courtesan. Stopping before him, she bowed deeply and asked, 'Would the gentleman care for some company?'

Akitada eyed her painted face and judged her to be quite young and pretty. He wanted to send her away, but then wondered if she knew Tora and had not wanted to say so in front of the other woman. Tora never paid for the services of his paramours. 'You're very kind,' he said. 'May I offer you a cup of wine?'

She clapped her hand for the proprietor to bring another cup and sat down gracefully beside him. 'Thank you, My Lord. I'm called Little Wave.'

Akitada reached for the flask to pour some wine for her, but she was quicker. 'Allow me,' she murmured and managed to touch his hand so lightly that it seemed like a caress. Then she moved closer on her knees, ostensibly to serve the wine. She refilled his cup first and offered it with both hands and a smile. When he took the cup, their hands touched again, and this time hers lingered. 'Oh,' she breathed, her eyes on his lips.

She was very good, and her intentions were obvious. Akitada knew this, but his heart started to beat a little faster anyway. 'I wondered, Little Wave,' he said, as she poured her own wine, 'if you had remembered Tora. He would not pass up a charming girl like you.'

She sipped daintily, fluttering her lashes at him over the rim of the cup. 'If he's half as handsome as you, sir, I wouldn't forget him. Some men turn a girl's head in an instant and she's quite lost.' She gave him a melting glance.

The expected rejoinder, 'Surely a gentleman would make every effort to find her again,' was on Akitada's tongue, but he blushed and said instead, 'You are a flatterer. Actually, he doesn't look much like me. He's much better-looking and has a very big smile.'

If she was disappointed at his refusal to flirt, she did not show it. Touching his arm lightly with

157

her fan, she said, 'However handsome he is, he cannot be like you. And I prefer clean-shaven gentlemen.' She bent a little closer to let her fingertips brush his upper lip and then trace his mouth. 'But you *are* very sad.'

Akitada became aware of her scent. It was strangely seductive. Sandalwood and something else, perhaps orange blossom. Tamako used orange blossom. He remembered their embrace earlier: the pleasant familiarity of her scent, the way her body fit against his. He took a deep breath and reached for his wine cup.

The wine had heated his body, and it was a long time since he had made love. He looked at the girl. In spite of the wine, his mouth suddenly felt dry. It would be so easy. She was young and charming and willing to give herself for a bit of silver. Such a thing was good for both of them and hurt no one. He looked into her smiling eyes and then down to where her breasts swelled above a small waist.

She smiled knowingly and leaned forward. Her scent was very pleasant and her gown gaped just a little, revealing a glimpse of rosy flesh. His fingers itched to reach inside her gown, to feel that soft roundness in his palm. He felt sweat beading his upper lip and gulped more wine.

'I have a room nearby,' she murmured. 'Beside the river, where it's cooler and the sound of the water will accompany our pleasure. Come with me. I will make you happy again. I'm not called Little Wave for nothing.'

He imagined making love to this young girl to the sound of the rushing waters, cradled in her arms, buoyant as on a wave, and he felt desire stir and sweat break out all over his body.

'It isn't far. Shall we go together? Or perhaps you would rather follow?' She took his hand and started to rise.

It would be so easy and pleasant to forget his troubles for a little, but Akitada was suddenly appalled at his weakness and snatched back his hand. 'Not today, Little Wave,' he said hoarsely. 'I must find Tora.'

She pouted charmingly. 'Oh, this Tora again. Can't we forget about him for just a little?'

He knew that she merely thought him a convenient customer. If he agreed, the older woman would join them to discuss the price. It served him right, and the realization helped to cool his blood. He said, 'I won't mention him again, but perhaps you know a girl called Hanae?'

She drew back, suddenly looking desolated. 'Don't you like me at all?' Her voice trembled a little.

He felt sorry for hurting her. She was very young, too young for this coarse business. 'I find you very attractive, Little Wave,' he said more gently, 'but I must find Tora and Hanae quickly.' She still hung her head, and he lied, 'Perhaps we can meet some other time, when I'm not so busy.'

She cast a despairing glance towards the others, but then gave him a tremulous smile. Putting down her empty cup, she bowed. 'Thank you for the wine. I'm sorry I troubled you.'

He was a little ashamed of himself and wondered if her failure would get her a reprimand. She had good manners for a prostitute and

159

certainly played her game very well. 'Wait,' he said and saw hope flash in her eyes. He fished a piece of silver from his sash. 'Here. For your time. I came for information and am paying for detaining you. If you don't know Tora, nor Hanae, perhaps you can tell me who might.'

She tucked the coin between her breasts. 'Thank you,' she said, smiling again. 'I owe for my rent.' Her relief was not very flattering, but she went on, 'There's a new dancer called Hanae. She and Kohata perform at the big parties. You could ask Kohata. I heard Hanae's married.' She shook her head. 'If it's true, she's a fool. She could be a courtesan of the first rank.'

'Perhaps she wanted a family.'

Little Wave laughed bitterly. 'That's what I thought, and now look at me. He left me with a child, and I'm just scraping by on chance meetings. It used to be that people had my name on their list and I was always busy.'

Akitada stared at her. 'You have a child?' He would have judged her to be no more than sixteen.

'At least she's a girl. In another five years I can sell her into the trade.' She was matter-of-fact about it. Women in her profession had little chance to settle down with a decent man, and no place to go but back to the old life. And their children followed them into misery. Akitada thought of the deaf-mute boy, but Little Wave was too young to have known the dead courtesan. The world was full of tragic events and lives that ended in disaster. With a sigh, he took out another silver coin he could ill spare and gave it

160

to her. 'This is no life for you and your daughter. Leave this business while you are still young.' Then he rose.

She looked up at him, clutching the money. 'It's only because I'm young that men want to lie with me,' she said sadly. 'Well, some men. I wish you'd stay. I really like you.'

She looked so forlorn that Akitada blushed. 'I am sorry,' he said and turned to walk away.

She ran after him. 'Will you really be back?'

He shook his head.

She extended her hand and pushed something in his sash. 'I wasn't worth this much,' she said and ran back to the others.

Outside, Akitada found that she had returned one of the silver coins.

The dancer Kohata rented a private pavilion behind one of the better restaurants. Her maid answered his knock and informed him that 'her lady' was at work.

'At this time of day?' Akitada asked suspiciously.

The maid gave him a pitying look. 'My lady is much sought after. She is a great dancer and works very hard. She has not yet returned from Lord Sadanori's party last night.'

And what that meant was pretty clear: someone had requested entertainment of a more private nature. He would never understand the lifestyle of these people. Somewhere he had heard the name Sadanori recently, but he could not recall where. He was one of the Fujiwaras, an important one, though they had never met.

161

He decided to call on the dancer. Leaving the quarter, he walked southward through streets where merchants, artisans, and the upper servants and retainers of great families lived in small, neat houses with modest gardens. The area gradually became more rural. Here and there he passed a mansion, heavily walled and gated against riff-raff. Then the streets became footpaths, and the footpaths mere tracks. The wooden houses shrank in size, and in the surrounding fields people grew vegetables to sell in the market. Children played among chickens and ducks.

In a weedy field beside the road, an ox grazed, tied by a long rope to a post and watched over by a small boy. Instantly, Akitada was reminded of the child he had left behind in Otsu. He asked directions of the boy and turned down another weedy road. A bridge of timbers and boards passed over a canal where ducks and geese splashed and squawked. A woman was washing clothes on the bank, while her children chased each other and a black-and-white puppy. It was a wholesome scene after the Willow Quarter, and Akitada was cheered by it.

The dancer's house was no more than a one-room shack, but its small veranda was overgrown with a flowering morning glory vine and a white cat sat on the top step. Someone had planted a few vegetables in a plot near the gate. The place looked deserted.

Akitada pushed open the gate and walked along the path. The cat rose and mewed plaintively. He leaned down to stroke its back.

'Nobody's home,' a shrill voice called out

to him.

He turned and saw a middle-aged female peering over the fence.

'I am looking for the dancer Hanae,' he said. 'Do you know where she is?'

She scanned him from head to toe before answering. 'Hanae left yesterday. In the morning. A sedan chair came for her.'

He should have expected it. Like Kohata, this Hanae had also spent the night with a client. 'When do you expect her back?'

The woman smirked. 'Couldn't say. She's in demand, that one, though she'd better make the most of her time. Noble suitors don't like being saddled with another man's child.'

So the famous dancer was pregnant. Like Little Wave, she had been careless or unlucky. Akitada eyed the woman's sharp face with distaste. His good humor evaporated, he turned to leave, when she said, 'I told the fool who knocked her up that she had better things to do than wait around for him.'

He walked over to the fence. 'I was told she was married. Can you describe her husband?'

She was taken aback by the question, then exploded with invective. 'Married, hah! He's just another good-looking, good-for-nothing lay-about. Never here when she needs him. I warned her, but she won't listen. Oh, she says, he works for a great lord and can't get much time off. A fine husband! He comes for meals and sex, that's all. The only thing he ever brought her was a mangy dog that kills my chickens, and when I complain he calls me names. Good riddance to

163

such scum.'

Akitada looked at her, then looked back at the little shack, the vine, the cat, and the vegetable plot. Could it be? Was this where Tora had been spending his time? He asked, 'This sedan chair that picked up the young woman, do you happen to know where it was taking her?'

She was pleased by this question. 'No, but it was Lord Sadanori himself who sent for her. A sedan chair. Imagine. Hanae may never come back here.'

'Sadanori? Fujiwara Sadanori?'

'That's the one.'

Akitada was appalled. If the dancer had played Tora wrong with Sadanori and Tora had gone after her, he could be getting into big trouble. 'Who would have information about Hanae's appointments?'

She gave a little cackle of amusement. 'If the gentleman is interested, her dancing master Ohiya is the one to talk to.'

Ohiya lived in the Willow Quarter, and Akitada trudged back the way he had come. By now it was well past midday, hotter than ever, and he had not eaten yet. Besides, the unaccustomed walking caused unpleasant spasms to the old wound in his injured leg. By the time he reached the quarter again, he was limping. He decided to rest and fortify himself first and entered a large restaurant called The Crane Grove.

The restaurant was busy, but his clothes marked him as an upper-level official, and he was shown to a seat near the window. His waiter, a thin, eager young man, was chatty in hopes of a fat tip

164

from the important customer. 'We get many gentlemen during the day, this being the best restaurant in the city,' he informed Akitada. 'I particularly recommend the fish soup. And afterwards a dish of eel?'

Akitada nodded and glanced through the latticed window at the willows drooping in the afternoon heat. He felt glum. If the dancer expected his child, Tora's concern for her was reasonable. But he had chosen to keep everyone in the dark and sneak off in this shameful manner because he was ashamed of the liaison. Finding Tora was not the only problem.

When the waiter returned with wine, Akitada asked him if he had seen anyone resembling Tora.

The waiter had not, but he dashed off to check with the other waiters. He was a helpful young man, but it was hard to get in more than one question at a time. Akitada sipped the wine and looked out at the street. Early customers were arriving in the quarter, well-dressed men in search of a bit of relaxation or dalliance before returning to their families after a day in their offices and bureaus.

The fish soup arrived, along with the information that one of the waiter's colleagues remembered meeting Tora, but had not seen him in weeks. Would the gentleman like to question the other waiter?

No, Akitada saw no point in it, but asked about Hanae.

'Hanae?' The waiter's eyes lit up. 'Such a dancer,' he cried. 'I know her well. So graceful.

165

Like a celestial fairy. So light on her feet that she seems to float. Even those who live above the clouds are bewitched by her. They say she's already won the heart of a great lord. And when she sings ... it's like hearing a nightingale.' He paused and leaned forward. 'Don't mention this, but she was to dance here last night. When she didn't show up, we sent for Kohata instead, but Kohata was engaged. It was a disaster, and my boss was wild because he thought he would lose a very important client. But the client canceled before we could tell him.'

This agreed with the neighbor's story. Akitada nodded and began to eat. The soup was excellent, but the more he heard about the dancer, the less he liked her. Hanae had found a rich and powerful protector and had better things to do than wait for Tora or dance at a party. She had gone off to give a private performance to her benefactor instead.

In due course, the eel arrived, accompanied by a bowl of fragrant rice and several dishes of tasty condiments. Akitada had just sampled the pickled chestnuts when some sort of disturbance broke out on the street. People were running and shouting, and several red-coated constables trotted past the window. Akitada's waiter dashed out the door and reappeared an instant later, chattering to two burly constables who pushed him aside to make a cursory check of the guests before disappearing into the kitchen, where loud curses and a clatter of pans greeted their invasion.

The waiter returned to Akitada. 'I thought that

you must be wondering what happened, sir,' he said, slightly out of breath. 'I went to find out for you. The constables are looking for a madman. He attacked the owner of the Fragrant Plum Blossom and the dancer Kohata, the same one I mentioned. I'm not sure, but he may have killed them.' Seeing Akitada's startled expression, he had second thoughts. 'Nothing to worry about, sir,' he reassured the valued guest. 'The constables will catch him shortly. We don't allow trouble in the quarter. It's safer here than anywhere. Is the eel to your liking?'

Akitada ignored this glowing testimonial for the Willow Quarter, popped a last bite of eel into his mouth, and approved of the food.

He paid, leaving the waiter a generous tip – though not as generous as that young man had expected – and walked to the house of the dancing master, a modest building marked with a sign that read: 'Master of the Dance. Teacher of all forms of court dancing – *bugaku* (both the left and the right), *gosechi*, *sarugaku*, and *dengaku*. Students accepted only after interviews.'

A couple of passers-by had stopped and were looking at the open door. The sound of excited voices could be heard from inside. Akitada knocked and, when no one came, entered. He followed the voices to a large room.

Several people were in it, all talking at the same time. A thin middle-aged male in a peculiar black silk robe seemed to be having hysterics, while an older woman and four small girls clung to him, adding their anguish to his.

'What is going on here?' Akitada demanded.

167

All six fell silent and turned startled eyes his way. The man disengaged himself from the clinging females. He touched his throat and croaked, 'I've been attacked. I, Ohiya. Attacked in my own house. If the police had not arrived in time ... heavens ... I cannot think. Look at me. I'm shaking like a leaf.' He held out limp hands, then put one to his forehead. 'I feel faint,' he moaned. 'Help me, girls. I must sit down.'

The older woman and the four little girls, dressed as richly as the little girl who had accosted Akitada earlier that morning, rushed to his rescue. They supported the man to his cushion, where he sat, his eyes closed, taking deep breaths to calm himself.

Akitada guessed that this was where the constables had run the madman to ground. The maniac did not seem to have done much damage, however, except to Master Ohiya's nerves. Akitada waited until the master calmed down. Then he introduced himself and said, 'I'm told that you are the teacher of the dancer Hanae?'

Ohiya closed his eyes and moaned again.

Akitada cleared his throat. 'I seem to have arrived inopportunely. If you will oblige me with a little information, I shall be on my way.'

Ohiya cried, 'I wish I'd never laid eyes on her. She'll be my death one of these days. Oh, the pain in my chest.' He gasped and clutched at himself. The older woman rushed forward to dab at his face with a square of soft paper, and the girls wailed again and clung to him. He said irritably, 'Let go of me. I'm having trouble breathing with all of you crushing me like that.'

They retreated, murmuring apologies.

Akitada decided that there was nothing wrong with the man and snapped, 'Master Ohiya. I have taken a lot of trouble finding you. May I have your attention for a moment?'

His tone had the desired result. Ohiya sat up and gave him an appraising look. Then he made a slight bow. 'I do beg your pardon, sir. I was overcome. My constitution is frail, I'm afraid, and the least thing upsets it.' He paused. 'Not that this was a small matter. He was murderous.'

'Pull yourself together, man. You're alive.'

'Yes, well.' Ohiya felt himself all over, then said, 'If you're looking for Hanae, I'm afraid I cannot help you. She seems to have disappeared.' He added more querulously, 'I cannot imagine why anyone would think I had something to do with it. These women are always getting into trouble.'

This echoed almost exactly Akitada's own thoughts, but he was more interested in something else. 'Who else is looking for her?'

'Why, that madman. Her husband. How dare he? I told her from the very start to leave him alone. "You are going to ruin your chances," I said. "A girl like you can rise to the top of the profession." But she wouldn't listen. He turned her head, and she married him, a penniless servant who lives and works elsewhere.' Ohiya threw up his hands. 'Because he's handsome! I ask you. If she must roll about in the bedding with a man, let it at least be a wealthy patron. His little fling pays off handsomely, and they return to work richer and with a reputation that makes

169

them more attractive. But her lout of a husband got her pregnant and now plays the jealous lover. What fools these people are.'

ELEVEN

Making Amends

Thunder was rumbling overhead when Akitada reached the police headquarters. Superintendent Kobe was in his office and greeted Akitada warmly. He knew of Yori's death, but several months had passed since then, and he expressed surprise and concern at Akitada's haggard appearance.

Akitada brushed this aside and said, 'I came because Tora's in prison again. As far as I can make out, it was just a matter of breaking the peace, but some people may lay charges against him.'

It had only been months since Kobe had helped clear Tora of a murder charge, and he raised his brows. 'Really? Did the rascal inflict serious wounds?'

'I don't believe so. It happened in the Willow Quarter about an hour ago.'

Kobe cast up his eyes. 'Of course, where else?'

'I haven't spoken to Tora in several days, but I think this is more complicated than just rowdiness. Tora seems to have taken up with a dancer

170

called Hanae. The girl may be pregnant with his child. Yesterday she took off with Fujiwara Sadanori.'

'She must be a beauty then. Yes, I see your problem. The hot-head won't see reason. If we turn him loose, he'll confront His Lordship and the charmer.'

'Precisely.'

They sat, pondering the problem. Outside, thunder growled again, and gusts of wind rattled the shutters. Finally, Kobe said, 'I assume your interest is less in finding the girl than in stopping Tora from doing something foolish?'

'Yes, of course. Or rather, it would be, except...' Akitada paused. How to put his uneasiness into words? 'Mind you, everything points to her having left of her own will, but what if she didn't go freely? There's something peculiar about all this.'

'Out with it. It's not like you to hold back on opinions.'

'I'm no longer sure of much. There was another disappearance from the quarter about six years ago. A courtesan of the first rank left abruptly and was not heard of again. Sadanori was linked to her also.'

'Ah, the beautiful Peony. As I said, he's a well-known connoisseur of female beauty, and his power and wealth make him desirable to such women, even if his personality doesn't.'

'I've never met the man. Is he involved in anything of a criminal nature?'

'I wouldn't go that far.'

'I only know he holds several high positions in

171

the administration – in spite of poor performance – but this is common enough and throws no light on his private life.'

Kobe sighed. 'We have nothing very substantial. Two women have complained of mistreatment. Their stories could not be proven, and in one case the victim was not sure herself. The first, a courtesan, claims that he raped her. Since she regularly sells her charms and admits that Sadanori paid her generously, we had a good laugh. The other story is more difficult. It involves a very young girl. She was only thirteen at the time and in training with a registered entertainer. She claims that Sadanori made advances to her, and that she was kidnapped and raped.'

'Aha!'

'Not so fast. It is true that she was raped. The prison matron examined her. But the girl was blindfolded at the time. She did not see who raped her.'

'Did you confront Sadanori?'

'Of course not. He would have laughed me out of his house and then seen to it that I was replaced by someone more easily bribed in case of future trouble.'

Akitada frowned. 'But you believed him guilty.' He raised his voice over another roll of thunder. 'Apparently, intimidation works as well as bribery to pervert justice.'

Kobe was angry. 'Be careful what you say.'

'Sorry, I didn't mean that. Things have been more than usually difficult. Tora's problem is not my only one. I've been charged with stealing a child.'

172

'What?'

'A fisherman and his wife from a village near Otsu say I took the boy for improper purposes.'

Kobe's eyebrows shot up. 'You mean sex?'

'Yes.'

'What in heaven's name have you been up to?'

Akitada said wearily, 'It's a long story. I found a ragged, starving child and took pity on him. The alleged parents have abused him and now see a chance to get quite a lot of money from me. Sadanori's activities with courtesans may tie in with the boy somehow.'

'Forgive me, but you always manage to become involved in impossible situations. If you say that those peculiar events of the dancer and the boy are somehow connected, I'll take your word for it, but frankly...' He shook his head.

'I don't feel happy about it. The boy is only about five, and he is mute.'

Kobe's eyes narrowed speculatively. 'Your son was that age, wasn't he?'

'That has nothing to do with it,' Akitada snapped. 'This child was lost. In the rain at nightfall. Anyone would have stopped for him.'

Kobe shook his head. 'Well, let's go talk to Tora. Perhaps something will come to us when we hear what he has to say.'

The first heavy drops of the storm struck them as they crossed the courtyard to the jail. There, Kobe read the charges and shook his head again.

They found Tora manacled and chained to a heavy column and clinging to it like a ship-wrecked man to flotsam. Two guards stood over him with whips. His blue gown had been pulled down for the flogging, and angry red stripes marked his bare back. His head was pressed against the column.

'Stop that,' Kobe snapped.

The guards saluted, but Tora did not bother to open his eyes. Akitada was suddenly afraid. This was not Tora's first arrest or whipping, but in the past he had always borne the experience defiantly. He went to him. Up close, Tora was filthy and stank.

'Tora?' Akitada's voice was unsteady, so he tried again. 'Tora, are you all right?'

There was a slight tensing of the shoulders, but no other sign that the chained man had heard.

Akitada turned to the nearest guard. 'Untie him.' The guard looked at Kobe, who nodded.

When his arms were released, Tora slumped and sat, his head bowed between his knees.

Akitada knelt beside him and put his hand on his arm. 'Tora, look at me. I've searched for you all day.'

Tora muttered, 'Go away, sir. I'm no good to you anymore.'

'Nonsense. I need you, and you need me. What about Hanae?'

Tora's head finally came up. He looked at Akitada from bloodshot eyes and said, through a split lip, 'You know about Hanae?'

'I know she may be in some sort of trouble,' Akitada said cautiously. 'What happened?'

'Some rich bastard's got her. I was trying to find her, but the scum in the quarter all cover up for the cursed nobles. I got a bit impatient. When that she-man Ohiya refused to help me, I knew he was in on it, too. I was going to squeeze the truth out of that perfumed piece of dung when the constables jumped me.'

Kobe interrupted with: 'We'd better discuss the rest in my office.'

Tora staggered to his feet with Akitada's help and limped on one bare foot. Akitada asked, 'What happened to your clothes, and your other boot, and...?' He ran out of words to express his shock.

'I walked to Uji and back. Never mind. Did you mean it? About helping me find Hanae?' When Akitada nodded, Tora's hand shot out and grasped Akitada's fiercely. 'Even after I left you in Otsu?'

Akitada nodded again. 'I meant it,' he said and felt some of the tightness in his chest giving way. He put his hand on Tora's shoulder.

'I'm not too proud to beg, sir,' Tora said. 'I left you because I was afraid for Hanae. You'd do the same for your lady, I think.'

The comparison made Akitada uncomfortable. Tora's assumption that he, too, would set aside every other consideration, even the most sacred obligations, to protect Tamako troubled him. It had been a long time since he had felt this strongly about his wife.

As they crossed the courtyard, Tora said, 'Hanae's my wife, and she's going to have my child, sir. Can you make the superintendent turn me loose so I can find her?'

'Your wife?' Akitada still did not want to believe this. A woman from the Willow Quarter? Tora had never needed to marry his women, or to pay for prostitutes. He almost said so, but Tora's face stopped him. He said instead, 'Why didn't you tell me? How long has this been going on?'

'We met after Yori died. I didn't want to bother you and your lady with my concerns so I kept waiting for a chance, but it never came.'

Akitada opened his mouth and closed it again. He should have looked after his family better. There was more to be mended than the roof of his house.

In Kobe's office, Akitada asked, 'Can we get the charges dismissed?'

Kobe said, 'Of course not.'

'There must be something you can do.'

'Not unless you can persuade the injured parties to withdraw their charges.'

'That dancing master?'

'And the owner of the restaurant. He claims personal injury and damage to his property.'

Akitada grimaced. 'Perhaps I can pay them off.'

Kobe continued, 'Also, the courtesan Kohata. She says Tora has caused her to be ridiculed and this has permanently damaged her reputation. I doubt she'll come cheap.'

'I may not have enough money,' Akitada said to Tora. 'The judge in Otsu kept all the gold I had with me.'

Tora looked blank. 'Why?'

'I was also arrested. We are both charged with kidnapping the boy.'

Tora sucked in his breath. 'What? How can they do that? We saved the kid from that witch of a mother. And why take all your gold? Have the

176

judges turned to highway robbery now?'

'The money is to cover damages. The Mimuras claim I misused the child.'

Tora stared at him, brow wrinkled. '"Misused"?' Understanding dawned, and with it a look of such outrage that Akitada almost smiled. 'Filthy-minded scum. Have they lost their minds?'

'The Mimuras want money.'

Kobe had followed the exchange with interest and grinned. 'I suppose you'll have to decide whether to bribe yourself out of your legal difficulties first or take care of Tora's problem.'

Akitada said, 'It isn't funny, Kobe.'

'I couldn't resist after you accused me of accommodating Sadanori.'

Akitada sighed. 'I'll go back and see what I can do about getting Tora's charges dropped. Then I'll look for Hanae.'

Tora said quickly, 'Never mind the charges. Just find Hanae. Please?'

'I promise.'

Tora looked grateful. 'You'll like her, sir.'

Akitada doubted it, but he nodded.

Trudging back to the amusement quarter in a steady drizzle, Akitada was not optimistic. Two days and a night had passed. Either Hanae had chosen her new life freely, or she had already been violated. He would take care of Tora's problems first.

Dusk had fallen early. In the quarter, lanterns glimmered like fireflies in the darkness. From the open doors of wine houses and restaurants came the sound of music and laughter. In spite of the weather, the Willow Quarter was doing a fine business.

The Fragrant Plumblossom was crammed with guests. Chikamura, his head bandaged, was entertaining everybody with the story of the attack. When Akitada asked to speak to him privately, Chikamura led him into a small back room.

Akitada said courteously, 'I deeply regret the incident earlier today. The man who caused your injury is my retainer, Tora. He was desperate at the time because his wife had been kidnapped. He begs your forgiveness, and I came to pay for the damages.'

If he had not been so worried about his slender funds, Akitada would have been amused. Chikamura's face expressed his gratification at an apology from a nobleman, delight at the thought of generous reimbursement, and finally doubt and regret that it might not be a good idea to appear too greedy. He hemmed and hawed, said he understood, but there was the matter of the broken wall and the cost of the doctor, and...

'Can you show me the damage?'

'I had it fixed. The carpenter charged two pieces of silver for a rush job, but I had to have the restaurant open for tonight.'

'Yes, quite. And the physician?'

'Another two pieces of silver. He's a terrible crook.'

'Very well. If you stop by the prison early tomorrow and withdraw the charges, you shall have ten pieces of silver. Is that agreeable?'

It was. Chikamura bowed him out of his restaurant, pleased that he had kept the gentleman's goodwill while collecting many times over what he had paid.

Akitada's spirits rose a little.

Kohata was next. She was home and sullen. Akitada looked at her expensive costume and the costly appointments of her room and took an instant dislike to her. He cut through her lamentations with the comment that he had many friends among the aristocracy and hoped that he would be able to say nice things about her. Kohata pouted and then agreed that perhaps the incident might be forgotten if her business continued to flourish. Akitada felt little guilt over threatening a woman who depended on the goodwill of men like himself. After all, she had been ready enough to grind a poor man under her dainty foot.

The dancing master was also at home. Akitada was admitted by a young male servant in a surprisingly handsome silk robe. A worried-looking Ohiya lounged alone and in informal attire, leaning against a lacquered armrest. He wore a deep-red silk robe and a voluminous open jacket of golden yellow brocade with purple trim over full lavender silk trousers that were embroidered with black flowers. Akitada averted his eyes from this costume and accepted a seat on a plump cushion. Strongly scented incense rose in delicate spirals from a censer, and a flask of wine stood by. The servant whisked one of the two cups away and brought another.

Ohiya fanned himself with a gilded fan and

asked for news of Hanae. When Akitada told him that she had not been found, his face fell. 'Oh, dear, oh, dear,' he moaned. 'That *is* worrisome. I shouldn't have spoken ill of her. No wonder her young man was so distracted.'

This was encouraging, and Akitada said cautiously, 'Tora works for me. I've come to see if I can convince you to forgive him.'

Ohiya hesitated. 'Well, he was very abusive. I don't wish to mention the names he called me! Shocking and very crude. I'm an artist and was merely training Hanae.'

Akitada guessed from this that Tora had called Ohiya a pimp. He said, 'I'm sorry. Tora was perhaps jealous of your influence over the young woman.'

Ohiya nodded. 'Exactly. Young people do not handle romantic attachments very well.'

Akitada agreed, mentioned Tora's devotion to Hanae, and hinted at compensation for Ohiya's suffering.

At this, Ohiya sat up. 'Oh no, I couldn't. After all, I'm quite unhurt. He only gave me a bad fright. In fact, I had already made up my mind to go to the police and drop the charges. Tora's headstrong and rude, but I'm willing to concede that he does seem to care for the poor girl.'

Akitada was so surprised by this sudden change in Ohiya that he felt a niggling suspicion that all was not as it seemed. 'That's very generous of you,' he said. 'I am going to search for Hanae. I wonder, can you tell me anything about Lord Sadanori? He seems to have had an interest in her. Could he be involved in her disappearance?'

Ohiya gulped. 'Lord Sadanori?' He reached for his cup and drank before answering. 'Very unlikely, I would say. It's true, he engaged Hanae quite often, and he pays very well. But no, I think Lord Sadanori's position argues against such suspicions.'

Akitada said grimly, 'I disagree. He seems to have a bad reputation with women. A man's rank and power do not excuse wanton disregard of decency.'

Ohiya flushed. 'My dear sir, do please remember that you are in the Willow Quarter. Our careers and our livelihood depend on men like Lord Sadanori. You'll forgive me, I'm sure, if I point out that if our clients were held to such high moral standards, we would all starve.'

Akitada recalled the young woman in pink. He had come very close to paying for the services of Little Wave. Besides, Ohiya had been decent about Tora. He decided not to pursue the matter, thanked the dancing master, and left.

It was fully dark, but the rain had stopped. Akitada was soaked, he was tired, and the amount of walking he had done made his bad leg hurt, but he owed Tora this and much more. He needed to pick up the trail of the sedan chair that had taken Hanae away. If only he had questioned the neighbor more thoroughly earlier. Well, there was nothing for it. At least the woman should be home this time of night.

The streets had become quagmires after the rain, and he sloshed through puddles, ruining his boots and trousers. Worse, he lost his way in the dark. A lantern would have helped, but thieves roamed the streets of the capital at night. It was better not to announce your presence by carrying a light.

When he heard the lowing of the tethered ox, he knew he was on the right street. An impenetrable blackness seemed to weigh down on the city. Akitada almost missed Hanae's house because it showed a glow of light. This was strange, but perhaps the nosy neighbor had come to snoop.

The little gate squeaked after the rain. Akitada walked quickly up the walk.

The door of the house flew open, and, for a moment, a girl's figure stood outlined against the light. Then she rushed down the steps and flung herself into Akitada's arms.

TWELVE

Hanae's Story

Akitada thought he was holding a child. She was small, and her body felt as fragile of bone and flexible of limb as a child's. The perception lasted only a moment, because she gasped and started flailing and kicking to get free. Akitada released her instantly, saw she was falling, and reached to catch her. A stinging slap landed on his cheek, followed by a series of punches from small fists. She cried, 'Take your hands off me!'

and screamed for help.

A light came on next door. The girl backed away, and Akitada saw a small oval face that was painted so white that it seemed all eyes. It expressed panic and fury in equal parts. He took a wild guess: 'Hanae? Are you Tora's Hanae? We've been looking for you everywhere.'

She still looked frightened. 'Who are you?'

'I am Sugawara. Tora works for me.'

A small hand covered her lips. 'Oh, no,' she moaned. 'I didn't know. Forgive me, sir.' She bowed deeply.

'You couldn't know. You *are* Hanae, then?'

'Yes, I'm Hanae. Where's Tora?'

The neighbor's door flew open. 'What's going on over there?' she shouted.

The slender girl cried back, 'It's me, Hanae, Mrs Hamada. Sorry. I was startled, but everything's all right.'

If she had hoped that Mrs Hamada would close her door and leave them in peace she was mistaken. The woman immediately came to the fence. 'Hanae? You're back?' she cried. 'That man of yours was looking for you and a noble gentleman also. How was your visit? I expect you'll leave us now.'

Akitada snapped, 'Go back inside, woman. You can gossip tomorrow.'

Mrs Hamada gave him a startled look. 'Oh, you're back, sir. I see.' She giggled. 'You've become very popular, Hanae.'

'She'll think the worst now,' Hanae muttered.

Akitada had taken note of the fact that Hanae was wearing the gaudy costume of a professional dancer. Irritation at Tora's taste in women surfaced again. He wanted to get to the bottom of this affair as quickly as possible so he could take care of his own problems. 'Let's go inside,' he said curtly.

She hesitated just a moment, then led the way. The little house was painstakingly clean, but so cramped for space that Akitada could see all of it at one glance. A single oil lamp cast some light. He saw Tora's sword hanging on the wall and looked again at his wife's dance costume and her heavy make-up. Her childlike size made him wonder how old she was, but he had had proof enough that day that women fell early into the life of pleasure.

She also gave him an appraising look, then placed a cushion for him, knelt, bowed, and apologized for the humble surroundings. Her hands were shaking badly, and as Akitada looked, he saw rips in the sleeves of her embroidered robe. The brilliant blue silk was wet all over and mud stained her skirt. None of this made up for the trouble she had caused.

'Where have you been?' he demanded, ignoring her courteous welcome.

She lifted her hands helplessly. 'I don't know.'

'You don't know?'

'I was picked up in a closed sedan chair. The bearers took me to a house. There an old woman gave me some wine to drink. The wine made me sleepy, but I was very thirsty and drank a lot of it. When I woke up, I was alone and my hands and feet were tied. After a while I got loose and escaped, but it was dark outside and I ran so hard that I don't remember the street.'

Akitada found this hard to believe. The very economical account left out a great deal. What of the elaborate costume and make-up? 'You went to perform for Lord Sadanori?' he guessed, gesturing to her costume.

'No,' she cried and pulled at the gown in disgust. 'This isn't mine. I don't know what happened to my own clothes. I was wearing a plain gown when I left. I thought I was to be a nursemaid.' She touched the thick white paste on her face. 'Someone else did all this after I passed out.'

'Really?'

They stared at each other. The make-up looked as if it had been applied by an expert, but Akitada was no judge of such matters. She was probably very pretty under all that paint. Kobe was right: Tora had good taste in women. Her hair was long and loose, and her small hands graceful. Whatever her age, she was certainly no child and knew all the tricks to attract a man like Tora. And that childlike fragility would appeal to his protectiveness.

As if she guessed his thoughts, she asked again, 'Where is Tora, sir?'

'In jail.'

She jumped a little at that. 'In jail? Why? Because of me?'

Akitada nodded. 'When he couldn't get any answers about your whereabouts, he attacked a few people in the Willow Quarter.'

Her eyes filled with tears. He thought, she won't really cry because it will smudge all that black paint around her eyes. But the tears fell and left black streaks in the white paint.

Akitada was ashamed. 'He should be released tomorrow.'

'He didn't attack Lord Sadanori?'

This made him wonder if she had been raped after all. 'No. Should he have?'

'Of course not. They would kill him.'

He raised his brows at that. 'Will you tell Tora what *really* happened?'

She flushed. 'I told you the truth. I don't know what happened after I passed out. Nothing, I think.'

He nodded. 'Much the safest way. But he'll want better answers than you gave me.'

She looked around helplessly. 'I cannot stay here,' she said. 'I'm not sure where I'll be.'

'Why can't you stay?'

'They may come after me when they find me gone.'

Akitada opened his mouth, but thought better of it. He rose. 'You'd better come with me,' he said.

She shook her head. 'Oh, no, I couldn't. What would your lady say?' She got to her feet and gestured to her costume. 'I have worked in the Willow Quarter,' she said, adding defiantly, 'as a dancer.'

'Tora says you're his wife.'

'Yes. We wanted to tell you, but—' She broke off and sighed. 'Did he tell you we are going to have a child?'

Akitada eyed her flamboyant costume and slender waist. 'Yes,' he said coldly. 'Under the

186

circumstances, you should not have had dealings of any kind with a man like Sadanori. You must have known of his reputation, even if Tora did not.'

She started trembling again, but her voice was steady. 'You're right, sir. I was a fool and know that now. But I was offered a great deal of money, and we needed it if I was going to give up dancing.'

He turned away. 'Get your things and let's go.' He went out onto the small porch and waited. When she joined him, she had washed her face and changed into a plain blue hemp gown. A large covered basket hung over her arm, and she clutched Tora's sword. He gave a grunt and set off.

The truth was, he would rather not insult Tamako by introducing a dancer from the amusement quarter into their house, but neither did he want Hanae to disappear again. She had caused him enough trouble when he needed to concentrate on rescuing the child. He thought about the situation in Otsu and became distracted by its difficulties.

When he reached his home, he remembered her and turned. 'We are here.' She was behind him, her face perfectly white and her breathing labored. 'What's the matter?' he asked. 'Are you sick?'

'Your legs are longer than mine.' She gasped and dropped her basket. The white cat emerged from it, mewing her protest. Her mistress pressed a hand to her belly and tottered to the wall, leaning against it, her eyes closed.

Akitada pounded on the gate and shouted, 'Genba! Genba!' A dog started barking. He turned back to Hanae. 'I'm sorry. My mind was on other things. It was very thoughtless of me. You should have told me to slow down.'

She gave him an exasperated look, then bent for the cat.

'Let me.' He snatched up the basket and put the cat back in it, then pounded on the gate again. The dog went into a frenzy of snarling. 'What is a dog doing here?' Akitada muttered.

'It's Trouble,' she said in a tired voice.

'Trouble?' he asked, confused.

She chuckled weakly. 'That's what Tora calls him.'

The dog's growls turned to excited snuffling and whining. When the gate finally opened, he shot out, a large, shaggy gray ball of energy. He jumped up on Akitada first, leaving muddy stains on his robe, then abandoned him to greet Hanae. He licked her face and then bounced around her, yipping with joy. The cat hissed from its basket.

Genba appeared and took the basket from Akitada, then caught the dog by the remnant of rope around his neck.

Akitada looked at the three unexpected additions to his household. Then he looked down at his wet, and now muddy, robe and said bitterly, 'I take it Trouble has come to stay.'

No one corrected him. They walked into the courtyard before Akitada remembered introductions. 'Hanae,' he said, 'this is Genba. Genba, Hanae is Tora's ... wife. She'll stay here until he gets out of jail tomorrow.'

Genba's face broke into a broad smile. 'Hanae! Tora's been beside himself. He'll be so happy you're safe.' He turned to Akitada. 'Did you say "jail", sir? Is he all right? Nothing serious, I hope.'

'Not now,' Akitada said sourly. 'Let's not discuss this now. It's been a long, miserable day.'

He took Hanae to Tamako, a meeting which proved once again that he knew nothing about women. He hoped to leave matters to his wife and escape to get out of his wet clothes. 'This is Hanae,' he said.

Hanae waited, and when he said nothing else, she explained, 'I'm Tora's wife.'

'Tora's wife?' Tamako looked startled. 'Oh, dear. I'm afraid he did not tell us about you.'

Hanae shuffled her feet. 'I'm sorry,' she said. 'I shouldn't have come. Please forgive the intrusion.'

Tamako said quickly, 'Of course you didn't intrude. Sit down, Hanae. You look exhausted.

Hanae blushed. 'I'm quite well, but it's been an exciting day and I'm a little tired.' She paused, glanced at Akitada, and murmured, 'And I'm expecting a child.'

Tamako went to put her arms around her. 'Men,' she muttered, with an accusing look at Akitada. 'Such nonsense, to hide you away like this. I have wished all along that Tora and Genba would bring home wives and raise their families here. You are most welcome in this house, my dear Hanae. I want to hear all about your marriage.' The two women clung to each other, and Akitada turned coward and slipped out of the room.

Seimei was waiting for him, his face all smiles. 'You found both of them, sir. Wonderful! Such a relief, even if Tora is in jail again. How did that happen?'

Akitada gave him a sketchy account while he shed his wet and dirty clothes. Seimei helped him into his house robe and poured hot tea. 'You must be very proud,' he said, 'to have solved the matter so quickly and easily.'

Exhaustion finally caught up with Akitada, who had not slept much the previous night in Warden Takechi's cell in Otsu and had walked too many miles today. He looked at Seimei blearily. 'Not at all easily, old friend. I think I shall sleep for days.'

Seimei immediately busied himself spreading his master's bedding and left.

Akitada was too tired for a bath. But he had barely extinguished his candle and placed his head on his pillow when his door opened. Tamako came in, already dressed for bed in a thin white underrobe with a pale rose-colored gown thrown over it. In the light of her candle, she looked like some delectable celestial being. The pink gown reminded Akitada of Little Wave and of making love to the sound of the river. Tamako floated nearer on bare feet, her body faintly visible under the thin silk where the light fell on it. He felt a jolt of desire for his wife and flung aside his covers to invite her into his bed.

But Tamako's eyes flashed for reasons other than love. She was very angry. 'How could you?' she demanded, stopping before him.

'How could I what?' he asked, blinking against the light.

'That poor young woman! She's been through a hellish time, and escaped with incredible courage. You must have seen her bloody wrists and ankles. She tore the skin off when she fought against her bonds until she broke them. She finally used her teeth. And you made her, frail as a child and pregnant, walk all the way here. Why didn't you get a sedan chair for her?'

'A sedan chair?' Akitada wanted to point out that he was no Sadanori and doubted that she would have felt comfortable taking another chair if she had indeed been abducted, but he did not get the chance. Tamako was not done with him.

'Yes, a sedan chair. And then, instead of making her welcome here, you told her she could only stay the night. And she the wife of a Sugawara retainer! Tora's wife! The mother of his unborn child! What were you thinking of?'

Akitada looked at his wife in dazed wonder. She was extremely attractive in her anger. There was a rosy color in her face, and her breasts strained against the thin silk with every angry breath. He sat up. She had been his companion for the past six years, a woman who should be as familiar to him as the old robe he was wearing, though not perhaps as comfortable. Certainly not in her present mood. But she was very desirable indeed. He smiled at her and let his eyes explore the half-obscured secrets of her body underneath the silk. 'The devil with Hanae. Come here.'

'Oh!' she cried, pulling the pink robe around her and flushing even more rosily before running from the room.

Wishing Hanae to the devil again, Akitada lay back and tried to subdue his mutinous body. Whatever Tamako's outrage, the dancer was safe, and tomorrow Tora would be back.

He smiled. Suddenly, he felt more optimistic about bringing home the boy he had grown fond of. He wondered what he would call him and fell asleep considering the possibilities.

He woke at dawn to the barking of Tora's dog. As soon as he had identified the unaccustomed sound, he put aside his irritation and stretched. The barking stopped. Perhaps, he thought, a guard dog would not be a bad idea. If Tora looked after the beast, it might be possible to become used to him. As for the cat, there were enough mice scurrying about in the walls and nesting in the thatch of the roof to keep the animal occupied for years.

But there was still Hanae. And, in time, Hanae's child. Akitada frowned. No, it would be much better if they all moved back to their own house and left him to his quiet life. On this thought, he closed his eyes and dozed off again.

The next disturbance was the sound of hammering and sawing. It was quite close to Akitada's room, and more sleep was out of the question. He sat up and rubbed his eyes. Sunlight filtered through the shutters and made striped patterns on the wooden floor.

Seimei scratched softly at the door before coming in with Akitada's tea.

'What is this infernal racket?' his master demanded.

'Sorry, sir. It's the new carpenter.'

Akitada brightened. 'Really?' He got up and accepted a cup of steaming tea. 'That was very efficient of you. I'm glad the repairs have begun.' He drank his tea.

'It's not my doing, sir. Tora sent the man yesterday.' Seimei pursed his lips. 'He's quite old, I'm afraid.'

Akitada eyed Seimei, who was well into his seventies and had become frail. If Seimei called the carpenter old, he must be truly ancient and well beyond being useful. Putting his cup down, Akitada raised the shutter and walked outside. He followed the carpentry sounds to his wife's pavilion. There he found a small wreck of a man with hair that was an astonishing color, somewhere between black and orange. The odd character was ponderously measuring a board, while the shaggy dog watched. The man's skin was as deeply wrinkled and brown as a walnut shell, and every bone and tendon in his thin arms and legs was visible. He straightened up with a groan and limped to the broken veranda step to fit the board in place. The dog followed and sat, head cocked attentively to observe the operation.

'Good morning,' said Akitada.

The carpenter did not hear him, but the dog spun around and charged, barking loudly. Akitada stepped back, but the animal paused only long enough to recognize a recent acquaintance and then jumped. Off balance already, Akitada sat down hard. The dog pushed him down and proceeded to wash his face with an enormous wet tongue.

Akitada shouted at the animal and flung him off. Getting to his feet was another matter. The dog circled with happy barks, ready to pounce again. The carpenter finally noticed. He approached and bowed deeply. The man must be given credit for recognizing authority even under humiliating circumstances, but he was not much help at the moment.

The door of the pavilion opened. 'Trouble!' Tamako looked down at the scene. The dog abandoned Akitada and raced to her.

Remembering his wife's anger the night before, Akitada got up nervously, but she smiled, wished him a good morning, and invited him in.

She still looked delicious, standing there in a pretty gown with that welcoming smile on her face, and he accepted eagerly. Bounding over the broken step and leaping across the hole in the veranda floor, he fetched up practically nose-to-nose with his wife. He caught the scent of orange blossoms, and took her in his arms. If the old carpenter was shocked at such behavior, Akitada did not care. Tamako had forgiven him, and he planned to take his time making love to her.

'Akitada.' Tamako's tone was firm.

'Yes, my dear?' He swept her inside the room, dropping the shutter with his free hand behind them. The room was dim, but Akitada saw that his wife's bedding had not been rolled up yet. Someone moved in the shadows.

'You can let me go now,' said Tamako. 'Really, the veranda was quite safe.' Akitada released his wife. Tamako went on brightly, 'Hanae and I had hoped to have a word with you before you left for work. It's good of you to come so early.'

Hanae again! Akitada felt a surge of resentment against that young woman. His eyes adjusted, and he saw her hovering near the door, looking embarrassed, though why a woman from the quarter should be embarrassed at what passed between men and women was beyond him.

Before he could sort out the situation, Tamako suggested, 'Let's sit down and discuss what is to be done about Lord Sadanori.'

Akitada sat down obediently. 'Done? Nothing can be done.'

Tamako bristled. 'Nothing? After what he did to Hanae?'

'Unless I missed something, nothing happened to her.'

'How can you call the abduction of a respectable young woman from her home for the pleasure of a depraved nobleman nothing?'

Respectable? Tamako had not led so sheltered a life that she did not know what passed in the amusement quarter. Hanae made a small noise of protest, and Akitada said peaceably, 'I'm sure it must have been very unpleasant, but we don't have any proof that Sadanori was involved – even if it were wise to charge a man of his stature.'

'Wise?' Tamako cried. 'What has wisdom got to do with it? Shall he continue to prey on defenseless women because everyone is too afraid to oppose him? Will you risk Tora's ruin by leaving this to him?'

Akitada opened his mouth and closed it again. He wanted to tell his wife that you don't pull the tiger's tail, but then he had never been very wise in such situations in the past. He tried reason. 'Hanae has assured me that she never saw Sadanori. She says she was unconscious.' A thought struck him, and he looked at Hanae. 'You're quite sure that – er – nothing happened to you?'

Hanae blushed. 'I wasn't raped,' she said. 'Oh, please, you must make Tora believe that nothing happened. I just want to forget the whole business.'

Tamako said, 'Don't be so timid, Hanae. My husband can put a stop to that monster. If he didn't rape you, he probably had just not got around to it yet.'

Akitada considered. Perhaps Hanae would know if she had been raped while she was unconscious. Coroners could usually determine recent intercourse in a dead woman. But Hanae might well cover up certain details because of Tora. He said firmly, 'There's no evidence against anyone, let alone Lord Sadanori. The sedan chair could have been sent by another admirer.'

Hanae said stubbornly, 'It was he who asked me to be a nursemaid. And he sent a woman to arrange for my visit to his wife. That's the only reason I went with them.'

'But you have no proof that it was not some other man who wanted your company. The woman could have lied.' Akitada was more and more convinced that Hanae herself was lying. 'I was told Lord Sadanori expected you to perform at a party that day. Kohata was asked to fill in for you when you didn't show up.'

Hanae clenched her small fists. 'I turned down the job. He knew I wouldn't perform because my husband objected. He was angry with me. They say he has some strange fancies. Only, I didn't think he felt that way about me.' She sighed. 'Can't we forget about it? I was very foolish.'

Tamako said, 'Whatever we decide to do, you cannot go back to your house. It's too dangerous. Besides, as Tora's wife you belong here, and this house is big enough for all of us.'

Akitada looked at her in dismay. His wife put an arm around Hanae. 'Oh, I am so glad that we shall soon have another child in this empty house.'

Akitada thought about the boy in Otsu – the as yet nameless child who had no voice to plead for himself and no one to take him in. Tamako had disregarded his own feelings in favor of Hanae's unborn child. Poor boy, he would not be welcome here.

Getting to his feet, he said soberly, 'My wife is quite right, Hanae. Tora's wife and child belong here. I hope that you will feel comfortable in this house.' Then he nodded to both of them and left.

Tora returned towards midday. When Akitada heard the news, he went to the courtyard, where he caught Tora swinging Hanae in his arms. They separated hastily when they saw him, and Tora came to greet him.

'How did you manage it, sir?' he asked, his face shining with happiness. 'Where was she?' He turned to look at Hanae, who hung back a little. 'Is she all right?'

'She says so. In fact, as she'll tell you herself, she escaped on her own and I merely brought her home. What about you?'

The charges against Tora had been withdrawn. He still looked the worse for wear, but a bath and tender care from his wife would soon improve that. Akitada returned to his study, where he went over his accounts again and thought about the Otsu problem. He was ready to write off the exorbitant amount of gold held by the Otsu judge if it bought the child's freedom. He had, after all, intended to do this in the first place.

Shortly after his midday meal, Tora and Hanae came to see him.

They entered shyly and expressed their thanks for accepting Hanae into the Sugawara family. Hanae looked very ill at ease and kept glancing at Tora as if she had to remind herself that this was what he wished to do.

Akitada was pleasant, said the right things, and then added, 'My wife will make the proper living arrangements for you.'

The Sugawara property was not in good repair, but it was large. One whole wing, once occupied by the late dowager, stood empty. Akitada had given it a cursory inspection; he still disliked being reminded of his stepmother. Now he remembered another matter. 'That carpenter you hired, Tora. Isn't he a very old man?'

Tora looked uneasy. 'He's a good carpenter. Sadanori's overseer fired him for being slow, but he's experienced and I thought...' He faltered.

'Yes. Quite. Well, set him to work on giving you two a dry abode.'

'I can do that myself, sir. No need to take him from other chores.'

'I shall need you for something else.'

'Now?' asked Tora, astonished.

'Have you forgotten the child in Otsu?'

'Sorry, sir. Stupid of me. What will you do about those charges against you?'

'Against you, too, don't forget.'

Tora grinned. 'If yours are dismissed, mine will be too. Anyway, all we really have to do is prove that the boy doesn't belong to the Mimuras.'

'How?'

'We'll find his real parents.'

'If the courtesan Peony was not his mother, and apparently she was not, then I have not the slightest idea where to begin to look.'

Hanae interrupted, 'I beg your pardon. Is that the same Peony you asked me about, Tora?'

Tora said, 'Yes. Did you find out anything?'

'It may be nothing, but when I asked the old hag where I was, she said I was in Peony's house. And then she gave me that drugged wine.'

THIRTEEN

Peony's House

Peony again.

This time Akitada had to face the problem of the drowned courtesan. He had made only a token effort to trace her. Never mind that the child had recognized a cat, and that the cat had led him directly to the dead woman's house and a toy sword in the garden. He had stopped looking for the boy's family because what he had really wanted was the boy.

Without strings.

He looked at Tora and Hanae, sitting hand in hand across from him. Tora's bruised face shone with happiness, but Hanae still looked nervous. It occurred to Akitada that she did not trust him any more than he trusted her. Perhaps it was enough that she made Tora happy, though marriage was no guarantee that all would be well between them. He sighed. Who was he to judge their chances?

He said gravely, 'Thank you, Hanae. We have been trying to trace a young woman by that name, a courtesan of the first class who lived in Otsu under the protection of a nobleman.'

She nodded. 'I'm sorry I didn't have a chance

to find out more.'

Tora squeezed her hand and said, 'You see what it means, sir? That bastard Sadanori used to keep Peony in that house. When she ran off to be with her lover, he followed and killed her. Hanae thinks that he only cares for women who don't want him. He'll do anything to have them. Maybe that includes killing them.'

'A tempting theory, but our Peony lived in Otsu for years after she left the capital.' Akitada looked at Hanae. 'Did you reject Lord Sadanori's advances, Hanae?'

She shot Tora a glance. 'He made no advances, sir.'

Tora frowned. 'You told me he wanted you.'

Hanae said with dignity, 'Not that way. At least I did not think so.'

'Well, that was stupid,' exploded Tora. 'Look what happened.'

She lowered her eyes. 'Yes, Tora. I see that now. I'm very sorry.'

Akitada asked, 'What do you think, Hanae?'

Hanae raised her eyes. 'It's possible, sir. He gets angry when he can't have his way.'

'We must have a look at the house where you were held. Do you think you could find it again?'

'I doubt it, but I can try.'

Akitada remembered Tamako's anger with him the previous day. 'Please describe what you remember. Start at the beginning,' he said.

'The sedan chair stopped outside our house about mid morning two days ago. One of the bearers came to the door and said they had been sent for me. I thought it was for the interview.'

201

'Describe the sedan chair and the bearers.'

'It was ordinary, the kind you hire, and the bearer was the usual type. I explained that my husband was taking me, but he said they had instructions and couldn't wait. I left a message with my neighbor and got in.'

'You said you could not see where you were going, but did you get a sense of direction?'

'I know we went westward to start with and then turned north. But after that there were so many turns that I got confused. I knew it was going to be a very long trip and started dozing.'

Akitada said, 'Could they have circled the same block ten times to confuse you and make you think they were going to Uji?'

'Yes.'

'Close your eyes, and think for a moment about what you heard, or smelled.'

Hanae closed her eyes. 'We passed the market, one of the markets. I smelled fried rice cakes and heard hawkers crying their wares. And later I heard the great temple bells, but they were faint.' She sighed and looked at Akitada. 'That's all, I'm afraid. The rest was silence or just the noise of other people walking or riding.'

Akitada sighed. 'Now when you finally halted, you left the sedan chair. What did you see?'

'We were inside a small courtyard. The house had a thatched roof. There were two tall pine trees and a high fence. I couldn't see anything outside the courtyard.' She thought. 'There were more trees, not pines, and another roof on one side of the courtyard. And I saw a well and a shed or bath house. The gravel had been raked

202

recently.' She looked at Akitada anxiously. 'Does that help? I don't know what the house looks like from the street.'

'You're doing well. What sort of fence and gate was it?'

'Boards and woven bamboo segments. Nothing elegant. The gate was just a single one, but as tall as the fence and made of solid wood. You could not see in or out.'

'And the house was a gentleman's private home?'

'Yes, but small. I got the feeling it was close to other houses on a street. It's not anything I really know, though. I was becoming very worried by then because it didn't seem the sort of place I expected.'

Hanae was either a very good liar or her story was true. If it was true ... Well, Akitada had been wrong about people before. On the whole, he wanted to believe her for Tora's sake and for the sake of their friendship. He said, 'You must have been very frightened. Did anyone come out to greet you?'

'No. The bearers put me down at the door and told me to go inside. I thought of leaving, but they barred my way and so I did as I was told. The old woman was waiting inside for me. She called me by name and was so friendly that I was relieved. She said there had been a change in plans and she was to talk to me instead – to save me the long journey to Uji. I'm afraid I wanted to believe her. And then she served me wine.'

There were some large problems with Hanae's tale, but Akitada said, 'A very clever plot and, but

203

for your determination, it would have succeeded.'

Some of the tension left Hanae. She blushed a little at the compliment.

'You never saw anyone except the two bearers and the old woman?'

'That's all. It was night when I left. I wish I'd taken a good look around, but I was afraid they'd catch me.' She paused. 'I thought I heard the cry of a crane once or twice.'

'Possibly there was a lake nearby. Or the river. Describe the interior.'

She sat up a little straighter. 'I was in only one room, but it was very luxurious. I'd never seen so many costly things in one place. There were five or six beautiful painted screens and a lacquered curtain stand with mother-of-pearl inlay. We sat on a thick grass mat on cushions of red silk. The wine flask and cups on a small red-and-gilt stand were of porcelain. It looked like a room for an empress. I saw a large silver mirror and make-up cases and lovely lacquered and painted trunks. On the shelves were books and games and musical instruments. I kept expecting the lady of the house to appear. That's when I asked where I was, and the old one said it was "Peony's house". The way she said it was ... secretive. She kept looking at me and smiling.' Hanae gave a dainty shudder.

'Would you say,' Akitada asked, 'that it was the sort of place where a very rich man might keep his favorite concubine?'

'She would have to be very special.'

'Was there a garden? Could you see outside?'

'The shades were down and the outer shutters closed. We sat by candlelight.'

'Hmm. Describe the old woman.'

'She was about fifty years old, I think. A little taller than I. Broad in the hips, but not fat. She had small hands and feet, and a round face. Her hair was getting thin and gray.'

'Any recognizable features? Scars, moles, a limp?'

'No. She looked ... respectable.'

Tora muttered something under his breath. Akitada ignored him. 'So you drank the wine she offered. Did you talk about anything?'

'I was nervous and chattered about being a nursemaid and how I liked children very much and that I was so happy I was to have one of my own. She just nodded and smiled. Then I got dizzy. I remember that her teeth were blackened and thought that strange for a servant, but then she could have been a relative. I'm afraid I don't remember anything after that.'

Akitada cleared his throat. It was a convenient tale. 'When you woke up, you were alone?'

'Yes. It was completely dark. I was lying on the floor. My arms were tied behind my back and my ankles were tied. I was wearing the silk robe.'

Tora moved angrily and muttered again.

'Be quiet,' said his master. 'Go on, Hanae.'

'My head hurt. I felt quite sick for a while. But then I began to work on the rope. I thought the woman had gone to sleep and if I was as quiet as a mouse, I might get away. I managed to get the ropes off and felt my way out of the room and down a hallway. The outside door wasn't locked, but the gate was, so I climbed over the fence and started running. After a while I heard the bell of the East Temple and found my way home just before you came.'

Akitada said nothing for a few moments. Then he asked, 'Do you mean to say you were unconscious for more than a whole day and night?'

'I must have been.'

She had looked quite sick, but her story was still hard to believe. What drug would leave a woman unconscious that long? And if Sadanori had ordered her abduction, he had had plenty of time to take his pleasure. Why had he not done so? And how had she escaped so easily? But he said nothing of his doubts and thanked Hanae.

'Get your sword and saddle two horses, Tora,' he said, getting up. 'We'll look for the house and have a talk with that old woman.'

Akitada doubted the house or the old woman existed, but for Tora's sake, they had to look. On horseback, they covered more ground in less time, but the sun was setting before they trotted down a quiet residential street just north of the Willow Quarter. They had covered the areas south of both markets without seeing likely houses. This was a quiet area of small but well-kept homes.

And then Tora pointed. He had been scanning the skyline for pine trees and now he said, 'Look over there, in the next street. See the two pines, and one has a large bird's nest in it. I bet that's where a couple of cranes are roosting. Remember Hanae said she heard cranes?' He spurred his horse, and Akitada followed. In the next street was indeed a house behind a high fence, a fence that was part wood and part woven bamboo.

'Possibly,' Akitada said, grudgingly. 'It looks empty. No smoke.'

They pounded on the gate. Nobody came. Tora kicked at the gate with his foot and it flew back, crashing against the fence inside. A couple of mourning doves flew up with a clatter of wings; otherwise all remained silent. They rode into a small courtyard that looked exactly as Hanae had described it.

Tora dismounted, gave a couple of lusty shouts for servants, then tried the door of the house. 'It's open, sir. Let's have a look.'

The house was empty, and that meant they had lost the old woman, their only witness to Hanae's story. She would have been likely to run when she found that her prisoner had escaped.

They checked all the rooms quickly. There were five and a kitchen. The house was small, but well appointed. Even the kitchen was equipped to furnish elaborate meals at a moment's notice. It was exactly the sort of place a very rich noble-man would furnish for a treasured female who was not acceptable in his household. But this house had not been in use for a long time before Hanae's abduction. A great deal of dust lay everywhere, and cobwebs hung from all the ceil-ings. Only the main room had been cleaned. And strangely, while the furnishings were not new, they had seen little use, and that suggested that the house had stood empty for years. Was it Sadanori's? Had he built it for the courtesan

Peony, who had ended her life in another man's secret hideaway in Otsu?

Akitada inspected the main room. The pieces of rope still lay next to a bundle of plain clothing, proof of Hanae's tale and of the abrupt flight of the old woman. Tora pounced on the bundle and unrolled it. It consisted of a plain dark blue gown, a pair of matching trousers, and a white-and-blue figured sash. 'Hanae's,' he said.

Akitada nodded and raised the heavy reed blinds, bound in green brocade and tied with silk. Then he threw open the wooden shutters, looking out on a small, overgrown garden. More birds flew up. He turned and, in the remaining daylight, he saw the beautiful screens. Shimmering with gold dust and brilliant colors, they were painted with landscape scenes: a pond with a pair of ducks, a mountain gorge under a full moon, a garden scene with a pair of rabbits, and an assortment of baskets and birdcages suspended from a veranda roof. There were peonies on all of them, and colored paper squares covered with calligraphy were pasted into the design. The peonies' colors were white, pink, and deep red; there were doubles and singles, heavily fringed or plain; they grew from the ground, leaned over water, or filled baskets. The paper squares contained love poems.

'Peony's house,' Akitada muttered and went to read the poems.

Tora came to look. 'Oh, I see what you mean.'

'Peonies and love poems,' said Akitada.

'That sick bastard didn't look like a poet to me.'

'Oh, they're not Sadanori's.'

They looked briefly at the musical instruments and feminine possessions – the trunks were filled with exquisite robes – then closed the shutters again and left the house.

'Let's talk to the neighbors,' Akitada said.

They split up to knock on the gates of all the houses on this block. When they met again, they had little enough information. The property belonged to some noble family and had been closed up for years. A caretaker checked it from time to time, but nobody lived there.

'It's a miracle thieves haven't made off with everything the way they did in the villa in Otsu,' Akitada said.

'Sadanori keeps a watch on it.'

'Nobody mentioned his name. Too bad that old woman took to her heels. She would have known. I wonder where she went.'

'To report to him that another one got away,' said Tora grimly.

'Let's go home. Tomorrow we'll go back to Otsu to see if that Peony and this one are the same woman.'

FOURTEEN

A Death in Otsu

The next day was one of those delightful early autumn days when the summer heat has broken and the world looks deceptively fresh and young again. They rode to Otsu with lighter hearts than perhaps they had any right to.

Tora, the memory of Hanae's lovemaking vivid in his mind, whistled. If Akitada felt any regrets that his own bed had remained empty, he put them aside as he thought of the child. He still wished with all his heart that he could bring him home, but his conscience insisted that he at least try to uncover the child's parentage.

Akitada did remember fleetingly, and with a pang of guilt, that he should be at work. A whole week had passed since his return from Hikone, and he had yet to report to the ministry. Of course, he had a free hand nowadays – daily tasks were in the capable hands of a large staff of clerks and scribes, and the minister was in office – but they would wonder sooner or later what kept him in Hikone. He must try to settle affairs in Otsu today so that he could take up his duties again.

They reached Otsu by midday. The lake

stretched before them like an invitation to eternity, its far reaches melting into a blue horizon, and black-headed seagulls shrieked and spun in the air above. The brisk autumnal wind filled the sails of boats, moving them along swiftly. It was a day when it seemed easy and tempting to leave behind all one's troubles.

They left their horses at the post stables and walked to the warden's office. Tora was still a fugitive until his status could be cleared. They met Warden Takechi as he hurried out, his face grim and his mustache bristling with excitement. Three constables trotted at his heels and shouted, 'Make way.'

The warden stopped. 'It's you, sir,' he cried. 'The answer to a prayer. Would you mind coming along on a murder case?'

Akitada said cautiously, 'I'm Sugawara, Warden Takechi. I brought my retainer to answer the charges against him.'

The warden waved an impatient hand. 'I know.' His eyes flicked over Tora. 'He can come along too.'

Bemused, Akitada looked at Tora, who grinned, no doubt relieved that he was in no immediate danger of arrest. They followed the warden and his constables down the busy main street of Otsu and into a residential quarter.

The warden turned to speak to Akitada on the way. 'I wouldn't have troubled you, sir,' he said, belatedly apologetic, 'but it's Dr Inabe who's been murdered. He's the only doctor in Otsu. I'm told he's been bludgeoned to death in his home. I want to get my hands on the killers quick.'

Akitada hoped to settle his own affairs and return to the capital before dark, but he could not afford to alienate the warden. He said, 'I'm not sure I can be of much use, but I'll gladly take a look.' Then he asked, 'Is the boy well? Is he still with the widow Yozaemon and her son?'

'No problems there. The Mimuras have made no trouble.'

'I've decided to settle the matter with them.'

'Much the best way, though they don't deserve it.'

'I'd like to see him.'

'Go ahead. The judge is satisfied that you mean the child no harm.'

Tora gave a snort. 'About time.'

Fortunately, Warden Takechi seemed to take this as an expression of loyalty and only nodded. Akitada was grateful; he suspected that the warden had put in a good word for him. 'Tell me about your victim,' he said.

The warden's face fell. 'He's ... he was a good man. Everybody loved him. Getting on in years – past fifty – but still strong and healthy. No family. Never had children, and after his wife died he lived alone, like a monk almost, with only one old servant. He tended to the sick and served as our coroner. He'll be sorely missed.'

'I'm very sorry. Any idea who did this?'

'None. It makes no sense at all.'

The doctor's house was not far from that of the dead courtesan, though it was not on the lake. It lay hidden among thick, rustling trees. Birds chirped and chattered, and here and there a late cicada still sounded its shrill rasp. Outside the open gate a group of neighbors waited. To the side stood one of the itinerant monks. The neighbors greeted the warden with anxious questions, but he brushed off them off and left a constable at the gate to take their information.

The house had once been a fine one, but it was as sadly neglected as the Sugawara home. Shutters hung loose, and big wads of thatch were missing from the main roof; a kitchen building leaned crazily, and weeds grew everywhere. But the whole place was alive with birds. Swallows nested under the eaves, scattering bits of straw and thatch; doves cooed in the trees, suddenly swooping down in a swarm to fly across to a neighboring property and back again; somewhere finches chittered; and the courtyard's gravel seemed covered with tiny chirping sparrows, pecking and fluttering up at their approach.

'He loved the birds,' muttered the warden.

A distraught and trembling old man in a dusty robe and with a small black cap on his white hair waited for them. The warden nodded to him. 'Where is he?'

'The studio.' The old man led the way, shuffling in worn straw sandals through a derelict garden, where more birds fluttered and rustled in the shrubbery, to a small pavilion in better repair than the rest.

They took off their shoes at the door. 'This is where he lived,' Warden Takechi explained. 'His study, library, pharmacy, and living quarters all in one.'

The pavilion was small. Odd, Akitada thought, how the man's life had contracted to living in one room and with only one servant. Being childless, Inabe was alone in the world. He suddenly had a vision of himself, years from now, dying alone in his study while the Sugawara mansion lay in ruins about him. The image depressed him.

Leaving the constables and the servant outside, they stepped into a dim, oppressive space. Sickly sweet odors of rotting fruit, stale wine, and of something stranger and more upsetting hung in the warm air: the cloying smell of blood and death. There was an odd sound, a faint sibilant hum. The room was crowded with dimly seen objects.

Skirting something on the floor, the warden crossed the space and pushed open the shutters to the rear garden. Sunlight poured in, slanting through the branches and falling across the body as if to focus attention on it. The dead man lay face down near the center of the room, his head towards the garden, his arms and legs flung out like those of the rice straw manikin in the peasants' harvest rites. His black silk physician's gown was neat and the white socks clean, but the back of his head was covered by a strange black cap that was horribly alive and buzzing.

Hundreds of flies, disturbed in their feeding frenzy, hovered and clung, fighting like tiny vultures over their carrion.

All around, the necessities of Inabe's simple life cluttered up the modest space. Like most men, he had either not been a good housekeeper or had not really cared about such things. The walls were lined haphazardly with shelves, some crammed with books, others with a jumble of jars

214

of ointments and boxes of powders. Bundles of drying herbs hung from ceiling beams. On a small, low desk, notes, papers, scrolls, used wine cups, dirty rice bowls, and, incongruously, a straw rain hat kept disorderly company. A bamboo stand in the corner held more cups, chopsticks, a wine flask, three overripe plums in a chipped bowl, a burnt-down candle in a holder, and a dirty brazier. Several old leather-covered trunks probably contained his clothes and bedding. The doctor's case stood beside his walking staff at the door by which they had entered.

Tora growled, 'Amida, his head's a mess.'

They looked at the corpse. The warden brushed away the flies. They rose sluggishly, drunk and heavy from their meal, and revealed the wound, a mass of congealed blood mixed with hair, bone splinters, and brain matter. More blood had puddled, dark and viscous, under the head. The doctor's black silk cap lay nearby. Half under his upper body was a crushed bamboo birdcage.

The dead man had been tall and thin, his hair white until someone had turned it this unnatural shade of rust brown. The topknot had come undone under the force of the blow that shattered his skull. Death must have been instantaneous.

Warden Takechi muttered something, then became businesslike. He peered at the wound, touched the dead man's skin, glanced about the room, and turned to the servant who cowered at the door, his face white and his body trembling. 'Your master's been dead a while. How is it that you just now report this?'

The man bowed. 'Wasn't here. Just got back.

Cousin's funeral. More death.' He shook his head. 'Found the master and went for help. A neighbor. My legs are no good.' He wrung his hands and shivered.

The warden growled, 'We'll check your story. When did you last see the doctor?'

'Two days ago. In the morning. Eating his gruel. Feeding the birds. He said not to worry. He could manage.' The old man stopped as if exhausted by so many words.

'Your cousin's funeral was not in Otsu?'

'In Ohara. I walked. Gone two days.'

'I see. Did your master expect visitors while you were away?'

'No.'

Akitada thought again of his own childless state. It seemed to be what lay in store for old men who had no families and only lived on to do their jobs. Or, like the old Masuda lord, they went quietly mad and left their affairs to women. The doctor had become a recluse. He had subsisted here, in this one room, served by another old man, puttering about among his books and medicines or in his overgrown garden unless he was called out on a case. A dreary, hopeless condition.

Tora went to peer at the body. 'Nasty blow,' he said.

The warden looked glum. 'He's been our coroner for thirty years or more. It's a disaster. Now who'll tell me when he died?'

'Well,' said Akitada, 'I can give you my opinion for what it's worth, but you'd better appoint some other medical man until you can hire a suitable replacement. If nobody is available, send

216

to the capital for Dr Masayoshi.' He bent to scrutinize the corpse, then felt the dead man's neck. It was cold, dry, and a little stiff to the touch. The dead are no longer quite human.

Outside, a cicada struck up its strident song again and put him in mind of the Buddhist image of the empty cicada shell. Man shed his body to become reincarnated. That fly returning to the wound was another image of the shortness of human life and of rebirth. Soon that wound would crawl with maggots. In fact, he could see a scattering of their eggs and some slight movement in one of the clusters of pale grains. They had already begun their cycle of destruction and renewal, the bond that tied man to the smallest living creature. What karma would bring a man back as a maggot?

'He's been dead a while, I think,' Warden Takechi said again.

'So has his bird.' Tora went across the room and bent to pick up a large black crow by one stiff leg. 'It had something wrong with its wing.'

The servant piped up from the doorway, 'Master put on a splint.'

'Well, somebody bounced it off the wall.' Tora dropped the bird. 'I hate bastards who do things like that to helpless creatures.' He drifted off to inspect the rest of the room.

Akitada said, 'The doctor died some time before yesterday, I think. The wound was caused by a single massive blow from behind. He fell forward, was probably dead before he hit the floor.'

The warden came closer and looked.

Akitada gestured at the wound from several angles. 'See here? That cut is quite deep. Bone splinters protrude. It took great force to make that wound. And it slants. He was hit with something heavy and round, a cudgel perhaps, and by someone a little taller than he is.'

'Why taller?' asked the warden.

Akitada straightened up, his eyes searching the room. Tora was at the door, his eyes on the doctor's staff. It was a long one, made of thick bamboo, and resembled those that itinerant monks carried. Theirs had metal rings at the top, which jingled as they walked, but this one was plain and lacquered black. When Tora picked it up and hefted it, the old servant said helpfully, 'The master's staff. Calls it his friend. Because he leans on it.'

'Well, his friend turned on him,' said Tora, holding it out to show what he meant. The servant backed away with a whimper. 'At least the bastard that killed him is a neat fellow. Puts things back after using them.'

Warden Takechi took the staff. 'He's right,' he said. 'There's blood and hair on it.'

Akitada nodded and turned to the body again. He lifted one shoulder to get a look at the dead man's face. More fat flies rose from his nostrils and mouth and from the open, glazed eyes. Dr Inabe's face had probably been narrow and scholarly and showed his age. Now it was puffy and one cheek was suffused with the blood which had gathered under the skin after death. There was a greenish tinge to it. Akitada sniffed. 'Yes,' he said, 'As I thought. A noticeable smell.' He lowered the body again. 'I would say he's been dead for at least a day and a night. The murder happened the day before yesterday, and most likely it was still daytime. The neighbors may have seen something. The killer was a tall man and strong, because it takes strength to kill another man with only one blow. You asked why I thought he was taller than his victim? The position of the wound shows that. He had to strike almost horizontally because the ceiling is too low to swing the staff downward.'

The warden, looking a little dazed, nodded and barked out orders. The two constables disappeared.

Akitada inspected the dead bird, then looked around the room. He turned to the servant. 'I wonder,' he asked, 'if your master was likely to receive strangers in here?'

The old man shook his head. 'Never. People ring the bell. I go and tell the master. He packs his medicines and goes with them.'

Akitada said to the warden, 'You see what that means, don't you?'

Warden Takechi blinked. 'A thief? Someone climbing the wall to rob him? Yes, I guess that's what happened.'

'Not likely,' said Tora.

The warden frowned. Tora grinned back impudently. 'Can you see a common thief being tidy? Or taking the time to play kickball with a bird?'

'Hmm,' said Akitada. He turned to the warden. 'The doctor's servant can check if anything is missing, but I suspect that the doctor admitted his killer himself. I'm afraid that's all I can tell you until you get more information.' He paused. 'Now I would really like to go and visit the boy. Suppose we stop by your office later?'

Takechi looked unhappy, but nodded.

When they were outside, Akitada said to Tora, 'You really should not volunteer your opinions. Even when you are right. The warden was getting irritated. Remember, he can still lock you up.'

Tora grinned. 'Sorry.'

'This murder is very inconvenient. Inabe must have been the coroner in Peony's drowning.'

'Hah! You think someone killed him because of her?'

'No. I just wanted to speak to the man about that drowning, and now he is dead.'

Tora was not listening. 'Murdered! Both of them! And that means ... What does it mean?'

'Nothing. Come on, let's go and visit the boy.'

But Tora was not to be moved until he had thought it through. 'Sadanori talks to Ishikawa, Ishikawa goes to Otsu, and Peony's coroner dies. Coincidence? I don't think so. Maybe Ishikawa was being a good boy and visiting his old mom, but what if he wasn't? What if he bashed the doc instead?' He clapped a hand to his head. 'Amida! I told the bastard in Uji that you were in Otsu, and he dashed back to the capital to tell Sadanori. That's it. That must be it. That's when Sadanori sent Ishikawa to kill the doctor. And that means the doctor knew something about Peony's death.'

Akitada said sourly, 'A brilliant deduction. You have solved all of our problems, along with the warden's case.'

'Well, nothing else explains it.'

'On the contrary. There could be a thousand different explanations for what happened. Yours is a wild tale based on wishful thinking because you hate Sadanori. At this point we don't even know that Peony was murdered, let alone by whom.'

Tora flushed. 'How can you say that with Sadanori's reputation? If you won't believe it, then I'll find the proof myself. They're devils. And we've got stop them.'

Akitada had no particular feelings about Fujiwara Sadanori, but accusing a man of his rank of abduction, rape, and now murder was going a little too far. Tora had always disliked the ruling class, and the incident with Hanae had apparently stirred up all the old loathing. He said, 'Your sort of thinking creates trumped up charges against the innocent.'

'Innocent? Crap! Ishikawa's always been a crook. And that bastard Sadanori. Men like him live above the clouds and think they're above the law. They know they can get away with anything. And when it comes to our women, they don't even believe in common decency.' He glowered and kicked a clod of dirt into a patch of weeds. A rabbit erupted with a high-pitched squeal and shot across the road. Tora chortled, his good mood restored. After a moment, he said more calmly, 'So what do you think?'

Akitada was a little shaken by that outburst. Tora's theory was not without some logic. He also distrusted both Ishikawa and recent events. Perhaps Ishikawa had come to Otsu on Sadanori's instruction. And Sadanori was implicated in at least two prior abductions of women from the amusement quarter. He was also linked to Peony, if she was the same woman who had once lived in the house they had visited. But until there was proof, neither her death nor the murder of the doctor could be laid at his door, nor Ishikawa's.

He sighed. The scene at Inabe's house had depressed him for purely personal reasons. 'I don't know what to think, Tora. We'll question Peony's neighbors, but I want to go see the child first,' he said.

Akitada stopped in the market to purchase a bright-red wooden top and tucked it in his sleeve. 'A small gift,' he said, a little embarrassed. 'He has no toys.'

Tora grinned.

The Yozaemons lived in a poor little house near the market. Mrs Yozaemon, as round and neat as a brown hen, was hanging her washing over the brush fence. There were small shirts and diminutive pants among the larger clothes, but the boy was nowhere to be seen.

She saw them and her round face broke into a wide smile. Wiping her hands down her sides, she bustled to open the gate. 'Welcome, welcome.' She bobbed a bow with each 'welcome'.

'Thank you.' Akitada scanned the yard. 'Is the boy here?'

She laughed. 'A little boy likes to hide.' She cried, 'Nori.'

'Nori?' Akitada asked, astonished. And then: 'Can he hear you?'

222

'Of course he can hear.'

It was good news. 'How do you know his name? Has he found his voice?'

'No, not that. Manjiro and I kept calling out names and that one made him look up. So that's what we call him. He answers to it.'

How simple it had been for this woman and her son to name the child, while he had cast about in vain and called him 'boy' or 'child'. Nori? He recalled how he had stopped in the dark woods and thought the small palc figure was the ghost of his dead son. He had called, 'Yori,' and the boy had come to him.

Mrs Yozaemon raised her voice again. 'Nori? Come here. You have visitors.'

And there he was. Or rather, there was his head, peering around the corner of the house. A moment later he came towards them, slowly and with a solemn face. Akitada was disappointed. He had imagined a gleeful dash into his arms. There was not even a smile. Was he afraid? No, not that. But he was distant, reserved, if a child that age could be reserved.

They had trimmed his hair and tied it above each ear. Just so had Yori worn his hair, and this boy, though he was probably a little older, was small for his age and looked a little like Yori. The sharp pain of Akitada's loss was back, made sharper by this child's new coolness towards him.

Nori stopped beside Mrs Yozaemon. He remembered them, Akitada was certain of it, but apparently he no longer considered them friends. Heartsick, Akitada crouched and opened his

223

arms, but the boy shook his head, his eyes distrustful.

Forcing a smile, Akitada said, 'I see you blame me for leaving you. I could not help it, but I didn't forget you. Not for a moment.'

The boy said nothing. He seemed to wait patiently for his dismissal.

Akitada produced the top and held it out. The child promptly put his hands behind his back and glanced away.

Mrs Yozaemon cried, 'Oh, go on, Nori, take it! The gentleman brought you the pretty toy. And he's come a long way to visit you.'

There was no reaction, and Akitada stood up, helpless in the face of such rejection.

Tora scooped up the child and said, 'Hey, Nori, what's the matter? Let's have a smile. Look, the sun's shining and there's a nice wind. Suppose we go buy a kite and fly it this afternoon?'

But Nori struggled, and Tora put him down with a sigh. Akitada said, 'Never mind. He's not used to kindness, poor little fellow.' He hid his disappointment, reminding himself that he had come to make sure the child was well taken care of and he had now done so. Nori was clean and looked much healthier. He stood clutching Mrs Yozaemon's skirt, waiting for them to leave. Akitada thanked his caretaker and gave her the red top. Still smarting from the rejection, he said, 'We'll try to find his family so he won't have to return to the Mimuras. If that fails, I'll pay them to let me raise him.'

She clapped her hands. 'What a lucky boy! You will like living in the capital, Nori, won't you?'

The boy looked at her, but gave no sign that he had understood.

Akitada left, feeling lonelier than before. To shake off this mood, he tried to think about the warden's murder case as they walked back to the lake, but his disappointment about the child was stronger than his sense of justice. It seemed a betrayal of the dead man, and he brooded on this.

Tora glanced at him from time to time, but did not speak. At the dead courtesan's villa, Akitada sent Tora to talk to the neighbors while he pushed through the wilderness to the dilapidated house. The scene was even more depressing by daylight. He looked around for the cat, but did not see it.

Down by the water, he disturbed a pair of ducks in the reeds near a broken boat dock and watched them paddle away, the male protectively herding the female. Ducks were faithful to their mate, a pair for life and a symbol of harmony between a man and woman. Such harmony had not been possible for him and Tamako, and apparently not for Peony and her lover either. The night watchman had claimed that the man had deserted her.

Akitada looked across the sparkling water. Boats of all sizes bobbed and moved across it – carrying other lives and, no doubt, happier ones. Suddenly, in broad daylight and sunny weather, Akitada felt again that cold shiver, that sense of lurking death.

He turned away abruptly, irritated by his morbid fancies.

They walked up and down the street, knocking on gates and talking to servants, but the results were disappointing. It became clear that Peony, or her protector, had taken measures to keep the curious away. She had rarely appeared in public, and then only deeply veiled. Her servants, a maid and a porter, had been from the capital and had rarely spoken to other servants. Her death had surprised them because they had believed the house empty at the time.

Tora pounced on certain rumors that started after Peony's death. She had been heard weeping because her child had died, her lover had left her, her lover had died, she had contracted smallpox and lost her beauty – all these, separately or in combination, were in people's minds reasons for her suicide, and so her vengeful ghost was born. Tora, of course, rejected the suicide theory. He was still convinced that Sadanori had murdered Peony, and he proposed they return to the capital and confront her killer.

Akitada grumbled, 'Nothing but rumors. We're a long way from being done here. We still have no proof that the boy was hers or that she was murdered. And we still do not know that she is the woman from the capital.'

Tora protested, 'It's the same name. And the time fits. The neighbors called her a courtesan, and they mentioned a child.'

'A child that died. I wonder what happened to her servants.'

'They left before she died. The neighbors thought the house was empty. Why did they leave? And who reported her death?'

Akitada stopped. 'Yes. Someone had to find her in the water and get the warden. A neighbor? If we assume that Peony was kept by the Masuda heir, the family's role in all of this is, to say the least, suspicious.' He glanced up at the green hillside above the town where the many curved roofs of the Masuda mansion glistened in the sun. 'We'd better ask Warden Takechi.'

But when they reached the warden's office, Akitada had second thoughts about Tora's presence. 'Let me do the talking,' he said. 'We can't afford to have you locked up.'

The warden was looking glum, but he brighened when he saw them. 'Thank heaven you're back, sir. This is a very difficult case. Would you believe it, nobody has seen anything.'

Akitada sat down, and Tora squatted near the door.

'It's still early,' Akitada said consolingly and wondered how to divert the man's attention to their own problems. 'Er, if you have the time, I would like to discuss Tora's case.'

Warden Takechi glanced across at Tora. 'If you're wondering about the charges against your servant, I sent a message to the judge while you were visiting the child.' He rummaged among the papers on his desk. 'Here's his answer.' He passed across a note.

Akitada scanned it. The judge mentioned the rank of Secretary Sugawara and the fact that His Lordship had posted a considerable sum of gold as security. He concluded that, as His Lordship had now brought the young man in himself, there was no longer any reason to arrest anyone. In the unlikely event of a trial, the judge trusted that Secretary Sugawara would produce Tora.

Akitada returned the letter with mixed feelings. The judge had checked up on him and his noble birth, and rank had paid off. He said, 'Thank you. I'd planned to go back today, but now Tora can take care of business and I'll stay on until tomorrow.'

The warden smiled. 'I'm deeply grateful for your generous assistance, sir.'

Akitada did not correct him. He asked, 'Perhaps you can tell me who reported the death of the courtesan Peony?'

'Peony?' Takechi blinked. 'Oh, that one.' He got up and searched among the ledgers. Selecting one, he ran his finger down the entries. 'Her maid. I have a vague memory that she'd come from the capital for a visit and found her drowned in the lake.' He closed the ledger.

Akitada was startled. The maid had come from the capital? How long had the body been in the water? He asked, 'You spoke to the woman?'

'No. It was a suicide, sir. There was no need to investigate.'

'The maid's name and address?'

The warden shook his head and spread his hands. 'We were too busy.'

Akitada suppressed a sharp reproof for such slovenly work.

'I hope the child was well?' Warden Takechi said.

'Yes, thank you. He seems healthy.'

'Good.' The warden looked uncertainly at Akitada. 'Well then, have you had any ideas about the doctor's murder?'

This was going to be difficult. Akitada took a

228

deep breath and made a stab at it. 'Have you considered motive? Who wanted Inabe dead? Who benefits from his death?'

'Surely it was a robbery? Some villain came to steal and was discovered by the doctor.' The warden added glumly, 'The bastard's probably long gone by now. We're close to the capital, and once there, a man may disappear and never be found again.'

Akitada knew this was true enough. 'Was anything taken?'

'Nothing apparently. I think the thief was surprised and ran.'

Behind Akitada, Tora grunted. To forestall an interruption, Akitada said quickly, 'Nothing? You had the servant check?'

The warden looked uncomfortable. 'A small amount of silver was still in one of the trunks. The servant says there's never been more than that in the house. The doctor doesn't charge his poor patients.'

'Was it known that the doctor was poor?'

'In Otsu, yes. Mind you, he wasn't always poor. After his wife's death, he started treating the poor for free. You saw the place.'

'Yes.' The memory depressed Akitada. 'I don't think your self-respecting professional thief would break into a poor man's home, and if he did, he would certainly take a quick look around before departing. Of course, this may have been an amateur. But think of the position of the body. If the doctor had surprised a thief, he would have faced the man. Even if he had been frightened, he would not have taken his eyes off him. He would

229

have backed away perhaps, but in that case the staff would have struck the front or side of his head, and he would have fallen backward. In this instance, he had turned his back on his visitor. That suggests that he knew him and wasn't afraid.'

'But who would kill him? He was respected and loved by all. People depended on him.'

'As I said, Warden, you need to find a motive besides robbery.'

Warden Takechi shook his head hopelessly. 'I cannot think of one. He was a good man.'

'And a good coroner?'

'The best.'

Akitada let a brief silence fall, then said, 'I suppose he was the coroner who pronounced the courtesan's death a suicide?'

The warden frowned at this return to the earlier topic. 'Yes, of course.'

'I have some questions about that case.'

Takechi said nothing.

'The neighbors think a child was living there.'

'There was no child.'

'And you found no other body in the water?'

'No, but people drown and disappear in the lake all the time.'

Akitada shook his head impatiently. 'I think the boy I found is Peony's son.'

'What? Why? And how would the Mimuras end up with him?'

'I don't have all the answers yet, but I intend to find out. Perhaps the child ran away after his mother's death, or was placed in their care by someone else. Mimura's a fisherman. Maybe he fished the child out of the lake. Cheap labor for the cost of a few bowls of millet and some rotten fish.'

The warden shook his head dubiously.

Akitada was groping in the dark and knew it. He thought that Nori was young Masuda's son, but would that family want him? Should he even meddle in a matter that was none of his business? Who was to say that he was doing the child a favor? The Masuda family had certainly made no effort to help Peony or her child.

But he pressed on anyway. 'Mrs Ishikawa, the Masudas' nurse, knew of the boy but refused to talk about him because Peony and her child are forbidden topics in that household.'

The warden sat up. 'Funny you should mention her, sir. Her son stopped by, the day before yesterday. Maybe she sent him to ask about you.'

Tora's growl, 'There, I knew it,' startled the warden.

Akitada rose. 'Forgive me for a moment. It's getting late, and Tora must leave for the capital.'

Outside, Akitada ignored Tora's excitement and said, 'It appears there may be something to your theory after all. Ishikawa is behaving strangely. I want you to check on him. Go back and see if he's returned to the capital and what he's up to. Then find Peony's maid. She's probably still connected with the Willow Quarter. You'll know whom to ask. I'll be back tomorrow.'

Tora beamed. 'Thanks, sir. But don't you need me here?'

'No. I'm going to have another talk with the Masuda family. Good luck.'

231

FIFTEEN

Family Secrets

When Akitada rejoined the warden, he asked, 'I wonder why Ishikawa was interested in my affairs. What did you tell him?'

'Well, he asked about your arrest. I said you'd taken an interest in a lost child, and his parents were trying to extort money. He seemed satisfied with that.'

Akitada could well imagine Ishikawa gloating at the news. 'I had rather not alert anyone else to my investigation at this point,' he said. 'To get back to Peony's death, why is there so little information available?'

'It was in the third month, sir. Not a good time. We had our hands full.'

Akitada frowned. 'The maid must have spoken to a constable. Is he available?'

'No, sir. He died.'

'Great heaven,' cried Akitada in frustration. 'Don't you keep track of people?'

'Impossible, even in good times. We register who owns property, but not who uses it. The house belongs to the Masudas. We don't count transients.'

Akitada shook his head. 'Incredible.'

232

The warden said, 'Otsu is a city with special problems, sir. We have a busy harbor here, and everybody who travels to and from the eastern and northern provinces passes through.'

Akitada nodded grudgingly. 'But Peony was no transient. She had been living here for about five years,' he pointed out. 'I'm told she used to be a courtesan of the first class and was under the protection of the Masuda heir. You would think the authorities would have taken notice of her household.'

The warden shook his head. 'We don't interfere with the Masudas' private affairs. And when she died, we had the epidemic to worry about.'

It seemed incredible that he had forgotten. It certainly explained the superficial investigation and the lack of interest in the child's fate. Conditions would have been as chaotic here as they had been in the capital. 'I'm sorry, Warden,' he said, embarrassed. 'I forgot. Of course. But the coroner did have a look at the body and was sure she had drowned?'

Takechi sighed at Akitada's persistence. 'He was sure she drowned.'

Akitada accepted it. If Peony had died from drowning, a coroner would have known the signs. It meant Sadanori was not responsible. Unless...' Could someone have drowned her? Taken her into the water and held her down?'

'I don't know,' the warden said. 'We were all terribly rushed, the doctor especially.'

Since the investigation into Peony's death had been the merest formality, Akitada could only guess at the reliability of Inabe's verdict. In times

233

of epidemics, individual deaths lost importance and, when tending many desperately sick patients, the doctor might well have rushed the job. Eventually, both she and her child had been forgotten among all the other tragedies.

Akitada sighed. 'I'm going to have another talk with the Masudas.'

He knocked at the Masuda gate, and the same old man opened the window in the porter's lodge and blinked at him.

'My name is Sugawara,' Akitada said, raising his voice. 'I called here before.'

The man nodded, disappeared, and the gate opened. Stepping in, Akitada said, 'I want to speak to your master this time.'

'The master sees no one.'

'He will see me. This concerns a murder.' And perhaps it did, at that.

The servant was taken aback. 'Who died, sir? We haven't heard.'

Akitada hesitated, then said, 'Dr Inabe.'

'The doctor? Murdered? Oh, you must not tell the master. It would kill him.'

'Why?'

'The doctor's his friend. He's been tending him like a brother. Oh, dear. What will I do?' To Akitada's surprise, the old man began to weep.

Akitada said gently, 'You must tell him, you know. Otherwise he will wonder why his friend isn't coming to see him anymore.'

'Oh, oh, oh.' Moaning to himself, the old man shuffled off, and Akitada followed. They climbed the steps to the main house and took off their

234

shoes. The servant held the heavy door for Akitada. They went through a dim hall with a painted, coffered ceiling and turned to the right, down a dark corridor. The old man's sniffling sounded unnaturally loud. The floors were dark with age and beautifully polished. A subtle scent of sandalwood incense hung in the still air.

The servant stopped at a carved door. Opening it softly, he put his head in and asked, 'May I trouble you, Master?'

Akitada heard nothing, but he could see part of a room lit by candles or oil lamps. After a moment, the servant opened the door a little wider and slipped in.

Akitada followed. The room was large, very clean, and very plain. A dais with silk cushions ran along one wall. On it sat a figure that resembled the ancient Chinese sages on old silk scrolls: a gaunt old man with long, loose white hair and a beard that fell into his lap. The old man's eyes were closed, and rosary beads twisted through the gnarled fingers of one hand.

The whole scene was vaguely religious. The old man wore a black silk robe and brocade stole like a Buddhist clergyman. A small Buddha statue rested on a carved table across from him, and two tall candles burned on either side of the figurine. Incense, expensive sandalwood incense, curled up from a gilt censer. Akitada thought the old man had fallen asleep at his prayer until he saw one of the beads move through his fingers and the thin lips form a soundless word. Lord Masuda was a lay monk. And he was either deaf or so immersed in his spiritual world that nothing else penetrated.

The servant approached him on soft feet, knelt, and bowed deeply. 'Master?' he said again, softly, pleadingly. There was no reaction.

Akitada stepped into the room and cleared his throat. The servant jumped and sent him a shocked glance. Akitada decided to wait.

Another bead slipped through the fingers.

He has hands like claws, thought Akitada. And a nose as sharp as a beak. A sleeping vulture. Old age takes away the softness of rabbit or mouse and turns us into creatures of prey.

The servant's voice rose a little. 'Master, Lord Sugawara is here.'

The rich brocade of the stole shimmered in the light of fat candles in two tall candlesticks. The room also contained a scroll painting of a young man seated in court robes. He was handsome, his face still round – though with the same bushy eyebrows and sharp nose as his father – but he was smiling, a proud young noble who knew he was among the fortunate. Someone had placed flowers before the painting: bronze chrysanthemums and white hydrangeas.

'Master.' The servant's voice rose in desperation. 'Bad news. Dr Inabe is dead.'

There was no reaction. Another bead fell, and one of the candles sputtered. The old lord had not moved except for the infinitesimal release of a finger on the rosary.

The old servant's voice was now quite loud. 'Lord Sugawara says the doctor has been *murdered*! Do you wish to speak to him, Master?'

Apparently not. The eyes remained shuttered

behind the thin lids. Another bead was released and made a tiny clicking noise. Some wax spilled over, a drop sliding slowly down the candle into the holder where it congealed. The old servant sighed. He bowed again, touching his head to the polished floor, then rose and came to Akitada.

They left the room without speaking. The servant slid the door to very softly and said, 'I'm sorry, sir. This is not one of his good days.'

'Is your master deaf?'

'No. His spirit has left.'

'But he was praying.'

'Maybe.' The servant shook his head. 'I bathe and dress him every morning. Then I feed him some gruel and put the rosary in his hand, and he sits like this all day. If I don't give him his rosary, he weeps.'

'Dear gods. How long has he been this way?'

'Ever since the young lord died. A year or more. Some days he's a little better. The doctor can get him to open his eyes and speak a few words. Oh, dear. What will happen to him now? They used to sit together, and the doctor would tell him what was happening in the town and what the weather was like and what he planned to have for his supper that night. I always listened, for the master would eat a little of that same food that night. He doesn't eat well as a rule. And now, who knows? Maybe he'll just give up and die.'

The darkness of the heart. The death of his son had taken the father's will to live.

Akitada suppressed a wave of empathy for the old lord and asked, 'You do all this work by yourself? Are there no other servants?'

'There's only Mrs Ishikawa. And she's not really a servant. The ladies help.'

'But surely there's enough money for a large staff.'

The old man turned away and started back towards the front of the house. 'The first lady pays people from the town to come and clean the rooms and do odd jobs,' he said. 'A cook comes every day. Sometimes there's a seamstress. But nobody lives here except the family.'

'Do His Lordship's daughters-in-law keep him company during the day?'

'No.' It was a statement of fact, neither rancorous nor complaining.

Akitada wondered at the strangeness of this household run by women. The fact that only workers from outside were being used suggested that the family had something to hide. Surely that something was Peony and her relationship with the younger Masuda. When they reached the main hall, Akitada asked, 'Was the picture of Lord Masuda's son?'

The old man's face softened. 'Yes. It's just like him. Wasn't he handsome?'

'I expect the ladies thought so. What did Lord Masuda think about his keeping a courtesan from the Willow Quarter in the lake villa?'

The old man's face closed and he shuffled away. Akitada caught up and stepped in his path. 'Come, you know very well what I mean. Young Masuda fell in love with the courtesan from the capital and installed her in the lakeside villa. Everyone knows.'

The servant bowed his head. 'We're not to talk

about it, sir.'

Akitada said acidly, 'Yes, I heard. His first wife has forbidden the subject. She who also holds the purse strings. She had reason to be jealous of the beautiful woman from the capital who took her husband's heart and gave him a son.' The old man said nothing. Akitada snapped, 'There was a son, wasn't there?' Silence. 'Why did his father not take care of the young woman and her child, his own grandchild?'

To his surprise, the servant became angry. 'The first lady doesn't tell me what to do,' he said. 'I've served His Lordship since we were boys. It was His Lordship who forbade mention of the woman's name in this house.'

'But why in heaven? She gave him an heir.'

'Because she killed the young lord.'

'What?'

'That devil woman – that cursed demon...' The old man trembled with fury and choked on the words.

Akitada put a steadying hand on his bony shoulder and said, 'Calm down. The story I heard is that he deserted her and his son and later died of an illness. Now you tell me he was murdered?'

The servant dabbed his sleeve to his eyes, sniffed, and said fiercely, 'He left her when his father insisted, but she bewitched him with her tears, and he went back to her. That's when the vengeful demon poisoned him. He died at her house.'

Akitada stared at the old man. 'He died there? When?'

'My young master died on the tenth day of the

third month after many days of pain and suffering. Oh, the she-devil!'

'But she was not accused of the crime or arrested. In fact, she stayed on in the house for another year.'

'They couldn't prove it. She was too sly. Called the doctor in. But it was too late. The young master died, and his father lost his mind. There was nobody left to punish her. The first lady's son was still a baby, and he died, too. They said it was the curse.' He suddenly raised a finger towards the coffered ceiling. 'Heaven's net is large, and nothing escapes it.' Giving an odd dry chuckle, he hobbled away.

Akitada looked after him, appalled. The humble and devoted old man had sounded positively malevolent. He pieced this new information together with what he already knew. If the servant was right, then someone other than Sadanori had had a motive to kill Peony, a much stronger motive. It certainly explained the puzzling behavior of the Masudas towards Peony and her son. If Peony had murdered the Masuda heir, then it was far more likely that her death was the work of someone in this family.

Had Peony really killed her lover? Akitada decided that it did not matter if she had, so long as the killer *thought* she had. And who in this household would have had such a motive? The old lord? His servant? One of the wives?

The empty hall lay dim and silent around him. He thought of the passions that had torn this family apart and the guilty secrets they hid from the outside world. The dead man's wives must have hated the beautiful woman from the capital. His father seemed to have disliked the relationship from the beginning, and he certainly hated her after his son's death. And, being loyal in every way, so did his servant. What about Mrs Ishikawa? Her role seemed negligible, but she had visited Peony and her son. Why had she done so, when the ladies she served were hostile to their husband's concubine?

And what was her son's role in all of this? Akitada knew Ishikawa well enough to be convinced that he would look for profit in a situation of this sort. Ishikawa was a blackmailer.

And there was another thing. Whatever had happened, whatever Peony had done or someone had done to her, nobody here would claim her son. Akitada heaved a deep sigh. Perhaps this was, after all, just another interesting murder case, and he would return home with a small boy.

He started to leave when he heard a silken rustling in the dark recesses of the hall. A moment later, a woman entered the back of the hall on soft feet. She came from the left and headed towards Lord Masuda's room. She carried a footed tray and vaguely resembled one of the Buddha's handmaidens as she glided across the polished floor towards the corridor.

The younger wife. What was her name again? Lady Kohime.

When he spoke her name, she gave a little cry and stopped, peering at him through the gloom. 'I'm sorry if I startled you,' he said quickly. 'I'm Sugawara. We met a few days ago. I paid a visit to your father-in-law and was on my way out.'

She came, still clutching the tray, her eyes on his face. 'Oh, it *is* you,' she cried, as if she had not believed him.

He saw that her dress was a brilliant copper red, and that she wore white paint and rouge on her face. She smiled at him with red lips and blackened teeth. An upper-class lady would not have revealed an open mouth to a strange male visitor, nor stood so close to him that he could smell her scent. He moved away a little.

'How silly of me to be frightened of you, sir,' she simpered. 'Only, we never have company here. It's very dull. But why did you visit Lord Masuda? He never says anything. He just sits there like a statue.' She lifted the tray a little. 'I was just going to feed him. He's like a baby.' She heaved a sigh.

He looked at her round face with its round, childish eyes, and at her half-open mouth, and disliked her stupid coyness. It seemed unfair to take advantage of a silly woman, but there had been murder, and Akitada had no more patience with family secrets. He put on a smile and made her a little bow. 'You're right, Lady Kohime. He didn't speak to me either. What a pleasure, therefore, to see you.'

She giggled and fluttered her lids. 'Oh, I'm nobody. A widow with two daughters. Not much more than a servant here, really.'

He let his eyes travel over the rich silk of her gown, which covered lush curves underneath. If he was not mistaken, she was flirting with him. Lady Kohime had struck him from the first as a

242

silly and shallow woman of common back-ground. Clearly, she was bored with her life, even if it entailed wearing fine silks and living in a great mansion. Putting aside his remaining scruples, he said, 'Surely not. You are entirely charming. It would have given me much greater pleasure to chat with you, but I'm afraid I brought bad news. Dr. Inabe is dead.'

She gave a small gasp. 'Dead? But then he was quite old, so ... I mean, old people die, don't they?' She cast a glance towards Lord Masuda's room. 'Eventually.'

More than shallow, thought Akitada, she is as blatantly self-centered and uninhibited as a small child. He wondered if Inabe's murder had been news to her. Something had not rung true in her reaction. He said, 'Sometimes even young people die. Forgive me for raking up old pain, but I understand you lost your husband last year. Was it some illness?'

'Something he ate didn't agree with him.' She eyed the covered bowl on her tray thoughtfully and added, 'My husband was very fond of *warabi* shoots. I used to gather them and cook them for him the way my mother and grandmother did. He loved that, especially *warabi mochi*. Perhaps someone was careless.'

It was artlessly said. Fern shoots were a springtime delicacy, but if they were not picked at the right stage and cooked properly, they could make a person very ill ... and possibly kill them.

'He died from eating *warabi* shoots?'

Her eyes widened in shock. 'Oh, no. I didn't say that.'

'You said someone may have been careless in the preparation of his food. He didn't die here?'

'My husband had gone elsewhere when he became ill.'

A vague answer, and uttered primly. Akitada asked, 'Was it in Peony's house that he died? In the house by the lake?'

She cast a glance over her shoulder. 'Shh! We're not to speak of her.'

'Was a doctor called?'

'Dr Inabe. He couldn't help.'

'Did the doctor suggest your husband had been poisoned?'

The sound of a sliding door, then quick firm footsteps and more silken rustling: Lady Masuda appeared. Akitada almost took her for a ghost because she wore a very dark gown today, so dark that it looked black, and her narrow, pale face seemed to float across the hall, disembodied.

Lady Kohime gasped and moved away from Akitada with a small nervous laugh. 'Just look who's here, sister,' she cried in a girlish voice. 'I was just taking Father's gruel when Lord Sugawara surprised me.' She made it sound as if he had made improper advances.

Lady Masuda changed course and approached like an angry spirit. Giving Akitada a hostile glare, she said sharply, 'I wondered what had happened to you, Kohime. That gruel must be quite cold by now.' She whisked the lid off the bowl and bent over the pale rice broth. 'Just as I thought. Back to the kitchen and reheat it. Hurry. Father must be quite famished by now.'

Lady Kohime pouted, but she made a small bow in Akitada's direction and danced off towards the kitchen, her colorful gown fluttering around her as if she were a bright butterfly.

The contrast between the two women could not be greater. Kohime had been all childlike softness and gayety, while tall Lady Masuda, for all her well-bred elegance, was stern discipline. The eyes that regarded him coldly were intelligent. He would not be able to trap this woman into indiscretions.

Her silence meant that she waited for him to account for his presence. He cleared his throat and said, 'As I explained to Lady Kohime, I brought news of Dr Inabe's death. Lord Masuda's servant admitted me.'

She frowned. 'Foolish man.' For a moment Akitada took the comment personally, but she went on: 'He should not have done so. Servants get old and make mistakes. My father does not receive visitors.'

He thought it interesting that she had not seen fit to comment on the doctor's death. 'Yes,' he said, 'I could see that it was a mistake.'

'He actually took you to meet my father?'

Lord Masuda was not really her father, though it was customary for a wife to accept a husband's parents as her own. Still, the emphasis was unnecessary here. She was establishing her position in the household. Akitada nodded. 'It was an honor to meet him, though I'm afraid he took little notice of me.'

She said nothing, but her eyes were wary.

'I understand that Dr Inabe treated his son, your

245

husband, during his final illness?'

Was there a flicker of fear in her eyes? But she only said, 'Yes.'

Lady Masuda was not a type Akitada admired: unemotional, intelligent, and with a man's authority in her voice and manner that was confrontational. On the whole he preferred the silly and seductive Kohime. What were these women hiding? For he was convinced, by now, that there was a dangerous secret in their past. And what had possessed the dashing young Masuda to choose two such dissimilar women as his wives and then rush off to the arms of a former courtesan?

'Well,' Akitada said, retreating after a moment of being stared down, 'I shall be on my way then. I regret having been the bearer of bad news. I understood Dr Inabe was the family physician and Lord Masuda's friend.'

She waved this away with an impatient hand. 'Naturally, it is sad. I am sorry you were troubled. We do not receive visitors. This arrangement seems much safer for two women and an ailing old man.'

And what did that mean, apart from the fact that she had just warned him away from future visits? His face set, and without acknowledging her words, he gave her the merest nod, and left. Let her think she had offended him. He was irritated with both the Masuda women.

He was walking down the winding road, through the trees and past the small shrines and modest houses, wondering what he should do next, when it struck him suddenly that the one name that had cropped up again and again, the name that linked Peony most closely to the Masudas, was that of Dr Inabe.

SIXTEEN

The Little Abbess

The morning after Tora returned from Otsu, he went back to the Willow Quarter. His first visit was to Ohiya. He disliked this intensely, but Ohiya knew everything that happened in the quarter. He was admitted by a boy servant who wore a woman's red silk gown and a condescending expression.

Ohiya was at breakfast. He greeted Tora with unexpected courtesy and accepted his apologies graciously, then invited him to have a cup of wine with him. Tora relaxed a little, but kept a wary eye on the servant. The fellow was wearing make-up, he decided. They locked eyes, and the boy blew him a kiss. Tora flushed and glared at him.

Ohiya assured himself that Hanae had come to no harm, then said, 'My dear Tora, you look much improved. I quite see now what attracted Hanae to you.'

Tora was pleased by this. He was almost sincere when he said, 'Only my desperation made me behave as I did, Master Ohiya.'

247

Ohiya smiled. 'I understand completely. Your concern does you great credit, as I told Lord Sugawara.'

Tora relaxed a little more and drank some wine. It was excellent, and the boy kept his cup full. 'There's another matter, Master Ohiya. My master and I are investigating the disappearance of the courtesan Peony six years ago. Do you remember that?'

Ohiya said, 'Oh, yes. You assist in the investigation of crimes, do you? How very clever of you!'

Tora let Senju fill his cup again. 'I give the master a hand,' he said modestly. 'Very nice wine. Anyway, this Peony is why I came. My wife insists you know everything worth knowing in the quarter.'

Ohiya smiled back. 'I do.'

'I would be very grateful to hear the story.'

'Would you?' Ohiya gave him a long look. 'Well, I must try to do my best then.' He turned to his servant, 'Senju, my dear, this will interfere with your shopping. I'm quite safe with Tora, I promise you.'

'Now?' exclaimed the boy. 'Traipse across town looking like this?' He gestured at his clothes.

'Of course not, my treasure,' said Ohiya. 'Go and change into something very manly and fear-inspiring so you'll look like Tora here.'

Senju looked at Tora and back at Ohiya. 'I won't be gone long,' he said, his voice heavy with sarcasm, 'and I hope I'll find things as I left them.'

Ohiya chuckled as the door closed behind him and said, 'Senju's such a show-off, but he's very entertaining.'

He began Peony's story with her rapid rise to fame. 'Nobody had heard of her when she first came, but the girl could read and write and was a lady. One of the top courtesans, Evergreen, took her into her service and trained her. Evergreen brought Peony to me for lessons in singing and dancing. She was a quick learner and eager to make her career.'

'She was a lady? What was she doing here if she was one of the good people?'

'Ah,' said Ohiya, 'good question. What does a young girl of that class need money for?' He laughed softly. 'I never found out, but she soon made very good money. She was a courtesan of the first rank within a year. A remarkable career, but she was a remarkable girl.'

Tora thought about it. 'What she was like?' he asked.

'Delightful, and desirable to many men, but stubborn.' Ohiya grimaced. 'Like your wife, she preferred a lusty lover to a career.' He gave Tora a wink. Tora flushed. 'Charming,' murmured Ohiya.

Tora asked, 'Who was that lover?'

'I've been trying to remember his name,' said Ohiya. 'A very handsome young man, but not from here. I imagine she ran away with him.'

'She disappeared six years ago, right?'

Ohiya nodded.

'Do you know where she lived, who her clients were, and if any of her family, friends, or former

249

servants still live in the city?'

Ohiya laughed. 'Not so fast. We have time.' He refilled their cups. 'Remember, it was a long time ago, and I never knew Peony well.'

Tora said, 'Are you sure she could read and write? A woman who worked in the quarter?'

Ohiya winced. 'Not everyone in the quarter is illiterate. I have quite a good education myself.'

'But you're a man,' Tora said generously.

'Hanae can read and write. Or didn't you know?'

Tora flushed. 'Of course I know. Go on.' He emptied his cup.

Ohiya smiled and refilled it. 'Let's see. She had her own establishment on the Horikawa River, near the Reizei Palace. She rented a small private house with a garden on the river. Very nice. I went there once to give her lessons. By that time, people were saying that she had imperial blood. Nonsense, of course, but she had class. And noble suitors.'

'When did she move to Matsubara?'

'Matsubara?' Ohiya looked shocked. 'You must have misheard.'

'Maybe. Who were her suitors?'

'Oh, she played hard to get.'

'Sadanori?'

'Yes, he was enamored of her.'

Tora relaxed. 'Did she ever complain about him? You know, that he was rough or threatened her?'

Ohiya laughed. He reached over and tapped Tora's cheek. 'Silly boy. Of course not. No first-class courtesan ever complains about her clients.

250

She's not, in any case, ever alone with them unless she chooses to be. She attends parties or gives them. If a top-class courtesan wants to take a lover, she may do so, but most hold out for a permanent arrangement. Quite different from the sort of girls you may have met in your callow youth.'

Stung by this comment, Tora blustered, 'There's still only one way of doing it unless she liked an audience.'

Ohiya laughed heartily and patted Tora's knee. 'You're delightful. Actually there are quite a lot of ways – some that may never have occurred to you.' He moved a little closer.

'Oh?' Tora wanted to leave, but the wine had made him warm, and he lacked the energy. Ohiya smiled. Tora shifted in his seat and pretended to glance about the room.

'My dear boy,' Ohiya said softly, 'I do think we got off on the wrong foot. Shall we try again now that we've settled our differences?'

Tora was becoming very uncomfortable, but there was the matter of the money owed to Ohiya. 'About Peony...' he began when Ohiya's hand crept up his thigh. Tora shifted it. 'Er, Peony. She must've had a maid ... some female who was close to her?'

'Another cup of wine?' asked Ohiya and leaned over so he could refill Tora's cup. His other hand slipped inside Tora's robe.

Tora gasped. 'No, thank you,' he said. 'I've had too much already.'

Ohiya removed his hand and smiled at him. 'Good. Yes, there was a maid, or maybe a nurse.

251

I'm not sure. She had an odd name.' As he pondered, he studied Tora's face. 'You know, Tora,' he murmured, 'you have beautiful teeth and a delightful smile. It's quite painful to me when you glower. Why are you so angry with me?'

'I'm not angry.' Tora gulped and looked around the room for inspiration. 'And last time, I was worried about Hanae.'

'Yes.' Ohiya chuckled softly. 'You did look like a wild man then. Very fierce. I was quite frightened. But when you had me backed against the wall and were leaning right into my face with your wild eyes and growling voice, like this –' he demonstrated by bringing his own face close to Tora's – 'you took my breath away. Such force, such manliness. My knees turned to water.'

Tora got a noseful of scent and leaned away as far as he could. He was afraid that this perfumed and painted man had designs on him. 'That maid,' he asked. 'Her name? Or where I can find her?'

Ohiya drew back with a sigh. 'Women, that's all you're interested in. Her name was Little Abbess. And I cannot tell you where she is now.'

Tora scrambled to his feet. His face felt as if it were on fire. 'Well,' he said hoarsely, 'I suppose that's all. Thank you for your help and, er, for not laying charges.'

Ohiya rose with the grace of the trained dancer. 'But my dear boy,' he said, 'I haven't even begun to tell you all.'

Tora swallowed and croaked, 'I'll have to come back another time. No time today,' and backed towards the door.

Ohiya followed, all gracious host. 'Please do, dear boy. Please do.'

Back on the street outside Ohiya's house, Tora leaned against the wall and gulped air. No telling what would have happened if he had stayed a moment longer. Remembering Ohiya's fixation with his teeth, he shuddered. The things a man had to do to gather information. It struck him that his master and Genba, and even Hanae, would think his troubles hilarious.

He next went back to Rikiju. Skirting garbage and a ragged body, prone on the ground and either drunk or dead, he knocked and heard someone coughing inside. After a long time, Rikiju opened the door a crack and peered out.

'It's you again,' she said without much enthusiasm. 'I was trying to sleep.'

Tora went in and closed the door behind him. 'Had a good evening then?' he asked, turning up his nose at the smell of stale bodies and dirty bedding spread on the floor.

'No. I've been sick, you oaf.' She sat down on her rumpled quilts and coughed again, great gulping, hacking coughs that seemed to wring her out. When it was over, she pushed her matted hair out of her sweaty face. 'What do you want? You ever find Hanae?'

'Yes. What's wrong with you?' She looked flushed, but the room was warm.

'Never mind. What happened?'

Tora leaned against the door and told her.

When he was done, she shook her head. 'You two get into horrible trouble and manage to get

253

back out. Me, I just have the usual bad luck, only mine doesn't change.' She went into another paroxysm of deep, rattling coughing. She staggered up to scoop some water from a wooden pail.

'You need money?' Tora fished out a string of coppers and peeled off half. She protested it was too much and staggered back to her bedding. He added half of the remainder to it and laid the money beside her. 'When did you eat last?'

She licked cracked lips. 'I don't know. When were you here?'

He looked at her, aghast. 'Three days ago? Have you had a doctor?'

'Don't be an idiot. If I don't work, I don't eat. And I can't afford a doctor even when I'm working.'

'All right,' said Tora, scooping up some of the coins, 'I'll be right back with some hot food.'

He left, trotted to the market where he purchased fried fish and a large serving of rice and vegetables, all of which the vendor wrapped in a sheet of oiled paper. Tora spent some of his own money on a flask of good wine. When he got back to Rikiju, she had tidied up the room a little, washed her face, and combed her hair. But the dreadful cough still racked her thin body and she ate little. The wine seemed to help. It put some color into her pasty skin, and she could speak a little more easily. Tora asked her if she'd ever heard of Peony and her maid, the Little Abbess.

To his surprise, Rikiju said immediately, 'Peony's dead. Drowned herself in Lake Biwa, but Little Abbess lives only a block from me.

Why?'

She was beginning to take a little interest in the world around her, so Tora told her about the case. She was pleased. 'Nice to know somebody cares,' she said. 'Even if it's a little late for Peony. Men are bastards.'

Tora thought that ungrateful and said so. She tried to laugh, but choked and started coughing again. 'You're a friend, Tora,' she finally managed. 'Not the same thing. Thank you.'

Tora took his leave, slightly mollified because friends evidently didn't count as men for her, but he worried. Rikiju did not look like she was getting better. He made her promise to send for a doctor and use the money he had left to pay for medicine.

Little Abbess lived in another tenement like Rikiju's, but in larger quarters. She had two small rooms and had turned the larger into a seamstress's shop. A striped curtain covered an opening to what was probably a kitchen area. The room was filled with stacks and piles of multicolored fabric scraps and lengths, mostly ordinary stuff, dyed hemp, some ramie, and linen, but also odd pieces of silk. Tora realized she made a living from buying old clothes and painstakingly removing the stitches. Then she would wash the fabric and sew new clothes from it for those who could not afford to buy lengths of new fabric.

Little Abbess was a squat, middle-aged woman with a bun of thick gray hair, who wore one of her own patched garments. She was busy convincing a middle-aged couple to buy the warm jacket the portly man was trying on. It was brown-and-white quilted ramie and had faded in places. The man's tiny sharp-faced wife stood by, making disparaging remarks in hopes of getting a better price.

The seamstress abandoned her clients for a moment to bring Tora a patched cushion and ask him to wait a moment. She looked like a motherly type, unlike the harpy who pursed her lips and plucked at the jacket while her fat husband scowled at Tora.

Tora said, 'By the gods, that's a very handsome jacket. Looks warm, too. And just the color I like.' He got up to feel the thickness of the fabric.

The fat man jerked it out of his hand and snapped, 'It's mine.'

With the purchase completed, Little Abbess turned to Tora. 'If you'd like a jacket like that one, I could make you one.'

Tora would not be caught dead in such a thing. 'Sorry, but I'm broke. Are you the one they call Little Abbess?'

'Nobody calls me that any more,' she said crossly.

'Rikiju sent me. She says you worked for a courtesan called Peony?'

The woman's face crumpled. 'My lady's dead.'

Tora sat down again. This was going to be easier than he had thought. 'Tell me about her.'

But she was wary now. 'Who are you? Why are you asking questions? Nobody cared when she needed help.'

'I'm Tora.' He tried one of his disarming smiles. 'I work for Lord Sugawara. We investigate crimes the police can't figure out, and we

256

think your lady was murdered.'

'Then you think wrong. She drowned herself. I saw her with my own eyes. Floating in the lake.' She brushed away angry tears. 'But you're right about one thing. It was a crime the way they treated her. To me they are murderers, just as if they'd plunged a knife into her poor body.'

'Are you sure she killed herself? What were you doing there?'

She eyed him for a moment, then said, 'I have no time for this. I have a living to make.' She whisked up a garment and sat down to sew.

'You can talk while you're working, can't you?'

She said nothing, just glowered.

Tora wheedled, 'Look, I'd buy something, only I'm down to my last few coppers.' He held up the depleted string. 'My parents were peasants, and I work for a few coppers just like you. I'm on your side, yours and Peony's. We can't let the bastards get away with abusing us. Just tell me if Lord Sadanori is responsible.'

Her head came up. 'Lord Sadanori?' She snorted. 'If she'd stayed with him, she'd still be alive. Good looks aren't everything in a man. Mostly, they're poison where a poor girl's concerned. Go pester someone else.'

Blast the woman. She was insulting. As a rule, Tora had an easy time chatting up females of all ages, but this one was charm-proof. He was not about to give up so easily on his theory, though. 'What about a guy called Ishikawa?'

'Never heard that name.'

'Was your mistress afraid of Sadanori? Or of

257

somebody else?'

'No.'

'But he kept her in a house here? A house he decorated for her?'

'We both lived there, and he treated her like a princess.'

The curtain to the room was flung aside. An old man staggered in, leaning heavily on his stick. 'You done, woman?' he wheezed.

'Just about, Grandfather Shida.'

Defeated, Tora rose. If she had told the truth about Sadanori, his master was right and he was wrong. At least she had confirmed that the Peony in Otsu and the famous courtesan Sadanori had courted were the same. At the door, he remembered to ask, 'Your mistress had a son, didn't she?'

She looked up, needle poised, eyes suddenly intent. 'They found him?'

'What?' wheezed the old man. 'Round? I don't want my pants round.' He gave the garment in her lap a poke with his cane.

Tora sidled back. 'Maybe.'

She pushed aside the old man's cane and got up, her face filled with sudden hope. 'He's alive?' she asked. 'You've heard something? Maybe even seen him? Please tell me he's alive.'

'What wife? I have no wife.' The old customer limped forward and poked her shoulder with a sharp finger. 'I want my pants. You promised them.'

Tora folded his arms. 'I don't know that I should tell you. You weren't very nice.'

But she would not be teased. She grasped his

258

arm with a painful grip and shook it. 'You have to tell me, curse you. He's all that's left of her. She loved that child.' And then the tears ran down her face, and she clutched him, sobbing and muttering in her grief.

'Hah!' cried the old-timer. 'Making out in the middle of the day. Stop that.' He stuck his cane between them and tried to wrench them apart. 'Disgusting,' he croaked, swinging the stick dangerously close to their heads.

'Sit down and wait, old man,' Tora roared. He caught the end of the cane and pushed. The man stumbled back and sat down hard on the floor.

'Help,' he squawked. 'Help. They're attacking me.' He crawled to the door, where he became tangled in the curtain in his hurry. Once outside, he could be heard shouting for the constables.

'All right,' Tora said to the Little Abbess. 'Don't cry. I'll tell you what I know, but you've got to help me.'

'They were all I had,' she mumbled, sniffling into her sleeve. 'All I had in life.'

'My master found a little boy in the rain, standing beside the road outside Otsu. He was about five years old and in rags. Skinny little fellow with big eyes.' She watched him avidly, her face blotchy with tears and her mouth open. 'The kid doesn't speak, and my master took him for a deaf-mute.' Her eyes dulled and she started to shake her head. 'Wait,' Tora said. 'We figured out he can hear all right; he's just not talking.'

With a sigh, she dabbed at her face and turned away. 'My lady's son could speak very well. He was always prattling away. He was a bright and

259

lively child.'

'This boy was living with fishermen in Awazu. He'd been mistreated.'

'Awazu? That's outside Otsu? I'll go see for myself.'

Tora explained that the child was in better hands now, and finally she was satisfied and sat back down.

'Your turn now,' Tora said. 'What about her family?'

She took up her sewing again and gestured to the cushion. 'My lady's mother was born into a good family, but she was only a concubine in her husband's house,' she said. 'She gave her husband a son and a daughter before she died. But when my lady's father also died, the oldest son drove us away. My lady's brother left, and we never heard of him again. My lady and I came here. What else were we to do, two women alone?'

Tora raised his brows. 'You turned a little lady into a working girl?'

Anger flared. 'I made sure she could earn a living by her beauty and talent. She was never a common prostitute. Peony had all the great lords at her feet. Lord Sadanori wanted to make her his wife.'

'Are you serious?'

She nodded. 'I talked and talked until I lost my voice, but she was in love with young Masuda. She could've had servants and fine gowns. She could've been again what she once was. Sadanori was mad about her. He settled us in a fine house until new quarters could be built for her at his mansion. He spoiled her with gifts. Life was good, but she wasn't happy. One morning she made me pack her things and hire a sedan chair. She ran away to become a kept woman instead of a wife! And then not even that. When he died, his people left her to starve.'

As Tora followed the story, a niggling suspicion arose. Mrs Yozaemon had called the lost boy 'Nori'. Nori – Sadanori. He asked, 'Whose child was the boy? Sadanori's or young Masuda's?'

She glared. 'What does it matter?'

Tora smelled a rat. 'It matters to the boy.'

'No. He only had his mother and me. And I'm too poor and too old to raise a small child, but I will if this child turns out to be hers.'

As a courtesan, Peony might have slept with many men, regardless of her nurse's assertions. There was a good chance that her child was neither man's. 'What about her family? They might want him.'

She hesitated just a moment too long before saying, 'No.'

'What do you mean? What was her father's name? Her mother's? How can there be nobody?'

Her anger flared up again. 'She was nobody to them because her mother was an Ezo chieftain's daughter.'

'Oh.' The Ezo were the barbarians of the north. They were treated like outcasts. Tora looked on Little Abbess with kindlier eyes. The woman had been a devoted nurse and had followed her charge into destitution. 'Why are you so sure she

261

killed herself? Couldn't somebody have drowned her?'

She looked startled, then shook her head. 'When the man she loved had died, what else could she do, poor little bird? There was no going back to her old life. She tried for more than a year. I saw her poor body. She was so thin.' She started to weep again. 'I used to take her what I could scrape together: a few coppers, some food, little treats, clothes for the boy. But it wasn't enough.'

'It must've been bad, finding her dead.'

She nodded. 'I blame myself. I was too lazy, and one of the boy's jackets wasn't done. Such foolishness! If I'd left a day before, it wouldn't have happened.' She dabbed at her wet and puffy face. 'And when she'd sent for me.'

'She sent for you?'

'She wanted me to come back to her.'

'You're sure the message was from her?'

'Yes. Who else would've written such a thing?'

Tora did not know, but had a notion that Peony's message was somehow important. 'Did she say why she wanted you back?' She shook her head. 'She didn't mention Sadanori? Or the child?' She shook her head again. Tora bit his lip. 'If she was starving, I don't see how she expected to feed you.'

'I thought she'd come into some money, that maybe the old lord had finally seen fit to take care of them as he should've in the first place. More fool me!'

Tora got up with a sigh. 'Thanks for your help.' She nodded. 'You're not such a bad guy. How's

262

Rikiju?'

The memory of that cough-racked figure returned. 'Very sick. I left her some money and told her to send for a doctor.'

'I'll make sure she does. Poor Rikiju. At least my lady was spared that.'

It was what all the women of the quarter feared more than pain or violence: to lose their appeal to men and die alone and penniless in some slum hole. It looked more and more like Peony had taken the quick way out.

SEVENTEEN

Birds and Rhubarb

After his second visit to the Masudas, Akitada debated talking to the warden again, but it was getting late. He had not eaten since that morning, and by the time he did, it would be dark. Besides, there was the problem of where he was to sleep. He rebelled against returning for a third time to the inn where he had been publicly humiliated, and where the fat innkeeper might well balk at admitting such a guest, even without a small boy victim in tow.

He settled the problem of food by stopping in the main restaurant in Otsu. It was busy, and he felt reasonably anonymous. He enjoyed the steamed dumplings with shrimp and yams, and then found a quiet backstreet lodging house.

Feeling pleasantly tired, he opened the doors to the garden to let in the cool breeze, and then lay down where he could look up at the starry sky.

He had much to mull over. Foremost, of course, was the servant's shocking charge that Peony had poisoned young Masuda. The second lady, while not precisely charging Peony with murder, had hinted at the same thing. But improperly prepared *warabi* was an uncertain method of killing a healthy young male, no matter how much of it he ate.

Still, the idea of poison was troublesome. The Masuda ladies both had motives. They were the scorned wives. And Akitada had not liked the way Lady Kohime had glanced at the old lord's dish while she had chattered about poisons. Everything about her suggested that she had been raised in the country, where they had a good knowledge of herbs and plants. The old man stood between her and her daughters and a very large fortune.

Still, if young Masuda had been poisoned, Dr Inabe would have known. He would certainly have reported a murder. Or would he? His friendship with the Masudas might have kept him silent.

The doctor's room had contained shelves of stacked papers and books. Chances were the man had kept records of young Masuda's illness. Perhaps he had even left notes about his post-mortem findings on Peony. Akitada also wondered where the boy fitted into the tangled relationships and motives, but the child was no

264

longer his only reason for searching for answers.

The stars were extraordinarily clear, as was the great river created by the God of the Sky to separate his daughter from her lover. What importance the *Tanabata* legend attached to bringing people together! He was suddenly overwhelmed by loneliness.

The stars blurred as his eyes moistened with self-pity. Ashamed, he fought the emotion. It was a long time before the hurt faded and he slept.

Akitada decided to share some of the information with the warden, but when he mentioned the servant's story that young Masuda had been poisoned by Peony, Takechi became agitated.

'Not a word of truth to it,' he cried, waving his hands. 'It's their grief talking. That death hit them hard and so they have to blame it on someone. His Lordship went mad, and the old man is simple-minded and loyal to his master. If the old lord had not lost his mind, he'd have seen the truth in time and that tale would never have started.'

Akitada raised his brows. 'So there's gossip about it. I understood the servant and the second lady to say that young Masuda became ill at Peony's house and that Dr Inabe was consulted?'

'Young Masuda had the flux. A common enough ailment around here. People will drink or eat the wrong things.'

'Like *warabi* shoots?'

'*Warabi*?' The warden looked blank. 'If it was, nobody mentioned it to me. Anyway, it wasn't a police matter.' They looked at each other, and the warden became anxious. 'You don't think this is connected to the doctor's murder, do you?'

'I don't know. When you have an unexplained murder, you tend to wonder about everything. I'd like your permission to return to the doctor's house to go through his papers in case they contain a clue to his death and young Masuda's.'

'Of course. Shall I send a constable along to give you a hand?'

'Thank you, no. I think you need your men. Do you want me to reseal the place when I finish?'

'No need for a seal. The servant's watching.'

Akitada started to point out the need for keeping the scene of a crime secured until an investigation was complete, but thought better of it. He asked instead, 'Who inherits the property?'

'A nephew. We're trying to contact him.'

'Then he does not live here?'

'He's not been around for years. The servant says the young man travels a lot.'

'Hmm.'

The warden chuckled. 'If you're thinking he might've returned to kill his uncle for the house, I doubt it. It's practically a ruin, and there was no money apart from the little bit of silver in the trunk.'

This saintly reputation was beginning to irritate Akitada. 'Did the neighbors see anyone?

'Just the usual. Servants leaving and returning from shopping. A mendicant monk. A post boy with a letter for someone. A sedan chair that picked up one of the ladies for a visit to her shrine and brought her back again.' He shuffled among his papers. 'And, yes, the fishmonger

266

with a basket of fish for one of the houses.'

'You checked them all?'

'Yes.' Gloom settled over the warden again. 'I hope you turn up something.'

Warden Takechi had not bothered to leave a constable at the gate, and so Akitada wandered in uninvited. The doctor's old servant was sweeping the courtyard.

He blinked, trying to recall Akitada's name.

'I'm Sugawara. The warden and I came yesterday. I have permission to look through your master's papers.'

The servant nodded and put his broom aside. 'The ladies asked about the funeral,' he muttered as they walked through the tangled garden. 'Couldn't say. The body's gone. Not even monks chanting. Disrespectful.'

'The arrangements should be made by Dr Inabe's relatives. He has a nephew, I hear.'

'That one.' The old man spat.

'Wait until you hear from Warden Takechi.' Akitada glanced around the lush wilderness. The garden was filled with sound. Birds were singing and chirping, calling out to each other and answering, challenging rivals or warning of the human presence among them. 'The birds are doing their best to make up for the lack of chanting,' he said with a smile.

The servant nodded. 'They know,' he said quite seriously. 'Waiting to be fed. I'll get some food.'

Akitada looked up into the dense branches. The foliage was alive. Did they know their benefactor was dead? They must have seen Inabe's killer come with murder on his mind and watched him leave, his hands stained with the blood of their friend and that of one of their own. It was a foolish speculation, and Akitada turned to business.

The warden's people had left the door to the studio unsealed. Muttering angrily under his breath, Akitada walked in. If anything, the stench was worse today. Like the warden, Akitada went to raise the shutters to the back garden. Light, fresh air, and birdsong poured in.

The room looked the same, except that the body was gone. The doctor's blood still stained the floor, though, and attracted an occasional fly. More flies crawled on the dead crow. The warden had also taken the murder weapon, but the broken birdcage still lay there, and Akitada bent to pick up the pieces.

The old servant hovered at the door. He said, 'I haven't come in here.' He did not explain if he feared the dead man's spirit, thought to remain around its home for forty-nine days, or the warden's anger.

Akitada said, 'I'll be working with your master's papers. Don't let me keep you from your chores.'

The old man looked relieved and crept away. Strange, thought Akitada, how many old men and their old servants he had met on this case. First the old lord and his servant, and now the doctor and his. Or perhaps it was not so strange. If loyalty meant anything, then master and servant would grow old together. He thought of Seimei. The bond between them was as strong as blood.

The Masuda servant's passionate hatred for Peony was due to that loyalty. But the doctor's servant seemed more confused than grief-stricken or angry. Perhaps his claim that he had walked to his cousin's funeral was untrue.

Enough theorizing. He needed facts.

He prowled around the room, looking at everything but the books and papers. The clothes box held plain and badly worn black robes and under robes, loin cloths, socks with holes in them, and a moldy black cap. Some of the things were good silk twill, but green with age. The dishes were a similar mix. Some were of cheap earthenware and some of fine china, but the china was cracked and chipped. Two pale rectangles on the wall suggested that paintings had hung there once. Otherwise, there was little of a personal nature in the room. No games or musical instruments. Just the broken birdcage.

It supported what he had been told of the doctor: that he had become an individual who cared nothing for personal luxuries, though once he had been well-to-do and had led a different life.

Akitada inspected the shelves of drugs and ointments next. He opened jars and twists of paper and sniffed at the contents. The doctor must have known what all this was, but Akitada was in the dark. Seimei or Tamako might know. Seimei had always dabbled in herbal medicines, and Tamako was an avid gardener who would probably recognize the dried plants that hung from the doctor's rafters.

He looked at them: bunches of leaves, glaucous

or grey, glossy or downy, coarse and smooth, large, small, feathery and spiny, palmate and toothed. He recognized none. Black, white and brown tubers hung among them, twisted and shriveled in their dried death. They reminded him of the neglected garden at home, of the dead wisteria, and of the coldness that had come between him and his wife.

He turned to the books and papers.

The doctor had the medical texts, the *Ishimpo*, as well as a series of herbals and pharmacological treatises. These, along with the *Book of Changes*, the *Manyoshu*, and the four Confucian classics, made up his library. But there were also handwritten scrolls and notebooks. The notebooks were what he had come for. They seemed to cover interesting medical cases and diary entries. Just what he needed. He laid them aside.

In the rolled-up scrolls, each sheet was carefully pasted to the next, while the notebooks were sewn together along one edge. The scrolls contained drawings and poetry. Akitada recognized some of the lines. Apparently, the doctor had liked the poems and had copied them for his own satisfaction. One of the scrolls was devoted to bird studies. It had drawings, as well as observations about avian habits and wise sayings and legends. On the most recent page, he found drawings of a crow and a detailed sketch of its wing. Under the drawings, Inabe had written down the legend of the crow that was sent by the goddess Amaterasu to guide the first emperor and his army to their new homeland.

The doctor's peculiar obsession with birds

seemed harmless, even attractive, but what if it had affected his judgment? He turned to look at the dead crow. Making a face, he picked it up. The flies had done their work thoroughly; the black carcass was dusted with a snow of eggs and crawling with white maggots. Some fell off as he held the large bird by its foot and carried it outside to place it under a shrub. The birds fell silent for a moment. He looked up. Another crow sat on a low branch, its head cocked and its beady eyes staring at him accusingly. 'I didn't do it. I'm sorry,' he said and felt foolish. The crow gave a harsh squawk and flew off. The bird chatter started up again.

And here came the old man, carrying a small sack. When he reached the open area in front of the studio, he shouted, 'Here it is. Come and eat.'

Another one who talked to birds.

Akitada watched as the servant loosened the knot on the bag and swung it. An arc of golden grain flew out and spread in a shower of kernels across the ground. In an instant, the air was full of feathered bodies and fluttering wings.

Akitada and the old man stood as hundreds of birds landed and scuttled about, chirping and pecking. More and more arrived, alerted by some secret code of their own, until the ground around them was covered with small feathered bodies in all colors and shapes. Then they were done and flew away again in another rush of wings.

Akitada was enchanted.

The old man folded the empty cloth. 'The last of the rice,' he said mournfully. 'In his honor.'

'But what will you eat now?'

'Beans.'

He went back to whatever he had been doing, and Akitada looked after him, astonished that this man had thought it more important to honor his master than to fill his own belly. He had been wrong to suspect the man. This also was great loyalty and filled him with sadness. With a sigh, he returned to his work.

The medical notebooks turned out to be nearly incomprehensible. The doctor's brush strokes were often careless, and worse, he used a form of abbreviated language that meant that Akitada could only make out a few sentences here and there. Part of the problem was the medical vocabulary. Of course, the notebooks might be deciphered by another medical man, but Akitada wanted to locate pertinent material on his own.

It took him well past midday to make out Inabe's method of dating, and then another while to find the two notebooks that covered the dates of the two deaths. By that time, his stomach growled, his head ached, and his eyes no longer focused. He decided to stroll to the market to get a bite to eat.

The old man had disappeared. Akitada wondered if he was eating his meager meal of beans in some dark corner. The thought made him feel guilty. He decided that he could manage quite well with one bowl of noodles, purchased from a stand. But the noodles were surprisingly tasty and so he ate a second. After months with a listless appetite, he was beginning to take pleasure in food again. This also filled him with guilt. It seemed to him that it signified an end to his grief

272

for Yori. He bought a few rice cakes for the doctor's servant and chose to go back past Mrs Yozaemon's.

The boy was outside. Even better, he was playing with the red top. Akitada smiled to see him spin the toy with considerable skill. He was afraid of another rejection and just watched the child from a distance. He was a handsome boy for all his thinness, and the old desire to hold a child in his arms again, to hear him laugh, to feel small arms hugging his neck, was back. He turned to leave.

At the doctor's house, the old servant accepted the rice cakes with many bows and mumbled thanks, and Akitada returned to his work with a heavy heart and scant interest. He had barely started skimming the entries that dealt with the first smallpox cases when the old man appeared at the open door. He carried two ripe plums on a small footed tray, presenting them to Akitada with a bow.

'Late ones. Very sweet.' His eyes strayed towards the rotting plums his master had not lived to eat. 'Wasps,' he said worriedly, nodding towards them.

Akitada thanked him and said, 'There are worse things than wasps. Warden Takechi should be back later. We will ask him when you can clean this room.' When the old man still stood, looking around sadly, he asked, 'What are your plans now?'

'Plans?'

'I mean if the doctor's nephew decides to sell this place.'

'Oh, he'll sell it.'

'How do you know?'

'What the master said. Merchants want gold.'

'Merchants?' The old man abbreviated speech as his master had abbreviated his journal entries. Some people became garrulous when they were much alone. Apparently not these two.

'The master's family. He didn't like them.'

'But I'm told he left this property to his nephew.'

'Who else?'

To the old man's mind, family, no matter how unpleasant, came first. Akitada wondered if the property, even in its ruined state, might present a motive for a greedy man. 'The nephew has visited here?'

'Once.'

'When was that?'

'After the harvest. Spent the night.' The old man made a face. 'Quarreled and left.'

'They quarreled? What about?'

'Don't know. The master said, "Good riddance."'

Akitada sampled a plum. It was delicious. Perhaps he should plant another plum tree. The one in the south garden was too old to bear fruit. This reminded him again of Tamako's wisteria and other garden matters. He glanced up at the dried herbs. 'Where did your master get his herbs?'

'The garden. The monks. And the pharmacist.'

'There is a herb garden? Where?'

The old man took him. Down a narrow path through the shrubbery, there was a small clearing of cultivated land. A spade lay beside a newly-dug section. The old man said, 'Time to split the rhubarb.'

'Rhubarb?' Akitada was beginning to understand the way his mind worked. He had fed the birds all the rice, and now he was digging the herb garden. He was showing his respect to the dead man.

'*Daiou* root. For constipation,' said his companion.

'Are any of these plants poisonous? Like *warabi*, for example?'

The old man gave him a pitying look. '*Warabi*'s not medicine. Doctors heal.'

True enough. Akitada was hunting another murderer altogether. He thanked the old man and returned to his notebooks.

When he read the entry for Peony, he was disappointed and baffled. She was identified only as 'drowned woman'. The doctor had noted a bruise on her left temple and written 'not serious' next to it. And then came the puzzling part, for he had written in the margin, 'There is no end to my guilt.' What guilt?

Akitada put the notebook aside and reached for the one that covered the previous year. But no amount of searching produced an entry for the Masuda heir. It was as if his death had never happened, and yet Inabe had treated the young man. He went through the whole notebook again. There was not only no reference to a patient with the flux at the time, but also the pertinent days did not exist in the notebook. He saw no obvious break in the note-taking, no unfinished sentences, but he checked to see if pages had been removed. If so, it had been done so carefully that there was no trace of it.

EIGHTEEN

Fox Magic

After Tora left Little Abbess he made straight for Sadanori's mansion. As before, the gate stood open, but today no bearers delivered lumber and no carriage waited. At the gate stood one of the monks with a basket hat. When he saw Tora, he placed his wooden begging bowl on the ground between his bare feet and started to play softly on a long, straight bamboo flute. He was not playing very well.

Tora paused to dig out a couple of coppers and drop them in the bowl. The monk lowered his flute and bowed. 'May Amida bless you.'

'Your first visit to the capital?' asked Tora. He gestured at the empty street. 'Not much traffic here. You'd do a lot better at one of the bridges or in the markets.'

'Thank you. Do you work in this fine mansion?'

'No.' Tora had no time to chat with idle monks. He had his own questions to ask.

A few house servants in their white uniforms and black hats were busy with chores, and in the distance he heard hammering. The builders, apparently, were still busy. The same servant who had discovered Tora on his last intrusion approached.

Tora greeted him like a long-lost friend. 'Good morning, brother. I was hoping to catch you. We weren't introduced last time. I'm Tora.'

The other man looked surprised. 'I'm Genzo,' he said, nodding a greeting. 'How's the job coming?'

'We ran into a little hitch.' Tora was pleased with this fabrication. There was always some hitch on a building project. 'Nothing serious, but the boss wants to know when to expect another inspection. He was hoping Ishikawa was still out of town.'

'No such luck. He got back last night. But he hasn't talked to the master yet, so maybe that'll buy you some time.'

'Genzo!'

They turned. Sadanori stood at the veranda railing of the nearest building.

Genzo knelt and bowed. 'Yes, Master?'

Tora remained standing and stared up at his arch enemy. The lord's fleshy face was nearly round, and its features, a pair of small eyes, a button nose, and small pink lips under a tiny black mustache, struck him as ridiculous. He reached up to stroke his own handsome mustache.

Sadanori's eyes flicked over him. 'Who is that person?' he demanded.

'He assists the building supervisor, Master.'

'Oh.' Sadanori dismissed it. 'Is Ishikawa back?'

'Yes, Master.'

'I want to see him. Now. At the new pavilion.' Sadanori turned and went back inside.

Tora and the servant waved to each other and took off in opposite directions. Tora trotted towards the pavilion.

It looked almost complete and very pretty with its dark wood, white plaster, and shiny blue roof tiles. A bright red balustrade wrapped around the veranda. The building supervisor stood at the foot of the stairs talking to two men. This time, Tora walked up openly.

'Morning,' he said cheerfully. 'Almost done, eh? Looks nice.'

The supervisor stared. 'Who're you?'

'Oh, I'm from His Lordship's mother's household. On a visit to the capital. Thought I'd take a look and see how things are coming along here. Did you know that His Lordship is coming?'

'What? Now?'

Tora enjoyed the other man's consternation. 'Oh, yes. With Ishikawa.'

The supervisor cursed and charged up the steps, while the two workers melted away. Tora grinned and strolled around the building to the back where it overlooked the lake. The piles of lumber had disappeared, as had the stacks of tiles. The tiles covered the roof now and glinted in the sun. Another staircase led to the veranda here, and Tora went up and into the building. He looked for a hiding place, but found only bare rooms. They were quite elegant, beyond anything in the Sugawara household, their columns lacquered red like the balustrade outside, their ceilings decorated with stylized blossoms and birds, and brand-new shutters stood wide open to the gardens and the lake. The smell of fresh paint hung in the air. Tora could hear the supervisor in one of the rooms, shouting, 'I don't care if the paint is wet. Cover it up and work somewhere else. Hurry up. Here he comes.'

Tora peered out and saw Sadanori approaching from the main house. The tall Ishikawa walked beside him, and several servants followed. Tora ran down the stairs and ducked under the rear veranda. He wished he could hear Ishikawa's report, but that was hoping for too much.

He waited patiently and watched the ducks and swans on the lake. Above him, muffled footsteps and voices marked the progress of the inspection. Would they notice whatever the supervisor was covering up? Apparently not. He heard no angry shouts, just some calm muttering. Eventually, the footsteps reached the veranda above his head.

'The view is charming.' That was Ishikawa. 'It will be very pleasant for Your Lordship on moonlit summer evenings.'

Sadanori's high voice replied, 'Nothing pleases me any longer.'

The supervisor offered, 'Perhaps some chrysanthemums can be planted along the lake's shore, and iris for next spring. It's perfect as a gentleman's retreat and also suitable for moon-viewing parties. Your Lordship will spend many happy years here.'

Sadanori said coldly, 'You may return to your work now.'

'I hope Your Lordship is pleased with our

progress,' the supervisor pressed.

'Yes, yes. Run along now.' Sadanori sounded impatient.

Somewhere, a crow cawed.

Ishikawa said, 'A good place for shooting practice. Having too many birds around destroys the peace.'

Under the veranda, Tora held his breath. Would they have their private talk now?

No. Apparently, they had already exchanged the information Tora was interested in – that is, what Ishikawa had been doing in Otsu. Sadanori now wanted to know what Ishikawa thought of the supervisor.

'I don't like the fellow,' Ishikawa said. 'I think he takes a cut on every order and pads the workers' hourly wage list.'

'Then you should stop him. What do I pay you for?'

Ishikawa laughed softly. 'Unlike your other servants, I'm a man you can trust. That's worth a great deal, I should think.'

'You have gone too far this time.'

'Your safety was my only concern.'

Silence.

'That reminds me, how is your lovely daughter?'

'*No!*'

Tora jumped a little. Sadanori had practically shouted the word. What was going on?

Above him, Ishikawa laughed again. 'And to think of the risks I took for you. Sugawara was back in Otsu with that servant of his.'

'So what?'

'Don't forget, there is still another witness.'

'Your mother?' There was panic in Sadanori's voice.

'Of course not. No, this one is here.'

'Then you have been careless.'

'Not at all. I just found out that Sugawara is asking questions about the case.'

'He won't find anything.'

'I disagree.' Ishikawa moved above Tora's head. 'You forget that I know how Sugawara works. He doesn't give up easily once he catches a scent.'

Silence again. Tora strained his ears. Sadanori grunted, 'I can stop him.'

'So can I. There is a woman at Fushimi. She knows how to find her.'

'I don't like it. It goes on and on. You take too much on yourself, and things get worse. See if you can manage it another way. We'll discuss your ... fee when all is safe.'

One man's footsteps receded; Sadanori's, probably. What was Ishikawa doing? What witness had he been talking about? Tora felt a hollow in the pit of his stomach. What if it was Hanae? But Hanae was safe at the Sugawara house.

Ishikawa finally moved. He went to the stairs and came down. Tora shrank behind one of the supports and watched him walk to the water's edge. There Ishikawa stopped and looked up into a tree. Suddenly, he scooped up a stone and flung it into the branches. With a loud squawk, a black crow flew up and disappeared. Ishikawa cursed after it and walked away, his face a mask of fury.

More confused than ever, Tora crept from his hiding place and followed. Ishikawa left by the open back gate and turned north.

The Fushimi market adjoined a fox shrine outside the city. Tora was convinced that Ishikawa had killed the doctor in Otsu and planned to kill someone else. Perhaps he should return to Otsu to report, but there was a certain urgency about Ishikawa's errand that made Tora nervous.

He stayed as far back as he could, mingling with other travelers on the road. Ishikawa was easy to see and not, in any case, suspicious of being followed. He never once bothered to look back.

The shrine attracted many people from the capital, and a village had sprung up around the conical wooded hill sacred to the grain deity. The market stretched along the main street, and at this time, near sunset, it was crowded. Vendors sold food and wine. Ballad singers, monks, and dancers competed for the pilgrims' coppers and added to the cacophony of the sellers crying out their wares. From the market, a line of red-lacquered *torii* snaked up the hill towards the shrine to the abode of the three grain deities.

But Ishikawa was not making a spiritual journey. After surveying the crowd, he made his way purposefully along the stands. Tora followed much more closely now. Though Ishikawa was tall, it would be easy to lose him here.

Near the entrance to the shrine grounds, Ishikawa stopped at a stall where a woman was selling combs and fans. The conversation between them was brief. Even at this distance, Tora saw that the woman was nervous. She kept bowing and speaking quickly. After a few sentences, Ishikawa nodded and walked away without buying anything.

Tora was about to approach the stall when a mendicant monk drifted up and talked to the woman. Tora waited, muttering unkind words and scanning the crowd for Ishikawa. He had disappeared.

To console himself, Tora bought a cup of the hot spicy wine. The wine eased his parched throat and was delicious, so he had a second cup. Then he returned to the comb and fan seller. She was middle-aged, but wore the colorful clothes of someone much younger. The paint on her face and her clothes probably meant that she had started life as a 'fallen flower' and now eked out a living in this market. She looked glum.

'If I buy one of your pretty combs for my wife, charming lady,' Tora said, 'would you answer a question?'

Few women could resist Tora's charm when he put his mind to it. This one could. 'What question?' she asked listlessly.

He selected a comb. 'How much for this one?'

'Fifteen coppers. It's a very fine comb.' The answer was automatic. When Tora did not argue, she took the money.

'A tall man stopped by here a little while ago. Do you know him?'

Her face closed. 'I don't remember. A lot of people stop.'

'Come on,' Tora pressed her. 'It just happened. A guy with a sharp face and lousy manners. I saw

283

him. He didn't buy anything.' He paused, frustrated by her stubborn silence. 'Just before that monk talked to you.'

'He asked about the shrine. The monk asked, too.'

'He did? Which way did they go?'

She shook her head and turned to another customer.

Tora considered the shrine entrance. Two stone statues of foxes flanked it, their bushy tails reaching skyward. They smirked down at him. The climb was a long one. Tora decided that Ishikawa would not have bothered. He was in the crowd somewhere, probably being followed by the monk wearing a basket hat. That reminded him of the monk in front of Sadanori's gate. Whichever monk this one was, he was following Ishikawa. Find the monk and find Ishikawa.

He walked up and down between the stalls without seeing either of them. Eventually, he sighed and gave up. The monk was a puzzle. Anyone could hide under one of those basket hats.

Tora's depression lifted abruptly when he got to the bridge over the Kamo River and saw the monk walking ahead of him. The basket hat bobbed along briskly, and the monk was over the bridge and turning into the warren of streets and alleys before Tora was halfway across.

Cursing the 'holy' man's longer stride, and dodging other travelers, Tora broke into a run. He must not lose his prey again. Luck was with him, and in the light of a shop lantern he caught sight of the basket hat turning south, towards the

Willow Quarter. Even better, he was taking a street that was deserted at this time of evening.

Tora increased his speed and had almost caught up when the other man heard his running footsteps and gasping breath and swung around.

With a growl, Tora flung himself on him, carrying him backward a few steps and to the ground. He had surprised the monk by his sudden attack, but the man was fighting back. He was young, strong, and more knowledgeable about street brawling than a servant of Buddha had any right to be.

In the struggle, the basket hat came off and rolled away, and Tora saw that he had caught a stranger. A young, strong, and desperate stranger. In that moment of surprise, the monk managed to bloody Tora's nose, nearly rip off an ear, sink his teeth into Tora's forearm, and knee him in the groin.

Tora grunted and released his prey to curl up in agony. The other man was on his feet in an instant, snatched up his basket hat, and took off, running.

Doubts returned. Perhaps this was just an ordinary monk. Itinerant monks often came from humble backgrounds and, being suddenly attacked, might revert to old habits. Still, this man had been far more violent than a religious calling permitted. Shaking his head in confused disgust, Tora walked home.

Genba answered his knock. 'You're late,' he grumbled.

'Couldn't help it. All is well? No trouble of any sort?'

'Trouble? No. Unless you count your dog. Why?'

Tora suddenly felt very tired. 'I lost Ishikawa.' He went to the well and pulled up a bucket of water. He drank, then splashed his face. 'What's that howling?'

'The dog. I had to tie him up so he wouldn't wake everybody when you got home.'

Tora became defensive. 'He's a fine watchdog. Let him do his job.' He went to the stable.

After an affectionate greeting, Tora released the dog and tiptoed into the room he shared with Hanae. He made a moderate amount of noise removing his clothes and yawned loudly once or twice. When that produced no reaction from the sleeping form of his wife, he crawled under the blankets, sighed, and went to sleep.

His rest was disrupted when Trouble introduced himself to the night creatures roaming the Sugawara property, barking as he chased them through the shrubbery. With a sigh, Tora got up again to put him back in the stable.

In the morning, Tora informed the women that he was returning to Otsu, warning them about Ishikawa. Tamako and Hanae seemed unworried. Then, after eating a bowl of rice gruel, he saddled his horse and left.

His failure with Ishikawa gnawed at him. Besides, he had not exactly covered himself with glory in his questioning of Little Abbess. His master would want to know about young Masuda's death. And about the old lord and his relationship with Peony before and after his son's death. And why Ishikawa's mother had visited. Little Abbess knew the answers to those questions, but Tora had only asked about Sadanori. The more he thought about it, the more questions popped into his head. He simply could not return to Otsu before seeing Little Abbess again.

In the courtyard outside her tenement, women were busy chattering and scolding their half-naked children while they hung out clothing or beat the dirt out of the straw mats they had slept on. For a copper, one of the older boys held Tora's horse while he went to call on Little Abbess.

The elderly couple from the previous day already stood outside her door. The man had the brown-and-white jacket over his arm, and both looked put out. When they saw Tora, the wife cried, 'Maybe you can get the lazy slut to open up. And you can have the jacket. We won't buy such trash.' She jerked it from her husband's arm and pointed a sharp finger at some loose threads.

Tora knocked on the wooden door. It was broad daylight, and contrary to the mean-faced biddy's opinion, Little Abbess had not struck him as lazy about her small business. When there was no answer, he gave the door a sharp push. It swung in on creaky hinges, and the sharp-nosed female let loose a shrill scream.

Inside, among her colorful bits of cloth, lay the plain brown body of Little Abbess. She was quite dead, her head resting in a pool of darkening blood.

NINETEEN

The Bird Scroll

It was getting dark when Akitada finished with Doctor Inabe's papers. He had not found what he was looking for. He rose, stretched his stiff back, and cast a final glance around the room. Someone would soon clean out the doctor's possessions. He took the notebook that should have contained the entry for young Masuda's death and the scroll with the bird drawings with him. Then he left the studio, closing the door behind him.

He called out for the old servant, but got no answer. Shaking his head, he walked away, first to the restaurant, where he had another excellent meal, and then to his lodging house.

Tomorrow he would report his failure to the warden. Takechi would solve the doctor's murder – or perhaps not. It was time Akitada returned to the capital and his own work.

There was still the question of the boy's parentage, of course. If Mrs Ishikawa identified the child as Peony's, the Masudas or Peony's people must be informed. If not, Akitada could buy him from the Mimuras and raise him himself.

It had been a long day, but he felt restless. Something had changed. Somehow, without his volition, his thoughts had turned from the boy to the tangled puzzle surrounding the dead Peony. He could not get a clear image of the woman. Was she a scheming and vengeful beauty who had killed her lover out of pique – or a helpless young woman who had loved a man above herself?

Back in his room, he called for more light and pored over Inabe's notes. Again he scrutinized the pages, the dates, the entries carefully. This time, it seemed to him that the last entry before the break did not follow the system Inabe had established. Inabe normally identified his patients by gender, age, and complaint. Next he rendered his diagnosis and noted his treatment. Then he would leave a space, and at a later time – and with different ink – there would be a comment about the outcome. For some cases there were several visits and different prescriptions, but always an outcome would follow in the end.

Except for the last case before the break. The patient, a ten-year-old girl, had suffered from a fever, and over a period of two days Inabe's herbal teas had failed to stop the fever. But he had never indicated if the child survived or died.

Surely that must mean that a page, or several, had been removed. And equally certainly they had dealt with young Masuda's illness and death. But who had removed them? The doctor himself? Or his killer? The studio had not been sealed or guarded after the murder, and as Akitada had noted, the servant was not watching the place as the warden had assumed. Anyone could have taken the pages.

But whoever had removed them had been careful not to leave traces. The stitching was still quite tight. Akitada pursed his lips. Then he carefully tugged off the last sheet of blank paper. It ripped cleanly where it had been stitched. When he held it up against the light, he saw that next to the rips were old pin holes. The notebook had been taken apart and then sewn together again, and the new stitches had not quite met the old pin holes.

He sat back and considered this. The process of removing pages and then painstakingly re-sewing the rest seemed to him not the work of a man who had just committed a murder. It was totally out of character for the person who had bludgeoned the doctor and kicked a wounded crow to death. Neither was it likely that this person, or an accomplice, had returned later to do such time-consuming work. In that case, the whole notebook would have been taken. Therefore Inabe himself must have removed the pages.

The simplest answer to the 'why' was that something had been wrong about the young man's death and that Inabe had been at least partially responsible. It might explain that note next to the entry about Peony's drowning: 'There is no end to my guilt.' Inabe must have assumed, with the maid, that Peony had committed suicide after struggling hopelessly for another year after the young man's death. Poison is readily available to a doctor, but would a man who tended so lovingly to birds kill a patient? And what was his motive? It made no sense.

Akitada sighed, blew out the candle, and went to sleep.

The next morning when he went to see the warden he found him with a youngish man who was short and corpulent and wore a mournful expression. His slightly flashy green-checked robe, black hat, and boots made Akitada think of a traveling peddler.

'This is fortunate, sir,' Warden Takechi said. 'Mr Usuki here is the doctor's nephew. He's come to make the arrangements.' He turned to the nephew. 'Lord Sugawara is kindly taking an interest in your uncle's murder. Perhaps he has some news for us.'

Mr Usuki bowed deeply, but the small, watchful eyes were suspicious. 'Deeply honored,' he murmured.

'I have very little news, I'm afraid,' Akitada said, seating himself. He expressed his condolences to the nephew, who became more mournful.

Akitada brought out the notebook, showed them the missing section, and explained his theory that Inabe had removed the pages himself. 'Both Lord Masuda's personal attendant and Lady Kohime attest to the close friendship between Dr Inabe and Lord Masuda. And as they accuse Peony of having poisoned young Masuda, I cannot help feeling that the doctor's death is somehow connected with hers.'

The nephew, his eyes intent, leaned forward to hear better.

But Takechi did not like Akitada's theories. 'I don't see it,' he said. 'To be sure, the Masudas took the young lord's death hard and had their reasons to dislike the young woman, but that doesn't mean they were right.'

'It gave them a motive to kill her.'

The warden shot a glance at Inabe's nephew, who was following the conversation avidly, and said quite sharply, 'We've been over that, sir. Unless Dr Inabe lied, the woman drowned, and Dr Inabe wouldn't lie.'

Akitada persisted. 'I don't think the drowning was natural. I believe someone put her in the lake and held her under. And by the way, when I informed Lady Masuda of Dr. Inabe's death, she expressed no surprise whatsoever.'

The warden threw up his hands. 'It means nothing. She's not very emotional.'

Usuki could not contain himself any longer. 'Forgive me, do I understand that His Lordship suspects the Masuda family had something to do with my uncle's murder?'

'No,' the warden cried. 'Not at all. His Lordship has been working on a different case altogether. There's no connection between that and your uncle's death.'

Akitada met Usuki's sly eyes and bit his lip. This was awkward. The doctor's servant had called the nephew greedy and selfish. Faced with a nearly worthless inheritance, he might well smell a chance to collect damages from the wealthy Masudas. 'Warden Takechi is right,' he said, 'I was merely sharing some random thoughts on separate investigations.' He glanced at the warden, who was still upset. 'I'm sorry I haven't been very helpful in the Inabe case. I came to tell you that I have to return to the capital today.'

The warden said quickly, 'Of course. It was very good of you to look at the doctor's papers for me. It hasn't helped to find his killer, but it saved us some time.' He rose.

Akitada suppressed a smile at the somewhat ungracious thanks and got up, but then he remembered the scroll. 'Oh,' he said to the nephew, 'I borrowed your uncle's scroll of bird drawings. They are quite charming.' He took it from his sleeve and showed Usuki the pictures of the crow. 'Your uncle was tending this wounded bird when he died. I wonder if I might borrow this for a few days?'

The nephew looked bored. 'Keep it, sir. It's of no use to anyone. Uncle was eccentric about those birds. It was a worry to me. We argued about it last time I saw him. I'd just as soon not be reminded. He's turned the whole place into bird land. Of course, since he'd fallen into the habit of treating everyone for free and giving his money away, I really shouldn't expect common sense.' A look of cunning crossed his face. 'I've come to make funeral arrangements and settle his estate, but I doubt there's enough to pay expenses. Shall we say that in exchange for the drawings, you'll let me know if you discover who murdered poor uncle?'

'Certainly,' said Akitada, 'but since the investigation will be in Warden Takechi's hands, perhaps you will allow me to reimburse you now?' As he fished in his sash, he remembered his confiscated funds. But Tamako would like the

293

bird scroll. 'Would two pieces of silver be fair?'

The man smiled with surprised pleasure. 'Quite generous, My Lord. If you insist—' His hand shot forward and grasped the coins eagerly.

The nephew's views of his uncle's lifestyle had made Akitada curious about another matter. 'Tell me,' he asked the two men, 'was Dr Inabe's changed behavior by any chance a sudden and recent thing?'

They exchanged looks. The warden said, 'I first heard about it a year ago. People told me that he wasn't charging them. And when I met him, he seemed different. Sort of quiet and ... humble. He'd always been very energetic and self-confident, as most physicians are. I never could figure out what happened.'

'Old age.' The nephew shook his head. 'He should have listened and sold the place. I offered him a room in my house. He would be alive today if he'd had any sense.'

But at a price, Akitada thought.

The warden, somewhat surprisingly, walked him out. When they were outside, he said, 'Usuki's not a very nice man. No filial sentiment. But he's been eliminated as a suspect. He was taking care of his business on the day of the murder and is vouched for by family and customers. I'm afraid it's an impossible case. We'll question the neighbors a bit more, but then—' He spread his hands and did not finish.

Akitada had one more errand before leaving Otsu. He took the road up the hill to the Masuda mansion with a sense of fatalism. It would be his final effort to find the boy's family. All along there had been two people who could have identified Peony's son: her maid, and the Masuda's nurse, Mrs Ishikawa. He had no idea if Tora had found the maid, but he could not wait any longer. Whether or not Lady Masuda had forbidden his visits or Mrs Ishikawa felt under obligation to her mistress, she must be made to see the boy and tell him if the child was Peony's or a stranger's.

He knocked at the gate and, as before, the old servant responded. Obviously few visitors called, or the man would have been kept too busy answering the gate to look after his master. The old man recognized Akitada and, shaking his head, started to close the gate.

'Wait.' Akitada held it open. 'I'm not here to speak to your master. It's Mrs Ishikawa I must see.'

The servant kept shaking his head and trying to close the gate. The contest was silly: Akitada, being much younger and stronger, could easily force his way in. He did not do so, because he was unwelcome in this house. 'Please,' he begged. 'Just have her come to the gate, or meet me outside. It's very important.'

The pressure on the gate eased. The old man said, 'I can't, sir. Mrs Ishikawa is gone.'

'Gone?' Akitada dropped his hand. They stood looking at each other through the narrow opening. 'Where is she?' Akitada asked.

'Gone on a pilgrimage. The first lady gave her approval.'

'When did she leave?'

295

'Two days ago. Her son came for her.'

'Ishikawa was here two days ago? When will she be back?'

The old man relented. 'He said it was just a little outing, a visit to a few temples before the cold weather starts. She'll be back in two weeks. Sorry, sir.' And now he closed the gate firmly.

Akitada stood outside and heard the bars slide into place and footsteps recede. After a moment, he turned and walked away, his mind in turmoil. It was pointless to be so upset. Tora should be back soon. Perhaps he had found the maid. In any case, they would return together to the capital and his old life. The child was safe for the time being, and he was content to leave him there. It had been madness to think that he could be a father again.

Not having anything else to do, he got his saddlebag from the lodging house and rode to the outskirts of Otsu, where he settled himself on one of the benches outside a wine shop to await Tora. The bench was under a spreading cherry tree and the weather was pleasant. The summer heat had passed, and a light breeze came from the lake, where seagulls swooped and cried to each other. A cheerful waiter brought him some wine and a bowl of salted vegetables without bothering him with small talk. His horse grazed quietly on a patch of weeds. Akitada watched the road and the lake for a while, then pulled Inabe's bird scroll from his sleeve.

The crow was really very well drawn. Inabe had had a gift as an artist. And his comments suggested a well-educated mind, even if he seemed

296

somewhat obsessive about the supernatural significance of birds. Looking at the pictures, Akitada wondered if the splinted wing would have healed and if the crow would eventually have flown back to the wild. Probably so. Perhaps the place was full of birds the doctor had healed. No wonder they were so tame. The birds would have been company of sorts for a very lonely man.

Something had happened to turn Inabe inward. The loss of his wife? No, that had been earlier. Akitada knew all about loss and what it could do to a man, but he put thoughts of his own loneliness from his mind and unrolled more of the scroll.

Two magpies on a pine branch. Inabe had written down the Tanabata legend about the bridge of magpies. Cranes. It appeared that cranes were as faithful to their mates as mandarin ducks. They symbolized a long life. Auspicious birds! Ah, here was a story about a wounded crane's gratitude to a human. It had turned itself into a beautiful maiden for the lonely young man who had saved it. Akitada smiled at the fanciful thought that Inabe's loneliness had caused him to devote his skills to healing birds in the hope of finding a wife.

A series of sketches of small birds: a water-rail, snipes, a fly-catcher, a cuckoo. The drawing of a plover carried a legend about its grieving for a lost mate. The nightingale was said never to sing in the gardens of the imperial palace. Why not? Akitada knew that white doves were sacred to the god of war, Hachiman, and he also knew the story of a pair of wagtails teaching the first deities how to make love and create life.

Akitada thought of Tamako. She really would enjoy this scroll.

Apparently, Inabe had loved the common sparrows better than any other bird. Several sheets were filled with their sketches and tales. He searched for and found the story he remembered from his own childhood. He had told it to Yori. It was about the sparrow with the broken wing who rewarded the poor woman who healed him with an unceasing supply of food until her jealous neighbor caught the little bird. But remembering his son brought tears to his eyes, and the characters swam crazily on the paper.

Akitada blinked and unrolled the scroll a little more to read the rest of the story, but the text changed suddenly. There were no more drawings. The writing was dense and professional and hard to decipher. It was the same writing as in Inabe's medical notebooks. His heart beating faster, he unrolled a large section. There were four sheets of medical notes altogether before the bird pictures continued. The story of the wounded sparrow had no ending because the medical notes had been glued over it.

What was more, these were the four sheets missing from the notebook. Inabe had hidden the pages by removing them carefully, and then he had sacrificed four sections of his treasured bird drawings to make sure they were hidden. Why? And from whom?

He read and learned that the ten-year-old girl had recovered. But it was the next patient who mattered: a thirty-year-old male who had complained of acute cramping in his belly, along with vomiting, and burning in his mouth and throat.

It had to be young Masuda.

There was no mention of *warabi mochi*. The doctor had merely poked and questioned the patient. He had noted spasms and tightness in the lower belly, especially on the right side, and had prescribed a dose of powdered *daiou* and *moutan*. The next day he had been called back and found the patient improved. But then, the day after, young Masuda had become much worse. He was now suffering from severe dysentery. Palpitation of the belly had produced fluid sounds. Inabe had again prescribed *daiou* and added *persica*. On this occasion he had noted a *yang* pulse and a yellow, dry coating of the tongue, and had identified them as the symptoms of an intestinal inflammation.

An inflammation? What had been wrong with the patient? There were two more visits, the comments increasingly shorter and more ominous: shallow breathing, cold sweats, and severe pain on the first of these, and on the last Inabe had noted that the patient was unresponsive and suffered from seizures. The outcome was, of course, death.

And that was all. Except that Inabe had scribbled some obscure comments in the margin of the last sheet. Akitada turned the scroll sideways and squinted at it. 'For lovesickness there is no medicine.' Love sickness? The other was a bit of Chinese which looked like 'Yue-sun's gruel'. He took it for the name of an obscure medicine.

More puzzled than ever, Akitada looked up, dazzled from close reading, and squinted at the sun. It was midday already, and that made Tora very late indeed. He decided not to wait any longer.

TWENTY

Scent of Orange Blossom

When Akitada got home, he went directly to Tamako's room. Since he had become a stranger there after their son's death, he announced himself outside the door and asked for permission to enter. She answered in her familiar, cool voice, and he went in.

She sat near the open door to the overgrown garden. He was struck by how very attractive she looked in the dark-grey gown that mourning still dictated and was glad that she was alone. But his heart fell when he saw that she was bent over two lacquer trunks he recognized. They had belonged to their son Yori and held his summer and autumn clothing. That she was taking out and handling his small garments depressed him immeasurably.

He expected grief, but she was calm. 'Was your journey successful?' she asked, giving him a searching look.

He came a little closer, wondering if he should sit down. 'In some ways,' he said cautiously, hoping for an invitation.

Her face lit up. 'You brought the child with you?' Her hands made a small, fluttering gesture at the clothes boxes.

He understood, and his heart fell further. 'No, but he's safe for the time being. I meant that there is more information about the Masuda case. And perhaps about the boy's paternity. But there are still many unanswered questions.'

She was silent for a little. 'Then you will leave again,' she said finally.

He was taken aback. He had just arrived. Was she so eager to have him gone? 'No. I ... I must return to my duties at the ministry.'

She nodded, closed the trunks, and rose. 'I had better tell cook to get more provisions.'

He did not step out of her way. For a moment they stood face to face, and he knew she was going to brush past him. In an awkward effort to keep her, he pulled the bird scroll from his sleeve and held it out. 'I thought you might like this.'

She took it warily. 'For me?' She held the scroll as if it were either precious or deadly.

'I found it among the victim's papers,' he said nervously. 'He loved birds and made a study of them. The scroll has his drawings and little legends and tales about birds. When I saw it, I thought of you. I bought it from his heir.'

She blushed. 'Oh, Akitada,' she murmured and undid the ribbon.

He saw the delicate color rise on her pale skin and thought how much more beautiful it was than the white paste worn by many women. 'The nephew was not a very nice man and had no love for birds or for his uncle, I think. You won't mind that it belonged to a dead man?' he asked anxiously. 'His murder is what kept me in Otsu.'

She looked up. 'Of course I don't mind. Poor man. I shall treasure this. Thank you, Akitada.' She unrolled the scroll and exclaimed at the drawings.

Akitada felt pleased with himself so far and said on an impulse, 'It also contains an important clue. See here.' He showed her the pasted pages. 'I'd be glad of your advice on the doctor's prescriptions for a very sick young man. You know much more about medicines than I do.'

She clutched the scroll to her chest, her eyes shining. 'Oh, Akitada.'

He smiled uncertainly. 'Do you mind?'

'Oh, no. I'm deeply honored by your confidence. I promise I shall study this very carefully.' She paused and her face fell a little. 'But I'm not an expert. Please don't expect too much. May I consult with Seimei?'

He heaved a sigh of relief. 'By all means. Excellent idea.' For a moment they stood smiling at each other, and then Akitada, suddenly afraid to spoil so good a beginning, fled.

In his room, he changed into his second-best silk robe and court hat, gathered his long overdue report on the Hikone affair, and set out for the ministry. He was almost light-hearted. Perhaps he might yet make his peace with Tamako. And the convoluted Masuda case had reached the interesting phase where it must begin to unravel, if only he could lay his finger on the right thread.

His desire to adopt the mute boy had faded to a

302

more distant benevolence. This fact, however, he had no wish to examine more closely because it would bring back the old grief and loneliness.

At the ministry, he met startled glances from junior clerks and was immediately ushered into the minister's office.

His exalted superior was a Fujiwara noble: not the worst of them, and certainly far better than his predecessor, who had made Akitada's life a misery until his death in the recent smallpox epidemic. The current incumbent was younger than Akitada and had no legal training – such things were irrelevant for senior appointments – but at least he made a show of taking an interest. Their relationship had been cordial from the beginning.

At least until now.

As soon as Akitada entered the minister's room, he became aware of a distinctly chilly reception. There was no smile on the minister's normally cheerful face. He looked like someone embarked on an unpleasant task.

He did not invite Akitada to sit and said crisply, 'We expected you earlier.'

Akitada searched his mind. Had he sent a message that the Hikone affair was taking longer than expected? The past ten days had preoccupied his mind to the exclusion of everything else. He said cautiously, 'Well, it has taken a while, but the report is finally done.' He held up the papers. 'It turned out to be a fairly clear-cut case after all. The local authorities—'

'I was not referring to the Hikone matter,' the minister interrupted. 'Rumor has reached the government that you were arrested in Otsu.'

Akitada's heart skipped a beat. He should have been prepared. Of course the Otsu affair would leak out. He knew that the judge had requested information about him, and the only way that could have been done was by turning to the central council and giving a reason. How could he have been so stupid? The truth was, he had been obsessed with the boy, and for his sake he had cheerfully risked his career and fortune. Buggery, if engaged in discreetly, would only raise an amused eyebrow, but the abduction and rape of a child was another matter.

He pulled himself together with an effort. 'A foolish mistake by the Otsu authorities,' he said, keeping his voice as clipped as the minister's. 'I have a good mind to lay charges against everyone involved.'

The minister relaxed a little. 'I thought there must be an explanation,' he said in a more conciliatory tone. 'Perhaps you'd better explain. The allegations have raised questions in, er, higher quarters, and I am to report.'

Worse and worse. It meant the chancellor had taken notice and given orders to the Censors' Office. The censors, in turn, had started proceedings by instructing the minister to conduct a full-scale investigation into the incident. That he could not have expected, and it struck him as so extraordinary that he asked, 'Do you mean this unfortunate, but essentially trivial mistake has become a matter of official concern?'

The minister nodded grimly. 'Afraid so. In our position, criminal charges are a serious matter.'

304

His expression softened a little. 'Sit down and take your time. Just an unofficial version to start with. Then we'll have a scribe take down your story for the final report.'

Akitada felt sick. He began with meeting the child in the forest. Diffidence made him give only the rough facts, and he watched with chilling foreboding as the minister's face lengthened more and more and doubt began to creep into his eyes. When Akitada was done, an uncomfortable silence fell. Akitada shifted, wondering what else he could say to convince the man of his innocence.

The minister forestalled him. 'I know you lost a son during the recent epidemic, but even so ... Don't you consider your behavior in this matter highly ... unusual?'

It had not seemed so at the time. Stung by the suggestion that he might be mentally unstable, Akitada defended himself. 'I only took pity on a lost child. I would have thought that a good thing. I cannot help it if ignorant and malicious people choose to interpret my motives in a salacious manner.'

The minister flushed and compressed his lips. 'I'm afraid,' he said, 'you're not helping me. Because I have only a short acquaintance with you, I must rely on what you say in your defense.'

This smacked more and more of the notion that he was on trial here. Akitada tried to control his anger. He also knew little about the minister's background. He had simply assumed that a high-ranking noble would not involve himself unduly in the work of the ministry and leave matters to him.

And so it had been. Yori's death had filled Akitada's thoughts day and night, and he had attempted to banish the memories with work. His new superior had not hindered Akitada's frenzied activity. Now, for the first time, it occurred to him to wonder about the man. He must be in his late twenties and had probably had the usual university training and private tutors. Unlike many of the court nobles, he looked like an active young man, healthy and without the softness that marked the more self-indulgent members of his family. But that did not tell him how he would deal with the present case.

Akitada felt a moment's foolish resentment and said coldly, 'Since I don't seem to be able to make a convincing defense to you, I must rely on my good name to speak for my character.'

The minister sighed. He reached for a sheaf of documents and passed them across the desk. Akitada bit his lip. They were the annual evaluations of his performance under the previous minister, probably complete and going back to the year when he had started as a very junior clerk. Most accused him of neglecting his duties to meddle in outside affairs in direct disobedience to orders and had haunted him before.

He said bitterly, 'These mean nothing. Your predecessor took every opportunity to attack me. His Excellency, the chancellor, and other high-ranking officials know of my service. I have received several high commendations and promotions for my work.'

'But in this case...' began the minister.

Akitada, very angry by now, rose. 'I absolutely deny those ridiculous charges. Perhaps you will consult further about my moral character with those who can speak to it. It will be best if I await your decision at home.' He bowed and walked out.

He stormed home and rushed into the courtyard at such a pace that the dozing Trouble thought it a new game and joined him, bouncing up and down and around him with a noisy welcome. Akitada cursed and pushed the dog away roughly, but Trouble simply increased his efforts and responded by taking small nips of Akitada's good robe.

'Tora!' shouted Akitada.

Tora and Genba appeared simultaneously and flung themselves into the fray.

The dog yipped with joy. A free-for-all! A chase! Three humans against one splendid dog.

Akitada withdrew from the contest and stood glowering on the steps until Tora collared his dog. Then he said, 'Get rid of him!' and stalked into the house.

He had been going to see Tamako to tell her of his dilemma, but decided to take off his torn and dirty robe first. Perhaps he would never have need for his formal clothes again. Slipping on his house robe, he tied its sash and went to give his wife the bad news.

Tora intercepted him in the hall. He looked upset. 'Sir, about the dog—'

'Not now,' Akitada snapped and brushed past him.

307

Tamako and Seimei were bent over the bird scroll. They looked up.

'Is something wrong?' Tamako asked. 'We heard Trouble.'

The dog's name seemed ominously appropriate. 'Tora should never have brought that miserable cur here,' Akitada said angrily. 'And yes, there is something wrong, though it has nothing to do with the dog. It seems I am under official investigation for the Otsu incident.'

Seimei sucked in his breath, but Tamako merely said coolly, 'Surely that was always a possibility?'

He glowered and sat down. 'I rather thought my credit was good enough to speak for my character.'

She sighed. 'Yes, I know. It's very disappointing. I don't blame you for being angry. It's really too bad that it had to happen just now.'

'Why?' he asked, surprised.

She blushed. 'I just meant ... You were so calm and ... content earlier. So eager to take up your responsibilities again.' She bit her lip, and lowered her eyes.

Akitada stared at her. His wife was positively glowing with embarrassment.

Seimei got up. 'I beg your pardon, sir, My Lady, but I was about to go and check on the poison.' He hurried from the room.

Akitada frowned after him. 'What poison?'

'Monkshood. It's a very poisonous plant,' Tamako explained. 'We wondered what could have made the young man so sick.'

'Oh.' Having come back down to earth so

painfully in the minister's office, Akitada had trouble refocusing for a moment. But really, if he was no longer wanted in his official function, nothing prevented him from using his free time as he wished. He took a deep breath. 'Yes, of course. I suspected *warabi* dumplings. According to one of his wives, they were a favorite of his.'

'Fern fiddle heads?' Tamako shook her head. 'They can make you sick, but surely not deathly ill. People eat them all the time. You yourself have found them tasty. What we need is something much more deadly. Seimei thought monkshood would fit what the doctor observed.'

Akitada frowned. 'If he had been given such a well-known poison, surely Inabe would have known.'

'Perhaps not, if the young man was already ill from something else and being treated. His symptoms from the treatment might have been indistinguishable from the poison.'

Akitada looked at his wife with admiration. 'How clever you are,' he said. 'What is *daiou* root prescribed for, and what happens after a few doses of the stuff?'

'Rhubarb root,' Tamako said with a smile. 'It cures constipation. You may imagine the effect for yourself.'

'Ah.' Akitada brightened more. 'The warden said young Masuda died from the flux.'

Tamako unrolled the scroll and reread the pasted pages. 'The doctor should have suspected something. But there is nothing. Unless—'

Akitada moved closer so that he could look at the scroll with her. 'Unless what?'

309

'Unless this note about Yue-Sun's gruel means something.'

'Some Chinese medicine?'

'I don't think so, and neither does Seimei.'

'It may just be a scribble. Like the one about lovesickness. Inabe liked to jot down stories. Whatever he saw reminded him of something else. The bird scroll is full of bird tales.'

'Yes. I noticed that too.' Tamako gave him a sidelong glance. 'I suppose there was opportunity for lovesickness in the Masuda household. Two wives and a mistress? And the mistress had been deserted at one point?'

'True. What about this Yue-Sun?'

'She's a character in a Chinese tale. Yue-Sun poisoned someone with a bowl of gruel. I forgot the details, but the victim died.'

'What? Old Lord Masuda believes that Peony killed his son. Who was the victim in the story?'

'Some very important person, and she was a servant or his handmaiden.'

'Hah!' Akitada jumped up and started to pace. 'So it *was* murder. Young Masuda was poisoned. By a woman. But Peony had no motive. He had returned to her, and she and her son depended on him. No, someone else killed him. I think a woman brought a certain food to the patient, and Inabe remembered that later when he became suspicious.'

'Very likely. Did Masuda's wives visit him at Peony's house?'

'Hardly. But Mrs Ishikawa admitted going there. She could have been sent by them.' Akitada sat down again. 'But there's no proof, and

I'm afraid it doesn't explain what happened later.'

They were sitting close to each other, and he became aware of his wife's scent. Feeling suddenly awkward, he stole a glance at Tamako's profile, a shell-like ear, and graceful neck. He wanted to trace that elegant hairline with his finger, to bury his face in the hollow between that soft and fragrant neck and her shoulder. He wanted to make love to his wife.

Caught between fear and daring, he was struck by the ridiculousness of his hesitation. They were alone. They were married. He had every right to caress her.

His hand was half raised when Tamako turned her head. Their eyes met, and her lips parted. Tender, moist, and welcoming lips. Eyes that became soft and warm. His hand found the warmth of her skin just above her collar, smooth as silk, strange and yet familiar. He felt an intense pleasure at her response, at the way she leaned into his hand and raised her face to him. Murmuring her name, he was about to reach for her with his other hand when the door opened and Seimei returned.

The old man stopped. 'Oh,' he said and started to back out again.

The spell broke. They moved apart and were again Akitada and Tamako, husband and wife with years of marital familiarity and distance between them. Tamako sighed softly.

Suppressing his frustration, Akitada said, 'Come in, come in. Did you find anything?'

If the old man's skin had not been so bloodless,

Akitada could have sworn he blushed. 'Yes, indeed, sir. Her Ladyship was quite right. The powdered root of *torikabuto* is recommended for a belly ache, also for colic and pain. But it is very powerful and must be given in extremely small doses.'

'Or it will kill?' asked Akitada.

'Oh, yes. Quickly. It is said that it takes the breath away and chills the blood, and the patient dies in great pain.'

Akitada looked at Inabe's scroll. 'It fits. But surely the poison was not administered as a medicine.'

Tamako leaned closer and extended a slender hand to point. 'Look. The symptoms did not occur until the doctor's third visit.'

Akitada was distracted by her perfume and nearness. He moved a little and for a moment their bodies touched warmly before she moved away.

Seimei cleared his throat. 'Tora was very anxious to speak to you.'

Akitada sighed. 'It's about his miserable cur. Come to think of it, I never had a chance to ask him why he did not meet me in Otsu.'

Seimei was startled. 'You don't know, sir? He found a murdered woman early this morning and was kept by the police.'

'What?' Akitada was on his feet. 'Why didn't anybody tell me?'

'I'm sure he tried to, sir.' There was a note of reproof in Seimei's voice.

Akitada grunted and dashed from the room.

It was getting dark outside. Genba was drawing

water at the well. From the corner of the house came the sound of coughing. The ancient carpenter was shuffling off to his evening rice.

'Where is Tora?' Akitada called out to Genba.

Genba put down the wooden bucket. 'He left, sir.'

'Left? To do what?'

'You told him to get rid of Trouble.' Seeing Akitada's frown, Genba explained. 'He's trying to find a home for him. It won't be easy. Trouble's not a handsome animal. And letting him loose will just mean he'll be killed. Tora's very fond of that dog.'

Akitada had not intended this. Shaking his head at the misunderstanding, he sat down abruptly on one of the steps. It creaked alarmingly, and when he looked, he saw that a large crack had opened up. This reminded him of the condition of his home. 'I'm afraid the next earthquake will bring the roof down around our ears,' he muttered. 'I've been neglectful of my responsibilities.'

Genba tried to cheer him up. 'The house is very solid, sir. The carpenter comes every day, and with three of us working together, we'll have all the problems fixed in no time.'

But Akitada knew better. For one thing there was no money. He had no idea how long he could pay the ancient carpenter. For another, his neglect extended to his family as well as his home. It was a miracle Tora had stayed with him all these years – that any of them had stayed. He looked at Genba, a huge man, a former wrestler gone to seed. His short, bristly hair was grizzled, and the massive body had turned soft and flabby. When he and Hitomaro had first joined Akitada's family, they had both been strong young men. Hitomaro had given his life for him, and Genba, in his own way, was still doing so. Genba had never married and had served him quietly, never making demands, never complaining about his lost chances in the ring. Akitada had begun to treat him as a fixture, almost with the same disrespect that Yori used to show him. Genba had been there to be made use of. They had taken his devotion for granted, and Akitada had even begrudged him the food that was Genba's only weakness.

'I'm sorry, Genba,' Akitada said now. 'I'm truly sorry about many things. I haven't been myself lately. Tora need not have given the dog away, just confined him somewhere.'

Genba's anxious face brightened. 'I'll tell him. He'll be very happy, sir.'

Akitada sighed. 'Are you happy here, Genba?'

Panic appeared in Genba's face. 'Why do you ask, sir? Have I done something wrong?'

'No.' Akitada rose to put a hand on Genba's shoulder. 'No, my old friend. Not you. The fault is mine. I beg your forgiveness. You must tell me next time I'm unreasonable or ... cruel.'

'Oh, I could never do that ... I mean you never ... You could never be cruel, sir. As for being a bit distracted, well, we know you don't mean it.' He broke off helplessly.

Akitada embraced him. 'Thank you,' he said, very moved. 'And thank you for watching over all of us while I ... was busy elsewhere and Tora had his own problems. I don't know what I would have done if it hadn't been for you and Seimei.'

Genba blinked rapidly and muttered, 'It was nothing, sir.'

'Did Tora by any chance tell you about a murder he discovered this morning?'

'No. He'd just got back from talking to the police and was depressed and very anxious to see you.'

'I was in a hurry and thought it was about the dog. Tell Tora to bring the dog back and then come to report to me.'

But Akitada waited in vain for Tora to return. Eventually, he spread his bedding in his room and went to sleep there.

In the morning, he got up and looked immediately for Tora. He found him sitting on the bottom step of the stairs, his shoulders slumped and his head in his hands. There was no sign of the dog.

'Where's Trouble?' Akitada asked. 'Didn't Genba tell you to bring him back?'

Tora rose and turned. It was obvious that he had not slept. 'I tried, sir,' he said. 'I went back last night, but he's gone. They took him away. I shouldn't have left him there. I could tell they'd mistreat him. But they had children, and I thought Trouble would like that. Someone to play with. He's just never had that before. I think that's what made him the way he was. There wasn't a bad bone in that dog's body. He was bored.'

Tora sounded near to tears, and Akitada felt very guilty. 'I'm sorry, Tora. I suppose Genba mentioned that I didn't mean it. Do you know where these people took the dog?'

Tora shook his head. 'I didn't ask. They're travelers. Vagrants. The whole family works at temple fairs. The kids tumble and beg a few coppers from the pilgrims. The husband and wife are jugglers and musicians. The husband thought he could train Trouble to do tricks.'

'Dear Heaven.' Akitada pictured that clumsy, big, unattractive animal trying to dance on a ball or jump through flying hoops. 'What gave him that idea?'

Tora looked shamefaced. 'Me. I was getting pretty desperate by then, so I talked him up a bit. Funny thing was, as I was talking, Trouble had that intelligent expression he gets sometimes. But you're right. He'll never learn any tricks. They'll beat him first, and then maybe they'll kill him. He gave me such a look when I walked away.'

Akitada remembered how it had felt walking away from the boy in Otsu and did not know what to say. Tora had a beaten manner about him that he did not like. When they had fallen out over Hanae, he had been angry and defiant. Now he just looked hopeless.

As they stood together in front of the house, neither knew what to say. Genba watched them from the stable door, and the old carpenter shuffled past, carrying some boards and making them a creaking bow. Akitada almost suggested getting another dog, but bit it off in time.

Tora said, 'Trouble was a lot like me. Couldn't do anything right, but he was loyal.'

More guilt.

Akitada muttered, 'Don't blame yourself. It was my fault. All of it was my fault.' He paused. 'What happened with that maid?'

'That's another thing I couldn't do right. The bastard murdered Little Abbess before I could talk to her. Beat her head in just like the doctor's.'

'Who is Little Abbess?'

'Peony's maid. She sells old clothes now. Sold, I mean.' He sighed.

Akitada frowned. 'So you got no information?'

'I talked to her a little the day before. She told me some things, but she was very close-mouthed about others. That's why I went back before reporting to you in Otsu. Only by then that bastard Ishikawa or the monk had got to her. She might still be alive if I hadn't gone chasing after Ishikawa.'

'What monk? You had better tell me the whole story from the beginning.' Akitada sat down on the steps.

Tora told him.

Akitada asked, 'What did the maid say about the child's father?'

'She wouldn't say if it was Sadanori or young Masuda. A customer came in, and I left to look for Ishikawa.'

Akitada had Tora repeat the conversation between Sadanori and Ishikawa twice. It puzzled him also. 'Sadanori's anger must be due to Ishikawa's blackmail,' he said, 'but it isn't clear if Sadanori ordered the murders or Ishikawa acted on his own and afterwards held the crimes over

317

Sadanori's head. What is the monk's part in all this?'

'I wish I knew. Every time I turned around I saw one of those begging monks. Maybe it was just one guy. Anybody could hide under one of those basket hats.'

Akitada frowned, remembering the monk in the warden's office in Otsu. He had identified the boy as belonging to the Mimuras. And had there not been an itinerant monk outside the doctor's house on the day of the murder? 'Where did you see all these monks?'

'The first one was outside Sadanori's residence. I told him it was a stupid place to beg. He wanted to know if I worked there. Then, at the shrine market, he was talking to the fan seller right after Ishikawa. I caught up with the bastard in the capital—'

'Wait. How do you know it was the same man every time?'

'I don't. But they were all about the same size and height. Anyway, his basket hat came off then and he was a stranger. I let him get away. But then, there he was again the next day, right outside Little Abbess's place. Right after her murder.'

'What? Did you speak to him?'

'No. He ducked into the crowd when he saw me.'

Akitada shook his head. 'Strange. A monk was also seen outside the doctor's place. Hmm. I'm not sure about this monk, but I have a feeling he's part of Peony's story. In any case, the facts now point to Ishikawa and Sadanori. You were right all along. I have other news. The doctor's notes show that he may have been killed because he knew someone poisoned young Masuda.' He smiled. 'You've done excellent work.'

'Thank you, sir.' Tora cheered up a little. 'What's next?'

'Get some rest. It's time I paid Lord Sadanori a visit.'

TWENTY-ONE

Lady Saisho

Akitada went to tell his wife about Tora's news. She listened, interrupted a few times to ask a question, but did not offer any comments until he was done.

'Oh, that poor, poor young woman,' she murmured. 'Rejected by everyone. And the boy. You must bring him to us, Akitada, whatever happens. We cannot let him down again.' Bypassing Tora's exciting tale of monks and murder, she had gone straight to what mattered most to her: the lost child.

He nodded reluctantly. 'Yes, I suppose so.'

Her eyes widened at his tone. 'I thought you were quite determined. Have you changed your mind?'

How could he admit his selfishness to her? 'My efforts have been grossly misinterpreted,' he said

319

evasively.

'But that is nonsense. You cared for the child because your heart is kind.'

'No, Tamako,' he said bitterly. 'I was not kind. I was lonely and behaved like a spoiled child who wanted an expensive toy. I was going to buy him. Now all our funds are gone, and so is my career. And the child doesn't even like me.'

He knew he had sounded petulant and started to leave, but Tamako caught his sleeve. 'No. You're wrong. You missed Yori and wanted someone to love again. I, too—' She took his hand and begged, 'Can we not try together to accept what happened?'

Akitada had no words, but he squeezed her hand and nodded.

She said, 'It helps to reach out when we stumble.'

Emotion choked Akitada. He made an effort and managed to say quite steadily, 'Yes, well, I've certainly fallen down many times on this case. But remember, if the child is really the son of Peony and Masuda, he has a family. Though it may be impossible to prove it, now the maid is dead and Mrs Ishikawa has been spirited away by her son.'

'Mrs Ishikawa is the key. Tora said her son expects to marry Sadanori's daughter.'

A misalliance, if ever there was one. 'It's hardly likely that Sadanori would agree.'

'He might if he were forced to,' insisted Tamako.

'Sadanori is very secure in his position at court. Besides, I don't see a man like Sadanori taking such risks. Seduction and abduction, even rape of women from the amusement quarter, are more in his line. Nobody pays attention to a man's sexual peccadilloes.' But that was not entirely true. He, Akitada, was under sharp scrutiny at this moment for sexual misconduct. However, he was hardly of Sadanori's rank and connections.

'What do *you* think?' asked Tamako.

'I don't know what to think. Ishikawa is repulsive, but I've never thought him capable of murder. When he cornered me six years ago at the university, he could have killed me, but he intended only a beating.' Akitada would always feel a remnant of sympathy for the handsome and brilliant student whose ambition and poverty had led him into crime.

'We must find Mrs Ishikawa.'

'Yes. You're quite right. I'm on my way to speak to Sadanori. After that we'll know better how to proceed.' Akitada rose with new energy. 'Thank you. You've been most helpful.'

Tamako gave him a trembling smile.

Akitada changed into his second-best silk robe and clean silk trousers before calling on the great lord. At the Sadanori compound, Akitada checked the gate for begging monks, but saw none.

Fujiwara Sadanori received him formally in the main house. The reception hall was lit by several candles on tall stands. Sadanori sat on a cushion on a thick grass mat, one elbow on a lacquered armrest and a *go* board by his side as if he had been interrupted in a game against himself. He returned Akitada's bow, calculated carefully to be just less than polite, and gestured to another

321

cushion.

'Have I had the pleasure?' he asked with the vagueness of a great man who cannot be expected to remember those who seek his favor every day, but his eyes were watchful.

'No, sir.' Akitada made no attempt to add the customary flattery, and the watchful eyes sharpened.

Sadanori was in his early forties and slightly corpulent. He had a round, smooth-shaven face with thin lips that turned downwards when he was not smiling. He was not smiling now. 'In that case, perhaps you will be brief. I am very busy.'

'Yes, I see. Briefly then: one of the women in my household claims that you had her abducted and confined in a house in the *Gojibomon* quarter. She managed to escape the day after the abduction. I found the story difficult to believe and came to verify the matter.'

Sadanori was clearly startled, but then his face cleared. He said coldly, 'An extraordinary story. I wonder you troubled to come here.'

'Her name is Hanae. She used to be a dancer in the Willow Quarter. I believe you know her?'

Sadanori laughed. 'Did you buy the girl? My compliments. She is a charmer, though I found her less than accommodating myself.'

Akitada corrected him. 'I did not buy her. She is the wife of one of my retainers. Perhaps you might care to answer my question.'

The other man snapped, 'I don't like your tone. And I certainly have no intention of answering rude and ridiculous questions.'

'You just admitted to knowing Hanae well

322

enough to have made her an offer of sorts, and I believe you own the house she was taken to.'

Sadanori's hands clenched. 'I have nothing to say to you,' he said. 'This visit was ill-advised.'

'I have seen the house myself and thought it perfectly suited for a concubine,' remarked Akitada, making no move to leave. 'I was particularly struck by the theme of the decoration. Peonies. Wasn't there a first-class courtesan called "Peony" a few years ago? Her sudden disappearance raised many eyebrows.'

Sadanori jumped up and pointed a shaking finger at Akitada. 'Get out!' he shouted. 'How dare you – you, a man who plays with little boys. Aren't you in enough trouble already?'

Akitada rose with a smile. Sadanori had been involved with Peony – deeply involved, to judge by this outburst – and he had known all along who Akitada was and why he had come. In fact, Akitada now suspected that Sadanori had been behind his troubles with the chancellor. He would have liked to pursue the matter, but Sadanori's raised voice had brought the servants, and so he bowed and left.

When he got home, he found Tamako dressed for travel. She greeted him with the news that she wished him to go to Otsu with her.

Akitada gaped at his wife. Tamako had withdrawn so completely from all outside interests after Yori's death that this new forthright demand startled him. She used to have a mind of her own, charmingly most of the time and irritatingly so when they had first begun to quarrel, but she had never taken matters into her own hands and issued commands to her husband.

'A ... a delightful offer,' he stammered helplessly, because he did not want to destroy their hard-won reconciliation, 'but there is another urgent matter.'

She gave him a questioning look.

'Sadanori. Tora was quite right to suspect him. We must find Ishikawa's mother and find her quickly.'

Tamako frowned. 'Is she in danger?'

'Perhaps, though I don't think Ishikawa would kill his own mother. More importantly, Sadanori knows that I suspect him.'

Tamako protested, 'But no one seems to know where she is. Surely you won't be searching the temples for her?'

Since this had crossed his mind, Akitada said defensively, 'I thought Tora and I could visit a few near the capital. Most likely she would leave an offering, and those are recorded. We would eventually catch up with her.'

Tamako shook her head. 'I think getting the child is more important.'

Her sudden, high-handed decision dismayed Akitada, but he called Tora, who arrived looking more rested and cheerful, and explained the situation to him.

Tora glanced from Akitada to Tamako, saw the firm set of his lady's chin, and said, 'I bet Ishikawa's taken his old lady to Uji, to Sadanori's mother.'

'To Uji?' Akitada considered this. 'By heaven, yes. Why didn't I think of that?'

'He has taken his mother to Lady Saisho?'

Tamako asked. 'But why?'

'He thinks we won't look there.' The more Akitada thought about it, the better he liked it. 'Tora, you've outdone yourself. I should have realized that the pilgrimage story was meant to throw us off the track.'

Tora grinned complacently.

'We can go to Otsu via Uji,' Tamako decided. 'It will make a pleasant journey.'

Akitada agreed meekly.

Uji had long been the refuge of the wealthy and powerful from the hectic life of the capital. The air was clean and pine-scented, and the sun glinted off the burbling waters and gilded the trees. Here and there, a maple already showed the first touch of red, and birds seemed to sing more loudly, perhaps to compete with the roar of the river.

At Lady Saisho's house, Tamako dismounted before Akitada could assist her and ran to admire the view of the river gorge.

Tora said, 'It's not like this at night, sir. It's dark as hell itself, and that noise gives you goose-flesh. You can't hear what's creeping up on you. You couldn't pay me to live here.'

Akitada watched Tamako. 'Yours is not a poetic soul, Tora,' he said. 'You probably only thought of demons and specters.'

Since this was true, Tora did not answer. Instead he belabored the gate.

Akitada found another reason to be grateful for his wife's presence. The servant at first refused to admit them, but upon being informed that Lady

Sugawara was of the party, he disappeared for instructions. He returned to take Tamako and Akitada to Lady Saisho's pavilion.

There, the sun slanted in through the open veranda doors and the sound of the river filled the room. Paintings of picturesque trees and rocks, waterfalls, river bends, and steep cliffs mirrored the scenery outside.

Lady Saisho was elegantly and elaborately gowned in multicolored silks and brocade. She had not bothered with screens and was with Mrs Ishikawa, who sat beside her in her customary black and with a distinctly nervous look on her plain face.

Akitada had not met Sadanori's mother before, but he knew that she had been lady-in-waiting to the emperor's mother until her marriage to Sadanori's father. She was still very handsome, though her long hair was white. She studied Akitada and Tamako as she made polite conversation.

Tamako pleased her by praising the view and reciting softly some famous lines from the novel *Genji*.

Lady Saisho smiled. 'Yes, I dearly love this place and find the river's sound soothing, but Lady Murasaki's hero was troubled by it, I think. There are those who cannot bear the unceasing roar. They claim it is so deafening they cannot sleep.' She glanced at Mrs Ishikawa, whose face reddened.

Akitada, impatient with pleasantries, said quickly, 'Mrs Ishikawa and I are acquainted, and I am very glad to find her here. I tried in vain to

326

speak to her a few days ago in Otsu.'

Mrs Ishikawa's hands clenched, but Lady Saisho was interested. 'Really? How very auspicious your visit was in that case. Would you like some privacy?'

'Not at all. I only have a small favor to ask.' Akitada smiled pleasantly at the ladies. Mrs Ishikawa's hands relaxed slightly. 'It concerns a little boy I found near Otsu. He has lost his voice and cannot speak for himself. I've been trying to find his family and think he may be the son of a dead woman who had ties to the Masuda family. If so, Mrs Ishikawa can identify the child.'

Mrs Ishikawa cried, 'Oh, no, I couldn't. I know nothing of the child. I cannot speak about the matter.'

This astonished Lady Saisho. 'My dear,' she said, 'calm yourself and allow Lord Sugawara to explain. We must try to assist him.'

Akitada told about finding the child, and Lady Saisho was enchanted. 'Oh, the poor boy. What a very moving tale!' She turned to Mrs Ishikawa. 'Why were you told not to speak about this?'

'I ... I m–made a mistake,' Mrs Ishikawa gasped. 'It had nothing to do with that boy.'

She was not a good liar.

'I think,' said Akitada, 'that the senior lady of the Masuda household did not wish the name of the boy's mother mentioned. Her name was Peony, and she was a former courtesan from the capital. Lady Masuda's young husband kept her in the lake villa.' He paused. 'Peony was quite famous in her former life.'

Lady Saisho stared at him. 'Peony was in Otsu?

327

How old is this child?'

'I guessed about five, but Mrs Ishikawa will know more precisely.'

They all looked at her. She flushed and cried again, 'I know nothing. Why ask me? I told you it's all a mistake. It has nothing to do with me.'

But Lady Saisho grasped Mrs Ishikawa's arm so firmly that she winced. 'I think not, my dear,' she said sharply. 'You must tell us what you know about this. My son had a connection with this woman. He searched for her for many years.'

Mrs Ishikawa whimpered, 'My Lady, don't ask me. Your son would not want to know.' She burst into a torrent of tears and rushed from the room.

Lady Saisho compressed her lips and turned to Akitada. 'You must leave this matter to me. She is too upset to talk now. Perhaps you can come back later?' Akitada hesitated. Leaving the two women at this point was risky. Lady Saisho pleaded, 'I give you my word that you shall have your answer.'

He rose and helped his wife up. 'Thank you,' he said. 'Please forgive my troubling you with this. We're on our way to Otsu to get the child and will return this way tomorrow.'

Lady Saisho nodded eagerly. 'Yes, that is an excellent idea. Please do. I would very much like to see the boy myself.'

Outside, Akitada helped his wife on her horse. Tamako said, 'Lady Saisho seems to believe she has found a grandson. Is she short of grandchildren?'

'Perhaps,' said Akitada. 'Sadanori has only a grown daughter, I think.'

* * *

They reached Otsu at sunset. To Akitada's dismay, Tamako insisted on spending the night in the inn where he had been arrested.

The oily host was visibly taken aback when he saw them arrive together. No doubt he was wondering why a man who had preferred the company of small boys in his bed would reappear with a grown woman in tow.

Akitada snapped, 'Don't stand there gawking. I need lodging for myself, my wife, and my servant.' Then he saw a dilemma. Tamako would want her privacy.

Tamako clarified, 'One large room for my husband and myself, and a smaller one for a retainer.'

The host bowed. He pushed the register across for Akitada to sign and stared at Tamako.

'Mind your manners,' snapped Akitada. Turning to Tora, he said, 'You'd better see the warden and also ask around town in case Ishikawa is here. I don't feel at all easy about not knowing what he's up to.'

'As for us,' Tamako said briskly when Tora had left, 'what shall we do first?'

They spent an agreeable evening wandering around Otsu so that Tamako could see the courtesan's house and the Masuda mansion on the hill. They paid brief visits to Warden Takechi and Judge Nakano, and Tamako managed to charm both men. The judge gave permission for the boy's visit to the capital.

Then they went to Mrs Yozaemon's. She was outside with Nori, feeding her chickens. The boy

329

clung to her skirt when he saw Akitada. She invited them into her house, finding cushions and something to drink and eat while telling Tamako how Akitada had saved her son from the false charge.

Tamako smiled at Nori, but the boy did not smile back. Akitada said gently, 'The lady is my wife. I told her about you, and she wanted to meet you.'

Tamako said, 'I used to have a little boy just like you, Nori. He was four years old when he died. How old are you?'

The boy held up a hand, five fingers extended.

Tamako nodded. 'Five. I thought so. We still have some of Yori's toys. Would you like to come for a visit and play with them?'

A visit? To play with his son's toys? Akitada was confused, but when the boy looked at him, he rallied and said, 'We would be very happy if you paid us a visit.'

Nori went to clutch Mrs Yozaemon's skirt.

'He's very shy,' she apologized, stroking his hair.

'Well,' said Tamako, 'we'll come back tomorrow. Then, if he changes his mind, he can ride back with us.' She said to the boy, 'We have horses, and we'd go back along the river where the fishermen catch fish with cormorants. Would you like to see that?' The child released his hold on Mrs Yozaemon's skirt. Tamako smiled. 'And then we'll go on to the capital. You could see the emperor's palace and see the guard exercising their horses and practicing with bows and arrows. And Cook would take you to the market. The

330

market there is much bigger than here. They have all sorts of entertainers and storytellers in the capital. And many animals are for sale. Cats, and dogs, and birds in cages. Even fish and singing crickets.'

The boy's eyes flew to Akitada again. Perhaps he recalled their visit to the Otsu market. Some of the resentment faded from his expression. Akitada admired Tamako's skill and offered, 'There's a cat at our house,' suppressing a twinge of guilt about Tora's dog.

The small face lit up. He came to stand between them. Looking from one to the other, he nodded with great solemnity.

'He loves cats,' said Mrs Yozaemon, clapping her hands. 'What a nice time you'll have, Nori.'

Night was falling when they returned to the inn. Tora was waiting for them. 'No sign of Ishikawa,' he said glumly.

Akitada shook his head. 'I don't like it. I'm worried about those women in Uji, especially now that his mother is aware of our suspicions. I think you should ride back there and keep an eye on the house.'

'Tonight?'

Seeing Tora's shock, Akitada relented. 'Well, I suppose it can wait till morning, but leave at daybreak. We'll follow later with the boy.'

They parted. Akitada walked close to his wife so he could catch a trace of the orange-blossom fragrance and brush her arm casually. He was intensely aware of her, and his heart was beating faster with hope. Would she allow him to make

331

love to her? He thought he could not bear it if she rejected him again, after all this time, when he wanted her so much. He stole a sideways glance at her face. How could he ever have forgotten how beautiful his wife was? And as he thought it, he saw her blushing.

'The bath is ready, sir, madam,' announced the inn's nosy maid and waited to see what they would do next.

'Thank you,' Tamako said. 'We'll find our way.'

'Would madam like me to assist?'

'No. My husband will assist me.'

The maid giggled and left.

Akitada looked at Tamako and murmured, 'I shall enjoy that.'

The corners of her mouth twitched. 'Shall you?'

'Oh, yes. Let's hurry,' he murmured into her ear.

Making love can take circuitous routes. Caresses are exchanged under the guise of untying a sash or removing silk socks for the other person, and it is only natural to help scrub a back or rinse it with a bucket of warm water. Such moments allow a man to admire his wife's body, and a wife to touch her husband while being merely helpful.

When they returned to their room, they found their bedding spread and food waiting. For all they knew it was delicious, but they were not hungry for food.

Much later, Akitada dozed off with his sleeping wife in his arms and a smile of complete happiness on his face.

TWENTY-TWO

The Deadly River Gorge

Tora arrived back at Lady Saisho's house early the following morning. He had left while it was still dark and ridden as fast as he could without breaking his horse's legs.

The house lay silent in the gray dawn amid the roaring of the waters and eerie drifts of mist rising from the river.

He was worried. Nothing had prevented the women from setting out for the capital to warn Sadanori and Ishikawa. He decided to make sure. After tying up his horse a little distance from the house, he walked along the fence to the back where Lady Saisho's rooms overlooked the river gorge. Worrying about waking the dog brought back unhappy memories of Trouble.

At the corner, he turned and followed a narrow footpath along a steep wooded slope until both fence and path ended at the cliff edge. There, he looked up at the house. He saw the moon-viewing platform outside Lady Saisho's room only twenty feet away, but the ground was treacherous with loose rocks, and below the river tumbled through a gorge so deep that it was impenetrable mist and noise. The very air above it seemed to suck at his body. He eased around the fence.

The thought of setting off a rock slide and plunging into the gaping darkness far below made him shudder. He began to crawl upward on his hands and knees. He had almost reached the platform, and could make out the dim light of a candle burning inside behind the closed blinds, when noise reached his ears. It was muffled by the roaring waters, but he thought he heard shouts and the dog barking. He reached the veranda and stood up.

Two women's shadows moved behind the blinds. Breathing a sigh of relief, Tora hoisted himself up on the veranda. The boards were slick with dew and treacherous, but he was not going back.

A third shadow appeared inside, a man who knelt and bowed. A servant or messenger? Tora crept up to the blinds and put his eye to a crack and suppressed a gasp. The face that had appeared for a moment was the face of Ishikawa. Then he heard voices.

'What is this? What do you want here at this hour?' Lady Saisho sounded angry.

Ishikawa said, 'Begging your pardon, My Lady, but my master was concerned about your safety. And I just heard from Seijiro that you had visitors.'

'What is that to you or my son?'

'Your son has reason to suspect that Lord Sugawara is plotting against him.'

Mrs Ishikawa cried, 'Oh, son, you're not in trouble again?'

'Nonsense, Mother.' Ishikawa's voice was

334

harsh. 'Beware of your rash tongue and remember the two noble houses we serve. Foolish words can do much harm.'

Lady Sadanori snapped, 'You will not speak that way to your mother in my presence. She is upset enough with your behavior. We are safe, and you may leave.'

'I'm sorry, My Lady. Seijiro says that Lord Sugawara's party is planning to return. It will be best if he finds you gone. You may gather a few things and return with me to the capital. Seijiro is getting the sedan chair ready.'

Tora cursed softly. He wondered how many men Ishikawa had with him.

Lady Saisho broke the short silence with an outraged: 'How dare you tell me what to do? I'm not going anywhere!'

Tora relaxed a little and wondered how Ishikawa would manage that one. He was beginning to like Sadanori's mother.

Ishikawa muttered something under his breath. 'We're wasting time,' he said. 'I have my orders. You must get dressed or you'll leave in your nightclothes.'

Mrs Ishikawa whimpered. 'Son, you mustn't speak that way to Her Ladyship. It isn't proper.'

'You will have to tie me up then,' snapped Lady Saisho, 'for I will not go.'

Ishikawa's voice sounded desperate. 'You must. Your son's life is at stake.'

Lady Saisho snorted. 'Ridiculous. I shall see you dismissed for this.'

Mrs Ishikawa burst into tears and rushed to her son. He pushed her aside, saying harshly, 'Get her ready, Mother. You're both leaving now. It's a fine thing when women set their minds against men.'

'You're nothing but a servant, Ishikawa.' Lady Saisho folded her arms and turned her back on him.

Outside, Tora considered. If he burst in on the scene, he might well find himself surrounded by Ishikawa's people and killed. That would not serve anyone. On the other hand, Ishikawa would prevail over Lady Saisho. He sounded determined enough. In that case, he, Tora, could do nothing but trail them to the capital.

He turned to cast an uneasy glance at the gorge gaping below, when he heard a woman's cry of pain.

Inside, behind the blinds, two figures were struggling; the third rushed to help and was flung aside so violently that she came stumbling through the blind, slipped on the boards, and fell. It was Mrs Ishikawa.

Lady Saisho cried for help, and Tora made up his mind. He flung aside the torn blind and jumped into the room.

Ishikawa had hold of Lady Saisho – in her night robe and with her white hair hanging loose.

'Let her go,' Tora growled.

They stared at him. Ishikawa released the old lady and reached for his sword.

Tora's own sword was tied to the saddle of his horse. He crouched, his eyes on Ishikawa.

Lady Saisho said, 'Put away that weapon, Ishikawa! How dare you bring a sword into my quarters?' When Ishikawa ignored her, she raised her voice. 'Seijiro!'

Ishikawa laughed. 'Seijiro isn't coming.'

But Seijiro did come. He slunk in nervously behind a couple of frightened maids, who burst into the room to clutch at Lady Saisho.

Tora decided Ishikawa was alone. 'Don't be a fool,' he said. 'Why kill more people?'

Ishikawa called to Seijiro, 'He's a robber. Grab him.'

Seijiro took a step forward.

'No.' Lady Saisho shook off the two maids. 'Ishikawa's gone mad, Seijiro,' she said. 'Disarm him and lock him up until we can send for my son.'

Seijiro blinked and stopped in indecision.

Tora said, 'Ishikawa's wanted for murder.'

Ishikawa laughed. 'Yes, yours.' He started forward. 'You won't live to repeat your slander.'

The tall candles flickered and spattered in the draft from the torn blind. Tora risked a glance, but this was a lady's room and contained no convenient weapons. The maids whimpered, and behind him, Mrs Ishikawa sobbed her heart out. Tora shivered. The current of air carried the musty smell of rotting things – the rank breath of the gorge. He feared having his back to it and moved away from the door.

Lady Saisho said, 'Only a coward would cut down an unarmed man.'

Ishikawa shot her a venomous glance. 'A gentleman does not cross swords with scum.'

Tora ignored the slur in the supreme confidence that he was a soldier and Ishikawa was not. Even an unarmed man could win against an inexperienced fighter, and this Ishikawa was a coward as well, as Lady Saisho had pointed out. Though he held a sword, the former student hesitated, not sure how to proceed. It was a great deal easier to strike an old man down when his back was turned than to use an unfamiliar sword against a young and alert adversary. Tora kept his eyes on Ishikawa's sword hand and waited.

Mrs Ishikawa scrabbled on the veranda behind him, and Ishikawa's hand tightened its grip. The next moment, he lunged at Tora. Tora spun away easily, catching Ishikawa's sword arm with his left hand and jerking it. Ishikawa gasped, stumbled, and fell to his knees.

Short and sweet, Tora thought, and twisted the sword from Ishikawa's hand. He was about to put its point against the other man's neck, when the women screamed, and a heavy weight hit his back, pitching him forward to the floor. He landed on his chin, jarring his teeth and nearly knocking himself out. Half dazed, he realized that Ishikawa's mother had come from behind and flung herself on him. She was clawing at his throat and head, and he was about to throw her off when someone stepped hard on his hand. He lost his grip on Ishikawa's sword as pain shot up his arm, but the pain cleared his head. With a curse, he tossed the woman off and rolled away. He heard rather than saw the blade strike the boards near his shoulder and rolled again until he came up against a wall. The room seemed filled with movement and noise, but he focused on Ishikawa. When the sword hissed down again, he flung himself forward and grabbed for Ishikawa's legs. Ishikawa skipped away, but his sword had missed.

Tora managed to get to his feet and put some distance between himself and his attacker. He was still a little dizzy and his hand throbbed, but he no longer had the river gorge behind his back. Ishikawa was now about ten feet away, his face contorted with rage.

His mother cowered on the floor, her mouth open in mute fear. The others huddled in a corner, Seijiro standing in front of Lady Saisho, and the maids cowering behind. The fight was between him and Ishikawa – and possibly that vicious mother of his.

Ishikawa laughed. He had found his courage at last. 'Look who's the coward now,' he cried. 'I think I'll kill you slowly. One cut at a time. Like this.' He darted for Tora with the quickness of a snake and struck at his thigh. Tora felt the blade sear his skin as he jumped out of the way. He was now close to the women's bedding and risked getting tangled in it, but his move had taken Ishikawa towards the platform. He danced about a little, then feinted again. Tora, cursing the other man's agility, jumped aside again, too far this time, so that he slipped on a silk quilt and almost fell.

Ishikawa laughed again, and so – horribly – did his mother.

Tora's patience was gone. Scooping up the quilt, he flung it at Ishikawa's face, then made a grab for one of the tall candlesticks. The candle fell and rolled away, but the candlestick was iron, and the moment he held it in his throbbing hand, he was filled with enough fury to kill.

Ishikawa was fighting free of the quilt, slashing about with his sword. His mother rushed to help him. Tora heard her scream and saw her fall, but Ishikawa was free and attacked. Tora deflected the sword with the candlestick. The blade clanged and jumped away, and he pressed forward immediately, swinging the iron candleholder at Ishikawa's head. He saw fear on Ishikawa's face as he backed away. Tora pursued, forcing him through the blind and out on to the platform.

There, with the river roaring below him, Ishikawa panicked. He rushed forward, slashing wildly, across boards that were too wet and slick for that sort of footwork. He slipped, tried to catch his balance, skidded, and fell over the edge of the veranda to sprawl on the rocks.

Tora followed more carefully. He stepped down from the platform and went across the stones towards the fallen man.

Ishikawa got up on his hands and knees and scrambled up the loose rocks.

Tora saw disaster coming and froze in place.

The rocks began to slide towards the edge – slowly at first, then faster – taking Ishikawa with them.

Ishikawa let go of his sword and scrabbled for something, anything, to hold on to. There was nothing. Tora flung himself down and stretched out an arm. Terror in his rolling eyes, Ishikawa reached for it, but the distance was too great. He made a desperate effort and loosened more stones beneath him, slipping downward towards the edge of the cliff. An ominous rumble began and gained in volume. The rock slide gathered momentum, and Tora flattened himself against the hillside.

He lay still and prayed. Through the rumbling, he heard Ishikawa scream once, shrilly, as he plunged over the edge. His wail faded away among the boiling mists of the gorge. The shifting stones slowed to a trickle. Then all was silent.

Tora raised his head. He was alone. Cautiously, he crept back up the hill until he reached the corner support of the platform. He was shaking so badly that he could not pull himself up right away.

Slowly, his relief at being alive gave way to the realization that his master would not approve of this night's work.

Nori seemed to enjoy the trip. There was no cormorant fishing in the daytime, but they stopped to see the birds and boats and all the paraphernalia that were used for it.

This pleasant mood changed abruptly when they reached Lady Saisho's. Akitada halted when he saw the gates standing wide open. He passed the child to Tamako, told her to wait outside, then drew his sword and rode in.

The corpse of a broken man lay in the middle of the yard in a puddle of blood and water, and Tora stepped down from the veranda where he had been sitting. Akitada heaved a sigh of relief, put away his sword, and looked at the body more closely.

'Ishikawa,' said Tora unnecessarily. 'We fished him out of the river after sunrise.'

'What happened?'

Tora gave him a brief outline of the night's events.

'And the women?'

'His mother's hurt. He caught her with his sword.'

Tamako, with Nori, came up to the gate and peered in. Akitada went back to explain. She nodded. 'Don't look, Nori,' she said to the boy. 'There has been an accident, but it does not concern us.'

Akitada said nothing; the 'accident' concerned the child very much indeed. He wondered what new complications the unexpected death of their prime suspect would bring to the case.

They dismounted at the steps to the villa. Akitada led them up and into the reception area, where he clapped his hands and shouted for the servant.

A pale-faced Seijiro appeared and bowed. 'My lady expects you, sir.' He led them to the same pavilion where Lady Saisho had received them the day before. Lady Saisho herself slid the door back.

Akitada's eyes scanned the room. The torn blind to the outside was lowered. Filtered sunlight fell on a floor that still showed traces of bloodstains. In a corner lay a swaddled shape under a layer of quilts. The boy clutched Akitada's hand.

'Thank heaven you are in time,' Lady Saisho said. 'She is very weak.' Her eyes went to the child. 'Oh, he is a handsome child. Are you sure he cannot speak?'

Akitada nodded.

'Well,' said Lady Saisho, 'we shall know more in a moment. Come.' She led them to the swaddled shape and lifted a corner of the quilt. Mrs Ishikawa lay on her back with her head supported by a wooden neck rest. Only her face and her hands showed. They were almost as white as snow, and her skin seemed transparent. Though her eyes were closed, Akitada guessed from the set of her lips that she was conscious and in pain.

Tamako came to kneel beside her. 'Mrs Ishikawa?' she asked, reaching for a frail hand. 'Can you hear me?' There was no response, and Tamako looked up at Lady Saisho. 'Has a physician been called?'

'Yes, but ... she lost so much blood. She is very weak. Look.' Lady Saisho moved forward. For a moment the two women bent over Mrs Ishikawa and Akitada could see nothing. They lifted the quilt, looked, and then replaced it.

When Lady Saisho stepped aside, Akitada saw that Tamako was very pale. She glanced up at him and shook her head slightly.

Feeling bitterly disappointed, Akitada turned to take the boy away. Once again, he had come too late.

But Lady Saisho said, 'Wait.' She bent over Mrs Ishikawa again. 'Listen to me,' she said quite sternly. 'You are dying. I'm very sorry for it, but you must be told. You have a chance to make good an evil that will otherwise destroy you and your son in the other world.'

Tamako bit her lip, and Akitada felt slightly sickened, though he knew the need for the

343

speech. He took the boy back to the dying woman.

Lady Saisho commanded, 'Open your eyes and look at this child.'

The thin lids fluttered and Mrs Ishikawa looked up at her. 'My son?' she whispered, and tears seeped from the corners of her eyes.

'He is dead. What you say cannot hurt him any longer.' Lady Saisho was matter-of-fact. 'Look at this boy, and tell me if he is the child of the woman Peony.'

'I must not tell.'

Lady Saisho gripped the other woman's shoulder. 'You must. There is no more time.'

Tamako half rose and protested, 'Oh, please don't.'

Mrs Ishikawa's eyes flicked to her. Then she turned her head slightly, letting her eyes pass over Akitada to the boy. She looked at him for a long moment. Then she turned her head away and nodded. 'Yes. That is Peony's son.'

'Ah.' Lady Saisho rose, her face alight with triumph.

Akitada passed the boy to Tamako, who took him from the room. He said, 'It proves only that the child's mother was Peony.'

Mrs Ishikawa was on the point of death. Her breath rattled ominously. Akitada bent over her. 'Mrs Ishikawa,' he said, 'forgive me for troubling you, but did you take some food, gruel perhaps, to Peony's house when young Lord Masuda was ill?'

The rattling in her throat stopped. She opened her eyes and raised her head. 'I didn't know,' she gasped. 'The gruel. I didn't know.' Her black eyes bored into his.

Akitada nodded. 'Yes, I'm afraid it was poisoned.'

'Oh!' She wailed and flung her head back so violently that the wooden neck rest tipped and her head hit the floor.

Lady Saisho cried, 'What are you doing? She has said all that matters.'

'There is still the matter of murder,' Akitada said. 'Young Masuda died of poison, and Mrs Ishikawa took it to him.' He knelt and lifted the dying woman's head on his knee.

Lady Saisho gasped. 'She murdered him?'

'No, I think her son used her.'

Mrs Ishikawa flailed weakly. The awful rattling began again. Her convulsion must have opened her wound because fresh blood was seeping from beneath the quilt. But she lay still now, her head on Akitada's knee, tears welling from her eyes.

'It was your son who sent you with the gruel, wasn't it?' Akitada asked softly.

She looked up at him and opened her mouth, perhaps to answer or to wail again, but all she managed was a harsh gurgle. Her stare became fixed and her jaw sagged. A thin trickle of saliva seeped from the corner of her mouth.

Akitada felt her neck and found no pulse. He placed her head back on the floor and got up. 'She is dead,' he said.

'Why do you look at me that way?' demanded Lady Saisho. 'It is not my fault she died. Her own son killed her.'

'I was told it was an accident.'

345

'You were not here. The man was deranged. He broke into my quarters and attacked both of us. He tried to kill your man, but he wounded his mother instead. We are well rid of such a man.'

Akitada controlled himself and said, 'We shall leave now. I regret extremely this upsetting experience for the child. Unfortunately, it was necessary.'

'No. The child must stay. My son will be here shortly.'

'I shall speak to Lord Sadanori another time.'

She barred his way. 'You cannot take my grandson away. I forbid it.'

Akitada suddenly felt pity instead of anger. 'Does your son have other children?'

'A grown daughter only. That is why...' She broke off. 'The boy is his. He must be. Sadanori looked just like him at that age.'

'He is most likely young Masuda's son.'

'No. Never.'

'I am truly sorry.'

She was silent for a moment. Then she said, 'You must prove that he is ours. They say you are clever. When you find the proof, I will pay you well and Sadanori will advance you at court. He is the chancellor's cousin and can raise you far beyond your dreams.'

Akitada bowed and walked out.

TWENTY-THREE

Trouble Returns

Akitada blamed himself for putting the child through a confrontation with the dying woman. Tora was also unhappy. Akitada thought his gloom was due to having inadvertently caused two deaths, but Tora seemed cool enough about the Ishikawas.

'I wish the bastard had confessed first,' Tora muttered. 'Now you've only got his mother's word about the poisoning. And you say she never blamed it on him.'

'No. But then she was his mother and she loved him. Having a child means protecting him, come what may.'

They were riding homeward, and he glanced over at Tamako and Nori. His wife's arms held the boy securely, and her head was bent to his. She seemed to be chatting, and the child smiled up at her. His heart warmed, but he feared that she might become too attached.

His own recent efforts at detachment made him see the child's situation in a new light. The tangled lines of the troubled history of two families formed a tight knot, and Nori was at its center. The child had at least part of the answer, and

Akitada wished he could speak. Perhaps he was as callous as Lady Saisho, but he wanted answers. Human obsessions, his own as much as those of the Masudas and of Sadanori and Ishikawa, had been responsible for the confusion and eventual disaster.

However, his comment about mothers' love had cheered Tora, who broke into Akitada's thoughts with: 'Hanae thinks we'll have a boy.'

Akitada smiled. 'Women know such things.' He looked over at his wife and said, 'I am deeply in your debt, Tamako. Thank you for your help.'

'What help?'

'For coming with me to Otsu. For your wise counsel. And for your patience and forgiveness.'

She blinked and looked away. 'Oh, Akitada, it was nothing,' she murmured.

'I'm sorry about the scene at Uji. If I'd taken the right steps earlier, I could have spared you that.'

She said earnestly, 'You must stop blaming yourself for everything. It's one thing to set things right for other people, and quite another to take on everyone's burdens.'

'I have been a fool, and look where it got me.'

'Nonsense. This is no worse than our usual predicaments.'

And that made him laugh.

They reached home at dusk and were greeted by the sound of barking. Tora gave a joyful whoop. 'I'd know that bark anywhere.' He pounded on the gate. 'Trouble!'

Inside, the dog yipped his excitement, and

348

heavy steps came running. Then Genba threw wide the gate, his face all smiles. 'Trouble found his way home on his own,' he cried. 'I heard him scratching and whining outside the gate last night, and there he was.'

It was a joyous and confused homecoming. The dog, looking thinner and missing part of an ear, rushed about, barking and jumping up at them. Hanae came running and flung herself into Tora's arms. Tamako's maid peered from the doorway and ran down the steps to greet her mistress. Seimei hobbled slowly to the top of the stairs. Even Cook ran out of the kitchen with a smile on her face.

Akitada went to greet Seimei. Seimei smiled, but he lost no time telling Akitada that the board of censors expected him to report.

This was a heavy blow because it meant that his case had been found serious enough to warrant an official investigation. An investigation alone carried the stigma of public disgrace. For a moment, Akitada's mind reeled, then he bit his lip and accompanied Seimei inside to read the document.

The letter was no more enlightening than Seimei's blunt report, but Akitada looked up from it and said, 'It must be Sadanori's doing. He did this to stop my meddling in his affairs. I wonder what he will say when I tell him that Ishikawa is dead and that he is suspected of several murders.'

Seimei looked nervous. 'You are not going to see Lord Sadanori again?'

'Even without the summons from the board, I

349

would have to speak to him. There are loose ends in this case, and the boy deserves to know what happened to his parents.'

Seimei twisted his thin old hands in silent protest.

Akitada touched his shoulder. 'Seimei, trust me. All will be well. Her Ladyship has taken us in hand.'

That made Seimei smile again. 'Oh, very good,' he said. 'Then happiness has indeed returned to this house.'

But 'trouble' had also returned, both figuratively and literally. While he was not certain how deep Sadanori's involvement in the murders went, Tora's report of the conversation between Ishikawa and his master suggested that Sadanori knew about them.

Akitada washed and changed his clothes, then went to tell Tamako about the summons from the board. Nori was sitting on the floor playing with Hanae's white cat. He looked like any happy, healthy little boy.

Tamako listened to his news and sighed. 'I suppose it had to happen. You will know how to answer them.' They had both learned that the decisions made by the mighty were not always based on reason and truth, and that punishment and reward were equally unpredictable.

'You won't mind living in poverty again?'

She shook her head and smiled at him.

His heart lifted with hope. 'I'm on my way to see Sadanori,' he said.

Her smile changed to alarm. 'Take Tora.'

'You know I must see Sadanori privately.'

'Yes, but ... he could wait outside.'

He laughed. 'You haven't seen Sadanori. I'm a much better fighter than he.'

'You will take your sword?'

'No, that's not what I meant. I wouldn't be admitted. I meant with my bare hands.' He flexed them and scowled ferociously.

Tamako giggled. She had always had a very pretty laugh. 'Be careful and hurry back, husband,' she murmured.

A short while later, when Akitada was sitting on the bottom step of the stairs, putting on his shoes, he noticed a strange rumbling sound that seemed to come from beneath his feet. He paused to listen. Trouble was barking furiously in the stable, and birds fluttered among the trees. Akitada got up and crossed the yard quickly, afraid that some part of a building or wall had collapsed.

But all seemed intact in the stable. Only the horses moved nervously and looked at him with large liquid eyes showing their whites. Trouble came, his fur standing in a ridge along his spine. He pushed his nose into Akitada's hand, whined and wagged his tail. Shaking his head, Akitada went back outside, glanced up at all the roofs and scanned the walls. Finding nothing out of the ordinary, he left on his errand.

Akitada was convinced that Sadanori had been an unwilling tool in Ishikawa's hands. He had a marriageable daughter who was his heiress, and Ishikawa had played a game of murder to implicate Sadanori until he was ripe for blackmail.

The last time Akitada and Ishikawa had crossed paths, the young man had also resorted to blackmail when he had discovered a guilty secret. This time he had created the guilty secret himself.

What Akitada was about to do would seem to Sadanori like more blackmail – all the more so because the powerful Fujiwara noble had caused serious problems for Akitada and was in a position not only to reverse them, but to further Akitada's career. Men like Sadanori were used to the greed of lesser mortals. It would be much wiser not to irritate Sadanori further, but that was impossible.

The great man's house lay quiet in the westering sun. There was little activity in the courtyard, and the servant who met Akitada seemed glad of a break in the tedium. He took Akitada into a small reception hall and disappeared to announce him to his master.

Time passed. Akitada was restless. After sitting for a while, he got up and paced. More time passed.

Akitada decided that Sadanori had left him waiting in order to be insulting. Thoroughly irritated, he pushed up a shutter and stepped out on to a veranda overlooking the lake and private gardens. The bright blue-tiled roof beyond the far trees must be the new pavilion. And there, in a distance, he saw his unwilling host – his plump figure in a blue gown unmistakable – jogging away past the lake to the pavilion.

Akitada turned and went back inside. The servant returned to inform him that his master was not at home and it was not known when he would return.

Suppressing anger, Akitada thanked the man and left. He walked quickly around the walled compound to the back gate. When there was no response to his knock, he pushed the gate open and took the path to the pavilion.

The garden seemed strangely silent. No birds sang. Near the water's edge some twenty ducks milled about nervously. Sadanori had had the building raised nearly five feet above ground level – probably for an unobstructed view across the lake to his residence and over the shining roofs of palaces beyond, all the way to the green hills outside the city.

Akitada climbed the stairs, and Sadanori called out, 'Who is there? I do not wish to be disturbed.'

Akitada said nothing and crossed the veranda.

'Go away!' Sadanori sounded irascible.

Akitada found him sitting at a desk in the nearest room, drumming his fingers and glaring at the door.

'You!' he gasped.

Akitada made him a mocking bow. 'A charming place for us to meet. Private, yet luxurious.' The room was not large, but the mats on the sparkling floor were very thick and bound in silk. Sadanori's desk was of the finest cedar wood and furnished with writing implements carved from ivory and jade.

Sadanori glowered. 'I don't want to see you. Who let you in?'

Akitada seated himself on a green silk cushion. 'What a very handsome robe,' he said lightly. It was in fact a very beautiful and expensive pale blue silk with a woven pattern of clouds. 'I happened to see you from the reception room and followed to bring you news from your mother.'

Sadanori's jaw clenched. 'My mother? You were trying to curry favor with my mother? I'm warning you, Sugawara, it won't do you any good.'

'I think,' said Akitada, 'you're under some misapprehension. I'm not here on my account.'

Sadanori's eyes narrowed. 'You're not? My mother is in good health, I hope?'

'Distraught, but well.'

'Distraught? What happened?'

'Two violent deaths are not reassuring events to witness.'

The other man's eyes widened. He gulped. Akitada let him wait. Finally, Sadanori gasped, 'Wh— who died?'

'Ishikawa died last night, and his mother this morning.'

Now Sadanori was frightened. 'Y–you k–killed them?'

'Of course not. But they talked before they died.'

Turning pale, Sadanori shouted, 'Get out. Get away from me. Help!'

His voice was not very loud, and the pavilion was a long way from the main house. Akitada sighed. 'You should be glad to be rid of your blackmailer.'

Sadanori stared at him as he thought about this. He still looked a little green and his hands still plucked nervously at his robe, but he weighed Akitada's words. 'Why are you here?'

'To tell you what happened.'

'I want to know what they said.'

So Sadanori was already beginning to fight back.

'You have been implicated in several murders.' It was not altogether an untruth, if you took in the conversation Tora had overheard here in this pavilion. Much now depended on manipulating Sadanori into making a mistake, a slip of the tongue that would confirm Akitada's suspicions.

Sadanori opened his mouth to speak when it happened.

The carved-ivory water container on his desk began to move. They both stared at it in astonishment. Akitada felt a faint trembling and wondered if Sadanori's agitation had transferred itself to the floor they were sitting on. Then all the implements on the desk started to slide about and the floor beneath him shook. Outside, the waterfowl took to the air with loud quacking and a clatter of wings. Akitada had the oddest impression of shifting, or rather of the walls around him shifting – or perhaps of the building sliding sideways. He caught his breath, trying to make sense of it, when Sadanori yelped, 'Earthquake!' and jumped to his feet to flee.

Before Akitada could follow, another rolling shake started, the ivory water container danced off the desk, and outside tiles crashed to the ground. The new wooden beams squealed like wounded animals, and a bamboo stand fell over, spilling Sadanori's library across the floor. Sadanori stumbled over them and out the door. Akitada heard him running down the staircase.

Akitada got up when the tremor ceased. It was safer outside, provided he was not hit by the tiles sliding down from the roof. Looking up at the ceiling, he saw small cracks. Massive timbers supported this floor and the heavy tile roof above him. Some dust sifted down, but the room looked stable enough. It depended on how long a quake lasted and how strong the shocks were. Perhaps the worst was over.

It was not. The next shock caused him to stumble. This time the floor under his feet rolled like a ship at sea. The building creaked and squealed. Akitada staggered to the door and on to the veranda. He clutched a pillar at the top of the stairs, gauging his chances of running down, when more tiles fell, smashing on the stairs and the ground. Dust rose as he clung on and wondered where Sadanori was. He thought of Tamako and the rest of his family and of his own house. It had withstood earthquakes before, but never in such a derelict condition. At least they had no tiles to worry about. He looked across the lake towards the city. It shimmered oddly in the sulphurous light of the sunset, but looked peaceful enough. The great danger in an earthquake was fire. All it would take was one oil lamp falling over, or a hot coal spilling from a brazier, and the flames would race quickly from house to house.

When the earth stopped moving and no more tiles fell, Akitada ran down the steps, leaping over the debris of broken tiles and putting some distance between himself and the pavilion. Then he looked back. A portion of the roof was bare of tiles, and a few veranda supports leaned here and there. In a distance he heard people shouting. There was no sign of Sadanori. Once again fate had interfered at the wrong moment.

Akitada was turning towards the gate when he caught a glimpse of blue. It was under the pavilion, where it had no business being. He approached the building cautiously to look, but he knew already. Sadanori, in his panic, had crept under his new pavilion.

'You'd better come out,' Akitada called. 'It's not safe down there.'

There was no answer. Akitada took another step and saw that one of the main supports of the pavilion, a huge beam that rested on a flat rock and held up, along with three others, the elegant, but fragile structure above, had slipped far enough off its foundation that another jolt would bring the whole pavilion down on top of Sadanori.

'Come out,' Akitada shouted. 'The building may fall. Hurry!'

There was still no reply. What was wrong with the man? Maybe a tile had stunned him. Or perhaps he was so afraid of Akitada that he would risk his life to avoid him.

It was a desperate choice. Someone in his own home might be hurt. Akitada hesitated, then ducked under the pavilion. Tora had hidden here when he overheard Sadanori speaking to Ishikawa. Sadanori was probably not worth saving, but watching him being crushed would be worse. He would grab him and drag him out into the open. And later, if all went well, he'd get the truth out of him.

Akitada bent double as he made his way to the cowering figure in the blue silk robe. Sadanori had lost his tall hat – Akitada stumbled over it – and sat with his head between his knees and covered by his arms.

'Sadanori,' said Akitada, 'stop this foolishness. There's no time. The building is slipping. You may be crushed at any moment. Come out.'

'No,' sobbed the other man. 'I'll die. It's my fate.'

Akitada cursed under his breath and took hold of Sadanori's arm. Jerking him up, he half carried, half dragged him towards light and safety.

But there was not enough time. The earth shook again, and the structure above them moaned in protest. Thinking of Tamako and his people, Akitada dropped Sadanori and scrambled towards the open. If he could at least reach the veranda overhang, he might be protected when the heavier timbers collapsed.

He managed a few more steps, then the ground under him rolled and heaved as if alive, and he fell to his knees. The large beam slipped with a slow squeal. One by one the horizontal supports above cracked, popped, tore, and splintered, and then the whole structure collapsed on him. For a moment the sound was deafening and it turned dark. Something heavy fell down in front of Akitada and blocked his way. The dust was thick and made his eyes burn and filled his nostrils until he choked. He was on his belly without knowing how he'd got there. Coughing, he tried to slide around the obstruction, to find a way out, but something pinned him from behind. When he used his right arm to feel around, he found that the floor of the pavilion was now within inches of his back and shoulders and touched his thighs. He could not reach any farther, and he could not move his legs.

An initial fear that he was injured severely and possibly paralyzed passed when he became aware of pain in his legs.

At about the same time, he heard Sadanori. The sound curdled Akitada's blood. The high keening noise was followed by a rattle and did not sound human.

Akitada guessed that Sadanori was less than five feet behind him, but debris separated them. He cleared his throat and called out, 'Sadanori?'

The keening paused.

'Are you hurt?' Akitada was not sure how badly he himself was hurt – the pain was mostly in his right leg – but he thought on the whole he had been lucky. Much depended on what happened next. Even if the main tremors were past, aftershocks were common, and the slightest movement might bring down the debris, which merely pinned his legs now, and crush him.

Sadanori said something, but his words were unintelligible.

'Somebody will come and get us out,' Akitada told him. That opened up new and frightening possibilities. Sadanori's servants scrambling about among the broken timbers could well cause a fatal collapse.

Sadanori suddenly raised his voice and said

clearly, 'I'm dying.'

Appalled, Akitada asked, 'Where are you hurt?'

'My arm hurts.'

That hardly sounded fatal, and Sadanori's voice was quite strong. Trust the man to wail over a small injury, thought Akitada. He put Sadanori's problems from his mind and concentrated on his own situation. His right leg still hurt. Worse, he had no feeling in the lower part of it any longer. For all he knew, part of the limb was gone. He gulped down fear and worked his right hand back to feel along his body. At his hip, he encountered the beam which seemed to rest on him. His left hand moved more freely, and his left leg seemed only pinned. He could move his foot. He began a cautious effort to free it, but something shifted as he moved and now pressed on his shoulder. It was becoming hard to breathe. Akitada tried to suppress a rising panic, but he still had night-mares of the weeks he had spent buried in a mine on Sado island. His heart started racing and he was gasping when Sadanori began his dreadful keening again.

Akitada forgot his own terror and got angry. 'Shut up!' he shouted.

Sadanori broke off.

'What makes you think you're worth saving?' Akitada asked nastily.

Sadanori sobbed.

Feeling better, Akitada put him from his mind and used his hands to dig away the dirt under-neath him. The ground was soft down here. He prayed that the beam, or whatever pinned him, was supported by something other than his body, and that he could get enough purchase to crawl out.

Sadanori suddenly said, 'I would not have hurt Hanae. I just wanted her to see what I could do for her. If the chancellor had not summoned me and kept me all day, this would not have happened.'

Akitada snarled, 'You lie. You had your servant drug her and tie her up. She escaped on her own a day later.'

'It's the stupid woman's fault. She exceeded her orders.'

Akitada did not think that worth a response.

Sadanori tried again. 'I did not intend any of it to happen. How can I be responsible for what Ishikawa did?'

Akitada stopped digging. What was he talking about? Still angry, he said, 'You're beyond the human law now, but the judge of the underworld will know exactly what you did.'

Sadanori wept noisily.

On an impulse, Akitada added, 'Your only option is to make a clean breast of it so that the living will not suffer for your deeds.'

Sadanori wept harder.

Akitada went on digging. He was sweating from the exertion, but so far nothing else had shifted and he could now twist his body a little.

'Am I really dying?'

Akitada almost laughed. 'How should I know?' he snapped. 'I thought you said you were.'

After a moment, Sadanori said sadly, 'Yes, I am. I hope it's quick.'

Akitada paused to rest. 'In that case you'd better confess now,' he said hopefully.

'We'll both die, so what's the point?'

'I'm not,' Akitada said with more conviction than he felt. 'I'm digging myself out.' And he started on his labors again.

And then the first of the aftershocks hit.

TWENTY-FOUR

The Truth

Akitada's first thought was that a quick death would have been preferable. It was not the pain in his arm and back that seemed unbearable, or that his chest felt crushed, but rather it was not being able to breathe. Or at least not enough. Every fiber in his body wanted to gulp air, but could not.

Panic seized him. He would die here, in minutes that would feel like hours. He was trapped and would suffocate. A fitting punishment for his cruelty to Yori, to Tamako, to Tora and Genba, and even to the dog. The gods had given him back a measure of happiness, only to snatch it all away.

Whatever weighed down on his chest had probably broken ribs, though breathing was not so much painful as very difficult. Except for the tiniest breath of dust-laden air, which choked him and teased his body into futile spasms that brought nothing but pain, he could not fully inhale.

He could still move his right arm, the one that did not hurt, and felt around with it. As far as he could make out, the last shock had settled the weight of the building on his body. His frantic efforts to breathe made matters worse. He concentrated on regulating his breathing. By taking slow, shallow breaths, he made his panic subside a little. He thought of Tamako. It seemed a pity that his life should end before they had a chance for another life together.

Perhaps he had thrown away that chance. Once disrespected, it was gone forever. But that was superstition. And he worried about Tamako. Heaven forbid she should be in such straits and he not there to help her. Then he thought about fire. What if she was trapped in a burning house?

His wrenching fear for her caused him to gulp for air, and he choked again on thick dust. After an agonizing sneezing and coughing fit, he pushed his terror aside. The others would look after Tamako. Unlike Sadanori's people, who seemed not to have missed him, Tora and Genba could be relied on. He listened for Sadanori and heard an odd snuffling noise.

'Sadanori?' he croaked.

Silence.

'Sadanori? Is that you?' Silly question, and no wonder he got no answer. But the snuffling had stopped. Speaking had wrought more havoc with his breathing, and Akitada gasped and rested. Then he tried again. 'Sadanori, did you tell your people where you were going?'

A sob and a soft, 'No.'

So the man who was responsible for his present condition still lived and was probably better off. Akitada felt resentful. The fool! No one would bother checking this building until other emergencies and damage to the main house had been taken care of. He took in more air and choked again. The blood pounded in his temples. It was not likely that he could last that long.

'She was so beautiful.' Sadanori's voice sounded dreamy.

'What?' Akitada was not sure he had heard correctly.

'Peony. She was mine. My wife to be. Did you know that I planned this place for her? We were to live here together. She left me before I could finish it.'

Akitada closed his eyes. He no longer cared to hear the dreary love confessions of a man who could have bought any woman he wanted.

'Masuda came like a thief and took her from me. Who would allow such a thing?'

Against his better intentions, Akitada asked, 'What did you do?'

'Clever Ishikawa found her in Otsu. She would not come back.'

'She died a pauper.'

Sadanori sobbed. 'I loved her. I will always love her.'

'Did you tell Ishikawa to kill them both?'

Silence. Then softly, 'No, oh no. I thought...' Sadanori's voice faded.

'He sent his mother to poison Masuda. And he

364

killed the doctor and Peony's maid because they knew about it. On your instructions.' Akitada gasped for air.

Sadanori said something very faintly, but Akitada was coughing and did not hear. 'Are you all right?' Akitada asked when he could speak again, surprising himself.

'I'm dying. May Amida help me.'

Perhaps he was dying, perhaps not. Akitada felt callous about the spoiled Fujiwara lord's fate. 'If you had told your people where you were going,' he said with a certain satisfaction, 'they would be here by now.'

Sadanori did not speak again for a long time, but the periodic sound of sobbing and whimpering meant that he was still alive. Akitada used his free hand to scratch away at the dirt again. It seemed hopeless; he could no longer get his fingers under his body except just below his chin. Mercifully, there were no more shocks, and after a lot of scratching and scraping, he breathed easier. Encouraged, he worked harder.

Sadanori said suddenly, 'I would never have allowed Ishikawa to kill Peony. He did not kill her. Masuda deserved to die. But not the others. I did not want that.'

Akitada managed to ease his left shoulder away from whatever had rested on it. His left arm was still caught, but hurt less. He ignored Sadanori and concentrated on freeing himself. After more grubbing under his body, the fingers of his right hand were bleeding. Never mind. He had certainly suffered worse in his lifetime, and Tamako was worth every effort.

Sadanori was still talking to himself. Something about stars. Perhaps he was reciting poetry. Or hallucinating. For that matter, there were some chinks and slivers of light in the murky darkness. Akitada bit down on his lip and gave his left arm a sharp jerk. Something shifted and his clothing tore and then he was blessedly free. Or rather, his upper body was free.

'Sugawara?'

'Hmm?' Akitada flexed his left arm and hand. They hurt too much to be useful. With a sigh he began scratching at the dirt with his bleeding right hand again.

'What will happen to me?'

'I thought you said you were dying.'

'You would like that, wouldn't you?'

'Well –' Akitada decided to take another chance and used all his strength to force his hips against the weight that rested on the small of his back – 'you took a life.' Something gave, and he held his breath in fear that he would be crushed. But all was well. He could twist his body now. It hurt like the devil, but he managed to pull up one leg, and then the other. Sadanori said something else, and Akitada snapped, 'Be quiet, I'm trying to get out of here.'

'Someone will come and get us.'

'If you're going to live, you'll have to stand trial.'

Sadanori clicked his tongue. 'If you believe that, you're a bigger fool than I thought. It's you who'll stand trial, and I'll watch you. Exile is very unpleasant, I hear.'

Akitada was familiar with exile. It was the most

common form of severe punishment bestowed on government officials who embarrassed their superiors and was rarely preferable to execution. His own legendary ancestor, Michizane, had died miserably in Kyushu.

He pushed himself forwards a few feet. Feeling around, he moved aside some smaller pieces of lumber, then crept around an obstruction and saw daylight ahead of him. It was like a gift from the gods, though he would have to find a way under or around a pile of broken boards and crazily tilting beams. There was no sign of help, but he felt reasonably sure now that he could eventually extricate himself.

'I take it you've decided you'll live,' he said dryly. 'In that case, perhaps you would not mind answering a few questions while we wait for rescue?'

There was a brief silence, then Sadanori said, 'Since we are alone, it cannot signify.'

'Peony gave birth to a child in Otsu. Is he your son?'

'No. They told me she drowned the boy along with herself.' Sadanori's voice broke. There was a long silence marked by faint sniffs.

Akitada managed to crawl over a pile of splintered wood after slipping off his good silk robe and abandoning it. Peony's fate still nagged at him. Had she really drowned herself? Her message to her maid could only have meant that she expected money and was no longer desperate. He called back to Sadanori, 'Could Ishikawa have killed Peony without your knowledge?'

The tearful noises ceased, and Sadanori said

faintly, 'No, he was here with me when it happened. Never, never did I think she would take her own life.'

Akitada registered the answer, but he had a new worry. He smelled smoke. Resting for a moment, he sniffed. Yes, and it was getting much stronger. All those reed screens and dry grass mats, all of Sadanori's paper scrolls and silk paintings would go up in a roar of flames any moment. Something had caught fire, and he had no time to lose on idle conversation.

The main obstruction between himself and the outside was one heavy beam that rested on smaller debris. He could neither squeeze through nor move things out of his way. There was a small space under it at one point, and he crawled in and heaved upward. But the beam was too heavy or lodged too firmly. Still, he tried again, and again. He heard a creaking and felt a slight movement. Using every ounce of his strength, he heaved again. Splinters cut into his back, and he could feel blood running down his sides, but the beam shifted and rolled a little. Something else shifted also and fell with a dull rumble somewhere behind him. Sadanori squealed briefly. Akitada paused to listen, but his ears now detected the crackling of flames, and he choked on smoke. Coughing, he frantically moved broken tiles and other debris. He thought he could already feel the heat searing his back.

When he found an opening that was just wide enough, Akitada squeezed through, shedding his under robe in the process. He emerged outside half-naked, dirty and bloody, and staggered to his feet. The pavilion was a leaning pile of rubble. Flames engulfed its north side and already licked eagerly at the near corner.

Sadanori was trapped.

Through the thick smoke, Akitada climbed on to the pile to see if he could reach Sadanori from above, but it would take more than one man to lift the heavy timbers, and the fire was getting very close.

Cradling his painful arm, he set off towards the main house at a limping trot. There was a fire here also, but he saw people milling about: servants, and a small huddle of colorfully robed ladies.

'Ho!' he shouted. 'Help! Over here. Your master's caught under the pavilion.'

They heard him and came. They tried their best, as Akitada stood by and directed their efforts. Some formed a chain to the lake and passed leather buckets of water up. The fire subsided in hissing steam.

Eventually, Sadanori was found. He was dead. It was not clear if he had died of suffocation from the smoke, been crushed, or had slowly bled to death. Akitada clambered on to the ruins and looked down at his corpse. He lay in a pool of blood from a deep wound in his upper leg. Everything considered, he looked quite peaceful. Perhaps he had been dying even as they spoke. Loss of blood made people light-headed, and Akitada remembered that Sadanori had sounded strangely calm. His last words had been of Peony.

Akitada limped home as quickly as he could,

frantic with worry. There were many fires in the city. In the west, the evening sun was setting against a lurid sky. Clouds of thick gray smoke turned its light to a copper glow. The scene was as frightening as any Akitada had known.

And everywhere he heard cries and shouts as people dealt with their individual disasters and tragedies. Earthen walls that once had hidden the mansions of the powerful had tumbled down and revealed leaning roofs and fallen galleries. Fine horses ran free in the streets, terrifying people who had fled their homes. A wailing woman came towards him with a child in her arms. The child looked dead. A monk wandered aimlessly, mumbling, *'Namu Amida butsu – Namu Amida butsu,'* over and over again.

TWENTY-FIVE

The Monk

When Akitada reached his house, he saw that the outer wall had fallen here also, but the rest still stood. Tora and Genba had brought the horses out and tied them to a pine tree. Now the two men were drawing water from the well. Tora dropped his bucket back into the well when he saw the half-naked, bloodied appearance of his master.

'Amida,' he cried, 'are you all right, sir?'

'Yes. What about the others?'

'All safe. Trouble made such a racket that everyone came out to see what was happening. So when it started, they just ran down from the veranda. Your lady and the others are in the garden. We thought it was safer there.'

'Thank heaven.' Akitada looked around dazedly, but was suddenly lighthearted. 'And give my thanks to your dog.'

Genba asked, 'What happened to you, sir? You look terrible.'

Akitada laughed. 'Never mind. We're alive.' His heart full with happiness, he hobbled into the garden, where he was greeted with cries of concern. Seimei inspected him and went for his medicine box.

Akitada smiled at his wife. 'Thank heaven. I had such fears.' Over her shoulder, he saw the boy sitting in the grass and he remembered their son, but even that memory was bearable. He was filled with such gratitude and hope. 'How did Nori fare?'

She chuckled. 'Very well. He thought it was a game.'

Seimei returned to treat his wounds. When Tora and Genba joined them also, Akitada told them what had happened and about Sadanori's confession and his death. 'The boy is young Masuda's son. We must return him, or at least make the attempt. I don't think he will be very welcome there.'

'No.' Tamako had tears in her eyes. 'You cannot be so indifferent as to abandon him again to the cruelty of others?'

'We have no choice, Tamako.'

'But if they don't want him?' she murmured.

'If they don't want him, I shall do my best for the boy.'

Perhaps she guessed how his feelings for the boy had changed. She pleaded, 'He's so small and has been hurt so badly.'

'The law demands that lost children be returned to their parents or relatives. But if it will make you feel better, you can come along. If no one in the Masuda household offers the child a home, we will bring him back with us.'

She said earnestly, 'You have always taken on the lost and wretched. First Tora, and later Genba and Hitomaro. Then our very ill-tempered cook. And now Hanae and Trouble.' She paused. 'And me, too.'

'No, not you. You found me, and I, fool that I was, almost lost you.'

Akitada was up early the next day to inspect the damage to the house. Old as it was, it had withstood the earthquake well. The stable, often patched, needed repairs, and there was the collapsed wall. He felt very lucky.

The old carpenter wandered in with his satchel of tools. 'Ah,' he said, contentedly looking around, 'I thought Your Honor would need me.'

'I'm very glad to see you, but surely today you can find work anywhere,' said Akitada.

'Oh, they're clamoring all right. Sent to my house last night, and then tried to hire me on my way here. And, for that matter, my own roof has fallen down, but I said to myself, "Go to him who helped you when you needed work," and here I am.' He gave Akitada a toothless grin.

'You are an honorable man,' Akitada said, his faith in human nature restored.

Life returned to normal – except for the visit from the monk.

Tora answered the knock at the gate to the barefooted figure in the drab gown, basket hat, and staff. He snapped, 'What do you want?'

The monk flinched when he recognized him, but said in a steady voice, 'I came to see your master.'

'Take off that hat.'

The monk sighed and removed the basket.

'Ha! I thought it was you. You'd better explain, that's all I can say.'

'I intend to.' The young monk's eyes narrowed. 'Did you have anything to do with the murder of the woman they called Little Abbess?'

'I was going to ask you the same thing.'

The monk gave a bitter laugh. 'She was a friend. I only wanted information.'

'So you say. What information?'

'I really must speak to your master. I came to get my nephew.'

'Your nephew?'

'The boy your master found in Otsu. I've been trying to find out what happened to my sister and her son and have only now traced the boy here.'

Tora wrestled with his surprise. It might be a lie, or it might be the truth, but their struggle for the boy had been too hard to give him up to this beggar monk. He glowered. 'You'd better leave or I'll make you sorry you ever bothered us.'

The monk rolled up his sleeves. 'I'll fight for what is mine.'

Akitada interrupted them. 'What's going on here, Tora?'

'He's the monk I told you about,' Tora said angrily. 'He says he wants his "nephew".'

Akitada nodded. 'Yes. I've been expecting him. Bring him in.' He turned and went back inside.

Tora muttered, 'Now what?' He looked at the monk. 'Does the master know you?'

The monk shook his head. 'I don't think so.'

'Oh, well, if you're here on legitimate business, sorry,' Tora said ungraciously and led the way to his master's study.

The monk's eyes were watchful and his expression guarded. 'I'm Shinyo,' he said. He fished some tattered papers from his robe. 'My travel permit, signed by my abbot, and letters of introduction to monasteries near the capital.' Akitada examined them briefly before returning them. The monk said, 'I'm told you have a homeless child in your care.'

'Yes. You must be Peony's brother. You led Tora a merry chase. No wonder he's taken a dislike to you.'

'An unfortunate mistake. I came for the boy. How did you know who I am?'

'You kept showing up, and Peony's long-lost brother was unaccounted for. Few other people could have such a persistent interest in her affairs. Your outfit is a useful disguise, but it raises suspicions.'

Tora pursed his lips and studied the ceiling.

'I wanted to find out about my sister's death

374

and what happened to her child. It became obvious that someone didn't want people to know.'

'I gather you eventually suspected Ishikawa?'

'Yes, he killed the doctor. I was going to see him about my sister's death when he came out of the gate, leaving it open. When I went in, I found the doctor murdered.'

Tora asked, 'Why didn't you report that?'

'I thought it more important to find out who the killer was, and so I followed him.'

Akitada shook his head. 'We've worked at cross purposes. Why has it taken you so long to look for your sister?'

'I live in a monastery on Mount Gassan in the far north. When I finally received permission to travel south, I found my sister dead and her child lost.'

The monks of Mount Gassan were ascetics who lived strictly cloistered lives and saw nothing of the outside world. 'I keep wondering if this tragedy could have been avoided. Your father was a nobleman.'

Shinyo stiffened. 'When he died, I was sixteen, and my sister fifteen. His family rejected us and we had to fend for ourselves. I became a monk, and my sister a courtesan. We did not choose freely. Such choices are given only to a few, and never to people like us.'

Akitada said gently, 'I don't know how much of your sister's story you know, but the two men responsible for her tragic end are both dead. It's time to let the past go.'

'You're right. I'm grateful that you found the

375

child. I have come to take him with me.'

Akitada looked at the ragged robe, the bare, calloused feet, the thin body. 'How do you propose to take care of a child?'

The monk lowered his head. 'I shall take him back to my monastery with me. He will be safe there.'

'To be trained as a mendicant monk, or a mountain priest? You made it very clear that you would not have chosen such a life for yourself. Why force the child to follow it?'

'The ways of this world are filled with death and pain. I've found contentment in the Buddha's way. The boy is my responsibility.'

Akitada shook his head. 'You can do nothing for him. Your nephew is a Masuda. His grandfather still lives.'

'The Masudas mistreated my sister and sold her son.'

'I know the old lord loved his son very much. For that reason, if for no other, he will adopt his grandson. But, in any case, by law paternal family ties take precedence over maternal ones.'

Shinyo frowned as he thought this over. 'Very well,' he finally said. 'Do this if you must. But promise that you will not leave the boy there if he's not made welcome.'

'You have my word. Would you like to meet Nori?'

The monk shook his head. 'I saw him in Otsu. If he's to live there, it will be better if I don't. Tell him that I shall visit him when I'm permitted to do so.'

* * *

The next day, the minister paid Akitada a surprise visit. He found him in a dirty old robe, carrying timbers to the carpenter. Tora was on the stable roof, hammering nails into boards, and Genba had gone into the city to bring back more supplies.

His Excellency gaped at Akitada. 'Is that you?' he asked, taking in the hatless topknot, the stained cotton robe and the short pants that revealed badly-scratched bare legs and dusty feet in straw sandals.

Akitada laughed, a new sound even to his own ears. He dropped the armful of wood, awkwardly because his left arm was still swollen and sore, wiped his hands on his robe, and bowed to his superior. 'Good morning, Excellency. Since I'm on leave of absence, I make myself useful.'

'Oh, dear,' murmured the minister, absent-mindedly brushing at his own fine green silk robe. 'Oh, dear, I had no idea you were reduced to this. I am so sorry, my dear fellow.'

'I like to keep busy,' Akitada said cheerfully. 'But perhaps we'd better go inside.' He stepped to the well, pulled up a leather bucket and rinsed the dirt off his face and hands.

Seimei was already waiting on the veranda, holding a drying cloth and Akitada's second best robe, trousers, and socks. The minister followed Akitada up the steps and watched as Akitada changed.

'Do you engage in violent exercise, Sugawara?' he asked, staring at the cuts and purple bruises.

'Not the kind that involves earthquakes. I do

377

hope Your Excellency's home and the ministry were spared serious damage?'

'Just minor damage, thank the gods.'

More suitably attired, Akitada led his guest through his study and out on the veranda. His small private garden with the fishpond was very pleasant at this hour of the morning. They sat on cushions, and Seimei brought wine and some small rice cakes. Akitada waited for the news.

'How very nice,' said the minister, after tasting the wine and looking about. 'I am sorry that you suffered in the collapse of Sadanori's pavilion. It must have been a terrible experience.'

'Being trapped was unpleasant, especially after I smelled smoke.'

'I can well imagine. The chancellor was very impressed that you should have risked your life to save his cousin.'

'Oh?' Everything considered, Akitada felt a bit guilty about Sadanori's death. He had relived his time under the pavilion repeatedly, especially those last moments, and knew that in the end he had worked to save himself without giving a thought to Sadanori. In fact, he thought his moving of that heavy beam could have caused the collapse that crushed Sadanori. He said, 'I regret that I failed to do so.'

'My dear fellow, you did what you could. It's a miracle you got out yourself. It is well-known in the highest circles that Sadanori had those ridiculous charges laid against you. I suppose you had gone to ask him to withdraw them?'

Akitada was momentarily speechless. He was not going to be dismissed or sent into exile after all. Amazingly, the chancellor's anger at him had changed to gratitude. He stared at the minister in surprise.

The minister fidgeted. 'I do hope you will forgive me for speaking to you the way I did?'

Akitada found his voice. 'There is nothing to forgive, sir. You acted very properly under the circumstances.'

The minister said warmly, 'That is very kind. Yes, I didn't have much choice, but I did not like doing it.' He flushed. His round black eyes became a little moist. 'The fact is, hmm, I like you, Sugawara. Your hard work is much appreciated. I don't know how I – how the ministry would manage without you, and that is the truth.'

Akitada was touched. 'You do me great honor, sir. I am deeply grateful for your patience. Losing my son as I did ... Well, I see now that I must have been a great trial to you. I apologize.'

The minister's round face widened with a smile. 'Not at all. Not at all. And about those charges, that has all been cleared up. The Otsu judge sent a report clearing you completely. Those people had no claim on the child you found. In fact, it appears the man was a notorious smuggler. The judge expressed great satisfaction with your help in the case.'

A smuggler? Akitada recalled the fine new storehouse next to the Mimuras' hovel. Of course. He should have guessed it. That would have gone a long way towards clearing his own character and freeing the boy.

'What about the poor child?' the minister asked. 'Will you keep him?'

'My wife has charge of him, but he should be returned to his family.'

The minister opened his mouth to ask, but said only, 'Ah,' and, 'well, I wish you success. Perhaps you will tell me what happens?' He rose. 'Time to get back. May we expect you when you have settled the matter?'

'Certainly, sir. In a day or so.'

In a burst of friendliness, the minister said, 'I look forward to it, my dear Akitada. You are always getting involved in the most fascinating situations.'

TWENTY-SIX

The Masuda Women

When Akitada returned to Otsu, Judge Nakano brushed away Akitada's thanks and returned his gold to him with many apologies. He greeted Tamako courteously, and then looked with interest at the boy. Dressed in Yori's clothes, and with his hair neatly parted and tied, he looked like a handsome noble child.

Nakano shook his head. 'I find it hard to believe that this is the same boy you found. Both Mimura and his wife were dealing in pirated goods. We found their storehouse filled to the rafters with evidence and put a stop to a notorious pirate who has been working on the lake.'

Akitada said, 'Good,' and added, 'we are on our way to speak to the Masudas.'

'You think the child is theirs? Come to think of it, young Masuda kept a courtesan. Is that it? Can you prove it?'

'Young Masuda acknowledged Peony as his concubine, and we know the boy is his son.'

'Extraordinary! Good blood shows, doesn't it? But the Masuda ladies will hardly welcome him.'

Akitada sighed. 'I must do my best for him. Thank you again for your support.'

At the Masuda mansion, the ancient servant opened the gatehouse window. He shook his head stubbornly when Akitada demanded to see the old lord. 'The first lady has forbidden it,' he said.

'This doesn't concern her. It concerns your master.'

'She doesn't wish my master to be upset again.'

'Life has a way of upsetting us, 'Akitada said coldly. 'If Lord Masuda had looked after his family better, his friend Inabe need not have died.'

The servant opened his mouth to object, but then just shook his head again. 'I don't dare, sir.'

'Look,' Akitada said, losing his patience, 'I have come with my wife and with Lord Masuda's grandson, his son's child by his concubine Peony. Would your master not wish to meet him before he dies?'

'B–but,' stammered the old man, 'that cannot be. You must be mistaken, sir. That child is dead. Lady Masuda said so herself.'

'Why is everyone in this household taking her word for things?'

381

The old man hesitated. 'Amida!' he whispered. 'Are you sure?'

'Yes,' Akitada said firmly.

The servant's resistance crumbled. 'Well, it is one of his good days, and the ladies are at a service for poor Mrs Ishikawa. Did you know she died on her pilgrimage?'

Akitada nodded.

'Surely a blessed occasion,' the servant said.

Akitada had no wish to discuss Mrs Ishikawa's blessed or unblessed state. He waited until the old man opened the gate. When the servant saw the child in Tamako's arms, his eyes widened. 'Amida,' he said. 'He's his father's image.'

'This is Lady Sugawara.' Akitada handed the child down to the old man and helped Tamako dismount.

The old man paid no attention. He held the boy and crooned, 'Oh, my little master, how very handsome you are. I used to serve your father when he was just your size.'

The boy smiled at him.

Akitada said, 'Perhaps we should have him meet his grandfather now.'

The old servant was still looking at the child with joy and amazement. 'Oh, dear, the ladies will be back any moment. I don't know what they'll say. Let's be quick.' He led the way.

Lord Masuda turned his head when they entered. He said nothing, but narrowed his eyes.

Akitada took Nori's hand and brought him to the old lord. 'My name is Sugawara,' he said. 'I was here once before, sir. Today I returned with my wife to bring you your grandson.' He told the child, 'Bow to your grandfather.'

Nori made a very creditable bow and a small noise in the back of his throat. Letting go of Akitada's hand, he went to touch the old lord's gnarled fingers with his small ones. Lord Masuda looked long and searchingly at the child and from the child to the painting of his son. Akitada held his breath.

'Yori?' Lord Masuda's voice was thin as a thread. 'Is that really you, Yori?'

The boy nodded, and Akitada's heart missed a beat. He looked at the servant.

The servant was wiping tears from his eyes. 'His son's name was Tadayori. The child looks just like him at that age. We used to call the young master Yori.' He gestured to the painting.

Akitada looked at the image of the younger Masuda and saw that his eyebrows almost grew together and slanted upward a little at the temples – as did the child's. He took a deep breath. His own Yori had been Yorinaga – but the coincidence moved him profoundly.

He had crossed paths with this child on that rainy night of the O-Bon festival. In the darkness of his heart he had mistaken him for his son's ghost and called out his name, and the child had come to him. For the span of that night and a day, he had lived in the dream of having a son again. They had encountered a cat who had led him to Peony's villa, and everything else had followed – so many things, including his own salvation. Somehow they had reached this moment, he and the boy – a grieving father and a fatherless child.

The old lord looked at him. 'Where did the

child come from?'

'My Lord, when I was here earlier, I spoke to you about your son and the courtesan Peony.'

'Peony?'

'They had a child, a boy, born five years ago. Your son acknowledged the boy as his. This is that child.' Akitada did not know this for certain, but young Masuda's return to Peony implied as much.

Lord Masuda looked from Akitada to the boy and then back again. 'He resembles my son,' he said. His gnarled hand stretched out and traced the child's eyebrows. 'What is your name, boy?'

The child was struggling to speak when the door opened abruptly and Lady Masuda swept in, followed by Kohime. 'What is going on here?' she demanded, taking in the scene and singling out Akitada, anger flaring in her face. 'I told you my father is not well.'

Akitada's eyes were on the boy. He had a sudden premonition of what was to come. Lady Masuda had finally met her retribution.

But the boy looked past the first lady. His face crumpled, and the small boy erupted into violent movement and speech.

'Sh–she ... k–killed her,' he screeched. Before Akitada could stop him, he dashed past Lady Masuda and threw himself at Kohime, fists flying. 'She killed my mother. She did it.'

Kohime screamed, gave the child a violent push, and fled from the room.

Akitada caught the boy in his arms. The child was shaking with a storm of grief and anger, but he was still talking, a flood of incomprehensible syllables of loss and anger. Akitada had guessed the wrong killer, but his heart was filled with joy. 'So you found your voice,' he said, hugging him. 'All will be well now.'

'M–my m–mother,' sobbed the child, pressing his wet face against his neck.

'Shh,' Akitada patted his back. 'Your grandfather will take care of it.' And somehow he knew that it would be so. The old man was far from senile; he had merely been submersed in grief and loneliness for too long. He was very alert now and fidgeted with suppressed emotion. And he was looking straight at Lady Masuda.

She was very pale, but her eyes devoured the child. 'Thank the gods, he is alive,' she whispered. 'Oh, thanks to the blessed Amida, he's alive. How did you find him? I have searched everywhere.'

'Are you responsible for this?' the old lord shouted, his eyes flashing. 'He looks like your husband. Is that why you tried to get rid of him?'

She ran to him and knelt, weeping. 'No, Father, I wanted him. I meant to give that woman all the money we had for him.'

The old man's claw-like hand pointed a shaking finger at her. 'You lied to me. You took my son's son from me.'

She shrank away.

Akitada said, 'If you would allow me...' He turned to the boy, 'What *is* your name?'

'Yori,' said the child, as if the question were foolish. 'Like my father.'

Lord Masuda's face softened. 'Yes, Yori, like his father.'

Akitada said, 'Well, then perhaps Yori might stay with my wife while Lady Masuda explains.'

'Oh, please let me take him,' cried Lady Masuda, rising to her knees.

'No,' said her father-in-law, 'you will stay here and make a clean breast of this.' He told the servant, 'Fetch my other daughter.' As soon as they had gone, he asked, 'Now, daughter, why did you lie to me about my grandson and his mother?'

She bowed her head. 'Forgive me, Father. I wished to spare you. You were so ill after my husband died. And you blamed that woman.'

'That does not excuse your lies.'

She cried, 'It's true I was a little jealous, especially after she gave him a son while I was still childless. But after my own son was born, I no longer minded so much.'

'My son wished to live with that woman and her child. I did not approve, but as he had given me an heir, I permitted it. It was none of your business.'

'When Mrs Ishikawa said Peony had killed my husband, I reported it to you, but nothing was done, and then my own son passed from this world—' Her voice broke, and she whispered, 'You should know what losing a child will do to a parent.'

The old lord compressed his lips, but his expression remained cold. 'Go on.'

For a moment she trembled on the verge of more tears, then she squared her shoulders and said, 'It was then that I became obsessed with my husband's paramour and her child. I had to see

386

her. Kohime was very understanding. She came with me. It was ... strange. She was very beautiful, much more beautiful than I. I could see they were poor, and I was glad. I saw the boy playing with his kitten, and I thought if we could buy the child from her, I could raise him. I told his mother I would return with money. She seemed grateful, and he was a sweet boy and my husband's son.' She looked pleadingly at Lord Masuda.

He grunted. 'Because I disliked and distrusted the woman, I believed you when you came to me with the story that she poisoned my son. But if you had brought the child to me, I would have adopted him.'

Lady Masuda wiped her eyes. 'I went home and gathered up all the gold I could find, and Kohime added what she had saved, and then we went back to her. We told her what we wanted, but she became hysterical and cried she would rather die than sell her child. She snatched up the boy and ran into the garden with him. I was afraid she would do him some harm. Kohime ran after her and tried to take the child.'

Lord Masuda raised a hand to stop her. 'Here is Kohime now. Let her speak for herself.'

Kohime's round face was splotchy from weeping, and her hair was disheveled. She threw herself on the floor beside her sister-in-law and knocked her head against the boards. 'I didn't mean to kill her,' she wailed. 'I thought she was running into the lake with the child and grabbed her. It was an accident, Father.'

The old lord sighed deeply. 'So *you* killed her.'

'We struggled and fell down. She bit and kicked me. She was very strong and I was afraid. My hand found a loose stone on the path and I hit her with it, but she didn't stop. So I kept hitting her until she stopped moving. I didn't mean to kill her. I just wanted her to let go of me.' She burst into more violent tears.

Lady Masuda stroked Kohime's hair. 'It was an accident, Father. The boy was trying to help his mother. He had a wooden sword, and he stabbed at Kohime with it. I saw it all from the veranda. When Kohime came running back to me, she was bleeding. I took her into the house to stop the bleeding. She said she had killed that woman.'

A heavy silence fell. Kohime wept quietly. After a moment, Akitada asked, 'Did you go back to make sure Peony was dead, Lady Masuda?'

She nodded. 'We were terrified, but we both crept out to look. She was still lying on the path. The boy was beside her, holding her hand. Kohime said, "We must hide the body." But there was the boy. We could not bring him back here after what had happened.' She paused and gave her father-in-law a pleading look. 'We were very frightened that this trouble would bring shame to the family. We thought perhaps we could make it look as if she had fallen into the lake by accident. I would take away the boy, while Kohime would hide the body because she is the stronger. I tried to talk to the child, but it was as if his spirit had fled. His eyes were open, but that was all. He let me take him, and I carried him away from the house. I did not know what to do with him. When

I came to the fish market, I saw a woman packing up to return to her village. I offered her all the money we had brought to take the child.'

Akitada muttered, 'All that gold, and the Mimuras beat and starved the boy.'

She flinched as if he had struck her.

Lord Masuda moved impatiently. 'And you, Kohime? What did you do?'

Kohime, the peasant girl in the fine silks of a noblewoman, said with childlike simplicity, 'I put Peony in the lake. It wasn't far. People thought she'd drowned herself.'

'Amida!' exclaimed Lord Masuda. 'What a fool you are. You are both fools and you deserve to be punished. I do not care what happens to either of you.'

Akitada looked at the two women who had caused such tragedy: one because she was a simpleton, and the other because she had been half mad with grief and jealousy. He thought what it must have been like to be the rejected wife tending to her dying child and remembered watching his own son die. He said, 'My Lord, no good can come from a public disclosure now. Peony's death was a tragic accident. It's her son's future that matters.'

The old lord said harshly, 'Kohime killed another human being.'

'Not intentionally. Peony drowned after she was put in the lake. I believe it was getting dark, and two hysterical women made the mistake of thinking an unconscious woman dead.'

'Kohime,' shouted the old man, his voice trembling with anger. 'Did you hear that? You idiot! She probably wasn't dead! You drowned her.'

Kohime stared at him. Her face was swollen, her nose ran, and her mouth gaped. She looked ugly and pathetic. 'No, she must have been dead.'

Lord Masuda turned from her in disgust.

Akitada cleared his throat. 'I think that the ladies, no matter how misguided, acted out of loyalty to you and your family. Let's not forget that they could not consult you in the matter and had no one to turn to.'

'You are generous,' Lord Masuda said after a long moment. 'I will, of course, adopt my grandson and raise him as my heir.' He glowered at his daughters-in-law. 'You two deserve to be beaten and sent away for what you did, but my son was unkind to both of you and yet you have stayed here and served me after his death. You shall be provided for if you obey my decision.'

Kohime sobbed, but Lady Masuda said quite humbly, 'Thank you, Father. We are both deeply grateful.'

Her father-in-law nodded. 'You, as my son's first lady, may stay to run this household and raise Peony's son to atone to him for his suffering. Kohime, you and your daughters will leave my house. You will reside in the lake villa. There you will pray daily for the soul of the poor woman you killed.' He looked sternly at the two women. 'Will you agree to this?'

They bowed and murmured their assent. Lady Masuda put her arm around the sobbing Kohime to support her on their way out of the room.

The old lord waited until the door had closed after them before his face cleared. 'I have a grandson. You have made an old man cling to life again,' he said to Akitada.

'There is one request, sir.'

'I am grateful. Only ask, and it shall be so.'

'The boy has an uncle. His mother's brother is a monk. He has only now found out the fate of his sister and her child and hopes to stay in touch. I think you will find him a pleasant and well-educated young man.'

'He shall be welcome.' The old lord clapped his hands. 'Bring my grandson to me,' he cried.

The boy returned and sat down beside his grandfather.

'Well, Yori,' the old man asked, 'how do you like it here? Will you come to live with your old grandfather?'

'Yes. Thank you, Grandfather. But I would like Patch to live here, too.'

The old lord stroked his hair. 'Who is Patch?'

'He's my cat.'

Lord Masuda looked at Akitada, who said with a smile, 'Patch still lives in the lake villa. He has been helpful in bringing you and your grandson together.'

'Then we shall bring him here,' said the old man and hugged the boy.

As they left the mansion, Akitada said to his wife, 'I'm sorry we couldn't keep him, my dear.'

She gave him a watery smile and touched his hand for a moment.

They told Tora what had happened on the

homeward journey. He received the news with great satisfaction, 'What a pair of vicious females! I bet poor Peony thought all was forgiven and that the money was to take care of them. That's what made her send for Little Abbess. It took a clever mind and a lot of legwork to figure out a nasty tangle like that Masuda affair. We did a fine job, sir, if I do say so myself.'

Akitada smiled. 'If I recall correctly, you were mostly working on the Fujiwara affair.'

'The Fuji—? Oh, you mean Sadanori?'

'Yes. Sadanori had nothing to do with the fate of the child, and he did not kill Peony. He was responsible for only one murder, young Masuda's, and even that might not have happened if Ishikawa hadn't urged Sadanori on.' He shook his head. 'It amazes me what lengths men will go to for love.' When nobody spoke, he looked up. 'Don't you agree?' he asked.

Tamako lowered her eyes and murmured, 'Yes.'

Tora grinned. 'I'm very glad *you* got over it, sir. Lately, there's been no telling what you might do next.'

Akitada looked at his wife, who blushed and said nothing. 'Oh,' he said, 'I must have behaved very badly.'

Tamako said, 'Not at all.'

Tora muttered, 'Forget what I said, sir. I didn't mean it.'

'No, you were right. I wanted that child's affection so badly because I miss Yori. Perhaps that's why I make excuses for Sadanori. And for Ishikawa's mother and those Masuda women.'

Tamako reached out to squeeze his hand. 'How they must have suffered! Poor Peony and poor child! And those two women, rejected by their husband and worried about their future. They only tried to buy the boy to give the old lord an heir, and then this terrible thing happened.'

'Some people are born with bad karma,' Tora pointed out.

Tamako frowned at him. 'Not in this case. Women like Peony have to sell their bodies and souls to men.'

Akitada thought guiltily of Little Wave in her pink-silk gown. He looked at his wife.

Tamako looked back and smiled, and suddenly, the sun was bright, the trees green, the colors of his wife's robe beautiful, and the air was filled with birdsong and the scent of flowers.

Their return journey was like a homecoming after a long absence. Some day they would return to Otsu to visit the child who had come into Akitada's grief so briefly.

Life places obligations on a man, and he had neglected his for too long.

HISTORICAL NOTE

Kyoto was founded in 794 A.D. as *Heian-Kyo* (Capital of Peace and Tranquility) and laid out on the pattern of the Chinese city of Ch'ang-An. Thus, its major and minor streets formed a grid-pattern along a north-south axis, with the walled Greater Imperial Palace (*Daidairi*) occupying the northern center. The Greater Imperial Palace encompassed the emperor's and crown prince's palaces, as well as the government buildings, imperial treasury, and guards' headquarters. The villas and mansions of the nobles and of members of the imperial family clustered around, while the rest of the population of about 200,000 – government officials, civil servants, craftsmen, merchants, laborers and entertainers – occupied the remaining two-thirds of the city. The city was divided into a right and left administration. Such divisions into right and left were common in the government structure and extended even to games and contests. *Suzaku* Avenue, a broad, willow-lined thoroughfare, formed the dividing line and led straight from the southernmost city gate (*Rashomon*) to the main gate of the Greater Imperial Palace (*Suzakumon*). The city is said to have been beautiful, with its broad avenues, its rivers and canals, its palaces and parks; and originally it probably contained some 80,000 dwellings, but by the eleventh century parts of it, notably the western and southern quarters, had begun to deteriorate and the population had shrunk. Among the disasters that preyed on the city and caused its decline were frequent earthquakes, fires, storms, and epidemics (from 806–1073 A.D. there were 653 earthquakes, 134 great fires, and 91 epidemics recorded). A certain amount of lawlessness accompanied disasters and further drove people to resettle elsewhere.

Heian-Kyo was carefully located to be protected from evil influences – in the north by mountains, in the east and west by the Kamo and Oi Rivers, and in the south by the confluence of these rivers and other rivers in the Ogura swamp. Major highways led south and west to the old capital of Nara and to the Inland Sea and the western provinces, and east to *Lake Biwa*, and from there to the Northern and Eastern provinces. In addition, there was much travel by water on the major rivers and on Lake Biwa. The foothills around the capital, the shores of Lake Biwa, and *Uji* (a picturesque setting on the Uji River southeast of the capital) were favored by the nobles for their country retreats or retirement temples. Uji is the famous setting in the final chapters of the eleventh-century novel *Genji* by Lady Murasaki.

Two state religions, *Shinto* (a native faith that venerates deities of agriculture) and *Buddhism* (imported from China via Korea and embraced by the court) coexisted peaceably. The fox shrine mentioned in this novel is a Shinto shrine, while the mysterious monk is a practicing Buddhist priest. The emperor, as a descendant of the native gods, celebrated Shinto rites during his tenure, but often took the tonsure as a Buddhist priest upon retirement or serious illness. A number of annual festivals have quasi-religious significance, among them the three day *O-bon* (or *urabon*) celebration, honoring the dead, who are thought to return briefly for a visit to their homes. This celebration has its origin in Chinese ancestral worship and Buddhism.

The *government* in eleventh-century Japan was also derived from the Chinese model, which was based on education and excellence, but by the eleventh century it had deteriorated into rule by the sons of a few noble families, primarily the large Fujiwara clan. Centrally located in Heian-Kyo, the government controlled, at least nominally, the rest of the country by imperially appointed governors. Akitada, who is essentially a civil servant, currently serves as senior secretary in the Ministry of Justice headed by a Fujiwara minister. Civil servants drew salaries commensurate with their rank and office. *Law enforcement* was in the hands of a police force and of local wardens, who were responsible for their district and reported serious crimes to the police. Judges worked as adjuncts to the police departments. Because of the Buddhist injunction against taking life, there were few executions. Prison terms were common, though often cut short by frequent imperial pardons, and exile was the preferred punishment for serious crimes.

Relations between men and women in Heian Japan were both more casual and more formal

396

than in western societies. Husbands and wives observed proper courtesies towards each other, but polygamy was permitted, probably because of high child mortality. It was generally practiced only by those who could afford to support large households. A gentleman might have several wives, ranked by importance, as well as several concubines, who might or might not live in the same household. Generally, customs favored males unless a wife had powerful parents. Wives could be divorced or deserted at the whim of the husband – in which case they returned to their families, or he moved out, because bridegrooms often took up residence in the house of the bride. Casual affairs were common for both sexes. Though there is no record of a 'Willow Quarter' in Heian-Kyo during the eleventh century, such places existed, most notably along the Yodo River, a mere river pleasure cruise away from the city.

Medicine, as practiced in eleventh-century Japan, was based on Chinese herbal treatises, acupuncture, moxibustion, and a good deal of superstition. Practitioners ranged from university-trained physicians to Buddhist monks and local pharmacists. The medicines mentioned in the novel were all available at the time.

Finally, the psychological concept called 'the darkness of the heart' serves to some extent as the theme of this novel. Almost a commonplace in the literature of the period, which made much of human emotions, it refers to the dilemma faced by parents who lose a child. Although Buddhist doctrine insists on denial of all worldly attachments, a parent's love for and the bitter grief attendant on the loss of a child cannot be denied. The term is found in both poetry and prose fiction of the time, for example in the *Tosa Diary* and Lady Murasaki's *Genji*.